WO T

ease return/renew this item by the last date shown

worcestershire
countycouncil
Libraries & Learning

BY LILITH SAINTCROW

Dante Valentine Novels

Working for the Devil

Dead Man Rising

The Devil's Right Hand

Saint City Sinners

To Hell and Back

Jill Kismet Novels

Night Shift

Hunter's Prayer

HUNTER'S PRAYER

★

LILITH SAINTCROW

orbit

www.orbitbooks.net

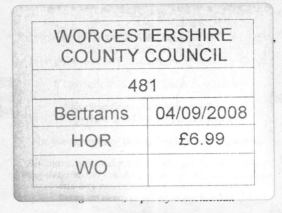
A CIP catalogue record for this book
is available from the British Library.

ISBN 978-1-84149-707-5

Typeset in Times
Printed and bound in Great Britain by
CPI Mackays, Chatham, ME5 8TD

Orbit
An imprint of
Little, Brown Book Group
100 Victoria Embankment
London EC4Y 0DY

An Hachette Livre UK Company
www.hachettelivre.co.uk

www.orbitbooks.net

For Miriam Kriss,
whose honor is impeccable.

From ghoulies and ghosties
And long-legged beasties
And things that go bump in the night,
Good Lord, deliver us . . .
—Traditional prayer

Thou Who hast given me to fight evil, protect me;
keep me from harm. Grant me strength in
battle, honor in living, and a swift clean death
when my time comes. Cover me with Thy shield,
and with my sword may Thy righteousness
be brought to earth, to keep Thy children safe.
Let me be the defender of the weak and
the protector of the innocent, the righter of
wrongs and the giver of charity.
O my Lord God, do not forsake me when
I face Hell's legions.
In Thy name and with Thy blessing,
I go forth to cleanse the night.
—The Hunter's Prayer

HUNTER'S PRAYER

1

It's not the type of work you can put on a business card.

I sometimes play the game with myself, though. What *would* I put on a business card?

Jill Kismet, Exorcist. Maybe on nice heavy cream-colored card stock, with a good font. Not pretentious, just something tasteful. Garamond, maybe, or Book Antiqua. In bold. Or one of those old-fashioned fonts, but no frilly Edwardian script.

Of course, there's slogans to be taken into account. *Jill Kismet, Dealer in Dark Things. Spiritual Exterminator. Slayer of Hell's Minions.*

Maybe the one Father MacKenzie labeled all females with back in grade school: *Whore of Babylon.* He did have a way with words, did Brimstone MacKenzie. Must have been the auld sod in him.

Then there's *my* personal favorite: *Jill Kismet, Kickass Bitch.* If I *was* to get a business card, that would probably be it. Not very high-class, is it?

In my line of work, high-class can cripple you.

I walked into the Monde Nuit like I owned the place. No spike heels, the combat boots were steel-toed and silver-buckled. The black leather trenchcoat flapped around my ankles.

Yeah, in my line of work, sometimes you have to look the part—like, *all* the time. Nobody takes you seriously if you show up in sweats.

So it was a skin-tight black T-shirt and leather pants, the chunk of carved ruby at my throat glimmering with its own brand of power, Mikhail's silver ring on my left third finger and the scar on my right wrist prickle-throbbing with heat in time with the music spilling through concrete and slamming me in the ribs. With my hair loose and my eyes wide open, maybe I even looked like I belonged, here where the black-leather crowd gathered. Bright eyes, hips like seashells, fishscale chains around slim supple waists—all glittering jewelry, silken hair, and cherry lips.

The damned are beautiful, really. Or here in the Monde they always are. Ugly 'breed don't come in here, or even ugly Traders. The bouncers at the door take care of that.

If it wasn't for my bargain, I probably would never have seen the inside of the place shaking and throbbing with hellbreed. Even the hunter who trained me had only come here as a last resort, and never at night.

I might have come here only to burn the place down.

Nobody paid any attention to me. I stalked right up to the bar. Riverson was on duty, slinging drinks, his blind eyes filmed with gray. His head rose as I approached, and his nostrils flared. He could sense me, of course. Riverson didn't miss much; it was why he was still alive. And I burn in the ether like a star, especially with the scar on my wrist prickling, the sensation tearing up my arm, reacting to all the dark hellbreed energy throttling the air.

Plus, a practicing exorcist looks *different* to those with the Sight. We have sea-urchin spikes all over us, a hard disciplined wall keeping us in our bodies and everything else *out*.

Riverson's blind, filmy gaze slid up and down me like cold jelly. "Kismet." He didn't sound happy, even over the pounding swell of music. "Thought I told you not to come back until he called."

I used my best, sunniest smile, stretching my lips wide. Showing my teeth, though it was probably lost on him. "Sorry, baby." My right hand rested on the butt of the gun. It was maybe a nod to my reputation that the bouncers hadn't tried to stop me. Either that, or Perry expected I'd show up early. "I just had to drop by. Pour me a vodka, will you? This won't take long."

After all, this was a hangout for the damned, higher-class Traders and hellbreed alike. I'd tracked my prey almost to the door, and with the presence of 'breed tainting the air it must have seemed like a tempting place to hide, a place a hunter might not follow.

It's enough to make any hunter snort with disgust. Really, they should know that there are precious few places on earth a hunter won't go when she has a serious hard-on for someone.

I turned around, put my back to the bar. Scanned the dance floor. One hand caressed the butt of the gun, sliding over the smooth metal, tapping fingers against the cross-hatch of the grip—blunt-ended fingers, because I bite my nails. Pale flesh writhed, the four-armed Trader deejay up on the altar suddenly backlit with blue flame, spreading

his lower arms as the music kicked up another notch and
the blastballs began to smash colored bits of light all over
the floor.

Soon. He's going to show up soon.

I leaned back, the little patch of instinctive skin between
my shoulder blades suddenly cold and goosebumped. Silver charms braided into my hair with red thread moved
uneasily, a tinkling audible through the assault of the
music. I had my back to Riverson, and I was standing in
the middle of a collage of the damned.

Life just don't get no better than this, do it, babydoll?

"You shouldn't be here," he yelled over the music as
he slammed the double shot of vodka down. "Perry's still
furious."

I shrugged. One shrug is worth a thousand words. If
Perry was still upset over the holy water incident or any
other time I'd disrupted his plans, the rest of my life might
be spent here leaning against the bar.

Well, might as well enjoy it. I grabbed the shot without
looking, downed it. "Another one," I yelled back. "And
put it on my tab."

Riverson kept them coming. I took down five—it's a
pity my metabolism just burns up the alcohol within seconds—before the air pressure changed and I *moved,* gun
coming up, left hand curling around the leather braided
hilt at my waist and the whip uncoiling.

People have got it all wrong about the bullwhip. In
order to use one, you've got to lead with the hip; you have
to think a few seconds ahead of where you want to be.
Like in a fast game of chess. You get a lot of assholes who
think they can sling a whip around ending up with their
faces scarred or just plain injured, forgetting to account

for that one simple fact. A whip's end cracks because it's moving past the speed of sound; little sonic booms mean the small metal diamonds attached to the laces at the end can flay skin from bone if applied properly—or improperly, for that matter.

Despite his ethnic-sounding name, Elizondo was a dirty-blond in blue T-shirt and jeans, dust-caked boots, his hair sticking up in a bird's nest over the face of a celluloid angel. His eyes had the flat hopeless look of the dusted, and I was willing to bet there was still dried blood under his fingernails. What he was doing here was anyone's guess. Was Perry involved in the smuggling? It wouldn't surprise me, but good luck proving it.

The whip curled, striking and wrapping around Elizondo's wrist; blood flew. I pushed off, my legs aching and the alcohol fumes igniting in my head, the butt of the gun striking across his cheekbone. *Not so pretty now, are we? When I get finished, you won't be.* I collided with his wiry-thin, muscular body, knocking him down. Heat blurred up through my belly, the familiar adrenaline kick of combat igniting somewhere too low to be my heart and too high to be my liver.

He went sprawling, landing hard on the dance floor, the thin graceful figures of Traders and hellbreed suddenly exploding away. They were used to sudden outbreaks of violence here, but not like this. It wasn't the usual dominance game played out for flesh or sex, or even darker hungers.

No, I was playing for keeps. As usual.

I landed hard, the barrel of the gun pressed against his temple, my knee in his ribs. "Milton Elizondo," I said, clearly and distinctly, "you are *under arrest.*"

I should have expected he'd fight.

Stunning impact against the side of my head. Judo stands me in good stead in this line of work; I spend a distressing amount of time wrestling on the floor. I got him a good one in the eye, my elbow being one of my best points. He had a few pounds on me, and the advantage of being a Trader; he'd made a good bargain.

Still, I put up a good fight. I was winning until he was torn off me, his fingers ripping free of my throat, and flung away.

A pair of blue eyes met mine. "Kiss." Perry's voice was even, almost excessively so. "Always causing trouble."

I made it up to my feet the hard way; pulling my knees up and *kicking,* back curving, gaining my balance and standing up. It was one of those little things you see in movies that's harder to do in real life but worth it if you want a nice theatrical touch. Nobody ever thinks a *girl* can do it.

The whip twitched as my arm tensed, flechettes chiming against the floor.

Perry is a few bare inches taller than me, and slim in a casual gray suit. Blue eyes, long nose, a thin mouth, and a shock of pale hair completes the picture. If he wasn't so damn *bland* he might be more frightening—but the fact that he's unassuming, that he blends in, that the eye just kind of slides past him, makes him scarier when you think about it.

Much scarier.

Especially with the kind of beautiful damned hanging around him.

I pointed the gun at him. He held Elizondo up with one

hand, the other hand in his pocket, casual as if he wasn't doing something no normal man would be able to do.

The music bled away in throbbing fits and starts. The scar on my right wrist turned molten-hot, the ruby at my throat began to vibrate, the silver charms tied with red thread in my hair tinkled. Mikhail's ring thrummed against my left ring finger; the finger that according to legend held a vein going directly to the heart. "He's under arrest, Perry. Put him down."

One blond eyebrow lifted slightly. He examined me the way a cat examines a nice, sleek bird, one the cat isn't quite sure if it's hungry enough to chase. A flicker of his tongue showed at the corner of his mouth, almost too fast for human vision to track.

The tip was scaled, and too wet cherry-red to be human. "Unwise to come in here, hunting."

Elizondo struggled, but Perry didn't even have the grace to pretend it mattered. Instead, his blue eyes held mine. I kept the Glock absolutely steady. Last time I'd shot Perry he'd bled buckets; I'd sent him a cashier's check to cover the damage to his suit. Which he promptly sent back with a dozen red roses and a little silver figurine of a scorpion that I'd picked up in a bit of newspaper and had Saul melt down. The silver had gone to coat more bullets, I burned the newspaper and the roses—and scattered salt all through the warehouse.

It pays to be cautious when dealing with the damned; especially hellbreed. The trouble is, nobody knows what *type* of damned Perry is, not even me, and he was a legitimate businessman. Deeply involved with all sorts of quasi-legal shit, but still legitimate, and able to afford a good lawyer. Or ten. Or twenty good lawyers, if it came down to it.

I cashed the check, though. I'm not a fool.

Then there was the holy water incident about a month ago. Which I was hoping he'd forgiven me for, or at least wasn't going to kill me over now.

Not when he could make me pay later, in private. I was banking on that, as I did so often. "I follow the prey, Perry. You know that. Hand him over, I'll cuff him, and the rest of you can get on with your revels. End of discussion." *And I'll even assume you have nothing to do with his business, but since he ran here like a rat once I blew his other hidey-holes I'm thinking it ain't a fair assumption. If I find out you're into slaving, Perry, our business relationship is going to undergo a drastic renegotiation.*

Perry's smile widened. "And what do I earn for my cooperation, Kiss? What is *this*," he shook Elizondo, negligently, "worth to you?"

Elizondo made a whimpering, whisper-screaming sound like an exhausted rabbit caught in a trap. I thumbed the hammer back with a solid click. Most women use baby Glocks because of their smaller wrists; I'm one of the stupid bitches who likes a big one. What can I say, I find it comforting. *Very* comforting. Plus I can handle the recoil, since I'm much stronger than your average girl.

Or even your average human. "Put him down, Perry. I'll cuff him." *I am not going to negotiate with you on this one.*

"A few moments of your time, Kiss? Since we are in such a very *special* place right now."

He's still mad about the holy water thing. Maybe it wasn't so easy for him to fix the scars. My throat went dry. I was acutely aware of the Traders and hellbreed, solemnly watching with their bright eyes and pale faces. I was outnumbered, and if Perry made it open season on me I was going to have a hell of a time.

Get it, Jill? A Hell of a time? Arf arf.

"Suck eggs, Pericles." I had four and three-quarter pounds of pressure on the five and change–pound trigger, and this time I lifted the gun. I would hit him right between the eyes, my pulse suddenly slowed and the sweat turned to ice on my skin. "Put him the fuck down before I blow your motherfucking head clean off your scrawny little body."

"Such ladylike language." But Perry dropped him. Elizondo hit with a thump and scrabbled briefly against the floor. "What is the nature of this one's sin, avenging angel?"

Sometimes hellbreed ask me that. *Do you really want to know? Are you sure?* "Child molester." I moved forward, carefully keeping the gun on Perry. Dropped the whip and gave the body on the floor a kick, he moaned and coughed. All the fight had gone out of him. I knelt, and managed to get the left bracelet on him. It took a bit of doing one-handed, but I also got his right hand wrapped, tested the silver-coated and bespelled cuffs, and decided it was good. "He had a thing for cutting out little kids' eyes. Once he finished raping them, that is. Then there's his habit of passing older kids along for a slave ring, that's what he's facing charges on now. Trouble is, this boy's a clairvoy. Always knows where the cops are going to be, jumps ship like a rat." My fingers curled in Elizondo's greasy hair, I wrenched his head up, examined his face. Yep, under his fluttering eyelids there was a sheen to his eyes. *Trader.* He'd bargained with one of Hell's denizens for an advantage over humans. It would be useless at this point to try to find out which one in town had given him what he'd asked for.

When Elizondo got to the jail Avery would exorcise him, and he'd go back to being a petty little meat-sack; he wouldn't have any clairvoyance left either. Psychic ability gets ripped out by the roots during a Trader exorcism, partly to deny hellspawn a further foothold inside a human being and partly because of the weird internal logic of exorcism ritual.

It would be excruciatingly painful.

Well, that was the price of being a Trader criminal in my town.

I dropped him, looked up at Perry, the gun still held steady. "Back up."

He shrugged, his hands in his pockets. "Your lack of faith wounds me, Kiss. It truly does."

Will you quit calling me that? I didn't say it. Giving Perry that opening would mean no end of trouble. "Back the fuck *up.*"

He took one single step back. "You owe me. I expect you here for two hours tomorrow. Midnight."

"I'm busy."

"With an attitude like that, you'll never pay your debt." His voice had turned silken.

Like I owe you for more than a month at this point. "I'm serious, Perry. This isn't my only job. I'll come on Sunday." I decided it was probably safe, holstered my gun. His eyelids dropped a little, but that was all. I tried not to feel relieved. "Midnight." *You don't own me. We just struck a deal, that's all. And it was a good deal, we both get something we want.*

You just don't get all *you want. You won't, either. Not while I'm breathing.*

He shrugged. "Two full hours, Kiss."

"You already said that." The bullwhip coiled back up as I flicked my wrist, I stowed it at my hip, and just for the hell of it I gave Elizondo another kick. My eyes never left Perry's. The pretty blond man on the floor vomited, a sudden sharp stink. I bent down, snagged the cuffs, and hauled him to his feet. "Sorry about that." My tone said clearly I wasn't sorry at all. "Thanks for the assist. I'll see you get some credit with the Chamber of Commerce."

A ripple ran through the ranks of the damned. Their eyes bored into me, bright little points of light; I heard Riverson mutter something under his breath. Something like *bitch.*

Perry's mouth twitched. If the smell bothered him, he made no sign. His eyes ran down my body, but his hands didn't leave his pockets. "A round for everyone, on the house." he said quietly. "Let's celebrate the end of a successful hunt, for our Kismet."

They shuffled, a polite and sarcastic cheer edging up from the crowd. I hauled Elizondo for the door as the movement to the bar started and the music began at low volume, ramping up slowly. They gave me a wide berth, and I heard the usual whispers.

I didn't mind. After all, next week I might be hunting any one of them; Trader, hellbreed, or whatever else hung out in the shadows. Once damned, *always* damned, it was a piece of hunter's wisdom.

What does that make me? The scar on my wrist ran

with cold prickling, Perry's attention on me the whole time.

Elizondo was an almost-dead weight by the time I shoved him out through the front door, past the glowering twin mountains of bouncer. My orange Impala was parked at the curb, in total violation of the fire lane, and Saul Dustcircle leaned against the hood, smoking a Charvil. He was tall and rangy, his skin a sweet burnished caramel; straight shoulder-length red-black hair glittering with sacred charms and small silver amulets tied with red thread. The tiny bottle of holy water on the chain around his neck, next to the small leather bag, glittered a sharp blue like a star. This close to so many Traders and hellbreed, the blessing in the water was reacting to the charge of power in the ether. To OtherSight, the Monde Nuit was a depression full of murky fluid, clearly a place where those allied with Hell came to party down.

Saul's dark eyes brightened as he saw me pushing Elizondo along. He shifted inside his hip-length leather coat, and his white teeth showed in a smile I was very glad to see.

I finally began to feel like I might have survived my latest trip into the Monde.

2

Every city has people like me. *Every* city. Usually the police and the local DA's office have us on payroll as consultants; when all's said and done it's law enforcement we're doing. Freelancers are rare, mostly because without the support system the regular cops provide we have a tougher time. Besides, even though most of us don't play well by rules or with others, we *are* on the side of the good guys. Our methods are a little different, but that's just because the criminals we catch are a little different.

Okay, a *lot* different. We do, after all, go after the things the cops can't. What ordinary cop can face down a Were or even an ordinary shapechanger, or an Assyrian demon? Not to mention the contagion of scurf or Black Mist bloodsuckers, the adepts of a Sorrows House trying to bring back the Elder Gods, or the Middle Way and their worship of Chaos? What ordinary cop stands a chance against a Trader, even? The very idea will send the more flighty of us into hysterical fits of not-very-nice laughter. We are what we are because we *know* what's out there in the darkness. People disappear all the time. It's a fucking epidemic; some of the disappearances are murder, some are fugitives, some are kidnapped by other human beings. Some of them are even found again.

But a good proportion of them are taken by the things that go bump in the night. And then it becomes a hunter's job to bump back.

Hard.

Morning isn't my best time, so I cradled a double vanilla mocha breve, extra whip, while I waited for the room to fill up. Bright, shiny new rookies; each one with a pretty badge and that look every rookie has, eager but trying to contain it, like a dog straining at the leash. Buzzcuts were in for both genders this year, and they came in laughing and joking, sobering when they saw me leaning against the dry-erase board. My back was to the defensible wall; it was why I taught in this room with its gallery of windows looking out onto the Vice squad's forest of cubicles. Each desk had an empty garbage can sitting next to it, and there were a couple of jokes about that, too.

I blinked sleepily and sipped at my coffee while they chose their seats, jostling and good-naturedly bantering back and forth.

On the other end of the dry-erase board, Captain Montaigne shifted his bulk. This was one of his less-favorite parts of the job. I heartily agreed.

I'd dressed normally, for me. Most hunters are sartorially odd, to say the least. So today it was leather pants, low on the hips; a tight *Mark Hunt* T-shirt, my long leather coat heavy on my shoulders. A gun rode my right hip, but I'd left the bullwhip at home. Instead, I wore extra knives. My hair was pulled back from my face with two thin braids, the rest of the long mass hanging down my back, silver amulets tied in with red thread. The braids were also woven with red thread and tiny silver charms; I wore the silver ankh earring in my left ear and the long fanged dagger earring on the right. A brown leather bracelet sat on my right wrist over my scar; my short-bitten nails were painted dried-blood red. The combat boots were steel-toed and scuffed; the tiger's-eye rosary dangled down and touched my belly while the black velvet choker with the medal of St. Christopher moved as I swallowed. Just below the choker, the chunk of carved ruby on its short supple silver chain was warm.

I also wore enough eyeliner to make me look like a hooker. My eyes stand out even more when I outline them with kohl. One blue, one brown, the mismatched gaze a lot of people find hard to meet.

I didn't paint them to accentuate it before. Not until I met Saul.

The rookies finished dribbling in, and Montaigne cleared his throat. I looked at the slide projector again, allowed a small smile to touch my lips.

Monty looked at the sheet in his hand, called roll. I let the names slip past me. They were like every other class of rookies, eyeing me nervously, wondering what I was, fiddling with the folders on their desks. Nobody had been brave enough to open one yet.

"Everyone's here." Monty shifted his weight again, a board creaking under his mirror-polished wingtips. He had a nice tie on, probably a gift from his wife. She had far more taste than he ever would. "Now listen up, boys and girls. This is Ms. Kismet. She's going to give you the class you've heard whispers about. Listen to her, and don't give her any shit. If you play nicely with her, she might even show you her tattoo, and believe me, it's worth it. You will be tested on this material, and it could save your life. So *no shit*." He glared at them with his watery gray eyes, and my smile widened. I could have repeated the speech word-for-word. Every class, though, some jerkass decided to get cute with me.

We'd see who it was this time.

"They're all yours. Don't kill anyone." Monty ran his eye over them one more time, then stalked away. The door closed behind him with a click.

I let the silence stretch out, taking a sip of my mocha. Then I set it down on the small teacher's desk set to one side, and folded my arms. "Good morning, class." I took perverse pleasure in speaking as if to a bunch of nine-year-olds. "I'm Jill Kismet. Technically, I'm an occult consultant for the Santa Luz metro area; my territory actually runs from Ridgefield to the southern edges of Santa Luz; Leon Budge in Viejarojas and I split some of the southern suburbs. If you *really* want to get precise and technical, I'm the resident head exorcist and spiritual exterminator, not to mention liaison between the paranormal community and the police. But the most popular term for what I am is a *hunter*. I hunt the things the cops can't catch."

A ripple went through the room. I waited. Phenomenal self-control, not one of them had made a smartass comment yet.

"I'm sure you all come from many diverse religious backgrounds, and you will probably think I'm doomed to go to some version of eternal torment after my inevitable demise. It is, I will tell you, too late. Strictly speaking, I've been to Hell and come back, and that's what gives me some of the abilities I possess. Most of you are probably wondering what the fuck I'm talking about, or wondering if this is a practical joke. Lights."

The lights flickered and died. Not a one of them glanced at the switch by the door. I snapped my fingers, and the slide projector hummed into life. "I assure you," I said into the thick silence, "I am not joking. These are crime-scene photos from a case you may recognize if you read the papers a year and a half ago."

"Jesus Christ," someone whispered.

"No. This is a rogue Were attack. Can anyone tell me what differentiates this from a regular homicide scene?"

Someone coughed. Choked.

"I didn't think so. By the end of this day, you'll be able to. If you'll open your file folders—"

"What the shit is this?" This from a tall, jarheaded rookie who smelled of Butch Wax.

Here it comes. I wasn't far wrong. He made the same little movement a lot of civilians do when confronted with the nightside—a jerk of the head as if shaking off oily water, like a dog or a horse. "This some kinda joke? What the fuck?"

"This isn't a joke, rookie. It's deadly serious. Your employment with the police force is contingent upon you passing this day-long course to my satisfaction. Because believe me, I do *not* want to visit any homicide scene starring any of you yahoos in the victim role. The simple rules I give you will keep you safe. Lights."

The lights flicked back on, and my smile wasn't nice at all. They stared at me, dumbfounded.

"I will be blunt, rookies. You'll all be required to memorize the number for my answering service, which will

page me. Pray you never have to use that number. Three
or four of you will have to. A few of you won't have time
to, but you can rest assured that when you come up against
the nightside and get slaughtered, I'll find your killer and
serve justice on him, her, or it. And I will also lay your
soul to rest if killing you is just the beginning."

Thick silence. Vacant stares. They were too stunned to
speak.

"Saul?"

He resolved out of the shadows in the far end of the
room, stalking between their desks. Several of them
jumped. It was a nice bit of theater, even if I do say so
myself. He reached the front of the room, a tall mahogany-
skinned man with his hair starred and hung with silver,
two streaks of bright red paint on his high, beautiful
cheekbones and lean muscle rippling under his T-shirt.
He was armed, too, and when he turned on his heel and
raked the rookies with his dark gaze, not a few of them
leaned back in their chairs.

"Saul here is a Were. You didn't know he was in the
room even when he flipped the light switch, and believe
me when I say he could have killed every motherfucking
one of you in here and walked out the front door of this
precinct without so much as breaking a sweat." I took two
steps away. "Do it."

Saul blinked, and complied.

No matter how often I see it, I always get a little shiver
down my spine when he *shifts*. The mind is trained by the
eyes to make a whole hell of a lot of assumptions about
things, and seeing a tall man who looks like the romance
novel ideal of a Native American melt and re-form, fur
crackling out through his skin, eyes becoming amber

lamps with slit pupils, can wallop those assumptions out from under you pretty damn quick. It doesn't help that my blue eye can *see* what he does, how he pulls on the ambient energy around him to break a few laws of thermodynamics and turn into a big-ass cougar.

Where Saul had stood, the cougar now sat back on its haunches. It blinked again, deliberately, and muscle rippled under its pelt.

Someone let out a thin breathy scream. The first vomiting spell began, in the back of the classroom. The blond jarhead's mouth worked like a fish's.

Saul *shifted* back, spreading his arms and shaking himself. Looked at me again. I nodded, he drifted over to the door, his step completely silent . . . and he proceeded to disappear from their sight again, the little camouflage trick Weres are so fond of.

The vomiting began in earnest, and I picked up my coffee, took a long drink and wrinkled my nose. When they were finished and the janitor had taken away all the puke-buckets, we'd get down to work.

3

Lunch was pizza, but none of them were in the mood to eat much. I had three pieces, Saul stopped at five; we didn't bother with dinner. I finally let them go at about six, mostly shell-shocked and bone-tired. The psych staff was on hand to give them each tranquilizers and a good talking-to. I was packing up the slide projector while Saul picked up all the leftover folders, when Montaigne breezed in the door again, this time accompanied by Carper from Homicide.

"Hey, Kiss." Carp could barely contain himself. "Another long day of bile?"

I wasn't in the mood. "How hard did *you* throw up when I trained you, Carp? I seem to remember you passing out and moaning near the end of the slide show."

Saul straightened. He didn't like Carp, and the feeling was mutual. His dark eyes fastened, unblinkingly, on the tall, broad-shouldered detective. My scar itched, under the leather cuff, prickling in the presence of antagonism.

Montaigne sighed. "Mellow out, both of you. How's it going, Saul?"

Saul shrugged. He went back to picking up the folders, each movement economical. "Good enough. Dragged one in last night."

"I heard; Avery was delighted." Monty finally dropped it. "There's something I need you to take a look at, Jill."

The script never varies. *Something I need you to take a look at, Jill.* Each time delivered wearily, as if Montaigne himself doesn't believe he's asking a woman just a little over half his age and half his size for help.

I gave my line. "Sure." I put the slide wheel back in its box. "Animal, vegetable, mineral?"

"Homicide. Carp examined the scene."

"Male or female?"

"Hooker."

Oh, for God's sake. "Male or female?"

"Female. The autopsy says so, at least."

"How fresh is the body?"

"Last seen last night. Out on Lucado."

Lucado, the flesh gallery. A cold finger touched my back. "Where was she found?"

"82nd and Varkell. On the side of the road, just on the margin of Idle Park." Carp finally spoke up. He might enjoy baiting Saul and giving me a hard time, but he was a good homicide deet and knew what to look for in a scene. If it had triggered his fine-tuned sense of the weird, I should definitely take a look.

I stretched, my lower back protesting as it often did after one of these things. "All right. Lead the way; send someone to box this up and put it back in the vault. Saul?"

"I'm with you." He fell into step behind me, and we left the file folders and the slide projector behind. "From Lucado to 82nd is a fair way."

"'Tis." I followed Monty's broad back and Carp's thinner, younger one. *And a body in what kind of shape that they can't tell male or female without an autopsy? That doesn't sound good.* Saul bumped into me, crowding me just like a Were. He liked physical contact, and herding me around was his way of showing it; it was also meant to make the point that I spent my off-duty time with him.

Weres get a little territorial like that.

I pushed him away, the leather cuff on my wrist brushing his arm. He jostled back as we strode down the hall. He was getting a little antsy; it would probably degenerate into a shoving match once we got home. We'd spar for a while, and it would end up very satisfactorily for all concerned.

He was always a little on edge whenever I had to go into the Monde. So was I.

We made it to the Homicide department, and a perceptible quiet entered the room when I did. I didn't pay attention, not anymore. Instead, we made it all the way through to Monty's office. Saul shut the door, not bothering to do his camouflage trick; he knew how Monty hated it. Instead he loomed behind me. One hand brushed the small of my back, a private caress.

I tried not to smile as I crossed the room to Monty's desk. He handed me the file. "Take a look. Want a drink?"

"Sounds good. Saul?"

"None for me." His voice was a pleasant rumble, he looked over my shoulder. I didn't flinch. I'd long since gotten used to hearing his voice in my ear, his heat brushing my back.

Monty handed me the bottle; I took a slug as I opened the file. The liquor burned all the way down, and I choked, slamming the bottle down on the desk. I nearly followed it with a fine mist of Jack Daniels, the picture snapping into coherent shapes behind my eyes. "Fuck." I backed away from both Monty's desk and Saul's heat, stalking over to the window. "Holy *fuck.*"

"All the internal organs are gone," Monty said quietly. "Took her eyes too. *Everything's* gone, there are chunks taken out of the upper arms and legs that look like . . . bites. The only reason the ME could make determination of sex was because of a lucky fingerprint. Her legs were still mostly there, but everything between them and her neck is *gone.*"

The picture was brutal, taken under the glaring high-intensity lights of autopsy. No wonder they'd had to get her on the table to find out *he* or *she.* The body was almost unrecognizable as human. *No hair. No clothes. Was she dumped naked? Are those claw marks? Teeth? What is this?* "She was seen on Lucado, and then found near Idle Park? How iron-clad is the sighting?"

"She was seen by Vice cops at ten-thirty. At two in the morning the body was found. Her right middle finger was left intact, they printed and ran it just on the off chance, got lucky. Sylvie Mondale, teen hooker and heroin addict." Monty's tone wasn't dismissive or harsh. Just blunt, to cover the aching sadness of it. I checked the vitals sheet.

She was fifteen. I'd been fifteen on Lucado once.

Jesus. They get younger all the time. Or is it that I'm

getting older? The picture glared at me, something about it still subtly wrong. *No breasts. And the viscera's gone. Where did it go?* "Parents?"

"Father's in Hunger Central, doing life for murder. Real winner. Domestic violence, petty theft, assault, grand theft auto, rape, breaking and entering. That's not counting the attempteds. Mom was a heroin addict, dead two years ago. Kid ran away from Blackman Hall and hit the streets, been in on prostitution charges every once in a while. Part of Diamond Ricky's gang."

"Grew up fast, this kid." Saul said it so I didn't have to. I turned the photo over, laid the file down on the desk, and began to look in earnest.

The pictures taken at the scene were also merciless. Someone had dumped her just at the edge of the park, right on a fringe of gravel bordering the road. Varkell Street slid away from 82nd at an angle, and she was left just at the dividing edge. Each photo was a different angle, with marks for triangulation. The body lay on its side, arms and legs flayed and crumpled together, blood soaking into the gravel. I looked, but didn't see any sign of entrails.

If they killed her somewhere else it's bound to be messy. Lots of trace evidence. But Carp's right. This is . . . this is something strange.

A chill finger caressed the back of my neck just as my pager jolted into life against my hip with a blurring buzz. The small sound made the sudden quiet in the room more noticeable.

I unclipped the pager, held it up, glanced at the number.

Christ. Never rains but it pours.

"This is one of mine." I gathered up the file with quick swipes. "Is this my copy?"

"Take it. I thought you'd want it." Carp had gone pale. "What's it look like, Kiss?"

I don't know, and that's a little disturbing. "We'll see. I'll be in touch. If another one like this shows up, call *and* page me. All right?"

"You got it."

I handed Saul the file and nodded to Montaigne, who was looking decidedly green. Of course, Monty hated it when I clammed up. Almost as much as he hated it when I opened my mouth and told him about the nightside. He'd run up against a Trader once, a guy who had bargained for near-invisibility and superstrength; Monty'd had the crap beat out of him and some good sense scared in by the time I showed up and dusted the Trader with four clips of ammo and a trick I picked up working the Santeria beat in Viejarojas under Leon's teacher Amadeus one summer.

It took Monty three months in the hospital to recover. He hasn't wanted to know shit about the nightside since.

Wise man.

"See ya round, Monty."

"See ya, Jill. Good luck."

It was the closest he ever came to thanking me. Or telling me goodbye.

4

Father Guillermo kept in shape by playing basketball, and his curly mop of black hair framed a face as pale, serene, and weary as a Byzantine angel's. "Daughter Jillian. Thank the gracious Lord."

I grimaced, but if anyone could get away with calling me that, he could. "Morning, Father. You rang?" Darkness pressed close behind me as I stepped over the threshold, from night chill into seminary quiet. Saul followed, his step silent, baring his teeth in a greeting to the priest, who was used to it by now and didn't flinch. Weres don't like the Church, and I can't say I blame them. There's only so much of being hunted an innocent species can take.

Of course, the fact that some Weres weren't so innocent didn't help. But still, they didn't deserve the Inquisition.

Nobody deserved the Inquisition, at least in my humble opinion. And the other half of Saul's heritage had suffered at the hands of Christianity too.

They remember, out on the Rez.

"I'm glad you've come." Guillermo, at least, was always happy to see me. Of all the priests I'd worked with, he was by far my favorite. "We have . . . another one."

Of course you do, otherwise you wouldn't call. I took a firm grip on my temper. Teaching a class of rookies always puts me in a bad mood. "Age, sex, details, Father. You know the drill."

He closed the high narrow door, locked it with shaking hands. I smelled incense, candles, the smell of men living together, and the peculiar fustiness that screams *Catholic.* My heartbeat kicked up a notch, and Saul bumped into me again, his hand this time smoothing down my hip through the tough leather of my coat. The brief touch was soothing, but I still moved away, following the priest's long black cassock. Sour fear roiled in the air behind Guillermo, despite the placidity of his face and the habitually clasped rosary. As a matter of fact, as soon as he was finished locking the door he clutched his rosary again, twisting it through his capable brown fingers.

"Twenty-four, male. The . . . it's odd."

Male? That *was* a little odd; women are statistically higher at risk for possession; it works out to about seventy-thirty. The Catholics blame it on Original Sin. I blame it on being taught to be a victim from birth, plus a higher incidence of psychic gifts—and less training for those very gifts, in our rational culture. We would just have to agree to disagree, the Catholics and me. "Odd how?" *You've had every conceivable type of person in here suffering from possession, Father. What makes this one different?*

Although I would have to admit there were patterns in possession, just like in everything else. Most victims are morbidly religious innocents, since Traders have the benefit of an agreement, no matter how shoddily phrased, to protect them from being taken over; also, the *arkeus* who comes through to sign the agreement usually loses out when the Trader's hauled in and exorcised. It's in their interest to make a good deal. Also, most victims are middle-to-upper-class; the poor seem to be ignored by the Possessors. For once, there was a predator who *didn't* feed on the lowest end of the economic pool.

The priest's footsteps echoed, mine brushed quietly along behind him, and Saul's were silent. "It's *different,*" Guillermo insisted. "This time it's . . . different."

I'm really starting to hate that phrase. I took a firmer grip on my temper. But then we reached the end of the hall, and instead of making the sharp right that would lead to the basement, the priest turned to the left and led us toward a smaller private chapel. I could see that the chapel door was barred, a four-by-four with a rosary hanging on it, swaying gently as whatever electric current was behind the door strained and swirled.

Uh-oh. Bad news. Why don't they have the victim downstairs in the exorcism chamber? "Gui? You want to give me a vowel or something here? Why aren't we heading to the chamber?"

"The victim is . . . a student, Jillian. It's Oscar."

My heartrate kicked up another notch. I didn't know Oscar, and the dreamy shocked tone in Father Guillermo's voice was beginning to worry me. "A seminary student? Victim to possession?"

"He was missing from evening prayers; Father Rosas found him in here."

Big fat Rosas, the jolly one. I eyed the chapel's high pointed doors. The four-by-four rested in iron brackets that hadn't been used since the great demonic outbreak of 1929. Now *that* had been a bad year for hunters all over. "Where's Father Rosas?"

"Father Ignacio took him to the hospital. He's suffered a heart attack. I entered the chapel and saw Oscar. He . . . he was *floating*. And gabbling in a strange tongue. I pronounced the name of Our Lord and he screamed in pain. Then I came out, barred the door, and called you. The rest of the students are in their dormitory; Father Rourke is standing watch there with the crossbow."

I heard the hiss-flare of a match, light briefly dappling the high narrow hall with its black-and-white tiles. Saul had lit a Charvil.

Oh, for Christ's sake. But I let it go. He had more than one reason to hate the Church. Guillermo didn't mention it, just pointed at the chapel doors. "He's in there. Please, be merciful. If . . . if he . . ."

I nodded, reached out. Touched the back of the good Father's hand. His fingers curled so tightly in the rosary it was a wonder his knuckles weren't creaking. "There." I pointed with my other hand, to a spot in the hall on the opposite wall, where a bench would provide him with a place to sit that was out of the way should the door get busted down, and out of the sight-line should it be busted down by whatever was in the chapel instead of by me. "Sit over there. Keep your rosary out, and repeat your Hail Mary. Okay?" That would keep him occupied and provide him with some protection—calling on a goddess is one of the oldest remedies against evil. Gui had once admitted to me that he loved God, certainly—but Mary was intercession, and a Jesuit is predisposed to Marianism anyway.

It was part of why I liked Gui. That, and his taste in microbrew beers.

I would have reassured him, but what priest would want reassurance from *me?* I'm a hunter, and condemned to Hell—or Purgatory at least—even as the Church quietly funds training for not a few of us.

Guillermo nodded. "Be . . . be merciful, Jillian."

"You know me, Father. I'm a regular angel of mercy." I regretted it as soon as it left my mouth. His face crumpled slightly, took back its serene mask. I saw just how badly shaken he was and regretted it even more. "Go sit down, Gui. I promise I'll take care of him."

A few moments later, with the priest out of the way and mumbling his prayer, Saul glanced at me. "Ready?" The cigarette fumed in his hand, resting casually on the four-by-four. His fingers brushed the dangling rosary. The wooden beads were charred.

Holy shit. What the hell's going on here?

I didn't reach for the whip. Instead, my left-hand fingers crept to my right wrist.

Saul's eyes widened a little. He dropped the cigarette to the tiles, stepped on it, ground it out. He said nothing.

The scar burned and buzzed under the cuff. I could feel my left eye—the blue one, the smart one—starting to get dry. I eyed the rosary as it swayed, the cross tapping the door with tiny little sounds. The closer I got to it, the more violently the cross swung.

Tap. Tap. Tap.

I took a deep breath. Saul's hand came up, the bone-hilted Bowie knife lying flat against his forearm. *Be careful,* his eyes said, though his mouth wouldn't shape the words. It would be an insult, implying I couldn't take care of myself. Weres are touchy about that sort of thing.

It briefly warmed me, that he would consider my pride. High praise, from a Were.

I unbuckled the cuff, and the shock of chill air meeting the scar made me inhale.

Did Perry, across town in the Monde—maybe sitting in his office, maybe in his apartment up over the dancefloor, staring at the walls or an empty chair—feel it when I did this? I'd never asked.

I didn't want to know.

Colors became sharper, the sting of cold air hitting the back of my throat, my skin suddenly sensitive to the faintest brush of air. My vision deepened, darkness taking on color and weight, new strength flooding my limbs.

As usual, the thing that scared me most was how *good* it felt. My hair lifted on a slight warm breeze that came from nowhere, and I lifted my eyes to find Saul smiling, a private little smile that reminded me of all *sorts* of delicious things.

The scar twinged. Open for business, working overtime.

"Ready," I whispered, and focused *through* the door.

Saul flipped the four-by-four out of its bracket as the charms tied in my hair made a low, sweet tinkling. The wood clattered on the floor, the rosary splitting, its beads kissing the tiles gently before shattering into fine ash. He kicked the door open, force splintering the wood in long vertical strokes as they flew wide. My boots brushed the floor lightly as I leapt through, right hand up and fingers spread, heatless black flame twisting at my fingertips.

Skidded as it darted for me, my hand twisting through a motion that sketched flame on the air.

I collided with a levinbolt, hit hard, the voice like brass bells stroked with a wire brush. It was muttering in Chaldean, and it had just thrown a concentrated bolt of energy at me.

Oh, for fuck's sake. Just what I need. The scar on my wrist flushed with heat, shunting the levinbolt aside and leaving me only breathless instead of knocked senseless on the floor.

Saul was suddenly *there,* appearing out of thin air, spinning into a crouch with the fingers of his free hand tented on the floor. The young boy in the long black seminary-student almost-frock (because they believed in old-fashioned clothing here at Grace) tumbled over him, the twisting ripping sound of Old Chaldean spoiling the air. I spun, the flame on my fingertips arcing, and caught him, boots skidding across the floor as kinetic energy transferred, mass times velocity equaling an elbow to my mouth.

That's why I don't get my nose pierced like I want to. I get clocked in the face too goddamn much.

Tasted blood; locked the kid's wrist and wrestled him to the ground. A few moments of heavy breathing and twisting, my coat rucking up, and I finally had him down on the floor. "Saul!" *For fuck's sake, where are you?*

He appeared, locking the boy's arms over his head. Pressed down with a Were's strength, his dark eyes meeting mine for just a moment and the paint streaked on his cheeks suddenly glaring in the darkness.

The chapel was narrow, pews on either side; the altar would have been beautiful if the *utt'huruk* hadn't leached all the life from the flowers, torn the cloth and the dead plant matter to shreds. It hadn't been able to breach the shell of belief and sanctity over the windows and walls, though; that was something to be grateful for.

Oscar was a tall blond corn-fed boy. I got my knee into his gut and held him down, his legs scrabbling uselessly against the tiled floor. *Don't crack his skull, Gui wants his deposit back on this mother.*

"Show thyself," I hissed in ceremonial Chaldean, the syllables harsh and curdled against my tongue. "Show thyself, unclean one, carrion one. *Show thyself! In the name of Vul I command thee!*"

It howled, and the smell of spoiled milk and dry dusty grave-wrappings coated the back of my throat. More important than the words of any exorcism is the psychic force put behind them, the undeniability of command. You have to be a little bossy with the bitches, or they start laughing at you.

Then you really have to kick some ass.

So I bore down, not physically but *mentally,* a long harsh breath of effort hissing out between my teeth. Struggling, my will locked against the *utt'huruk,* pressing, *pressing.*

A subliminal *pop!* and the world exploded. I passed out for a fraction of a second, the outward pressure I was expending slamming me out of my body and back in as the elastic defenses built around my mind snapped the thing away from me and deflected most of its blow. I came to with scaly, horny hands around my throat, digging in, and Saul's chilling cough-roar. The pews we'd landed on had shattered, wood-dust swirling crazily as the *utt'huruk*'s

bulbous red compound eyes stared into mine, its beak
click-snapping shut twice.

I'd pulled it out of the kid.

Good fucking deal.

I balled up my right fist, my left fingers scrabbling uselessly at its claws around my throat. The scar on my wrist
ran with flame, burrowing in toward the bone, *burning*.
The thing was wiry but tremendously strong, it hissed a
curse in Old Chaldean that would have turned a civilian's
hair white.

My right hand throbbed, the scar turning white hot
as if Perry had pressed his lips on the underside of my
arm again. A bolt of agonized desire lanced through me, I
punched the bird-headed demon right square between its
ugly eyes, where the seam of almost-flesh made an im-
perceptible weakness. *Utt'huruk* Anatomy 101: if you've
got a hellbreed-strong fist, use it on the thing's skull.

Its head exploded in gobbets of stinking meat, its predator's beak curling like plastic in an oven. The smell was
incredible. Choking, I scrabbled at the horn-tipped hands
digging into my throat, worked them free. My breath
came harshly. Little charms knotted into my hair dug into
the back of my head, my shoulders.

"Fuck." I coughed, rackingly. The *utt'huruk*'s body
slid bonelessly to the side, hitting the floor with a thump.
"Man, I hate it when they do that."

"You okay?" Saul, his voice low. But he didn't move
from his position, holding down the kid.

God, it was good working with him. "Peachy keen." I
rolled aside, made it up to my feet. My coat rustled as I
strode back to him. One boot on either side of the boy's
hips; I squatted down and ran my right hand down the

front of his cassock. Buttons parted, I pushed material aside, looked at his narrow pale chest.

No mark. The chest was the most traditional place, but . . .

I checked the inside of his wrists, his ankles, his knees. I even checked the inside of his thighs; Saul helped me turn him over and I checked his buttocks, the base of his spine, the *backs* of his knees.

His nape was covered by the high black collar. I tore the rest of the material aside, my heart beating thinly.

Nothing. I even smelled his *hair.* And checked his testicles.

"He doesn't appear to be a Sorrow," I said finally, and Saul let out a relieved sigh. I, however, was not relieved, not in the slightest. How could an *utt'huruk* get into a kid in a seminary? "Pick him up; let's go. Guillermo's probably having a fit by now."

Behind me, the *utt'huruk*'s body was caving in, noisome liquid running from its breaking skin in runnels of filth. Being a hunter was exhausting, but at least I wasn't a janitor.

Saul hefted the boy's weight, pale naked skin looking exotic against his more familiar mahogany darkness. "You hungry?"

My pulse was starting to come back to normal, the copper of adrenaline leaching out of my dry mouth. And despite the smell, my stomach rumbled. "Yeah. Want to go to Micky's?"

"Sounds good." His white teeth flashed in a smile that was like his hand on my back. "Bacon cheeseburger? Pancakes? Omelet?"

As if anything could match your omelets. "Tease."

5

Father Guillermo knew better than to be unhappy about the state of the chapel. He took the news calmly, all things considered, only almost-fainting; I held him up and made an appointment to come back and interview the kid's friends. I did search the kid's room and look over the visitors log, but none of the names seemed familiar or suspect; Oscar himself hadn't had any visitors and he would probably be in a coma for a good week before he woke up and could give any answers. There was nothing in his room. Nothing abnormal, that is.

It didn't matter. I'd find out. Chaldean meant the Sorrows, and if they were looking for fresh meat they would have to look somewhere else. I didn't allow a Sorrows House in my city.

That didn't mean they wouldn't try to sneak one in. Still, they should know better. Some hunters just keep an eye on the Sorrows and bitch-slap them every now and again to keep them in line.

I kill them on sight. And each time I do, I earn a little piece of myself back.

Saul and I hit Micky's at about midnight. Micky's is on Mayfair Hill, in the gay section of town; the nightclubs were just hitting their most frantic pace. But Micky's is a little more quiet, being an all-night restaurant of the quality the locals guard jealously and tourists only hear whispers of. Inside, the walls are covered with posters of film stars from the forties and fifties, and the bar is tucked in the back, smoky and murmuring but always well-mannered. Start trouble in Micky's, and your ass will be on the street in seconds flat.

Because along with being a safe place for the gay community to canoodle in the booths and kiss openly at the tables, Micky's is run by a Were and has Were kitchen staff. Some other nonhumans work there, too. Though a few of the waitstaff are civilian humans, Micky's is where nightsiders come to eat late at night.

Nightsiders on the right side of the law, that is.

I shrugged off my coat and slid into the red vinyl booth, giving Saul the side with his back to the wall. Chas was on duty, and he brought a martini and a Heineken, setting the beer down in front of Saul with a grin. "Heya, dude."

"Dude." Saul's answering grin lit up his eyes. "How you, Chas?"

"Can't complain. Hey, Jill." Chas looked like Puck on steroids, flirting his eyes at Saul while he put my martini down. Tonight his T-shirt was pink, with *Fancy Boy* in curlicue script across his broad chest. Jeans just short of indecent wrapped around his lower half. It was a safe bet that he was commando under them.

"Hey, Chas. What's the word?"

"All quiet around here. My sister says hello."

I stifled a smile. Marilyn thought she owed me for saving her baby brother's life. Chas had gotten tangled up with some trouble once, having to do with a circle of Traders running a dope-smuggling outfit from a house on Mayfair itself. Two SWAT teams had already been wasted by the time they called me in; I cleared the house and found Chas naked and shaking like a rabbit, chained in a small filthy room with only a mattress. I could still see the marks on his wrist from the chains if I looked closely. But after rehab and five-odd years of therapy, he was much better.

And Marilyn was everlastingly grateful.

I never told her that I'd almost killed Chas, I'd been trigger-happy after taking out five Traders and a little dog-like demon that looked disconcertingly like a Lhasa Apso. That had been before Saul, but only by a few months.

"Tell her I say hello back." I settled for empty cliché politeness. "How are you, Chas?"

"Better all the time. The usual?" The frightened-rabbit look had gone out of his eyes, and he'd stopped flinching when I moved too quickly.

After five years, that was a blessing. "The usual, hot stuff. Don't forget the strawberry jelly." I made a face, and was rewarded with Saul's slow smile. Chas bopped away, switching his cute little weightlifter ass, and Saul handed the file over the table.

"Dammit, I hate it when you anticipate me," I lied.

"You're just so transparent." Saul's smile widened, turned wolfish. "Rookies put you in a bad mood."

"I'm always in a bad mood. It's part of my girlish charm." I flipped the file open, turning over most of the grisly photos in the same motion. Instead, I studied other shots of the scene. "What do you think, Saul?"

His eyes met mine. Deep, dark eyes, as veiled as a cat's gaze, he rubbed his chin. No stubble yet; he doesn't have the usual Were problem of being hairier than an Armenian wrestler. The red paint was crackling, drying on his cheeks. It meant the day was over.

Thank God. I could do without days like today.

"Has it occurred to you," he said slowly, "that we've been really busy lately? You haven't had a week off since the spring equinox and that serial-rapist guy."

I thought about it, staring at the photo of the wet stain left under the body, gravel showing up sharp and slick under the glare of lights, evidence markers bright yellow.

He was right. It had been one thing after another. I hadn't even had a pedicure in months. Of course, being a hunter means being outnumbered. Most psychics are women, but most hunters are men; they can quite frankly take more damage.

We female hunters are a tough bunch, though.

Still, we have large territories, and even with Were and other alliances it's still hard work. Plenty hard, plenty dangerous, and unremitting.

But there should have been a lull or two since spring. We were just past New Year's, that made it almost a year since my last real break.

The trouble was, there wasn't anyone I'd even felt had a *chance* of surviving training, even if I had time to take on an apprentice or two. Saul was fast and tough, but he was a Were. There were some things a hunter dealt with that would kill him, if only because he didn't have the breadth of knowledge I did when it came to Possessors or *arkeus.* Or, say, a Sorrows adept.

Or, God forbid, a Black Mist infestation. No, Saul was great backup, the most marvelous backup in the world, but I couldn't train him to be a hunter. Even if he'd wanted to, which wasn't at all likely. He went with me because we were involved, not because he had any pressing need to even the scales. No *mission,* unless it was keeping his lover's skin whole.

Don't think I'm not grateful.

"Doesn't look like things are calming down much lately either." *I'd call for reinforcements, but who am I going to call? Leon? He can barely keep Viejarojas under control. Anderson up north? His territory's twice the size of mine. Anja, over the mountains? She's got all she can handle with the Weres fighting the scurf over there.* I tapped my fingers on the glassed-over tabletop.

"I miss you." The smile had fled. He picked up his beer, took a long draft, his throat working as he swallowed. Set it down, licked his lips. "I mean, I miss hanging out with you. We haven't been to a movie in months."

We spend every ever-loving day together. But you're right, our R&R has been sadly lacking of late. "I miss you too. What's playing?"

"Probably nothing much. The point is, you need to take a break, Kiss."

I made a face. "Don't I always. But you're right, we should spend some quality—"

"I want you to stop."

I actually dropped the file on the table, closing it. I stared at him. "What?"

It was his turn to make a face, a swift grimace. "Not

stop hunting, kitten. I know you too well. I want you to take a vacation with me. A real vacation, to someone else's territory. Where you're not always looking over your shoulder."

Do you think this is like a nine-to-five job, where if I leave I'll come back to paperwork and phone calls? I'll come back to dead bodies and mountains of work to catch up on. Christ, Saul, what are you thinking? "If I could get someone to cover—"

"Leon and Andy could both help; they've both got apprentices, for Christ's sake. Anja would be more than happy to ask a few Weres to come out on patrol—it'll be fun for them. Not to mention the Were population here in your own town. I want to get away." He nodded, sharply, as if he was finished speaking. Then he continued. "I want all your attention, for a change."

Were jealousy? Or something more? I glanced down at my right wrist, the scar covered and feeling flushed, full, ripe since I'd drawn on it. "Is this about—"

"It's not about that goddamn bastard and his goddamn Monde. I just want you to take a vacation. With me." He looked down at the tabletop, his long expressive fingers playing with the beer bottle. A ring of condensation marked the table, he moved the bottle slowly, blurring it, drawing it out. "Want to take you to meet my people."

Holy shit. My heart gave a leap that felt like zero-gravity had suddenly kicked into effect. "You want me to . . . meet your people." *Christ, I sound stunned. I feel stunned.*

He shot me a dark look from under his eyebrows, the charms in his hair stirring as he tilted his head. "That's what I said."

Oh, Lord. That was news. *Big* news, coming from a Were. I picked up my martini, downed half of it. It burned all the way down. "Sure." I tried to sound casual. "I want to dig a little deeper in this murder. But I'll call Andy and Leon tomorrow. Okay?"

His slow smile was a reward in itself. "You sure?"

As if I didn't know anything about Weres. I took a deep breath. "I'd be honored to meet your people, baby. Nobody better try to bite me, though."

"Aww, come on. I thought you liked that." The smile widened as he settled back in the seat, vinyl creaking and rubbing against his coat. I slid my boot over, touched his under the table, and had to catch my breath when his eyes half-lidded. Just like a big sleepy cat.

"Only from you, catkin. Only from you." I opened the folder again, looked down, and took the rest of my martini in one gulp, hoping Chas would come back soon with the food.

All of a sudden I couldn't wait to get home.

6

I woke up with Saul's heavy muscular arm around me so tight I could barely breathe, his face in my hair, and an ungodly racket right next to my ear. Late-afternoon sunlight came thick and golden through the blinds, and the sound echoed. One of the things about sleeping in a warehouse: the acoustics are screwed-up. Which means I can hear every sliding footstep, every insect in the walls . . . but it also means the phone's ring turns into something like an air-raid siren. Especially when I'm tired.

Saul stirred slightly. I pushed his arm away and stretched, yawning, fumbled for the phone. His fingers slid over my ribs, warm and delicate for all their strength. I finally managed to grab the phone and hit the talk button. "Talk." *This had better be good.*

The warehouse on Sarvedo Street was mine, a last gift from Mikhail. I'd been trained as a hunter by one of the best ever to take the field, and he'd left me this space; enough room for a fully equipped gym, a meditation space, a double kitchen for entertaining and cooking up supplies, and a nice big bedroom with plenty of space around the bed so I could be sure of nothing sneaking up on me. And since Saul had moved in, the place looked much better; he had a genius for finding thrift-store gems and bargain luxuries.

What can I say? Weres are domestic. He even does dishes.

The phone crackled in my ear. "Jill? It's Monty. Wake up."

Adrenaline slammed through me, cold and total. I curled up to a sitting position, Saul's hand sliding free and the green cotton sheets rustling. "I'm up. What do you have?"

"We have another body."

"Another . . ." *So far, Monty, this discussion is frighteningly familiar. How many times have we had this little talk?*

"Another dead hooker with all her guts and her eyes gone."

My mind clicked into overdrive. "Where? And where's the body?"

"Scene's at Holmer and Fifteenth. Recero Park. They're holding it for you, but it won't be long before the press jackals—"

"Recero? I'll be there in twenty. *Hold the scene.* Don't move even if the press finds it, put a tent over the body, and *leave it alone.* Okay?"

"Okay." But Monty didn't hang up. "Jill, if you know anything—"

"Who found it?" *Monty, I don't have anything yet, and even if I did I wouldn't tell you, dammit. You don't want to know.*

"Jogger. Being held at the scene. Medics are treating him for shock."

"I'm on my way." I hit the off button and bounced out of bed, heading for the bathroom at a dead run. My feet slapped the hardwood floor.

"Jill?" Saul's voice, all sleepiness gone.

"Another murder," I tossed back over my shoulder. "Get your coat."

I took one look at the body and my gorge rose. It takes a lot to upset my stomach, but this managed to do it. I stood at the edge of the crumbling sidewalk and contemplated the gentle rolling grassy strip, about six feet wide, that was the very edge of Recero Park. The trees started with a vengeance, erupting with scrub brush and thick trunks as if the forest couldn't wait to spill out; if it hadn't been the beginning of winter there would have been more shade. My breath hung in foggy ribbons in front of my face.

This one lay on her back, sprawled in the shade below a large oak tree right off a jogging path. Her ribcage was cracked open, her face savaged and the empty sockets of her almost-denuded skull were already hosting flies even in this chilly weather. There wasn't even enough hair left to mark her as female. I stood for a few moments, letting it sink in.

There was nothing left between the broken petals of her ribcage, and nothing left in her belly either. I could see the glaring gouges where something had ripped and gouged through the periosteum covering the lumbar vertebrae. Little shreds of what had to be her diaphragm hung from the broken arches of her ribs; her arms, like the other one's, were terribly flayed. Her legs weren't touched much, but they were oddly flattened, as if the bones had been crushed.

The femur's an amazing bone; it takes a hell of a lot of stress per square inch with every walking step and even more while running. To crush and splinter a femur so slim slivers of bone poke out through the quads is . . . well, it takes a lot of strength.

Saul had gone pale. I didn't blame him. He hung back at the very periphery of the makeshift tent that had been erected to shield the body from the press, who had just started to show up in droves.

I shut away the sound of people, slowly closing my awareness until I could hear the wind moving in the trees of Recero Park. Naked branches, most of them; there were evergreens further in the center of the park, but out here along the fringes it was scrub brush and sycamores, a pale beech standing like a sentinel at the corner of Fifteenth up to my left. Again, the body had been dumped less than ten feet from the street, just at the margin of the park. The sidewalk here was cracked and beaten; this was a for-lorn little stretch of road. Across the street a dilapidated baseball diamond for Little League stretched behind its rattling chain link fence, its dugout set off to the side, first base right across the street. The parking lot was a field of gravel and weeds behind the dugout and the stands, which looked rickety enough to collapse the first time someone sat on them.

Not a lot of witnesses, despite it being broad daylight. And nobody to hear her if she screamed. Assuming she was killed here. No, there's not enough blood.

The trees rustled.

Dumped here. Why? Anything that causes this much damage usually eats what it takes; why take the eyes? What is this?

I closed my dumb eye, the one that only saw the surface of the world. My blue eye stared, focusing *through* the scene, and I saw the faint fading marks of violence. She hadn't wanted to stick around, even as a disembodied soul; I didn't blame her. It was strange; she must have left in a hell of a hurry for the etheric strings tying her to her body to be torn like that. That wasn't too terribly out-of-the-ordinary for a violent death, but the scale of the damage was a little . . . odd.

"Paula Lee," Carp said, right next to me. I returned to myself, the sound of people swirling around me. "Those boots."

She did still have her boots on, distinctive pink leatherette numbers with stiletto heels. The pink was splashed with still-sticky crimson. "The boots are familiar?"

"I called Pico over in Vice, figured since the last one was a hooker and this one's wearing fuck-me hooves I might save myself some time. Peek knew the boots. She was also seen last night, early, on Lucado. Another one of Diamond Ricky's girls."

Crap. My stomach flipped, settled. "How old is this one?"

"Don't know. Caruso says she's young, though. Street name is Baby Jewel." Carp looked a little green, this morning he wore a thick gray sweater and jeans, a pair of battered Nikes. *Must have called him out of bed early. Was he sleeping in? It's almost 4 P.M.* His sharp blue eyes rested on the corpse; mine returned unwillingly to the ravaged face.

Baby Jewel. Christ. "I'd better have a talk with Diamond Ricky."

"He'll enjoy that." Carp's mouth pulled habitually down at the sides, making him look like the fish he was nicknamed for. He had run his hands back through his hair more than once today, I guessed. It stood up in messy spikes. His partner Rosenfeld was talking to one of the forensic techs; Rosie's short auburn hair caught fire in the afternoon light.

"You did the prelim, Carp. What's up?"

"Jogger came along, his usual route. Found the body, called it in from the pay phone at the corner of Fifteenth and Bride, two blocks up. Vomited right there before he did so, though. No tracks, even though the ground's fairly soft; there's some leaf scuff. It's the damnedest thing . . ."

I waited.

"Rosie looked at it and thought maybe the body had been *thrown* to land that way. Look at where her arms are, and where her head ended up. I think I agree."

You guys are amazing. "I'd carry that motion." I let out a heavy sigh. "Christ. Do you want to be there when I question Diamond Ricky?"

"Shit, yeah. Love to be a fly on the wall during that discussion. You gonna beat him up?"

I'd love to. "Only if he gets fresh with me. Try to keep your excitement under control." I motioned to Saul, who detached himself from the shadows he had begun to sink into and approached, his step light on the cracked pavement.

"I hate to ask." Carp's tone warned me. "But . . . Jill, do you have anything? Anything at all?"

"It's not a Were." That much, at least, I was sure of. "Mind if Saul does his thing?"

"Go ahead." Carp sounded relieved. I wondered when he'd figure out that I had no idea yet. Just like him.

And that bothered me. A kill like this was anything but subtle. When things shout this loud, they usually want a hunter to hear them.

Saul lifted his head and sniffed, rolling the air around in his mouth like champagne, tasting it. He stepped off the pavement, delicately, knowing the forensic techs were watching where he moved. His boots were soundless as he approached the body.

He paused four feet from the sticky pool of blood under the broken corpse. My gorge rose again; I pushed it down.

He bent his head, spreading his left hand, tendons standing out on the back, his fingers testing the air. Shuddered, his shoulders coming up.

He backed up without looking, retracing his steps. Reached the sidewalk, turned on his heel to face me. His dark eyes glittered, and under his dark coloring his face was cheesy-pale. His mouth turned down at both corners. He reached out blindly, his hand closing over my shoulder, fingers digging in.

I reached up, covering his hand with mine. Stared into his dark, dark eyes. He didn't speak—he would wait until he had everything clear inside his head before he gave me anything. But for the moment, we stood there, and copper filled my mouth.

In all the time I'd known him, I had never seen Saul Dustcircle look frightened before.

7

Failing sunlight dipped the flesh gallery in gold. The tenements slumped, tired as the women who walked below, go-go boots and hot pants, fake rabbitfur jackets, each on her prescribed piece of sidewalk. The overall impression of this section of Lucado Street has always been motion, hips swinging back and forth, eyes blinking and glittering under screens of makeup, teased hair, candy-glossed lips most often marred by cold sores. The older girls worked the north end, the bargain basement; Diamond Ricky's turf was further south, prime real estate I could remember pacing years ago when it was Val's territory.

I never like thinking about that, though. It was a whole lifetime and a trip to Hell away from me. Thank God.

Ricky had some of the best merchandise, the youngest and prettiest; teenage girls who each would have sworn that Ricky *loved* her and was *protecting* her. And of course, we suspected him of running an escort service that provided underage action for rich businessmen. No proof.

Yet.

His number one was a girl a little older than his usual crew; she tossed back her long brown hair, sniffed, and wiped at her nose with the back of her hand as I tilted my head, taking in the apartment: huge entertainment system, white leather couch, trendy-in-the-eighties Nagel print hanging on the wall. Ricky's tastes ran to chrome, glass, and leather, and every piece in here was bought with the money he took from the young girls outside, peddling their asses scraping together enough to feed his appetite for luxury. Normally he'd be sitting out on the street in his Cadillac with some muscle, overseeing the action, but we'd managed to catch him at home with nobody but his girl.

Lucky us.

I took a deep breath. Pulled the chair out from the dining-room table, dragged it across the spotless white carpet. You wouldn't think to look at this place that it was merely a modest brownstone sandwiched between sloping ramshackle apartment buildings filled with the desperate.

Slim greasy Ricky lounged on the white leather couch. He wore a black cowboy hat with silver scallops on the band, black silk button-down shirt, and leather pants. Cowboy boots with silver tips were propped on the low glass table in front of him. He gestured at the small square mirror tile laying on the table. Two lines of white powder were prominently on display.

Christ. Do pimps ever change? I shook my head, set the chair on the carpet at precisely the right angle. Saul leaned against the door next to Carp; Rosie was still at the scene. Carp's blue eyes were avid, flicking over every surface.

I settled down on the chair, folding my arms and resting them on the back, knees on either side. Turned my unblinking gaze on Ricky while the number one wiped at her nose again, snuffling, and padded into the kitchen.

Ricky grinned, his fingers dangling loosely in his lap, an advertisement. He indicated the powder on the spotless mirror again, with a nod of his hat. "Feel free, *puta*." His grin widened; we wouldn't bust him unless it got difficult. "Or you here to make some money? I turn you out after I test the merchandise, see."

You son of a bitch. The scar on my wrist throbbed. The smile began down deep, I let it rise to my lips. Waited for the right time to speak, as Ricky shifted. It was that tiny movement, a flinch, that told me I had already unsettled him. He was a man who lived off mindfucking women, and I was just aching to do a little in return. Even it out for the female species, so to speak.

I waited. Let the smile bloom. He was Puerto Rican, so I let the tiger's-eye rosary dangle, hunching my shoulders and resting my chin on my crossed forearms. My eyes would do half the work for me. It's funny how many cultures have weird legends about people born with different-colored eyes.

Only I was born with brown eyes. The blue one is a gift—or a curse. Whichever, as long as it worked.

I looked at Ricky's nose. If you stare right at the bridge of a man's nose, he thinks you're looking him in the eyes. The gaze grows piercing, intense, and the man starts to sweat. Especially if he's done something wrong.

"What you want, huh?" His eyes flicked past me to the door. Carp was probably grinning. Saul, of course, would be staring unblinkingly at Ricky, daring him to make a move. "What you want, *puta?*"

I slid the gun free of its holster, rested my elbow on the chair back and pointed the barrel at the ceiling. The pimp stiffened. "Call me a whore again, Ricky, and I'm going to shoot your balls off." My smile widened, became sunny. The charms tinkled in my hair as I moved slightly. "Baby Jewel."

His eyes widened. "What about her? Hey, man, she swears she's eighteen, you can't pick no—"

I leveled the gun, cutting him off midstride. "Did she get uppity with you, *cabron?* Stopped handing over her cash? What was it?"

I've never seen a man turn white as curdled milk so fast. There was a gasp from the kitchen, and his number-one girl came around the corner, her eyes as big as dinner plates. I didn't move—if she needed taking care of, Saul would handle it.

"Jewel? She . . ." His eyes flicked over to Carp, widened, came back to me. "Oh, shit. Listen, I did no—"

"Shut up, Ricky." I pulled the hammer back.

He shut up.

"Now. Jewel was working for you last night. When did you last see her? When did she drop off her last load of cash?"

He flinched. "Nine," he finally squeaked. "She work the early shift, man."

Vice had seen her at just past ten or thereabouts; she must have hit the street again, maybe trying to make her rent now that she'd paid Ricky off. Or had she? "How much did she give you, Rick? And keep in mind that I can smell a lie, you greasy little piece of shit."

The girl behind me was quivering with terror, exhaling a high hard musky smell dipped in copper. She knew something. Good luck getting her to spill; if she told us anything Ricky would probably demote her, a fate worse than death.

Still, I might be able to try, if I could catch her alone. A lot would depend on the next few minutes.

And a lot would depend on if I could keep my temper.

Ricky reached up, took his hat off. "Four, five hundred," he said cautiously. "Sent her back out, her pink ass can make four *times* that if she works. Lazy bitch. They all lazy."

And you're such a self-made man. "She didn't show up all day today, and you didn't check on her?"

"Check on her?" He laughed, snuggling back into the couch, his hips jerking up. It was macho, and I let it pass. *Let him get comfy. I'm going to make him pretty damn uncomfy soon enough.* "The bitch comes back. She begs for a little Ricky love, *bruja*. They all do."

So we've gone from calling me slut to witch. It's an improvement. I raised an eyebrow. "Just like Sylvie? Did she come back begging too?"

Despite being lazy, Ricky wasn't a fool. His eyes returned to Carp. "Oh, *shit*." He could barely get the breath to whisper.

I moved. The chair squealed, glass shattered as I brought it down squarely on the table; the sound was incredible. The girl screamed; Ricky let out a yell, and I was on him.

My knees sank into the leather of the couch. My left-hand fingers sank into his throat. I smelled *quesadilla* and cologne, not to mention the thin acrid funk of a coke fiend. I pressed the gun to his temple and smiled into his eyes.

This was pure terrorization for its own sake. I am not a very nice person, and if there's one thing I hate with a vengeance that surpasseth all understanding, it's *pimps*. I never pass up a chance to make a pimp feel my displeasure.

"I would as soon blow your head off as look at you, you greasy little cocksucker." My breath touched his lips. He shook like a rabbit in the snare. "I am going to ask you a few simple questions. Sylvie. Jewel. What did you do to them?"

I didn't think for a second that he had much to do with it. Mostly because the girls were worth more to him alive and peddling their wares. And also because Ricky was, like all pimps, a fucking coward.

He spilled a lot of babbling in Spanglish, enough for me to determine a few things: he hadn't even known Jewel was dead before we came calling. He also was more than willing to spill about the escort service, and I let him talk about that for a little while. Then he dropped one more piece of news.

I let go of him, reholstered the gun, and was off the couch in one motion. "You're sure?" The number-one girl stood by the entrance to the kitchen, her fingers pressed to her mouth and her eyes huge, dark, and full of tears.

"Course I'm sure, the stupid bitch!" Ricky moaned, turning his face into the couch. There was a ratty little gleam to his eyes I didn't like. "There's a doctor on Quincoa—Polish fucker, name's Kricekwesz, he takes care of that shit, but it ain't cheap. Stupid bitch. Stupid *fucking* bitch."

"You're a real prince, Ricky." I looked over at Carp, who was almost purple with restrained glee. It did him good to see me do something like this, something a regular cop wouldn't be able to do without worrying about a brutality lawsuit. "You want to take him in?"

Carp shook his head. He sounded excessively casual. "Not worth our time right now."

I silently agreed. Looked at the girl. Tears slicked her cheeks, and the way her eyes jittered away from mine told me there wasn't much hope of questioning her. There was a fading bruise just visible under the scoop collar of her pink shirt. She couldn't have been more than eighteen, but was already looking old.

"Do yourself a favor, honey." My voice was harsh.

"Get out of the biz." *Before you end up just as dead as those other two girls.*

Then I stalked for the door. *Pregnant. Sylvie was pregnant.*

This puts a little different shine on things, doesn't it. Two counts of murder for her and her baby; and all her internal organs gone. Why? What is this?

Outside in the hall, Carp eyed me while Saul curled his hand around my nape and reeled me in. I spent a few moments leaning against Saul's chest, hearing his heartbeat, the shakes going down slowly. Very slowly.

I'd never told him about Val, but it wouldn't surprise me if he guessed. I'd never told Mikhail either, even in the long, sun-filled afternoons we spent in the same bed. But I wouldn't be surprised if Mikhail had known, too—he had treated me so gently in that one space, the space where we became more than just teacher and student.

Saul didn't want to let me go, but after a few moments I slid away, and his hand fell back down to his side. But a little of his warmth remained against my skin, as much as I could hold on my own without his hands on me.

"Well?" Carp couldn't restrain himself.

I checked the hall, set off for the end of it, where stairs would take us down to the door and the street below. "My initial reaction? He's got nothing to do with it. Could be chance, you know how it is. The escort service, though . . ."

"Yeah?" Carp was almost begging for me to give him something, anything.

"It gives me an idea." More than an idea, in fact.

Shit. I'm going to have to go see him early.

8

Rosenfeld had short auburn hair, a strong-jawed, too-striking-to-be-pretty face, and wrists that put mine to shame even though mine are hellbreed-strong. She settled into the booth next to Carp and examined me suspiciously. "Don't suppose you've got anything useful."

"Not yet." I blew across my coffee to cool it.

Carp I could lie to, Monty encouraged me to keep it close to the vest—but Rosie liked it out where she could see it and tried to act like working with me didn't bother her.

Rosenfeld had only questioned my judgment once. That was during the Browder case; the next day she'd seen an *arkeus* up close and personal. I had almost been too late to save her—and she had seen me take my wrist-cuff off and battle the thing hand-to-hand. After a week in the hospital, she'd actually come down to the warehouse and *apologized,* something I had no idea a cop could do.

She was probably still dyeing her hair to cover up the

white streak. I had no idea if she was still undergoing therapy, and I didn't ask.

Carp snorted. "You shoulda seen it. Diamond Ricky pissed his pants."

Rosie's eyes didn't sparkle, but it was damn close. "I heard the Vice guys giggling about it. Are you really gonna eat that? My arteries are hardening just looking at it."

"I need protein." I smothered the pancakes in butter and strawberry jam; picked up two slices of bacon at once. "Got to keep my girlish figure."

"We should all be so lucky." She studied my face. "So what do you think?"

"Sylvie was pregnant. Ricky was going to send her to a doctor on Quincoa. I'll check him, leave you two to talk to the other hookers. See if they can describe the last trick of the night for either of our girls."

"I don't have to tell you we gotta work fast." Carp dumped more creamer in his coffee. "There are only so many man-hours they'll spend on this."

I knew. If the dead had been nice middle-class church-going girls, the public outcry would be tremendous and we'd have a whole task force paid for by John Taxpayer. As it was, the only thing drawing attention to this was the shock value of the killings. Who cared what happened to hookers? Certainly not the same John Taxpayer who handed over a twenty for a blowjob or a bendover in one of Lucado's dark corners.

Same old story, different day.

Saul stirred restlessly next to me, tucking into his hash browns. His eyes flicked over the inside of the restaurant, a hole-in-the-wall diner on Holmer. I passed him the salt

and the green Tabasco, shuddering at the thought of kissing him afterward.

I will never understand men and Tabasco sauce. "Two
dead women in two days. If this accelerates we're going
to have problems." I looked down at my cheese and ham
omelet. The pancakes were substandard, but the bacon
was crisp, at least.

"Thanks for that lovely thought." Rosie grimaced into
her yogurt and granola, produced from her purse. "Anything you want us to do other than talk to hookers and try
to keep the press off our backs?"

"I've got someone to visit who might be able to shed a
little light, after I talk to the doctor. At least, he'll be able
to tell me if someone's moved into town without permis-
sion." *And I've got to go back to the seminary and question a few kids, not to mention call Andy and . . . Christ,
my dance card's full. As per usual.* "Just be careful, okay?
This isn't looking good."

"Be more than careful," Saul piped up. "Be *cautious.*"

I glanced at him. He'd been extremely quiet since this
morning, and while I appreciated his restraint—he more
than other people understood how I felt about the sex
trade—I still felt a little alarmed at how pale he'd been.

But he probably didn't want to talk in front of the cops,
and I couldn't say I blamed him.

"Great." Rosie waved her spoon. "Be *cautious,* Tonto
says. Care to give any specific pointers, or will you just
settle for being cryptic?"

"Shooting our mouths off before we know precisely
what's going on will get us exactly nowhere," I pointed
out. "Don't give Saul a hard time. He works for me, not
for you."

"We all work for the taxpayers, baby," Carp weighed in.

Yeah. So do the hookers. I rolled my eyes, flicked a long, charm-weighted strand of hair back over my shoulder with a slight chime. "Eat up, boys and girls. There's work to do today."

The abortion clinic on Quincoa was closed by the time we got there. I used the payphone on the corner to leave a message on Carp's cell that we would try the doc tomorrow. Next we could either stop by the seminary or go to the Monde Nuit. I wanted to get the Monde out of the way first, and Saul just got that look again, so I drove. I left him in the Impala smoking a Charvil and staring at the building with narrowed eyes.

I walked up to the door, fitting the silver over my right hand. It was technically a set of brass knuckles, but made out of alloyed silver with just enough true content to hurt anything damned but enough other metal to be twice as hard.

The usual daylight bouncer was on duty, a massive guy with a tribal-tattooed neck; I nodded to him and strode past. My blue eye widened, taking in the flux of bruised hellbreed-tainted atmosphere.

It was still daylight, never mind that the sun was fading fast; the Monde was almost deserted. One or two Traders were in there drinking whatever it is the damned drink, and Riverson was at the bar again; a couple janitors were cleaning everything up and waitstaff were getting ready for dusk.

Perry was at a velvet-covered table in the back, three other hellbreed with him. They were playing what looked like a card game, and cigarette smoke fumed in the air. He didn't even glance up at me, but the scar on my wrist ran with throbbing prickles, a hurtful bloom on the underside of my arm.

I was glad it was covered.

"Hey! *Hey!*" Riverson yelled. I ignored him. There were a few musclebound idiots in the shadows, too far from the hellbreed to be any help; my pace had quickened. By the time I reached the table they were converging on me. Perry's profile was supremely unconcerned, bent over his cards. A low murmur like flies above a corpse filled the air.

Helletöng, the speech of the damned. The ruby warmed against my throat on its silver chain.

I kicked the chair out from under Perry and *punched,* catching him across the cheek and flinging him down and away. The next kick shattered the table; oversized cards, cigarettes, and a half-bottle of Glenlivet went flying.

I reached down, grabbed Perry's shirt, hauled him up left-handed, and punched him again. Blood flew, the silver armoring my fist would hurt him more than the force of the blow. I drew back, silver suddenly hot on my fingers, and did it *again,* dropped him, and kicked him twice. The gun left its holster left-handed, a feat I practiced long and hard to achieve in the dim first days of my training, and I set my feet on the floor, turning in a complete circle to see what I was up against.

Seven of 'em, not counting the goddamn breeds I just interrupted. Splendid.

Perry coughed, and the sound of his laughter cut the air into a thousand wet, shivering pieces. "Sweet nothings," he managed through a mouthful of blood. "Kiss. So nice to see you again."

The muscles stopped, each leather-clad mountainous one of them. I drew in a deep soft breath, the gun held level. "Back off," I told them. "Or I'll fucking kill you all."

Silver in my hair rattled just like a diamondback's tail.

They backed off. I reholstered the gun, bent down, and hauled Perry upright again. "I put up with a lot of shit from you, Pericles. You and the rest of your hellspawn scum. But *no underage cooch.* The rule's simple: no dabbling in the under-eighteen pool in my territory. Right?"

As usual, he got cute with me. "Would we dare disagree?"

I'd damaged one whole half of his bland pale face, his blood-masked eyes glared at me but he remained still, perfectly still.

Inhumanly still.

I let go of the front of his shirt. Blood dripped from his chin, the skin over his cheekbone mashed into hamburger, his lacerated eye puffing up. *Never pretty in the first place, and a whole lot worse now.* I discarded the thought, lifted my fist again.

"Spare me your kisses, Kismet." He raised his hands, loosely. But there was no shimmer of etheric force around them, he wasn't getting ready to throw anything nasty at me. "We know this decree of yours. We *obey.*"

Like shit you do, if you think you can get away with it. "Oh yeah? Someone's breaking it. Using Diamond Ricky's teenage whores to feed a few bad appetites. And right now my suspicion is squarely on the hellbreed population. I know how little self-control you bastards have."

His unwounded eye narrowed a little, that was all. I could tell nothing from his face, and he probably had the idea that I was just fishing.

Still, it was therapeutic to bash his face in every once in a while. It was also good for my image. "Whatever escort service supplying underage cooch you've got your fingers in, get out. Now. Or next time I come back I'll *shoot* you in the fucking face. *And* I'll see this place loses its incognito appeal with the police."

His lip curled—at least, the half of it that wasn't split and bleeding. "Human police?"

And whatever nightside help I can beg, borrow, and threaten to erase you from the face of the earth. "I'm sure they can be given a little help." I held his eyes, unblinking. The scar on my wrist sent waves of heat up my arm, each wave deep, soft, and deliciously warm. My heart rate rose a little, but I was trained too well to have a little sex magic distract me. "Don't fuck with me, Perry."

"Someday you might want me to." He reached up, touched his bleeding lip with delicate fingertips, and the smile in his blue eyes chilled my blood. "I'll live to hear you beg, hunter."

Not if I have anything to say about it. "Dream on, hellspawn. Do we understand each other, or do I have to kick your ass around this cheapshit little shack?" The back of my neck prickled. I could *feel* them moving in on me. *Got to think of something quick here.*

Perry waved them away. Thin black ichor spattered on the floor, the wounds closing slowly. Very slowly. Silver's deadly to them, something about the Moon and how she rules the tides of both sorcery and water. We don't fully understand *why* silver works, but no hunter I've ever run across cares. It's enough *that* it works.

Perry's eyes burned laser-blue. The tip of his cherry-red scaled tongue flicked over the black ichor oozing over his lips like a tiny crimson fish. "I understand you perfectly, dear Kiss. Do you even understand yourself?"

"Spare me the psychobabble." I turned on my heel, my hand throbbing inside the silver weight. My back ran with electricity—a damned I'd just punched in the face was right behind me. *Right* behind me. In front of me, two mountains of muscle, both wearing sunglasses, both armed with assault rifles. "See you Sunday, Perry. Maybe I'll ruin another one of your suits."

"I look forward to it. Try not to break anything next time."

"Don't piss me off, and maybe I won't. Keep your ears open." I strode straight for the muscle, and they moved aside to let me pass.

I let out a soft breath of relief, though I shouldn't have. Perry's voice floated through the air behind me, wet and chill with glee.

"You could've just asked, Kiss."

You fucker. "You wouldn't have told me jackshit," I tossed over my shoulder. *And I'm not so sure you don't know anything. This was an exercise in futility, but at least I got to hit you.* "Besides, maybe I like smashing your face in, *hellspawn.*"

With that, I hit the door. Mercifully, he didn't say anything else. Maybe he was getting smarter.

My orange Impala gleamed at the curb, once again in the fire zone, Saul's cigarette sending lazy whorls of smoke into the air out the passenger's-side window. I got in, dropping down in the driver's seat, and looked at the red fuzzy dice hanging from the mirror. Let out a sigh.

Saul said nothing.

"I think we're fucked." I stared through the windshield as the last of the daylight poured out of the sky's cup. "He knows something, maybe, but he won't give it up. Yet."

Saul exhaled a long sheaf of smoke. I worked the silver knuckles off my fingers; they were grimed with Perry's thin black blood.

They don't bleed red, Hell's scions. No, they bleed silt-black, in thin runnels like grapeseed oil, and it stinks as it decays.

"It isn't Were," Saul answered softly. "It isn't hell-breed, at least not any hellbreed or damned Perry has control over. It isn't a type of damned you've seen before. Whatever it is, it stinks of violence, and fur. I haven't ever smelled anything like this, Jill. It's definitely not human, but I don't know *what* it is."

I turned my head, meaning to look at him, but instead staring at the front door of the Monde guarded by its huge bouncer. Why the muscle kept letting me in I don't know, except for the scar on my arm and my bargain with Perry. Still, they should have roughed me up once or twice, just to keep things standard. "Something neither of us knows about. Something that attacks teenage hookers and divests them of their internal organs."

"It stinks of ice and rotting flesh. And magic. Bad, old, nasty magic."

I stared at the door as if I could will a part of the puzzle to come clear. "You think he's involved?"

"This isn't his style. But I wouldn't rule him out." Saul flicked the Charvil out the window. "What next?"

"The seminary. We need to figure out how an *utt'huruk* got into a nice corn-fed missionary boy. Then home to pick up a few things, and call Andy." I gave him a tight smile. "No, I haven't forgotten. And I want to pick his brains as well as ask him to send his apprentice down here to cover for me."

Saul looked troubled. I twisted the key and the Impala purred into life. Good old American heavy metal. "Jill."

"What?"

"Do you like visiting *him?*"

What? Saul had never directly referred to my bargain with Perry since coming back from the Rez after the rogue Were case two years ago. "What the hell are you talking about? One of these days, when I've figured out a lesser evil, I am going to kill him. He's useful, Saul. Don't start."

"I don't like the way he looks at you."

You're not the only one. I put the car in gear, released the parking brake, and pulled out. "Neither do I, baby. Neither do I."

9

I was on a hell of a run of bad luck, and more came in the form of information, as usual. The still-unconscious Oscar hadn't had any visitors, but he *had* been in the room when another seminary student's aunt had visited. The aunt had been tall, dark-haired, and nobody could describe her face; not even the priest who had signed her in and watched the visit—who just happened to be the heart-attack victim, Father Rosas. The kid who'd been visited was a transfer student from out of state, a thin ratlike teenage boy whose narrow eyes widened when I shoved the gun in his face and told him to strip.

Red-nosed Father Rourke choked, but Saul had him by the collar. Father Guillermo stood up so fast his chair scraped against the linoleum floor. "Jillian?" He sounded like the air had been punched out of him.

"Sorry, Father." And I was. "But this kid might be dangerous. It's insurance."

"You . . . *you*—" Father Rourke was having a little trouble with this. "You *witch!* Gui, you won't let her—"

"Paul." Gui's voice was firm. He backed up two steps from the teenager I had at gunpoint. "Remember your oath."

"The Church—"

"The archbishop *and* the cardinal have given me provisional powers once there is proved to be supernatural cause," I quoted, chapter and verse. "Keep yourself under control, Father, or Saul will drag you outside. Don't make him cranky, I don't recommend it." I nodded at the kid. "Strip. Slowly. The cassock first."

The boy trembled. The whites of his eyes were yellow, acne pocked his cheeks, and I was nine-tenths sure there would be a mark on him. Maybe not on his back, but somewhere on his body.

A Sorrow doesn't leave the House, living or dead, without a mark. One way or another, they claim their own, from a Queen Mother down to the lowliest male drone.

The question of just what a young Sorrow would be doing here in a seminary was the bigger concern, though.

And just as I was sure the kid wasn't going to strip, he slowly lifted his hands, palms out.

Uh-oh. This doesn't look go—

The spell hit me, *hard,* in the solar plexus, I choked and heard Saul yell. The cry shaded into a Were's roar, wood shattering, and I shook my head, blood flying from my lip. Found myself on my feet, instinctively crouching as the ratfaced Sorrow leapt for me; I caught his wrist, locked it, whirled, and had him on the ground. He was muttering in Chaldean.

Saul growled. I spared a look at him; his tail lashed and his teeth were bared. In full cougar form, but his eyes were incandescent—and he was larger than the usual mountain cat. Weres tend to run slightly big even in their animal forms. He made a deep hissing coughing sound, the tawny fur on the back of his neck standing straight up and his tail puffing up just like a housecat's. "Shift back," I snarled. "I need this bastard held down."

"What is she—what is she—" Father Rourke was having a little more trouble with the program. Gui had his arm, holding him back; Rourke's face was even more florid than usual. He was actually spluttering, and I felt a well of not-very-nice satisfaction.

I leaned down, the boy's wiry body struggling under me. "I can help you," I whispered in his ear. "I can help you, free you of the Sorrows, and give you your soul back. You know I can. Cooperate."

His struggles didn't cease; if anything, they grew more intense. He heaved back and forth, rattling in Old Chaldean like a snake.

It was always a fool's chance, to try to free a Sorrow. Hunters always offer, but they almost never take us up on it. The Mothers and sorceress-bitches have things just the way they want them, all the power and none of the accountability—and the boys are drones, born into Houses and trained to be nothing but mindless meat.

The Sorrows worship the Elder Gods, after all. And those gods—like all gods—demand blood. The difference is, the Elder Gods like their claret literally, with ceremony, and in bucketfuls.

Saul's hands came down; tensed, driving in. Immediately, it became *much* easier to keep the kid down. Working together, we got him flipped over; I held down the boy's hips while Saul took care of his upper torso. The Were's eyes were aflame with orange light, he was *furious*. He slid a long cord of braided leather into the kid's mouth, holding down one skinny wrist with his knee. "No poison tooth for you," he muttered. "Jill?"

"I'm fine." I spat blood, he'd socked me a good one in the mouth. Thank God my teeth don't come out easily. Sorcery is *occasionally* useful. "Hold him." *Where's the mark, got to find the mark, got to find it; what's a Sorrow doing in here?*

The boy's spine crackled as his eyes rolled into his head. He mumbled, and I wondered what he was cooking up next. *Goddammit, and he's gagged. Christ.* I tore the front of his shirt, ran my hand over his narrow hairless chest. No tingle. Where was the mark?

"Jillian?" Father Guillermo, by the door. He sounded choked.

"You *witch,* that's one of our *kids!*" Rourke was still having trouble with this one.

I snapped a glance back over my shoulder, checking. "Transferred from out of state? Your kid's in a ditch somewhere, Father. This is a *Sorrow.* Probably just a little baby viper instead of a full-grown one, though." *Or he'd have tried to crush my larynx instead of socking me in the gut.* I got his pants off with one swift jerk, breaking the button and jamming the zipper. "I suggest you wait outside in case he chews through the gag." Blood dripped into my right eye, I blinked it away, irritably. "The question is why the Sorrows are so interested in this seminary. And when I find the mark we'll find out."

I got lucky. It was on his right thigh, the three inter-locked circles in blue with the sigil of the Black Flame where they overlapped. He was a young soldier, not a man-drone only fit for sacrifice or a pleasure-slave. Of all the ranks a male could hold in a House, the soldiers had maybe the shortest life—but at least they weren't tied down and slaughtered to feed the Eldest Ones. "Bingo," I muttered, and held out my hand. The bone handle of Saul's Bowie landed solidly in my palm.

The Sorrow hissed and gurgled behind the gag. Saul reached down, cupped his chin, and yanked back, exposing the boy's throat and making sure he couldn't thrash his shoulders around.

I laid the flat of the knife against the mark and the kid screamed, audible even behind the gag. Steel against Chaldean sorcery, one of the oldest enmities known to magic.

The Elder Gods would have us all back in the Bronze Age if they could. They would have us killing each other to feed their hungry mouths as well. Still, there are some Elders the Sorrows don't invoke, because their very natures are inimical to the worship of darkness. Belief is a double-edged blade, and a hunter can use it as well as any other weapon.

"Thou shalt be released," I murmured in Old Chaldean. "Thou unclean, thou whom the gods have turned their face from, thou *shalt* be released, in the name of Vul the Magnificent, the lighter of fires—"

He screamed again. I paused. Next came sliding the knife up and flaying the skin to get the mark off. I could add it to my collection. Each little bit of skin, drying and stretching and marked with their hellish brand, was another brick in the wall between me and the guilt of my teacher's death. Each time I killed a Sorrow, I felt *good*.

Cleansed.

I am not a very nice person.

"Last chance," I said. "Before you go to your Hell." *And believe me when I say that's one place you don't want to visit even for a moment.*

The kid went limp.

There, that's more like it. I looked up at Saul, whose eyes still glowed. No, he was not in the least bit happy. But he nodded, a quick dip of his chin, and released the pressure on the gag just a little.

The rat-faced kid's eyes met mine. A spark flared in their tainted depths, swirling now he had revealed himself. His skin began to look gray too, the Chaldean twisting his tongue and staining his body.

Wait a second. He isn't even an Acolyte. What's he doing out of a House? "Ungag him."

Saul hesitated.

"Christ, Saul, ungag him."

The boy jerked. Leather slipped free. But Saul was tense, and I saw his right hand relax from a fist into a loose claw, nails sliding free and lengthening, turning razor-sharp. If the Sorrow made a move, my Were would open his throat.

"What are you out here for, Neophym? Who's holding your leash?"

He had apparently decided to talk. "Sister," he choked, gurgling. "My . . . sister . . . *please* . . ."

I bit my lip, weighing it. On the one hand, the Sorrows were trained to lie to outsiders.

And on the other, no Sorrow would ever use the word *sister*. The only word permitted for female within the House was *mistress*. Or occasionally, *bitch*.

Just like the only word for man was *slave*.

I considered this, staring into the Sorrow's eyes. "What's a Sorrow doing in my town, huh? You've been warned."

"Fleeing . . . *chutsharak*." His breath rattled in his throat.

Chutsharak? I've never heard of that. "The what?"

It was too late. He crunched down hard with his teeth,

bone cracking in his jaw; I whipped my head back and Saul did the same, scrambling away from the body in a flurry of Were-fast motion. I found myself between the body and the priests, watching as bones creaked, the neurotoxin forcing muscles to contract until only the crown of the head and the back of the heels touched the floor. A fine mist of blood burst out of the capillaries of his right eye.

Poison tooth. He'd committed suicide, cracking the false tooth embedded in his jaw.

Just as his heels slammed back, smashing into the back of his head, his sphincters released. Then the body slumped over on its side.

"Dammit." I rubbed at the cuff over my right wrist, reflectively. "*Damn* it."

"What's a *chutsharak?*" Saul's voice was hushed. Behind us, Father Rourke took in a deep endless breath.

I shook my head, the charms in my hair shifting and tinkling uneasily. "I don't know." My throat was full. "Gods above. Why are they sending children? I *hate* the Sorrows."

"It's probably mutual." Saul approached the body carefully, then began to mutter under his breath, the Were's prayer in the face of needless death. I left it alone. The poison was virulent, but it lost its potency on contact with a roomful of oxygen. He was in no danger.

"Jillian?" Father Guillermo sounded pale. He *was* pale, when I checked him. Two bright spots of color stood out on his cheeks. "What do we do next?"

"Any other transfers in the last year? Priest, worker, student, anyone?"

"N-no." He shook his head. "J-just K-Kit. Him." His eyes flickered past me to the body on the floor. The stink was incredible.

Father Rourke kept crossing himself. He was praying too. His rubbery lips moved slightly, wet with saliva. Probably an Our Father.

Sometimes I wished I was still wholly Catholic. The guilt sucks, but the comfort of rote prayer is nothing to sneeze at. There's nothing like prepackaged answers to make a human psyche feel nice and secure. "I'll need to go over the transfer records. Why would a Sorrow want to infiltrate a seminary? Are you holding anything?"

His face drained of color like wine spilling out of a cup.

"Gui? You're not holding anything I should know about, are you?" I watched him, he said nothing. "Guillermo?" My tone sharpened.

He flinched, almost guiltily. "It is . . . Jillian, I . . ."

"Oh, for *God's* sake. I can't *protect* you if you don't tell me what I need to know!"

"Sister Jillian—"

"What are you holding?"

"Jillian—"

I snapped. I grabbed the priest by the front of his cassock, lifted him up, and shook him before his shoulders hit the wall. "Guillermo." My mouth was dry, fine tremors of rage sliding through my hands. The scar on my wrist turned to molten lead. Behind me there was a whisper of cloth, and Rourke let out a blasphemy I never thought to hear from a priest.

"Take one more step and I hit you," Saul said, quietly, but with an edge.

"I could have died." I said each word clearly, enunciating each consonant. "*Saul* could have died. If I'd known you were holding something I could have questioned him far more effectively. You *cannot* keep information from me and *expect me to protect you!*"

"He's a Jesuit. He can't tell you anything." Rourke spat the words as if they'd personally offended him. "He took a vow."

I dropped Guillermo. *Fuck. I'm about to beat up a priest. Man, this is getting ridiculous.* "If you don't start talking in fifteen seconds, Gui, I'm going to start searching. I'm going to tear this place apart from altar to graveyard until I find whatever you're holding. You might as well tell me now. What is it? What are the Sorrows looking for?"

"It's nothing of any use to them." Gui rubbed at his throat. He was still pale, and the smell swirling in the air was beginning to be thick and choking. I was used to smelling death, but he wasn't. "Merely an artifact—"

"What. Are. You. Holding?" The scar pulsed in time to each word, and I was close to doing something unforgivable, like hauling off and slugging a *priest*. Dammit. This disturbed me more than I wanted to admit.

"The Spear of—" Rourke almost yelled.

"*No!*" Gui all but screamed.

"—*Saint Anthony!*" Rourke bellowed, his face turning crimson. Gui sagged.

I turned on my heel, eyed Rourke. *Come on, I used to be Catholic. Don't pull this shit on me.* "Saint Anthony didn't *have* a spear. He gave his staff to Saint Macarius."

"It is the spear he blessed with his blood when the citizens of a small town were overwhelmed with the hordes of Hell. He didn't use it; Marcus Silvacus used it." Father Rourke's flabby cheeks quivered, and he was pale too. I couldn't tell if I was smelling the stink of a lie on him, or the reek of fear.

*I am going to have to check that out. As far as I knew,
Marcus Silvacus never met Saint Anthony, and Saint Anthony didn't have a fucking spear.* I could feel my teeth
grind together. I tipped my head back, my jaw working.

"I'm sorry, Guillermo. But you took a vow." For once,
Rourke's tone wasn't blustering.

"An artifact here, and it somehow slipped your mind to
tell me? This isn't looking good, Gui. Years and years I've
trusted you, and I've done the Church's dirty work peeling demons out of people before I was even fully trained.
This is how you repay me?"

"The Sorrow said he was fleeing," Saul's voice cut
across mine. "It might be unrelated."

I wasn't mollified, but he did have a point. "Still, that's
something I needed to know."

"Agreed." His hand curled around my shoulder. "It
stinks of death in here. And we have work to do."

Damn the man. He was right again.

I shook out my right hand, my fingers popping as tendons loosened. "All right." I sounded strange even to myself. "Fine. But I won't forget this, Guillermo." *I will not
ever forget this.*

"I would have told you everything, Jillian. When I was
released from my vow." Gui slumped against the wall,
rubbing his throat, though I hadn't held him by anything
than his cassock. "I swear it, I would have. I didn't think
the two were connected, and I can't speak of it."

I waved it away. The charms tinkled in my hair, uneasily. "Get that cleaned up. And give him a decent burial; he
was only a kid."

"Not in consecra—" Rourke stopped when my eyes
rested on him. I felt my face harden. My blue eye began

to burn, and I knew it was glowing, a single pinprick of red in the center of my pupil.

"Give him his last rites," I said, very softly and distinctly. "If indulgence is required, *Father,* I'll pay. But for God's sake bury him kindly."

I left it at that. And for once, so did he.

Saul drove. I wasn't in the mood. We didn't speak on the way home. As soon as I swept the warehouse and determined it was safe I headed for the phone. Which began to ring as soon as I got within three feet of it.

I hooked it up. "This better be good news."

"Hello to you too." Avery sounded serious, as usual. "Jill, there's a problem."

Oh, Christ. Not another one. "The Trader I just brought in?"

A short, unamused laugh drifted through the phone line. Avery was a professional exorcist, not a hunter like me. It was his job to exorcise the Traders I brought in, just like it was Eva, Benito, and Wallace's job to handle other straight exorcisms in my city and refer the extraordinary ones to me. "No, he was an easy rip-and-stuff. Screamed like a damned soul, though. He's on meds. No, the problem's different. I wanted to talk to you about it."

I considered this. "Micky's? At—" I glanced at the clock, juggled his probable freedom from work. "Eleven?"

He agreed immediately. "Sounds good, I'll buy you a beer. Um . . ."

"Um, what?" I glanced over my shoulder as Saul began rummaging in the kitchen. He was probably hungry; I was too. The light shone mellow off his long red-black hair, silver glinting against the strands; his cheeks looked a little pale without the paint. He glanced up, probably feeling my eyes, and gave me a half-smile that made my legs feel decidedly mushy.

"Will Saul be there?"

What? "Of course he will. He's my partner." *And a damn fine one, too.*

"I just . . . well, yeah. Bring him. Sorry. Look, eleven o'clock. See you then."

I hung up feeling even more unsettled, and that was rare. Avery didn't have anything against Weres.

Not that I knew of, anyway. Nothing out of the ordinary.

I dialed Andy's number from memory and got his answering machine, left a message. The heavenly odor of sautéed onions tiptoed to my nose, and that meant steak. *Bless Weres and their domesticity.*

I stared at the phone after laying it back in the charger, my eyebrows drawing together. Then I picked it up again, and dialed another number from memory.

"Hutchinson's Books, Used and Rare." This was a slightly nasal, wheezing voice; I had to bite back a laugh.

"Hutch, it's Jill."

He actually spluttered. "Oh good Christ, what *now?*"

"Relax, baby. I just need to use the back room. Want to do some research for me?"

"I'd rather gouge my own eyes out." He was serious. Wise man.

"That makes you much more intelligent than a number of people I know. Listen, scour for everything you can find about the Sorrows. Brush up your ceremonial Chaldean and find me every mention of something called a *chutsharak.*"

"Zuphtarak?" He mangled the word. I could almost hear his teeth chattering. Cute, nervous Hutch was not cut out for hunter's work, but he was hell on wheels when it came to digging through dusty old tomes; which Hutchinson's Books held as a hunter's library in return for a number of very nice tax breaks that kept it afloat.

Hey, hunters believe in supporting local indie bookstores.

"Chutsharak." I spelled it for him. "But the *ch* is sometimes *j,* and sometimes—"

"—those goddamn seventeenth-century translations, I know. All right. Fine. You still have your key?"

"Of course I still have my key." *I am exceedingly unlikely to lose it, Hutch. And anyway, I built those fucking locks. They'll open for me anytime I want.* "I won't come by while you're in. Leave your notes in the usual place."

"Thank fucking God."

I snorted. "I thought you liked me, Hutch."

He gave an unsteady little laugh. I could almost see his hazel eyes behind his glasses and his thin biceps. "You're hot, yeah. But you're scary. I'll work on it. *Chutsharak.* Chaldean. Got it."

"One more thing."

"Oh, Christ."

"Can you look up Saint Anthony's spear?"

"Saint Anthony didn't have a—"

"I didn't think so either. But check it. And check to see if there's *any* connection between Anthony and Marcus Silvacus. Just to be sure." I rubbed at the bridge of my nose, feeling a headache beginning. Just my luck. But why would Rourke lie to me? Of course, I wasn't Catholic anymore, I wasn't a priest, and I was female; he would probably just confess and be forgiven and not lose any damn sleep over lying to *me*. And if Gui really was under orders not to say anything about an artifact hidden at the seminary, an artifact the Sorrows wanted for some unholy reason, things were getting stickier by the moment.

"Fine." Hutch said it like I had him by the balls—and not in a good way.

"Thanks, Hutch. I'll bring you a present."

"Keep me out of this."

I laughed, and he hung up. I laid the phone back in its cradle and stared at it, daring it to ring again.

It remained obstinately mute.

"Red-sauce penne with steak, and fresh asparagus." Saul made his happy sound, a low hum like a purr. "Want some wine?"

"Please." I rubbed at the back of my neck under my heavy hair. "You're a good partner, Saul."

His eyes met mine, he peered under the hanging cabinets. The copper-bottom pans glowed behind him. "Yeah?"

I folded my arms. "Yeah. Avery wants to meet us at Micky's. And then I've got some research to do."

"Research?"

I know, I know. I don't like it either. "Then we'll come back, and I'm all yours."

"I like the sound of that. Make yourself useful and open the wine, kitten."

10

Avery slumped in the booth, tapping his long fingers on the glass-topped table. Directly over him, Humphrey Bogart stared somberly out of a framed print. Curly brown hair fell in Ave's face, over sad brown eyes; he looked like a handsome little mournful beagle. Despite that, he was quick and ruthless during exorcisms, seeming to come alive only when a particular Possessor or *arkeus* was giving him trouble, or the victim started to thrash. Of all the exorcists I knew, he was the one who came closest to being a hunter, if only because of the sheer nail-biting joy he took in skating the edge of danger.

We are all adrenaline junkies, really. You have to be. Hunting is 95 percent boredom-laced waiting punctuated with the occasional bursts of sheer and total terror. No middle ground.

Ave's badge hung on a chain around his neck; he had shrugged out of his motorcycle jacket and was staring at his fingertips like he had bad news.

I was really getting a rotten feeling about this.

I slid into the booth, Saul right next to me. "Hey, baby." I gave a smile, but Ave didn't grin back. Not even a glimmer of his usual sleepy good humor. "Wow, looks grim."

Vixen swished her hips up to the table, her sleek brown hair clinging to her head like an otter's. "Hey." She plunked down three Fat Tires, her lip lifting as she glared at me, then smiled at Saul. He, as usual, looked supremely unconcerned.

She sighed, turned on her heel, and her tartan skirt ticked back and forth as she switched away with a Were's grace.

"In heat again, I see," Saul murmured, and I choked on my first sip of beer, the laugh bubbling up.

Avery didn't even crack a slight smile. I sighed. "So what's up, Ave?"

He finally shifted, picking up his beer and tipping a sarcastic salute to Saul. "Hey, furboy."

"Hey, skinman." Saul's tone was even, chill.

"I heard something." Avery addressed this to me.

"Yeah?" I waited, rolling my next sip of beer around in my mouth. Stifled a small pleasant burp; it tasted of grilled onions. At least I had the memory of dinner to get me through this. Whatever *this* was.

"One of my stoolies; he's a drunk. But he picks stuff up—it's amazing. He manages to get around. Anyway, he knows someone who saw something." Avery produced a white square of paper, held between his fingers like a card trick. "And the worst thing is, I believe him."

"What did he see?" *And what the fuck does this have to do with anything?* I shifted uneasily, the leather of my pants rubbing uncomfortably against the vinyl seat.

"Guy's called Robbie the Juicer. He saw them dumping Baby Jewel last night. Black van, no license plate. Said there were four of them, one looked to be a woman, and two men. The last one was . . . he said it was big, and it stank, and it threw the body like it weighed nothing."

Huh. I absorbed this. "Big. And stinky."

"Yeah. He said it looked like an ape. Like it was *furry.*" He darted a look at Saul. "Could it be a rogue Were? No offense, understand, I just thought I should ask."

It was a good question, considering what he'd been told. "A rogue Were would hide the bodies," I said, slowly. The memory of the last rogue to hit Santa Luz was far enough away that I could consider the notion without a gut-clenching burst of slick-palmed fear. "Wouldn't work with anyone else, that's why they're rogue. And wouldn't eat the organs unless it was starving; they like muscle-meat first. Who is this witness, and where was he?"

"My stoolie said something about a baseball diamond; the witness is homeless and sometimes sleeps in the dug-out. He heard the van's engine and looked out; the van sat there for a while and he decided to go take a look." He offered the square of white paper. "Here's his name and vitals, and a list of the places he usually hangs out. He's scared to death."

"He should be. This is nothing to mess with." I took the paper; it was thin and innocent against my fingers. "Thanks, Avery." *Christ, I bet I'm not going to sleep for a while.* Behind my eyes, the vision of the edge of the park and the baseball diamond flashed, and I cautiously decided it was possible. The dugout was at an angle and it was *extremely* possible someone hidden in there could have seen something. It was just *slightly* possible someone hidden in there could have been unremarked, which was the truly incredible part. Whoever this Robbie Juicer was, he'd probably used up his entire life's worth of luck.

Avery was decent, after all. He looked up, at my Were. "I'm sorry, Saul. I just—Christ. This thing's *awful*. There's talk going around."

My ears perked. "What kind of talk?"

"Talk of a bounty on Weres. Someone's saying that this is a rogue Were, and why shouldn't the rest of them suffer for it? And there's talk about you too, Jill, that you're marked and it's only a matter of time before the damned drag you back to Hell."

"Marked. By who?" *I've been marked all my life, Avery.* But if he was hearing whispers on the nightside, little bits of rumor from the occult shops and not-so-human stoolies that kept on the exorcists' good side, it could only mean bad trouble.

"I dunno. But you hear shit, you know. Something big is going down, and I can't get more than whispers." He hunched his shoulders, looking miserable. "You just be careful. We can't afford to lose you. *Or* your furry friend there."

Well, at least that was something. "Guess not." I bumped Saul with my elbow, but gently. Just to let him know I was there. He was still crowding me, a little closer than usual. Taking comfort in closeness. "We've got Sorrows adepts in town, Ave. At least one. I pulled an *utt'huruk* out of a kid the other day and there was a Neophym who gurgled something about *chutsharak* before biting his poison tooth. You know that term?"

"I never was good at that prehistoric shit." He shook his brown head, curls falling in his eyes. "I thought you didn't let the Sorrows in."

"I don't. When I find their bolthole I'm going to burn them. Just watch yourself. You hear anything that sounds like Chaldean, you *run*."

"You bet. Hey, be easy on this witness. He's not bolted too tight, I guess. And he doesn't want any police static, or I woulda met him and brought him to you."

Go easy? I'm an easygoing gal. "That goes without saying." I lifted my beer bottle and he lifted his, we clinked the glass together. He suddenly looked a lot easier about the whole thing. "I'll be gentle, I promise."

"Yeah, right." His color began to come back. "Sure you will."

I could almost feel my eyebrow raise. "You're a cynic, Avery. One day that's going to catch up to you." I lifted my beer again, and took a long hard swallow.

It tasted a little more sour than I liked. Or that could have been the taste of bad luck in my mouth.

Instead of research, we hit the street looking for Robbie the Juicer, the nervous witness. It was a cold night, clouds moving in from the river but not fast enough to give us rain before five or six in the morning; the hard points of braver stars pierced the veil of night and orange citylight. Outside the city limits, out in the near-desert, the waning moon would shine on yucca and sandstone. It was a night for sharp teeth and quick death. The air itself was knotted tight with expectation.

We canvassed the easier places on Avery's list first: the missions, Prosper Alley, the shooting gallery on Trask Street, the fountain in Plaskény Square. Nada. Not a whisper of our target.

Plenty of the people we saw that night had no idea we were there. I stayed close to Saul, and Were camouflage took care of hiding us both. Weres are traditionally hunters' allies, and plenty of times a hunter has been grateful for the furkind's ability to conceal. I was odd among hunters in that I actually slept with my backup, but by no means unique. Most Weres don't like bedplay with humans; we're too fragile.

But with the scar on my wrist, I was no longer so fragile. It made things interesting.

Just the way Saul's initial distrust and distaste for me and my helltainted self had made things interesting. Sometimes I wondered why he had come back.

You can find bums in any city. Looking for a *particular* homeless man in Santa Luz is needle-in-a-haystack frustrating. You just roll around a lot and hope to get stuck in the right place.

We were casing the second large mecca of the dispossessed in Santa Luz, Broadway. I walked beside Saul carefully, occasionally glancing down at the cracked sidewalk, threading between groups of street kids gathering in doorways and sharing cigarettes of both legal and nonlegal origin. Quite a few had bottles in brown paper bags, and a good number of them were younger than Baby Jewel. Dreadlocks, dyed hair, piercings, layers of clothing as they struggled to stay warm in the desert night, gangs and streetfamilies drawing together for comfort and protection—it was enough, really, to make a cynic out of anyone.

I caught sight of a thin, nervous-looking man with a scruff of brown hair, sharing hits off a bottle with a taller scarecrow of a black man in army fatigues. The brown-haired scruff wore a dun coat and a red backpack, black boots, and a shocking-blue T-shirt.

Saul marked him a full fifteen seconds after I did. "That him?"

"Coat, backpack, boots, and a serious case of nerves. Looks like it." I started forward, but Saul's hand closed around my arm. "What?"

He tilted his head. "Someone else is looking."

I looked. There, tucked into a slice of shadow like a professional, a skinny man in a long dirty duster finished un-smoking a cigarette. The red eye glowed as he dropped it, and he was too clean-shaven to be a homeless man. And it's not just strange to see a homeless man drop a smoke halfway to the filter, especially when he doesn't take a drag before he does it.

It rings every wrong bell in a hunter's head to see something like that.

"Got enough metal on him for me to smell, and he's hunting," Saul murmured in my ear. I barely nodded, letting him know I'd heard him.

Mercenary? Or something else?

I thought this over, examining our new player. Was he looking for Robbie or just for trouble? He didn't seem to have the nervous witness in his sights, but he was certainly up to no good. And if Saul could smell gunplay and violence on him, he was probably someone I should have a nice little chat with.

You can call me paranoid, but I rarely believe in pure coincidence. Usually coincidence gets a little help in a situation like this.

"Get our witness. Question him if you feel like it." I slid a slim, black-finished blade out of its sheath and reversed it along my arm. "I'll see what's up with our little friend over there."

"You got it. Where should I take the jitterboy?"

I did a rapid mental calculation of location and distance. "Take him to Woo Song's and buy him dinner, but don't let him drink any more. I'll meet you as soon as I can. Get *every* scrap of information you can from him. And play nice."

"I will." He looked, again, like he wanted to say *be careful*. But he didn't. He merely bent down, kissed my temple, and slid away, leaving me without a Were's camouflage.

I set off across the street at an angle calculated to bring me into our mysterious visitor's blind spot.

Unfortunately, I realized as I was halfway across Broadway, our friend wasn't alone. His backup was on the roof, and as bullets chewed into the pavement behind me and the screaming started, I realized that this wasn't normal at all. Nothing about this was usual. And that usually added up to one very *fucked* Jill Kismet.

I rolled, taking cover behind a parked car. Glass shattered; whoever it was had a fucking assault rifle and was spraying the car. The knife vanished, and I spared a brief prayer for the civilians on the street. *Let's have no casualties, Jill.*

That is, except for the ones you *want to inflict.*

11

A running gunfight is not like you see in the movies. Most gun battles are over in just under seven seconds, and most end with nobody getting hurt. Or at least, among the normal dayside population, that's what it's like.

A nightside gunfight is a different beast. We don't engage in them often, mostly because a lot of hellbreed and other things hunters deal with are tough enough not to need guns most of the time. A hunter is armed with heavy firepower merely to even the score.

These boys, however, were not nightsiders. They were human, and professional troublemakers unless I missed my guess. The one on the ground vanished as the one on the roof peppered the car I'd taken cover behind; I tore the cuff off my right wrist and stuffed it in my pocket, gasping as air hit the scar and a flush of chill heat slammed through my nervous system. I could have dealt with these jokers with the cuff on, but I was feeling a little unsettled. Besides, why not use near-invulnerability if you have it?

It used to be I wouldn't use it unless I *had* to. *God, Jill, you've changed.*

My own guns spun out, and I gathered my legs underneath me. Sighed, blew out between my teeth, and whirled, skipping back two or three steps before pitching forward, legs burning as I *pulled* on all the etheric force the scar could provide. My boots smashed into the car's hood, using the mass of the engine underneath to *push* against.

Wind screamed as I *flew,* gravity loosing its constraints for one brief glorious second.

The only trouble with doing this is a simple law of physics: the landing, once you're going that fast, is a lot harder than you think.

Impact.

I smashed into the man on the roof, heard human ribs snap like green wood, the rifle went flying. Skidded, my boots dragging and heating up with friction, hitting the roof *hard* as I lost my balance, teeth clicking together. The man let out a choked burble, I bounced up to my feet.

This is why I wear leather pants. Less goddamn road-rash when you hit a rooftop going faster than you should. Jeans would be shredded. It's not just a fashion statement—though they do make my ass look cute, as Saul so often reminds me.

I grabbed the man. He was in night-camo and streaky facepaint, and there was a whistling sound that told me one of his broken ribs had punctured a lung.

Shit.

"Who sent you?" *I'm going to take you to a hospital and have them patch you up so I can break every bone in your body for shooting down at one of my streets like that.*

You could have killed a bunch of innocents, you asshole.
My *innocents.* "Who? Tell me and you'll live." I held him
up one-handed, my fingers tangled in straps that were
some kind of harness to keep his weapons on, he was
armed to the teeth. He even had a couple of grenades. Just
the thing for urban combat. "*Who,* goddammit?"

He would have screamed if he could have gotten
enough air in.

Then it smashed through his chest, spraying me with
blood and chips of bone, I yelled and hit the ground for
cover, hearing the clack of pulleys as well as the meaty
thud of the body hitting the ground. *What the bloody blue
fuck?*

Silence. Sirens in the distance, screams and shrieks
from the street below. *Goddammit. What the fuck was
that?* I *extended* my senses, felt nothing.

The man in camo lay slumped on the rooftop, something protruding from his chest. I took a closer look.

It was an arrow. The head was heavy-duty, a nasty
piece of work; the sound of pulleys suddenly made sense.
Probably a compound hunting bow.

It took some doing to yank the arrow free of the meat.
I traced its path, both from sound and from instinct; came
up with a rooftop due east, higher up—a perfect place to
lie in wait and shoot. The bowman was gone now.

Who used *arrows* anymore? This was getting weirder
by the second.

The scar on my wrist pulsed, ripe and obscenely warm.
Silken warmth slid against my skin, under the dampness
of fear-sweat and sudden chilled adrenaline gooseflesh.
My breath came harsh, torturous, echoing in my ear.

What the fuck was going on?

The scar twinged. I let out a long frustrated breath. Laid the cuff back against my wrist. It was hard to cover the puckered, seamed mark back up. What if there was someone else out there with a bow trained on me? It might not kill me, but it would be a mite uncomfortable.

Well, there are Sorrows in town. A bow is just their speed, the filthy little Luddites. But why? Don't assume this is connected—but neither can you assume it's not. Great.

I stuffed the cuff back into my pocket. Hefted the arrow. Thought about it for a moment.

A sudden bite of bloodlust swam across the current of darkness. More of them, moving in. *Ah. More fun and games. I should have known an arrow wouldn't be the end of it.*

I stepped to the edge of the building and leapt out into space. Just as I did, the secondary team moved in, and bullets smashed into my chest. Blood tore across the night sky as I landed, and if I'd been human it would have killed me.

The knives slid into my hands. It was knives instead of guns this time because I wanted some of them left alive.

I hit *hard,* rolling, wet splotch of blood on the pavement as my bleeding back pressed down briefly, made it to my feet. A hunting cat's scream tore from my throat as I saw them, moving down the street in standard mercenary formation, with high-powered rifles and body armor.

I took the first one with a knee to the midriff, snapping a few ribs. The street behind me roiled with screams. *Get down and stay down, everyone, I'm on the job. Jill Kismet's going to work.*

Knocked the gun out of his hand; another kick sent

him careening away, crashing into the left flank guard. Punched the secondary through the faceshield of his helmet, a short kick dislocating his patella at the same time. The pounding of bullets didn't stop, one flicked past my cheek. *You boys are really starting to piss me off.*

"SURRENDER NOW!" I yelled, and threw my left-hand knife. It buried itself in on of the rear-guards. That left four of them on the left wing, they were moving in to surround me, bringing in the flanks. *Well-trained, they're well-trained, boys like this don't come cheap, who's paying for this?*

Oh, no. That isn't a combat pattern. That's a holding patte—

And then, it happened. The thing streaked down the street, tearing through dappled streetlamp light and shade, and it hit me squarely before I could even begin to move.

The massive impact smashed *through* me. Whatever it was, it was *big,* it was *fast,* and its claws tore through my right arm. The knife went clattering. *"Move move move!"* someone yelled. The mercenaries. They were retreating. The scar on my wrist gave out an agonized burst of heat.

It stank. It *stank,* a titanic massive smell that tore through my sinuses and made me gag, bile rising hot and whipping through my throat.

I hit the plate-glass window of a pawnshop, which wouldn't have been so bad if this part of town hadn't needed iron bars so badly. Agony as my ribs snapped, I fell to the concrete as it streaked for me, a low hulking shape that was *wrong,* my eyes refused to focus, even my blue eye refused to *see* what it was, blood hot and slick on my face, splashing against the pavement.

Cold. It was *cold,* frost starring the pavement. Little

curls of steam slid up from my skin, my breath pluming in the air as I gasped. It was so cold.

I lay there as it roared, coming for me again, I had to get up, couldn't, *there's a limit to the damage I can take even with the scar oh God oh God it hurts—*

The night turned peacock-iridescent with flame. The bolt hit it low on the side, hellfire crackling and fluorescing into blue, scarring my eyes. *Holy shit, that's hellfire in the blue spectrum! Who is it, a hellbreed come to dispatch me personally?*

The thing went flying, snarling. The sound was like adamant nails on the biggest fucking chalkboard ever. There was a crashing—metal and glass crumpled like paper. I choked on blood and tried to make my body obey me, struggling to turn over onto my side and push myself up. The frozen pavement burned my skin.

"Keep still, Kiss." The voice was familiar. *Too* familiar. "Let your body mend. This will only take a moment."

What the fuck is he *doing here?*

The thing snarled again. I pushed myself up on my feet, ribs snapping out and crackling as they melded back together but too *slow*. Far too slow. I coughed, bending over, a great gout of blood and lung-fluid fountaining out of my mouth and nose, splatting and steaming on the ice-starred sidewalk.

"Be *still,* Kismet." Now he sounded irritated.

I lifted my head.

Perry, in a loose, elegant gray suit, stood with his hands in his pants pockets, the streetlamps shining on his blond hair like a halo tilted just-so. He cocked his head as if listening, looking at the creature, which hunched in the middle of a shattered car. Hellflame dripped from its smoking hide, melting glass and metal, and I opened my mouth to scream.

The gas tank ignited. Flame belched, and the thing's squealing roar choked off midway. Glass whickered, metal shrapnel flew. I flinched, throwing up my unwounded left arm to shield my eyes. Grating pain tore all the way down my ribs.

Soft padding feet with claws snicking, retreating so quickly the sound blurred. The sound was distinctive, and habit noted it; if I hadn't had the cuff off I wouldn't have been able to track it as the sound faded a couple of miles away to the south. I coughed again, spat blood. Pain ran up my right arm from the scar, throbbing and delicious, sinking into torn muscle and broken bone.

His fingers sank into my left arm, a bolt of agonized heat going through me. Glass and metal groaned as the awful numbing cold retreated. "Idiot. Little *idiot*. Look at this mess."

I coughed again, choked on blood, bent over and vomited more blood. *I didn't know I had this much claret to lose. How many pints is that?*

I hate wondering things like that. But I usually only have time to wonder when the danger's past and I'm still breathing, so I guess it balances out.

Perry's fingers tightened. He propped me against the shattered glass and twisted iron. I'd made quite a dent, must have been going at a fair clip when I hit. The sirens were closer now, and everything was creaking as the terrible devouring cold fled the air.

Montaigne is going to have a fit. Pain ground through me again and I made a weak moaning noise.

My right arm hung in strips of meat, the humerus

snapped. "Look at this," Perry repeated, warming to his theme. "You idiot. You fool. You *stupid* little *id*iotic *feath-er*brained *ninny.*"

The scar pulsed hotly, pleasure rising with the pain, a horrible writhing python smashing through my nervous system. His other hand closed around my bloodslick wrist. I tried to fend him off, he slammed me back against the jagged metal, grinding the edges of my broken arm together with exquisite care, at just the angle to produce maximum agony.

I screamed, my ribs creaking. Choked on more blood. The ferocious cold was gone as if it had never existed.

He lifted my right hand, giving it an extra savage twist. Bone ground and I screamed again, weakly.

"Damage my fine work, will you? How is *this,* Kiss? Do you like the pain? *Do you?*"

I collapsed, panting, hanging onto consciousness by a thread. My lips were hot and slick with blood. "F-f-f-fuck . . . y-y-you . . ." I could barely shape the words.

"Promises, promises." His breath touched the scar, and the jolt of maggot pleasure that slid through me dipped me in fiery slime. It even drowned the pain for a moment, and I moaned. "Someday, Kismet. Some fine day, when I'm getting a little bored. We'll play a few games."

His lips met the scar, and mercifully it was pain again. Great roaring waves of pain as hellfire tore through my body, each wound rubbed with acid and ash, sadistic waves of agony as he took his time melding my shattered body back together. The scaled, hot, slick-wet touch of his tongue against the puckered tissue coated the roaring agony with slime, burrowed into my hindbrain, and ripped at the roots of my sanity.

When it was done, he dropped me. I hit the pavement hard, weak as a newborn but whole. Blood soaked into what clothes I had left. My coat was a mess. The charms in my hair tinkled, and my carved-ruby necklace sent waves of warmth spilling down my chest.

Perry turned on his heel, surveying the street. Smoke billowed up from the burning car, and condensation rose into the air as merely-chill met freezing and mixed. "This is highly unpleasant." His tone was too mild to be called *anger*. Distaste was as far as it went.

What, you think I'm having a ball? I lay against chill hard concrete, gasping like a landed fish.

"*Highly* unpleasant," he continued, meditatively. "I might almost suspect . . ." He seemed to remember I was at his feet. "You make this so fucking difficult, Kiss. I've broken stronger Traders with ease."

As usual, he picked exactly the right thing to say to piss me off and break the spell of lethargy. "I'm . . . not . . . Trader." Strength returned, the mark sending a wave of fiery pleasure up my arm. Flush, again. Full. Ripe. I could feel the warming trickle between my legs. My hips jerked forward. I gasped. "I'm *hunter*," I managed to say it all in one breath. "And some . . . day . . . it's going to be . . . you."

"Pray it never reaches that point, Kiss. You won't like being hunted."

I'm going to be the one hunting you, you bastard. "What was . . . that thing?" Blessed air whooped into my lungs. I was going to live. *Thank you, God.* I was going to *live.*

I can't explain the feeling. If you've ever been close to the edge of leaving the world entirely, you know what I'm talking about. If you haven't, I'm glad for you. But don't expect to understand. It's like every Christmas and every disappointment in your life wrapped up in cold air and set on fire with a napalm strike while your bones tremble inside the meat.

Something like that.

"How should I know?" Perry said, thoughtfully. Fog gemmed his blond hair with tiny jewels. "You're lucky it didn't kill you. Is this about your latest visit to the Monde?"

As if you can't guess. But Perry just liked to pretend he had his fingers in every pie; he really might have no idea. Strength returned, slowly. I pushed myself up to sitting, broken glass grinding against shredded leather. Levered myself up, balancing on unsteady feet. The sirens were getting closer. "Kind of." I had my breath back now. "What are you doing here?"

"Watching out for my investment, Kiss. I've put a lot of effort into you, and you're coming along quite nicely." The faint obscene happiness tinting his bland blond voice reminded me of maggots squirming in bloated meat.

Fuck you, Perry. God, I wish I could shoot you now. "Leave the mindfucks at home, Pericles."

"No mindfuck, Kiss. Strictly fact. Now, are you waiting around for the cops? I have other business to conduct tonight. You know, places to go, people to kill."

"Go bother someone else." I coughed, rackingly, my ribs reminding me they weren't designed for this kind of thing. The mark pulsed, wetly. Pleasure slid up my back like fevered sweating fingers, married to skincrawling loathing, like having a scaled tail run across your skin while you're dreaming safe in your bed.

He showed no sign of leaving. "Where's your pussy-cat? Have you finally sworn off bestiality?"

Lord, I wish Saul was here right now and there was a bullet or two in your head. That would make me very happy. "Lay off, Perry. I'm warning you."

"I only ask out of curiosity. See how patient I'm being? A good little hellspawn." He was smiling. I have only seen that smile on him once or twice, and each time it chills my blood. He looks so damn happy and interested, as if he's examining a fine piece of art—or ass. Something he knows he can pick up and is just stretching out the anticipation of. It makes his bland, nondescript face into the picture of "terrifying."

Especially when his eyes sparkle.

I finally felt as if I had enough air. "That was a trap for me." I didn't sound choked, but I was beginning to feel it.

"Gee, you think?" He didn't bother to weight the words with much sarcasm. But there was a ratty little gleam in his eyes I didn't like, though I was too tired and sore to think much about it.

Besides, there's *always* a gleam in Perry's eyes I don't like. I rolled my eyes. Dragged more sweet air in. "What are you really doing here?"

"I told you, looking after my investment. You think you can go for a few hours without getting shot or torn up? I really do have important things to do."

I waved my right hand experimentally. It worked just like it always had. The fog was retreating, evaporating up from the street in long white trails. "Thanks, Perry. Now get the fuck away from me."

"Sweet talk will get you nowhere." He grinned, his chin tilting up slightly. "I'll see you tomorrow night."

My heart thudded, my body too drained to even produce adrenaline. Still, the bite of fear just under my skin was sharp as a new blade, and hard to hide. "Midnight." I kept dragging in deep healing breaths. "I haven't forgotten."

The first cop cars arrived on-scene. I braced myself. When my eyes flicked back to where he had been standing, Perry was gone.

I hate it when he does that. I swallowed, tasting blood and bile, and peeled myself away from the twisted iron bars. *Monty is just going to die,* I thought, as flashing blue lights converged. The burning car smelled awful, and the stink of the creature still hung in the air. *Gah, that's foul.*

The shakes had me. Beating under every thought was the same sentence, repeated in frightened panicked-rabbit jumps across my brain.

I could have died. I could have died. Oh God, my God, I could have died.

12

$\mathcal{W}$oo Song's is a little hole in the wall, a neon dragon buzzing over a single door, no windows, and the smell of foreign cooking belching out each time someone entered or left. Since I was battered, bloody, and generally not in a good mood, I stood outside across the street until Saul appeared, shepherding our nervous witness. Once more I was grateful to have a good partner.

Robbie's eyes widened as he took me in; Saul himself barely raised an eyebrow. His gaze did flick to the leather cuff on my right wrist, which was conspicuously *not* blood-soaked. His hand was over Robbie's shoulder, and he moved with an awareness and grace that, as usual, comforted me and unsettled me a little at the same time.

Sometimes I wondered what would have happened if I'd still been just a human hunter when I met Saul. The scar was Perry's claim on me, true . . . but it also meant I wasn't so easily damaged during bedplay. And there were several times I could have died if not for the fact that I was tougher and quicker now, which would have put a distinct crimp in our relationship.

Go figure, I meet the perfect man after I'm in hock to a hellbreed, and if I wasn't tainted I couldn't have had a relationship with a Were.

Sometimes I don't just *think* God has a sadistic sense of humor.

I kept to the shadows, beckoning them into the alley across from Woo Song's. I suspected Robbie the Juicer would be a lot more comfortable where he couldn't see the bloody rags I wore. Half my left breast was peering out, my shirt was never going to be the same, and the tough leather of my pants was shredded. My long leather coat wasn't ever going to be the same either.

Clothes get expensive when you're a hunter. I was going to have a hell of a time getting the blood out of my sodden boots, if it was possible at all.

Dammit.

Monty hadn't been happy, but at least the Feeb on duty—sleek, dark Juan Rujillo—was actually a decent sort who wouldn't make any problems. Both of them were a little pale when I presented them with the scenario that scares everyone the most: something out there a hunter doesn't know about, and hasn't had any luck stopping.

Rujillo had promised to get me a list of all the professional operators in town, even if he had to twist a few interagency arms. That is one thing about being a hunter, you're usually assured of getting cooperation from even the stingiest intelligence agencies. Turf wars end up with a lot of dead civilians and uncomfortable media attention, and that's two things no intelligence or law enforcement agency wants. *Especially* the latter. There are very few spooks, Feebs, ghosts, or rubber pencils who want to interfere. The FBI has its own hunter division, the Martindale Squad, and it's whispered that the CIA has a few operatives that are a little more than strictly human.

I wouldn't know about that, though.

Though strictly speaking, a list of mercs in town wouldn't do much good. This had been a one-time shot; now I was wary and whatever mercenaries they'd set on me had suffered horrific casualties. It would be inefficient to send another mercenary cadre after me and expect it to delay me or hold me for the creature, whatever it was. And whoever was pulling the strings here wasn't stupid or inefficient.

That, at least, I was sure of.

Ruji had once again accused me of being a menace to property, but he'd done it with a twinkle in his eye. Monty was chewing Tums by the bucketload; he was the one who had to deal with the media showing up in droves and demanding an explanation.

And I was ready to explode from frustration.

"Start at the beginning," I said, and Robbie shot a nervous glance at Saul.

"You wanna come in and eat something?" Saul looked down at the alley floor, his shoulders hunching. It was a show of submission, almost shocking in a Were much taller and bulkier than me.

I must have been wearing my mad face.

"I don't think Wu-ma would like it if I showed up all bloody." I was trying for a light tone. *She'd probably feed me MSG just to express her displeasure, too.*

His nostrils flared. "You stink."

"Thanks. I just had a run-in with something big and

hairy that looks like a Were on steroids and reeks to high heaven." I eyed Robbie the Juicer, who was beginning to tremble. "Relax, Robbie. I'm not going to hurt you. As a matter of fact, I'm your new best friend. I'm going to keep you alive."

"Very goddamn kind of you." Robbie's voice was thin and reedy. His shock of dark hair was greasy, and he smelled like dumplings. "What the fuck happened?"

You do not want to know, civilian. Trust me. "Who did you tell? About the other night?"

His shoulders trembled. He stared at me like I was Banquo's ghost. "Couple people. Shit, man, after that I was happy to be alive. Got a cigarette?"

"I suggest we take him somewhere safe." Saul straightened, his eyes reflecting green-gold for a moment in the dimness. "I don't like this."

"I heard that." Even this alley wasn't likely safe. "Micky's? The bar, not the front?"

He nodded, the silver shifting in his hair; the little bottle of holy water at his neck sparkled summer-blue once, maybe reacting to the scar still pulsing hard and heavy under the cuff. Or maybe it was because I smelled of hellbreed, Perry's etheric fingerprints all over me from the work he'd done patching me up. "Good idea," he said. "I'll drive."

I didn't argue.

Robbie stared into his coffee cup while I scrubbed at my hands with baby wipes. I'd changed in the bathroom, into fresh pants and a T-shirt kept in the Impala's trunk, but my coat was still tacky-wet with blood and my boots were squishy. It had dried under my short bitten nails and crusted in my hair.

Thank God it was only *my* blood. One thing to be happy about: no civilian casualties. I'd managed to keep anyone innocent from being hurt.

It wasn't as comforting as it should have been, but it was enough for me.

The bartender, Theron, brought me a stack of damp washcloths and a beer. Ther was tall, lean, dark, and intense. He also happened to be a Werepanther. I'd only seen him *shift* once, during a fight with a nest of Middle Way Chaos-worshipping wannabes out on Chartres Street. I didn't want to see it again. Panther jaws can crack bones, and Theron was *big;* Weres tend to run bulkier than both humans and beasts but some of them just look too huge to be real. He was good backup but extremely unpredictable; not someone to call unless you wanted to play it his way. Still, he was a good sort, and part of the reason why nobody stepped out of line in Micky's.

"Stinks," he said, giving a nod to Saul.

Who visibly bristled. "I know, Theron. Thanks."

"Want a shot, Saul?"

"No. Thanks." Saul was extraordinarily still, his shoulders spread wide and his eyes luminous. Theron gave him a toothy smile, and retreated. In the dominance game between Weres, Saul and Ther were roughly equal; sometimes Ther pushed it a little, moving in on me, getting a little too close. It was a Were's version of social gameplaying, and I didn't like being a chit in the middle. Another night I might have been amused.

Not tonight, though. Getting almost-canceled will cut your sense of humor dead short.

"Why don't you start at the beginning, Robbie?" My temper was fraying badly. Saul's arm pressed against mine; I stopped wiping at the blood on my hands and leaned my head against his shoulder. He leaned back, subtly, then turned his head, his chin rubbing across my still-damp hair.

My chest eased a little bit. The shaking in my hands began to go down.

Robbie glanced up, looked hurriedly back down at his coffee. "I got ta the field at about ten-thirty. I wasn't drunk, but I was tired. So's I wanted a place where I could think, right? I pissed about back and got my sleeping bag all set up, got my stuff situated. Then I settled down and I was almost asleep, man. I thought of lighting a J to get myself all nice and mellow, but I was finally warmin' up. It was a cold fuckin' day, I tell you, out on the streets."

Well, yeah, we're past New Year's and in the chilliest part of the year. I sighed. Saul slid his arm around me, pulled me into his side. I wiped at my face with the first wet washcloth, scrubbing the wet terry across my cheeks, digging at my closed eyes. I can be covered in filth, but I like my face clean.

Call it a quirk.

The silver charms in my hair shifted, chiming softly. Saul's braid bumped my cheek as he turned his head, taking in the bar.

"So I dunno what time it was, but I heard an engine. And not a cop car or anything, just a very soft, nice purring engine." Robbie's dark eyes were wide, his spotted cheeks pasty. He was sweating, and he smelled like too few showers and too much drinking, with a healthy dash of fear-sweat on top. His fingernails were brutally short but still grimy.

The scar on my wrist tingled. *Perry.* What had he been doing out there? He didn't usually leave the Monde, preferring to sit in the middle of his web like a big fat waxy-pale spider.

That mental image made me shudder, and Saul kissed my temple.

"I got this weird feeling. Just a weird feeling. You live on the street long enough, you start to get a kind of feel for the nutzoid things. Like when the crazy shit is gonna start going down. Sometimes you don't get no warning, but most of the time there's this feeling before crazy shit starts up. Y'unnerstand?"

I certainly understood that. One of the things a hunter looks for in an apprentice is a certain amount of psychic ability; I wouldn't have survived to become an apprentice if I hadn't had more than my fair share to begin with. "Like instinct," I supplied.

His face brightened a little. He grinned into his coffee, with yellow teeth. "Yeah, instink. Thatza word. I just got that feeling. So I got up, and I went to the end of the dug-out, real low-like. Creeping. And I looked out."

His fingers tightened on the cup; dirt grimed into his knuckles and under his short-split nails. "I saw this black van sitting there. Just sittin'. And then I notice it ain't got no license plate, and I think maybe the cops are doing a sting, and I'm getting ready to get my ass out of there nice and quiet-like. Then the door opens up, and out jumps this thing. And damned if it don't look like a goddamn ape, but it hunches down—like them things you see in movies.

You seen that movie, where there's these things, they look human, but they don't move no human way?"

Honey, I don't need movies. I see them in living color. "I guess so." I didn't want to lead the witness, so to speak, so I didn't give him more.

"Like this movie where guys change into werewolves, and they run on their hands and feet, but their shoulders are all funny. And they've got weird-shaped heads. Lots of teeth. Anyway, the goddamn thing hopped out, and started snuffling. And I started thinking maybe it could smell me, 'cause I could smell it. Smelled like a wet dog puking its guts out in a whorehouse."

That was a revolting but extremely apt way of describing it. I leaned into Saul's side, for once not caring that my hair was crackling with drying blood and my toes were damp inside my boots. "Okay."

He continued. "Someone's gotten out, and they're moving around. A woman. Light hair, but not blonde. I can see her haircut, she's got it cut like that bitch on Channel Twelve—"

"Susan Zamora? The anchorwoman?" Zamora had a sleek, leonine bob dyed a fashionable chocolate-cherry color. She was a barracuda in human form.

There's no love lost between me and the press. I like to keep things quiet, because let's face it, normal people don't *want* to know about the nightside. Reporters have just enough orneriness to *think* they want to know, that's all. Which equals a huge pain in the ass for a hunter *and* the cops.

Don't get me wrong, I love the Fourth Estate like any red-blooded American. But Jesus *wept,* they make my job harder. Fortunately, they get stonewalled by everyone except UFO nutjobs and fake psychics.

Anyone who knows about the nightside knows not to talk about it.

"Yeah, her. That way. She's moving around, there's nobody else out there. And I've got a bad, bad feeling about this, because the furry smelly thing is snuffling, and I got this feeling like I'm going to throw up. Anyway, the woman barks something, and the furry thing leaps up into the back of the van and I can see the entire thing rock a little bit. Then it brings out something real pale, and I can see it's not right. The only thing that big is a body, but it handles it like it's nothing. The furry thing kind of shuffles to the edge of the sidewalk, and it *throws* the thing, and I see it is a body but something's wrong with it. It hits with a kind of thud and the furry thing is back in the van, and the woman gets in. Then the engine gets to purring again, and they're gone." He shivered, despite the close muggy warmth of Micky's. His eyes came up to meet mine, and they were dark enough that I reached up and pushed my beer across the table.

"Take it. It'll do you good."

He did, setting down his coffee, and took down about half the cold bottle in one long throat-working swallow. He wiped his mouth with the back of his dirty hand. "I bet it did smell me," he said miserably. "I bet it did."

"Don't worry about that right now. Was there anything else? Did she talk, laugh, move around the van at all?"

"Moved around looking up. That's all." He finished the rest of the beer. "What the fuck was that thing? It *warn't human*. I warn't drunk, ma'am. It warn't human 'tall."

The more worked-up he got, the more hillbilly he

sounded. "Maybe, maybe not," I soothed. *I'll take him to Galina's and leave him there; that's the safest place for him right now. And she won't stand for any street bullshit.* "But what's important for right now is to keep you out of sight. I've got someone you can stay with, if you don't mind a bit of work. It's either that or hit the streets where these people—whoever they are—are looking for you. Think back, and tell me everyone you told about this. *Everyone.*"

He did, and the list was depressingly long and imprecise, finishing with: "That kid who hangs around Plaskény Square, with the blue hair and the rings in his nose. Tall kid. I mentioned it to him. That's all."

That's all? Oh, man, this just keeps getting better and better.

"Tell her what you told me," Saul said suddenly. "About what the woman said."

"Oh, yeah. Almost forgot." His mournful face brightened. "It sounded like French."

Huh? "French?"

"I took four years of French in high school. I think that's what she was speakin'. Somethin' about . . . well, shit, I'm rusty. But I'd swear it was French."

"French." I nodded, my head resting on Saul's shoulder. Suddenly I was incredibly, bone-crunchingly weary. It's the reaction of coming very, very close to certain death: after the adrenaline and the urge for sex wear off, the only thing left was terrible exhaustion, as if every appendage is dipped in lead. "Okay."

Wonderful. A French-speaking broad with fancy hair, multiple murders and more on the way, and something so tough even Perry's frightened of it. Not to mention the fact that I think Perry knows more than he's telling. For a moment I closed my eyes, listening to the clink of glass from the bar, the clatter of silverware and murmur of voices from out in the restaurant, the sound of water and frying from the kitchen, a waitress's voice lifted in a snatch of song along with Bonnie Raitt on the restaurant's speaker system, giving "them" *something to talk about, a little mystery to figure out.*

Coincidence. Getting a little help again.

Saul was warm and solid beside me, his arm tightening, and he didn't let go until I opened my eyes and leaned away.

This just kept getting better. But for right now, all I wanted to do was go home and sleep.

13

Saul collapsed, his lax weight resting on me for a brief moment, his hipbones digging into the soft insides of my thighs. The tattoo high up on my right thigh writhed, its winged tingle running under my skin. I kissed along the edge of his jaw, found his mouth again. He tasted of night, of cold wind and wildness and the Scotch I'd taken down four mouthfuls of before he'd slid his arm around my waist and half-dragged me to the bed.

My hair was still wet, the charms tinkling slightly as the spillfire of orgasm tore through me again, my hips slamming up. The third was always the nicest; I gasped into his mouth and heard the low rumble of his contentment begin, a purr that shook through every cell, every bone, and chased away all remaining fear. Sweat mixed with the water from the shower, his smell of Ivory soap and animal musk making a pleasant heady brew.

"Shhh," he whispered against my mouth. "Kitten, shhh. It's all right."

I quieted, more air gasped in, flavored with his breath.

He kissed my cheek, my temple, my mouth again, bracing himself on his elbows.

As usual, he didn't want to let go, nuzzling along the line of my jaw and down to the hollow of my throat, teeth scraping delicately as aftershocks rippled through me. It had taken months of patient trying before I could let him touch me anywhere covered by a bikini, and even longer before I could rest there under his weight, utterly vulnerable. We were branching out, experimenting, and I finally felt like I'd trampled some of the demons of my adolescence.

But coming so close to death raised demons of its own. I went limp, closed my eyes, let him nibble at my throat. It was a highly erogenous zone for Weres, especially Weres of the cat persuasion. A sign of trust, and a sign of territorial marking. A hickey on the neck of a Were's mate means seriousness, means *don't touch this, it's mine.*

He was Were. He wasn't a human man, and sometimes I wondered if that was why I *could* let him touch me. With Mikhail it had been different—he had been my teacher, trusted absolutely even in the confines of the bed, always in control.

Until Mikhail had no longer wanted me.

My hands relaxed, slid down Saul's arms. The leather of the cuff touched his shoulder. He nuzzled deeper in my throat, the sharp edges of his teeth brushing the skin just over my pulse. A strand of his hair, freighted with a silver charm, lay across my chin.

"Saul," I whispered. He sucked at my throat, a spot of almost-pain, gauging it perfectly. I could feel the blood rising to the surface, blossoming on the skin, the bruise would be flawless. A dark mark, almost like a brand.

One last gentle kiss against my carotid artery and he moved, sliding out of me with exquisite slowness. Off to the side, the bed creaking as it accepted his weight, and the usual slow movement ended up with my head on his shoulder and his arm around me, my body slumped against his side. He was warm, flush with heat, and purring contentedly.

I thought he would fall asleep, as usual. But instead he pulled the covers up with his free hand, tucking us both in. "Better?" The rumble didn't fade when he spoke. Nobody could ever figure out where a cat Were's purr came from. If they know, they're not telling.

"Much." I kissed his shoulder. My neck pulsed with a sweet pain. "Good therapy."

"Happy to provide." He paused. "You looked pretty bloody."

It was the closest he would get to an accusation.

"It beat the shit out of me," I admitted. "I didn't hit it."

He was still. The rumble kept going. "A trap."

"Yep." I dropped the bombshell, even though he would have smelled it on me. "Perry showed up."

His purr stopped.

"Hellfire didn't even damage the thing, but he blew up a car and it ran off. Then he patched me up."

"Patched you up?"

"Says I'm an investment." I kissed his shoulder again. *Come on, Saul. Please.*

His silence was eloquent.

"Saul?"

He moved, a little, restlessly. A movement like a cat settling itself for the night, curling into a warm bed.

"Please, Saul. *Please.*" There was nobody else I would use this tone on. Pleading, cajoling, trying to convince. Almost—dare I say it—*begging.*

"I don't like it," he said, finally. He had gone tense, muscle standing out under his skin, the utter stillness of a hunting beast crouched low in the grass.

Oh, for God's sake. "You think *I* do? You think I *like* it?"

"Why keep going back?" As soon as he said it he made a restless movement, then stilled again.

"He's fucking useful. And if it hadn't been for the goddamn bargain I would have *died.*"

"I can take care of you." Stubborn. "If it wasn't for the goddamn bargain I wouldn't have left you there."

"And they might have killed us both and our witness as well. I'm a *hunter,* Saul. Perry's a tool. That's all. One day I'll kill him."

"Not soon enough."

Not soon enough for me either. "Amen to that." I rubbed my chin against his shoulder. My voice dropped to a whisper, I swallowed and felt the hickey on my throat pulse again. It was better than the scar on my wrist, a cleaner pain. "I love you, dammit."

"I know, kitten. I love you." But anger boiled under the words.

"It's just a tool," I repeated. The thought made me shudder with frantic loathing, remembering bargaining for the mark, remembering the press of that scaled tongue against my flesh. A hundred other unpleasant and downright horrific memories crowded behind that one, threatening like piled black clouds announcing a cataclysmic storm.

"I know." Saul's brushed my wet hair back from my face, I tilted my head against his fingers, savoring the touch that pushed bad dreams away. "I know. I just . . . I'm gonna breathe a sigh of relief when I see that hellspawn motherfucker draw his last breath. I wish I could tear out his throat myself."

You're not the only one. "I love you," I repeated, desperately. Under that desperation the deeper plea—*don't leave me. Please don't leave me.*

Not like he would. Weres settle down with their mates, and that's that. They do it much more easily and cleanly than humans manage to.

But I wasn't Were. I was an aberration.

The tension left him, bit by bit, and the rumbling purr returned. "Loved you the first minute I saw you, kitten. Covered in muck and swearing at the top of your lungs. God, you were a sight."

The memory made me smile, drowning the press of other memories not even half as pleasant. I could smile, now that I was almost two years away from that hunt. "Why do they always hide in storm drains? I hate that."

"Hm." He was sleepy now, going as boneless and languid as a cat in a patch of sunlight. The danger was past, thank God. "Go to sleep."

"I will," I whispered. "Stay with me."

Because if you leave me, I don't know what I'll do. As usual, the thought sent panic through me, plucking at my hard-won control over my pulse, tightening every muscle against postcoital lassitude.

"Not going anywhere, kitten." He held me tighter, even as he slid over the edge into sleep, the purr growing fitful but still comforting.

Thank God for you, Saul.

I listened to him breathing. It was the sound of safety, of good things, of comfort and pleasure and trust. After imagining what it might be like sometimes in the deep watches of the night, I now knew—and I had no desire to ever go back to being lonely.

My wrist prickled. The scar always felt like it was burrowing deeper, trying to reach bone. I'd given up wondering if it was phantom pain; it wasn't any more deeply scarred than it had ever been. It was just part of the deal.

If it came down to a choice, I was going to have to welsh on a deal with a hellbreed and take my chances. Damned if I did, possibly damned if I didn't . . . there was no winning here. The best I could hope for was as long with Saul as I could get.

Is that enough?

It didn't matter. It was all I was going to get. The bruise on my neck settled into a dimple of pleasant heat as I slid over the border into sleep's country. For once, I had no dreams.

The next day brought bad news, another body—and the first break. My pager was destroyed from last night's fun, and it would take me a day or so to get a new one; but they called me at home and I made the scene in less than half an hour.

"We don't know her name yet," Carp said. His hair was back to standing up in messy sandy-blond spikes. "Christ."

The abandoned parking lot was deserted under thin winter-afternoon sunshine, weeds forcing up through cracked old concrete. The body—if there was enough left of it to qualify as a body—lay slumped in the middle, blood lying sticky-wet on sharp thistle leaves and dead dandelion plants. The ribs were twisted aside, viscera and other organs gone, the eyes had been plucked from the skull and long strands of blood-matted hair stirred gently under the wind's stroking fingers.

Off in the ambulance, the kid who had found the body as he cut through the parking lot on his way to school made a low hurt sound. He was crying messily, and his mother was on her way to pick him up. No more shortcuts for him.

"God." I folded my arms. I'd gotten the blood off my coat, but it hung in tatters, clearly showing where the thing had clawed me. The right sleeve had needed patching before I could even put it on, and I wore my second-best pair of boots. "All I have is more questions."

"A black van with no license plate. A redhead who speaks French, and something that smells like—what was it?" Carp sounded grimly amused.

"A wet dog puking its guts out in a whorehouse," I quoted. I thought he'd enjoy that. Carp's laugh was sharp and jagged as a broken window.

Saul picked his way around the body, watching where he stepped. The sun touched the red-black of his hair and the silver of the charms tied in it, ran lovingly down his coat and brought out the glow in his dark skin. *A fine-looking man. A very fine-looking man.*

Saul stopped. He lowered himself slowly, staring intently at the ground. Then he reached down, his fingers delicate, and picked something up.

I held my breath.

He continued on his circuit, examining the cracked concrete and frost-dead weeds.

"Looks like Tonto's found something." Rosie arrived at my side. "How you feeling, Jill? Heard you caused some damage last night."

"Wasn't my fault. The Feebs treating you right?"

She shrugged, her eyes hidden behind mirrored sunglasses. Today she wore a hooded Santa Luz Wheelwrights sweatshirt jacket and a black leather coat, jeans and black Nikes. She looked like a fresh-scrubbed college kid, especially with the shades. "Rujillo. He's okay. Not like that bastard Astin."

I winced. Astin had been a good agent, but a rigid one; he believed the local cops were all incompetent or mismanaged. Having him reassigned had been a distinct relief. "Yeah, he's different. Little more flexible."

"You all right?" Her tone was excessively casual.

So you heard I was covered in blood. Rosie, I didn't know you cared. The thought was snide, unworthy of me. She *did* care. A cop who didn't care wouldn't have limped down to the warehouse in her bandages and apologized to me. "I got beat up a bit, but I'm okay."

"You know what's going on yet?" This from Carp.

"Not yet, Carp. Can't rush these things." *I'm beginning to feel distinctly out of temper.* Thin winter sunlight caressed my shoulders, the wind had veered and was coming from the faroff mountains; we would have deep frost. Living in semi-desert meant that winters were miserable cold times, especially with the war between the river wind and the mountains breathing on us.

"Wish you could. Press is crawling on our backs. All sorts of wackos coming out of the woodwork."

I knew. I'd seen the papers. *Serial Murderer Haunts Ladies of the Night!* was the kindest headline. Even the respectable rags were trotting out the Jack the Ripper comparisons. And the nightly TV news was in a frenzy. "Any incredibly weird, or just the usual weird?"

"Just the usual. Crystal-crawlin' psychics. Copycats. Nutcases." Carp sighed. "This is starting to piss me off."

"Me too." My tone was a little sharper than usual. I didn't like being in the dark, and I was failing them. "I'm working as hard as I can."

"We know," Rosie soothed. "We know, Jill." And they did. I'd worked with them for long enough that they *did* know, and I was grateful for that.

Saul approached. He held up his hand, and something dangled: three thin leather thongs, braided, interwoven with feathers and bits of fur. There were complex knots in a pattern that looked vaguely familiar. A single dart of darkness was braided into the end of it.

An obsidian arrowhead, carefully flaked and probably genuine. Saul's fingers flicked, and the arrowhead dangled. "Found something." His face was grim. "Smells awful. Probably related."

I plunged a hand in my pocket, already hunting for a drawstring bag. Found one, fished it out, and opened it. "Finally," I breathed. "Come to Mama."

He dropped it in, and wiped his fingers against his leather pants. The thing was oddly heavy, and coldly malignant. And he was right, it did smell. I caught a faint whiff of a familiar reek.

"I don't like this." Saul drew himself up, still scrubbing his fingers against his pants. "That thing is evil, Jill."

"They usually are." I was too relieved to finally have a

piece of usable evidence to mind much. "Do you recognize it?"

He shook his head, his jaw setting grimly. I stuffed the bag in another pocket, and studied the body. Now that Saul had circled it I approached, cautiously; he had point-blank refused to let me get near it until he had a chance to look. He stayed back as I edged closer, but I felt his eyes on me.

No, Saul wasn't happy either. But whether it was the case or Perry, I wasn't going to guess.

Now that I'd seen the creature, I could see marks that matched its claws. There were ragged slices in the flesh, chunks taken out of the thighs and the breasts gone, just divots with glaring-white splinters of rib poking through sodden meat.

I peered into the cavity left by the taking of the viscera, and my eyes narrowed. *Wait a second. Wait just a god-damn second.*

I looked through the rest of the scene, too, found exactly zilch. But my heart was beating quickly as I nodded at the forensic team and went back to Saul. "There's something else," I said.

Rosie and Carp both went still, attentive. Like bloodhounds straining at the leash. I took a deep breath, a chill finger sliding up my spine; it was the feeling of the first piece of a pattern falling into place. "There's claw marks and *other* marks. The thing I saw last night had claws shaped like *this*." My hands sketched briefly in the air. "The other marks, inside the abdominal cavity and around her eyes—those are too clean, and they're almost covered by the claw marks. The ones covered up are made by something *sharp*. Like a scalpel."

"A scalp—" Rosie trailed off. Her mouth pulled down, meditatively.

"Scalpel." Carp scratched at his chin. "Well. Okay. So?"

"I assumed the creature was eating what it took. It may be. But it might also be getting a little help. Or eating leftovers." I folded my arms against the chill in the air, the butt of a gun digging into my left hip.

Carp kept scratching at his chin. "Or it's covering something up."

"Either way." The smile pulled up my lips, baring my teeth in a feral grimace. "Cheer up, boys and girls. This constitutes our first bit of good luck."

"How so?" Rosie didn't sound convinced.

"Well, it's more than we had before. And if that little thing Saul found is from it, we can track it. Tracking it's the first step to finding it, which is the first step to taking its sorry ass apart. And that will make me very, very happy."

Saul stirred next to me, and I didn't have to read his mind. He was thinking that I'd run up against this thing once before and nearly died, so why should tracking it make me happy?

But I did. I felt irrationally happy. If it would make a mistake like dropping something, it could make other mistakes. Unless this was a challenge, a *fuck you, Kismet. We nearly got you last night; we'll get you eventually.*

"Do we know the time of death?"

"Hard to tell with the body so torn up. But it ain't frozen. And if it ain't frozen with this kind of cold, and on pavement, it's still pretty fresh." Carp sounded as unhappy as it was possible to sound without sarcasm.

"The blood's still a little tacky-wet too." I cast around. Good luck getting tire tracks on this concrete, and how did they get the van here? If they *did* get the van here. "The question is . . ." I sorted through all of the questions in my head, still far too many for my taste. I picked the most useful one. "The question is, why get rid of the bodies like this? What purpose does it serve?"

"Make our lives miserable," Carp muttered.

"Not as miserable as hers." Rosie jerked her chin toward the body, now being swarmed with forensic techs.

"I'm going to go do some research." I rocked back on my heels as Saul bumped into me, crowding me again. His heat was a comfort in the early morning chill. They were right, the body hadn't frozen yet. Whoever she was, she was freshly killed. "Buzz me if anyone else dies."

Black humor, maybe. Bleak gallows humor. But you spend enough time looking at dead bodies and hanging out with cops, and that kind of humor becomes necessary. It's a shield held up against the dark things we see, against the horrific things that can happen to anyone.

I'm lucky. I see inhuman things and how they prey on humanity. I see the aberrations, those who bargain away their souls for power, those who trade everything for the sweet seduction, the canker in the rose, the dominion of the earth. The cops have it so much worse.

They have to see the things human beings do to each other without any help from Hell.

Saul's chest brushed my back. He had stepped behind me, looming just like a Were. The fresh hickey on my neck throbbed.

"Yeah, we'll call you. Why don't you get a goddamn cell phone?" It was an old complaint. Carp hunched his shoulders, fishing a pair of latex gloves out of his jacket pocket.

"Can't afford to replace 'em, as many times as I get beat up and dumped in water. Not to mention electrocuted, stabbed, shot—"

"Okay, okay. I got it." Carp rolled his eyes. "Get this one corralled quick, Kiss. Rosie's getting pissy with the long hours."

Rosie wasn't amused. "Fuck you. Glad you're okay, Kiss."

I leaned back into Saul before moving away, feeling his hand brush mine. "Me too, Rosie. Thanks."

Saul followed me to the Impala, sitting tucked out of sight on Edgerton Street. He was sticking so close he might have been glued to me, and after dropping into the driver's seat I waited for him to come around and get in. He did, and I looked at the red fuzzy dice. They swung gently when I reached up and touched them, a gift from Galina.

I should go see her and have a cup of tea, it always helps me think clearer. But we had a witness stashed at her house, and it wouldn't do to go visiting her again and perhaps bring trouble to her door.

Saul didn't buckle his seat belt. Waited, staring out through the windshield. His profile was beautiful. I looked at his mouth—he had such a lovely mouth, his upper lip chiseled and his lower slightly full, a little bruised from kissing. *One of these days, I'm going to leave a hickey on him. He'll like that.*

"This is a break," I told him. "A good one."

He shrugged. "I don't like it. Broadway's only four blocks away."

Meaning they're playing with me. They dumped the body less than four blocks away from where they tried to kill me. Or did it come straight from dumping the body to mangle me? Either way, it's not good. "I know. But this is still a break."

"You're visiting Perry tonight."

Thanks for reminding me. The skin on my back roughened. I buckled myself in. He reached for his own seatbelt.

I twisted the key. The Impala's engine purred into life. *Sixty-seven was the best year in American car history.* My hands gripped the wheel. I decided silence was my best option.

What he said next destroyed *that* theory. "I want you to stay there."

"What the *fuck?*" I twisted my head to look at him so quickly a silver charm flew and smacked the window on my side, my hair ruffling out. It almost hit me in the eye, but thankfully the red thread held and it was snatched back as my head turned.

"I want to go do some research. I want you to stay at the Monde until I get back. It might take me a little while."

"Why? Where are *you* going?" I heard my voice hit the pitch just under "shriek."

"Just out to the barrio. I got a few things on my mind." He stared out the windshield.

"Like *what?*"

"Just a few things."

Fuck that. "I'll go with you."

"No, kitten. There are some places down there you shouldn't go."

It didn't help that he was right. The barrio was a good place for someone of my racial persuasion to end up dead; the Weres ran herd out there and only called me in if something boiled over. "People are dying, Saul. I'll go anywhere I need to." I settled back into the seat, listening to the engine's steady comforting purr.

"Please, kitten. If you're at the Monde, I know you're at least alive. I don't want to take you into the barrio." His eyes dropped, he looked at the dash.

"You'd rather leave me with Perry." Was that accusation in my voice? Wonders never cease.

"He's got a vested interest in keeping you alive, *you* keep reminding me of that. And he chased that thing off last night."

"I don't think he chased it off."

"It left when he showed up. Good enough for me. Come on, Kiss. Please."

This is something I never thought I'd hear from you, Saul. I looked at my knuckles, white against the steering wheel. Then I reached down, shifted into first to pull out onto Edgerton. "Jesus Christ, Saul. What the hell's going on?"

"I wish I knew, kitten. I really do." He did, too. I could hear it. Whatever he suspected, it had to be *really* bad if he was going into the barrio; doubly bad if he wanted me to spend any more time with Perry than was absolutely necessary. "I just want to ask some questions."

"Like what questions?"

"Like some Were questions. Watch your driving."

"Shut up about my driving." I took a right on Seventh, turning up toward downtown. "Talk to me, Saul. Come on."

"I just want to ask about that braid and knot pattern, that's all. It looks familiar, but I can't quite place it."

"Is the arrowhead genuine?"

"You're a sharp girl. I think it is." He shifted in his bucket seat, leather moving against the red fur of the seat covers; he fished a Charvil out of the box in his breast pocket. Rolled the window down a little, lit it with his wolf's-head Zippo. I reached down and yanked out the ashtray.

"The hair?"

"Human." His voice was shaded with distaste.

"Christ." I shifted into fourth, the tires chirped a little when I stamped on the gas. "Give me a vowel here, Saul."

"Wish I had one to give. It just *looks* familiar but I can't place it. Makes my hackles go up."

Yours too? "Instinct."

"Trust it."

"I do." *I have a healthy respect for a Were's instinct.* "All right."

He obviously hadn't expected me to give in so easily. "You'll stay there?"

"I will, Saul. If you want me to, I'll put up with Pericles. Just do what you have to and don't leave me there long, for God's sake. I suppose you want my car."

"I'll clean out the ashtray." He inhaled, blew out a long stream of cherry-scented smoke. His unhappiness mixed with mine, a steady tension between us. "And I won't grind the gears. We going to the hospital?"

"I want to check in on Father Rosas. Something about a Chaldean in a seminary after a Catholic artifact doesn't sit right with me. And an artifact I've never heard of—

and that Hutch hasn't, either?" I paused, hit the left-hand blinker and turned left on Pelizada Avenue. *Then we're going to visit that doctor on Quincoa.*

He inhaled a deep lungful of cherry-scented smoke, blew it out the window. "Catholic rites do offer protection against Chaldean sorcery and possession. That bird-thing couldn't get out of the chapel."

You've been studying, you naughty boy. My wrists weren't steady enough, a tremor running all the way up to my elbows I ignored. "Catholic immunity only started in the sixteenth century with the creation of the Jesuits and their Shadow Order. Loyola created the Society in 1534 and the Shadow Order in 1536 by secret charter; the Sorrows started to feel the pinch in 1588 when their House in Seville was cleared and torched. That was Juan de Alatriste." I knew I was babbling, couldn't help myself. "And then Alatriste went against the scurf in Granada and—"

"Breathe, Jill."

I took a deep breath. My knuckles almost creaked, my fingers were clenched so tightly. "The only thing worse than going there is anticipating it."

"He counts on that."

"And you want me to stay there after he's finished with me." *You hate him. The very first thing you learned about me was that I smelled like hellbreed. You hated me, as much as a Were can hate, I guess.*

His silence answered me. He inhaled again. Dry cold air bloomed through his slightly open window.

My heart twisted. I still didn't know why Saul had changed his mind about me. I didn't know what he got out of staying with me. All my life I've stayed alive by knowing the motivations of everyone around me, especially everyone who could hurt me. Anyone who made me vulnerable.

I could understand, I guess, why Saul wanted me somewhere he knew I'd be protected if that thing—whatever it was—came after me again. What I didn't understand was why he was with me at all. He was Were, and human rules didn't apply. I mostly thought that was a good thing.

Now I wondered.

I'd trusted him this far, with my body and whatever was left of my heart. I'd trusted him with everything Mikhail had left me. And I'd trusted him to watch my back more times than I could count.

It would have to be good enough.

"Okay." I downshifted as the light on Pelizada and Twelfth changed. "Okay. You got it. Okay."

14

*S*isters of Mercy rose above downtown like a giant brooding concrete bird. The old hospital was lost in a welter of pavement, but the great granite Jesus tacked on the roof still glowered in the direction of the financial district. We went in through the side entrance and suffered the immediate attack of linoleum, disinfectant, floor wax, and the smell of suffering.

Saul reached down and took my hand as soon as we walked in. I've grown to hate hospitals. Don't get me wrong—they're mostly wonderful places, staffed by some of the best and most dedicated around. But like schools, they just raise my hackles. So much suffering and free energy floating around, whether from illness and dying or from kids squeezed into little boxes and told to behave; so much *pain*. It's a charged atmosphere, which is good for a hunter—we kind of amp up to meet that charge—and bad for a hunter as well. There's only so long you can stay with your hackles up before going a little wack.

Of course, the case could be made that we're all permanently wack anyway.

We took the stairs up to the fifth floor, post-cardiac. My footsteps echoed in the hall, and I began to feel a little uneasy. My fingers tightened, and Saul gave me a single inquiring look.

I spotted Father Guillermo down the hall, and felt my face harden. It still rankled. The Church funded training for quite a few hunters, but it was an article of faith and doctrine that we were going to Hell for our traffic with and contamination by the nightside. Still, I'd thought I could *trust* Gui, that he wouldn't . . . well, hold out on me.

Treat me like just another layman.

God knew I'd handled enough exorcisms for him. I deserved a little bit of warning if his seminary was holding a relic or artifact—even if it was very likely that the Sorrows had no interest in the fucking thing.

Why were they there, then? What the hell's going on with that?

The scar tightened, sending a flush of heat up my arm. I stopped dead. My nostrils flared. Saul went still and dangerous beside me.

"You smell that?" I asked, as he let go of my hand and reached for the hilt of his Bowie.

"Incense," he replied. "And blood. A blue smell."

Not just a blue smell, but a smell I remembered. A smell that made my hackles not just rise, but stiffen into steel spikes and pulse with bloodlust.

God, how I hate them. Hate them.

"A Sorrows adept." I shook my hair back. The hallway was cluttered along the sides with little stations for doing paperwork, bits of medical paraphernalia, doctors in doors talking quietly or striding away purposefully—and Father Gui, his stare blank as he leaned against the wall three feet away from a door that was slightly ajar.

Probably Father Rosas's room.

I went for my guns, they cleared leather in a heartbeat. Kept them low, glanced up at Saul. His cheeks were pale under his darker coloring.

"Keep track of Gui," I whispered. "If he starts to act possessed, just back off and keep him in sight. Okay?"

"'Kay." He knew the drill. "Gonna kill a Sorrow, baby?"

As many of them as I can in this lifetime. "You better believe it." I started down the hall.

They don't tell you in training how the world slows down with each footstep as you approach a fight. Each breath takes forever. The palms get sweaty, the heart beats thick and fast, the hair on the back of the neck tries to stand straight up.

All in all, great fun.

Father Gui stared straight ahead. He made no move, and I didn't sense anything demonic in him. His tumbled black curls rested sleekly against his head, and his eyes were glazed, half-closed. The smoky oddness of a hypno-spell wove in the air around him, and I cursed inwardly. Finding out if the Sorrow had planted any triggers in him would be uncomfortable at best.

I pushed the hospital door in with my foot, every nerve aware of Gui leaning against the wall. If he moved with the eerie speed of the possessed, this could get really ugly really quick.

I saw a slice of the hospital room, a pale blue curtain drawn around the bed, the door to a small bathroom standing ajar. *Christ. Take your pick. Do you think a Sorrow's going to be hiding in the can, or behind the curtain? Standing next to Father Rosas with a knife to his carotid, maybe? It'd be just like a Sorrow to take a hostage and kill 'em anyway.*

I paused. The beeps of a heart monitor sounded, brightly ticking off cardiac squeezes. The sound came from behind the blue curtain, and the room was full of the blue, incense-laden smell of a Chaldean whore.

"You can come in," a familiar voice said. "I'm at the window. And I'm alone."

A woman's voice. My entire body went cold, then flushed with the heat of rage. I knew that voice. Of all the adepts of any Sorrows House, it was the last one I would think stupid enough to put herself in a room with me.

It was the bitch herself, Melisande Belisa.

The woman who had killed my teacher.

She *was* in the window, but I checked the bathroom and ripped aside the curtain. Jolly fat Father Rosas, his cheeks ashen, slumbered the sleep of a tranquilized and tired old man. The red blossoms on his nose and upper cheeks were testament to his love for the bottle, and his graying black hair was lank and greasy, beginning to go bald on top. But he was whole, and still alive—and he had a visitor.

She had long black hair, blue-black, and a hint of tilted-catlike to her eyes. Her skin was a little darker than the Sorrows usually preferred, but well within canons, and her eyes were the limitless black of the adept who has practiced for more than four cycles of their calendar; black from lid to lid, no iris or white to break the sheer gelid orbs. She wore delicate golden eardrops, and the bruising of Chaldean my blue eye could see in her aura was disciplined, a parasitical symbiote. A sickness that helped, like an *arkeus* helped a Trader.

The Elder Gods give to those who serve them well, almost as often as they consume them.

She wore blue silk, in utter defiance of passing for normal. A Chinese-collared shirt, loose pants, slipperlike shoes. As if she was still in a House's quiet, incense-laden darkness, shafts of sunlight piercing the dim smoke.

If it was the end of a cycle by their calendar, the air would be full of crackling expectation; and as night fell there would be a black flashing knife and the gurgle as a drugged prisoner—or more likely, one of their own, a male raised in the House's gloom for just this purpose—would wind up throat-slit, sacrificial death fueling ceremonies from a time when the Elder Gods walked the earth.

The Elder Gods were gone now, locked behind a wall so old even hunter legends only whisper of its making. But sometimes the smaller Chaldean demons come through and wreak havoc. The Sorrows accumulate what they can and spread their Houses like a sickness, praying for the return of their hungry masters.

I lifted both guns. My fingers tightened. Sunlight fell over her, bringing out the highlights in her hair, the mellow burnish of her skin.

"I need your help," she said.

Oh, for Christ's sake. I've had all I can stand of people saying utterly incomprehensible things. "For Mikhail," I whispered. Father Rosas's heart monitor beeped, incongruous in the charged, suddenly buzzing quiet.

She lifted both hands, palm-out but loose, with no tingle of sorcery surrounding them. "I loved him too. I just had to kill him."

I felt it again, Mikhail's body in my arms as he choked on blood and her mocking freezing laughter as she disappeared. As I screamed Mikhail's name until the Weres—small consolation that they were watching him just as I was—came to bear him away from the shitty little hotel room where he'd breathed his last and give him a clean-burning pyre.

And not so incidentally, to restrain me as I tried to throw myself after the Sorrows adept. She would have killed me then.

I was stronger now.

Shoot her now, goddammit! Shoot her! "I told you. No Sorrows in my city." My voice cracked, I could barely force out a whisper through my rage-tightened throat.

"You killed my brother." A swift grimace pulled down the corners of her pretty mouth. "We thought he could stay here unnoticed. In a seminary."

"Was an *utt'huruk* in one of his classmates part of the plan?" My voice was ragged. *Kill her. Kill her now.*

But she had used that word. *Brother.* It wasn't like a Sorrow. And he'd said, *sister.*

They lied, though. It was SOP when dealing with Sorrows: *don't believe a fucking word.* Masters of the mind-fuck, sometimes they even make Perry look simple.

And this one had taken in my teacher, probably the smartest fucking hunter on the face of the earth. She had done it so easily.

"The Chaser was sent to bring him back. It took you to kill him, hunter."

Like hell. How did it get in Oscar? By mistake? "He bit

his poison tooth." The words tasted like ash in my mouth. The situation began to resolve behind my eyes—maybe the Sorrows boy *had* been hiding out in the seminary. It was almost likely, and almost logical.

"I don't blame him. We know how . . . unkindly you view us." The sunlight faded, a cloud drifting across the sky. She looked out the window, presenting me with a profile I had only seen before in shadows, through a haze of bloodlust, rage, fear, grief. And a slice of her throat, visible above the Chinese collar. "I am in violation, hunter, and I've come here for your help. One of our adepts has escaped us, and is engaging in forbidden acts."

I felt one eyebrow raise. "I didn't think there were any acts forbidden to a Sorrows House adept. Except, of course, being a decent fucking human being." I eased back on the triggers a little, kept the guns pointed at her. Saw Mikhail's face again, the light dimming in his eyes, the last gurgle as blood pumped free of the gaping razor-made wound in his throat.

And oh, how he had loved her, meeting her in furtive alleys and motels, keeping his relationship with her a secret even from me. Even though I'd been his apprentice, closer to him than anyone else, Mikhail had kept his secrets. A hunter, snared in a Sorrow's net, Belisa's plaything in a game still murky to me. After his death the Weres and I had cleared the Sorrows House on Damietta Street.

I had not left a single one of them alive. But Belisa had already stolen Mikhail's amulet, the Eye of Sekhmet. It was probably in a Sorrows treasure-room right now, a pretty prize that had probably bought her the right to move up a few more ranks in the stifling cloister of priestesses.

True to form, she didn't even offer an apology. "Both

New Blasphemy priests are alive." She kept looking out the window. "And so is your pet cat. Be grateful."

Let me take off my cuff and thank you, bitch. "You have twenty seconds before I blast you out that window and into Hell," I informed her. *Calm and steady, Jill. See what she knows, if anything.* "You might want to start talking."

"Her name is Inez Germaine." She smiled as she dropped this piece of news. "Blood-colored hair, very sleek. From the North House in Alsace-Lorraine."

I stared at her. Could Robbie have mistaken Chaldean for French?

No way. They don't even sound similar. "I'm still not convinced." I thumbed the hammers back slowly, hearing two small clicks. *Ten. Nine. Eight. Seven. Six.*

"She is attempting an evocation, hunter. She is fueling it with death and acquiring funding from the sale of bodily—"

Four. Three. I'll admit it. I lost my temper and fired early.

I pulled both triggers at the same time, the sound was deafening. I kept firing, glass shattering, she was gone in a flurry of blue silk. I leapt to the window ledge, clearing the bed in one swift movement, and almost plunged out, just in time to see her land on the pavement below, roll gracefully, and bolt down Sarcado Avenue. Glass ground under my feet as I crouched on the windowsill, both guns leveled.

Five stories is nothing to a Sorrow, going after her now will just make everything messy. She had an escape route planned. This was the first step in the game. Just like she played with Mikhail.

No getting away this time, bitch. Not on my watch.

I took careful aim with my right-hand gun, closing out

everything around me, including Saul bursting through the door and the sudden scramble of sound from the hall. Sighted at her fleeing back, inhaling smoothly; *squeezed* the trigger.

Roaring sound, smell of cordite. I swear I could almost *see* the bullet as it leapt from the gun's barrel, a brief burst of muzzle flash lost in the weak cloudy winter light.

She stumbled, red blossoming as her right shoulder-blade shattered. *That's going to hurt as it heals, isn't it. No matter. I'll hunt you slowly. And before I'm done, bitch, you're going to beg. Just like Mikhail did.*

Six months I'd spent eating myself alive, wondering if I'd been too late to save my teacher because of jealousy, like any jilted lover. Until Saul and a hunt for a rogue Were had crossed into my city, and Perry's game to eat up whatever was left of my soul had shown me with stark clarity that I had not been to blame.

I had not killed my teacher. *She* had.

"Jill? *Jill?*" Saul. He grabbed my shoulders, dragged me back from the window. "What the *fuck?*"

"It's her," I was saying, in a monotone. "It's her. The bitch. It's her." The beeps of the heart monitor were steady in the background; Father Rosas hadn't even twitched. He must have been tranked out of his mind.

"Christ, was that really a Sorrow?" He shook me as I heard yells out in the corridor, running feet. "Jill? It reeks in here. *Jillian!*"

"It's okay." I shook my head. I was shaking, and my voice hit the level just a hair under "blood-chilling": soft, chanting in a singsong, tasting each word. "I'm okay. It's her. The bitch herself. I'm going to take her apart joint by fucking joint—"

"Come on." He pulled me under his arm and dragged me toward the door, the peculiar blurring of his Were camouflage beginning just at the corner of my vision. "Jesus Christ, you were only in here for a minute. Can't I leave you alone for ten seconds without gunfire? This is a *hospital.*"

Do you really want me to answer that, Saul? I let him pull me along, numbly. *It's her. The bitch. It's her.*

"To hell with dead whores," I heard myself say. "I'm going to hunt myself a Sorrow."

Then my left hand came up, I would have clapped it over my mouth if it hadn't still been full of heavy metal gun. "Christ," I choked. "I think I'm going to be fucking sick."

"Hold it for a few seconds," he replied, practically, palming the door open and dragging me out into the hall. He got me down the hall, neatly avoiding the chaos of security guards and running nurses, and out through a fire door, adding to the general fun. I felt sorry for the poor cardiac patients, fleetingly. And sorry for Father Rosas, though he probably hadn't heard a damn thing. She'd probably drugged him; poison and chemicals are a Sorrow's stock-in-trade. And Guillermo would mean less than nothing to her. Belisa's game right now was with me.

In an alley below I lost breakfast and everything I'd ever thought of eating for lunch. Saul held my hair back as I retched and swore, alternately, hearing the little gurgle of Mikhail's life bubbling out through his throat and her laughter like tinkling glass.

All in all, for facing down Belisa again, I handled it pretty well.

15

"This is beginning to piss me off." I stared at the small brick building. The office on Quincoa—Kricekwesz's—was closed again, this time at three in the afternoon. "Doesn't this doctor ever open up?"

Saul lit a Charvil. "You want to go in and take a look around?"

My stomach flipped. I studied the front of the place: windowless because of the chance of projectiles, *Family Planning Clinic* in gold on the door that had a peephole and an intercom box with the *Closed* sign hanging from it as well as a *UPS NO!* stenciled underneath on white-painted bricks. There weren't any protestors out here, and I supposed that was a good thing. A doctor who did abortions needed to be circumspect and safety-conscious; if he didn't have a crowd of Jesus freaks out front it meant that he hadn't pissed off the religious fanatics.

Yet.

I took my time, looking at the roof, the security cameras, the steel door. "Ricky didn't say anything about needing an appointment."

"Kind of odd for the doc not to be here."

"He doesn't keep night hours either." I sighed. My mouth tasted sour even through the cinnamon Altoid Saul had given me. My hands were no longer shaking, but I still felt a little . . . unsteady.

I couldn't believe something so callous had come out of my mouth. *To hell with dead whores. I'm going to hunt myself a Sorrow.*

It was exactly the sort of thing a hellbreed would say. Or a Middle Way adept, one of those selfish bastards. I couldn't *believe* myself.

"Christ." I let out a sharp breath. "If I'm going to do any breaking and entering, I want it to be for a good cause. We'll come back tomorrow. All the doc will be able to do anyway is confirm Baby Jewel wanted to get rid of a career impediment." Shame twisted under the words as soon as I heard my own voice. "Christ, Saul. I can't believe what I'm saying."

His hand closed over my nape, warm and hard. Saul reeled me in as he leaned back against the wall of the alley we'd chosen for surveillance. "Relax, kitten." He exhaled smoke over my head. "Just take a breath."

I closed my eyes and leaned against him, my head cradled below his collarbone and shoulder. My cheek rested against his T-shirt, and I pushed his coat aside and breathed him in.

His thumb worked along the tense muscles at the back of my neck. He took another sharp breath in, inhaling the smoke, and blew it out. "She really got to you."

"Mindfuck central." I jagged in another breath. *God,*

Saul, what did I ever do without you? But I knew. I worked myself into the ground and killed myself by inches, that's what I did. Just like every other hunter. "They probably have a dossier on me a mile thick." *And it doesn't fucking help that I have to visit Lucado again. I hate pimps. Jesus Christ, but I hate pimps.* I shoved the thought away. It went without protest, used to being pushed under the rug. I was no longer vulnerable, I was a grown-up, kickass hunter, and I wasn't going to forget it.

"What do you think the game is?"

"There's a vanishing possibility she actually knows something." My voice was muffled in his shirt. He was warm, warm as a Were, a higher metabolism radiating energy. "The trouble is, there's nothing Chaldean that does this. The demons like to possess, not eat. And the Sorrows don't *use* body parts. They like the whole person, bleeding and screaming. After they've mindfucked the hell out of them and torn them into little bits and slit their fucking throats and—"

"Jill."

"What?"

"Shut up."

I did.

"I need you calm, baby. Nice and calm. You start going off the deep end and your pheromones get all wacked-out, and that makes me *real* unhappy. 'Kay?"

I nodded, my cheek moving against his shirt. He smelled of spice, woodsmoke, Charvil cherry tobacco, and familiar musk. *I don't want to make Saul unhappy. That's the last thing I want.*

"'Cause I like you nice and sweet, kitten." His voice rumbled in his chest, not just the words but the sound soothing me. "I like you sleek and I like you purring. I don't like no fucking Sorrow playing with your head, and we'll fix it just as soon as we can. But for right now, baby, honey, kitten, Jilly-kiss, you need to calm the fuck down before I give you a *dose* of calm. Okay?"

"Okay." I heard his heartbeat, even and unhurried. This was rapidly getting out of hand. "I'm calm."

"No you're not." Amusement in his voice. "But close enough."

"I could still use a dose." *At least when you're in bed with me I'm sure you're not going to vanish.*

That thought vanished too, like bad gas in a mineshaft. I couldn't afford to start on that particular mental path right now.

"Bet you could. Me too." He moved a little, bumping me, I leaned into him. "Business before pleasure, baby." His voice rumbled against my ear.

"Who made up that rule?" *I am handling this very, very well. All things considered.*

"You did. Want to break it?"

Shit. "We'd better get to Hutch's. I've got books to hit before I have to face a few hours with a hellbreed."

"You want dinner?" Christ, did Saul sound *tentative?* Why? I wasn't going to break. I'd handled worse than this. The enemies I didn't like were the ones that surprised me, that's all. Once I knew they were in town, it became a clear-cut problem: seek and destroy.

Knowledge is the hunter's best friend, Mikhail always used to say.

Oh but it hurt to think of Mikhail. Hurt down deep, in a place I shut off from the rest of my life, the place that only bloomed when I was up alone at night with the wind mouthing the corners of the warehouse, low-moaning its song of streetcorners and loneliness. A place that hadn't shown up too often since Saul had waltzed into my life and first irritated the hell out of me, then worked his way inside my defenses and ended up twined around my heart. Worked in so deep I wasn't sure where he ended and I began.

The trouble with love is that it leaves you so fucking vulnerable. It's a weak spot. But without that weak spot, what the ever-living fuck is a hunter fighting for?

"No." I stepped reluctantly away from the shelter of his warmth. "I'd better not. Hanging around him tends to upset my stomach." I sighed, rolling my tense shoulders, and blew out a long breath. "Feel free, though. You can hit the stands for a burrito or something while I'm in Hutch's."

"You think I'm going to leave you alone in the bookstore with Hutch?" His eyebrow rose, and the world suddenly jolted back into its familiar configurations. "I know how hot he thinks you are."

Hutch's was a bust. Hutch hadn't had time to do more than pull the sources he thought were most likely and skim for translatable passages. The term *chutsharak* didn't appear to mean anything at all. Hutch himself turned white when he saw me, showed us into the back room, then closed down and hightailed it. Which meant we spent the better part of the day into the night poking through moldering books and not finding much that I didn't already know about the Sorrows.

He *also* hadn't managed to find anything on Saint An-

thony's spear. Which meant that either Hutch was slipping—or Rourke had lied to me.

Guess which one my money was laid on.

When the time came, Saul drove—my hands were a
little shaky. Our first stop was Mary of the Immaculate
Conception, and I spent twenty minutes in a back pew
with my eyes closed, smelling the peculiar odor of a
church. Incense, vestments, ritual wine, the dash of hope,
belief, terror, pleading. A familiar mix, comforting and
spurring in equal measure.

The beads of the tiger-eye rosary slipped through my
fingers as I sat, swaying slightly, the prayer repeating itself inside my head.

*Thou Who hast given me to fight evil, protect me. Keep
me from harm. Grant me strength in battle, honor in living, and a quick clean death when my time comes. Cover
me with Thy shield, and with my sword may Thy righteousness be brought to earth, to keep Thy children safe.
Let me be the defense of the weak and the protector of the
innocent, the righter of wrongs and the giver of charity.
In Thy name and with Thy blessing, I go forth to cleanse
the night.*

It is the Hunter's Prayer. Several different versions are
extant: Mikhail used to pray in gutter Russian, singing the
words with alien grace; I've heard it intoned in flamenco-
accented Spanish and spoken severely in Latin, I've heard
the greased wheels of German clicking and sliding, I've
even heard it chanted in Swedish and crooned in Greek,
spoken sonorously in Korean and sworn languidly in
French, and once, memorably, spat in Nahuatl from a
Mexican *vaduienne* while cordite filled the air and the
snarls of hellbreed echoed around us on every side. Me,

I say it in English, giving each word its own particular weight. It comforts me.

Faint comfort, maybe, that hunters all over the word had just said or were about to say this prayer at any particular time. Faint comfort that I was part of a chain stretching back to the very first hunters of recorded history, the sacred whores of Inanna who used the most ancient of magics—that of the body itself, with the magic of steel—to drive the nightside out beyond the city walls. The priestesses were themselves heirs to the naked female shamans of Paleolithic times; those who used menstrual blood, herbs, bronze, and the power of their belief to set the boundaries of their camps and settlements, codifying and solidifying the theories of attraction and repulsion forming the basis of all great hunter sorceries. They had been the first, those women who traced ley lines in dew-soaked grasses, drawing on the power of the earth itself to push back Hell's borders and make the world safe for regular people.

Faint goddamn comfort, yes. But I'd take it. Each woman in that chain had added something, each man who had sacrificed his life to keep the innocent safe had added something, and all uttered some form of this prayer. *God help me, for I go forth into darkness to fight. Be my strength, for I am doing what I can.*

When I was finished I genuflected, candles shimmering on the altar; an old woman eyed me curiously as I dipped both hands in the holy water. She looked faintly shocked when I smoothed the water on my hair and the shoulders of my ragged coat, wiping two slashes of the cool blessed water on my cheekbones like Saul's warpaint. I genuflected to the altar one last time, winked at the old woman, and met Saul in the foyer, where he was absorbed in staring at the stained-glass treatment of the Magdalene welcoming repentant sinners with open arms over the door. He dangled the obsidian arrowhead on its braided leather absently in his sensitive fingers, turning it over and over, smoothing the bits of hair and feathers.

He said nothing, and drove the speed limit all the way out to the familiar broken pavement of the industrial district, where the Monde Nuit crouched in its bruised pool of etheric stagnation.

He pulled up into the fire-zone, reached over, took my hand. Squeezed my fingers, *hard*. Let go, a centimeter at a time. Another ritual.

He would come into the Monde with me if he could. But a Were in a hellbreed bar like this would only spell trouble, and something told me Perry would love to have Saul on his territory.

That's exactly the wrong thing to think at a time like this, Jill. I stared out through the windshield. The long low front of the Monde beckoned, its arched doorway glowing with golden light. One hell of a false beacon.

"Stay here until I come get you, kitten. Okay?" If the words stuck in his throat, he didn't show it.

I nodded. The scar on my wrist was hard, hot, and hurtful, a reminder that Perry expected me. A reminder I did most emphatically *not* need. The silver charms in my hair tinkled uneasily.

"He doesn't own you." Now Saul's voice was thick. "He *doesn't*."

"I know." I barely recognized my own whisper. "He doesn't own me. You do." *You're the only man other than*

Mikhail who has ever owned *me, Saul. You mean you don't know that?*

"Christ, Jill—"

But I had the door open and was out, the chill of a winter night folding around me. I walked to the door, my bootheels clicking on the concrete; there was a line as usual. Hellbreed and others stared at me, whispering, I reached the door. The bouncers eyed me, the same twin mountains of muscle, their eyes normal except for red sparks glittering in their pupils.

Please, I prayed. *Let it be one of the nights he's bored with me. Let him have other business.*

Fat fucking chance. Last night he'd actually left the Monde Nuit and expended serious effort on me. Tonight I was probably going to pay for that.

Probably? Yeah. Like I was probably breathing right now.

I stalked between the bouncers, daring them to say anything; if they turned me away I could go back to the car and blame it on his own fucking security. But no, they didn't make a single move. In fact, one of them grinned at me, and the thumping cacophony of the music inside reached out, dragged me into the womblike dark pierced with scattered lights, the smell of hellbreed, and the jostling crowd of the nightside come out to have a little fun. The ruby at my throat warmed, and Saul's hickey pulsed.

Was it shameful of me to hope Perry wouldn't notice it?

I kept my chin up and a confident swing to my hips as I stalked for the bar. Riverson was on duty again, and his blind eyes widened. He immediately reached for the bottle of vodka.

Not a good sign.

I reached the bar, and he poured a shot for me, slammed it down. "You're supposed to go straight up," he shouted over the noise. "He's waiting for you."

I winced inwardly. Outwardly, I gave Riverson a smile, picked up the shot, and poured it down. It burned. "Not like you to give free drinks, blind man. But I guess my tab's still good."

His mouth pulled down, sourly. His filmy eyes flicked past me, evaluated the dance floor. There was very little he didn't notice. It used to be that a visit to the Monde would be during daylight, to visit Riverson and hear what he had to say, coming in as a hunter's apprentice and watching Mikhail's back. He'd never liked coming in here, even during the day. It was a very last resort, and one he hadn't had to use too often.

Perry had taken an interest the first time I'd covered Mikhail in this hole. Mikhail had nearly fired on him when he made that first appearance, leaning against the end of the bar and eyeing me.

Stop thinking about Mikhail, Jill. You have other things on your mind.

Of course, that was a losing battle. There wasn't a day passing by that I didn't think of him. After all, he'd rescued me, hadn't he? Better than any other father figure I'd ever had.

He had taken a shivering, skinny little girl in out of the cold, and he had trained me to be strong. Mikhail had pushed me, shaped me, molded me—and held the other end of my soul's silver cord as I descended into Hell to finish my apprenticeship.

Sometimes I wondered what he'd felt, watching my

lifeless body on the altar, holding the silver cord steady with the ruby I now wore pulsing and bleeding in his palm, wondering if I was going to come back. Wondering if I would survive the trip down into the place hellbreed call home.

Or did he not wonder? Did he know he'd trained me as best he could, and given me every weapon possible to use against the nightside? Had it been any comfort to him?

"You should stay away from here, goddammit." Riverson shook his head, his filmed eyes focusing past me. "You stink of Were."

"And you stink of Hell, Riverson. Keep your fucking advice to yourself." I slammed the shotglass back down on the bar, turned again, and walked toward the back as if I owned the place. My tattered coat swung like the fringe on a biker's jacket.

Feets don't fail me now.

In the back, the tables were full of hellbreed—playing cards, drinking quietly, murmuring in Helletöng that threaded under the blasting assault of the music thudding through shuddering stale air. Their glittering eyes followed me as I strode through, heading for the slender black iron door at the very back, behind its purple velvet rope.

A chair scraped, audible even under the noise. When one of them half-rose, reaching under his bottle-green velvet coat, I barely blinked. The gun was in my hand, pointed at him; his sharply handsome fine-boned face was a pale dish under the warm bath of electric yellow light. Cigarette smoke wreathed and fumed in the air. Yellow eyes glittered with the preternatural fury of a hellbreed, and a powerful one too.

Well, hello, whoever you are. What's your goddamn problem, you suddenly got tired of living? I kept the gun trained on him. The scar pulsed, hard and hot, on my wrist.

Give me a reason. Come on, just one little reason. Oh, please. Come on.

My finger tightened on the trigger. I could see the ether gathering, the black bruise of hellbreed swirling around him. I couldn't believe my luck. If he moved on me, I was well within my rights to shoot him and leave.

Then, out of nowhere, Perry's hand closed around my right wrist. The scar turned so hot under the leather I almost expected to smell scorching.

He said nothing, his fingers gentle, his bland interested face turned to the hellbreed who stood awkwardly, caught in the middle of pushing himself up to his feet and reaching under his jacket.

Without warning, Perry's fingers on my wrist turned to iron. He *squeezed,* I heard bones creaking, and he subtracted the gun from my grip with a negligent twist of his free hand. He leveled the gun, drew the hammer back, and pulled the trigger.

The shot sliced through thumping music, black blood flew. The hellbreed's head evaporated. The head is one of the surer places to kill a hellbreed—that is, if they're not actively leaping on you, being spooky-quick fuckers. And my ammo is coated with silver. True silver bullets are a bitch when it comes to ballistics. Luckily you only need enough of the moon-metal to pierce the hellbreed's shell and render them vulnerable. It poisons them as well; two for the price of one.

Perry replaced the gun in my hand. Then he guided my

hand down to holster it, his fingers still on the leather cuff over the scar, swelling up prickling and infected-painful to meet him.

The music swallowed echoes of the gunshot. Nobody moved. The hellbreed's body slumped to the floor, meat deprived of life, the mess of the head thocking wetly onto the laminate flooring back here in the inner court of the Monde Nuit.

Oh, fuck.

I didn't know who the 'breed was, or what his problem with me had been—hell, I was obviously a hunter, and he was probably wanted for something. But still, if Perry had wanted to make the point of just what I was here for, he could hardly have written it larger and underlined with neon. I was here because I had business with him, and I was under his protection.

In other words, Perry had done the hellbreed equivalent of a Were leaving a big ol' hickey on my neck. As if anyone in the room didn't already know my face.

Except the dead hellbreed in bottle-green velvet, that is.

Perry indicated the door, and let go of my wrist. I swallowed, set my jaw, and stalked forward. My back ran with tingling cold awareness. *He's behind me. Behind me. Oh God he's behind me.*

The door opened, a slice of blue light widening. I stepped behind the purple velvet rope, saw the stairs going up. My skin chilled all over.

Christ. I wish Saul was here.

No, no I don't. I'm glad he's nowhere near here. That means he's safe.

Behind me, Perry's soundless step filled the air as the

iron door swung shut. "A little touchy, aren't we, my Kismet?" His tone was even, interested, calm. "I wonder why."

Let the mindgames begin. I swallowed. "Lots of people trying to kill me lately."

"Not in my house." He didn't sound amused, for once.

"You can never tell when a hellspawn's going to get funny ideas." I kept my pace slow. This counted toward the two hours. Every moment I spent in the Monde counted toward the two hours.

God, get me through this.

"No. You never can." The soft, meditative tone was new, and gooseflesh began to swell on my back. I was glad I had my coat on. "Are you wondering what I'll ask of you tonight?"

"Safer not to wonder. Bound to be unpleasant." I reached the top of the stairs, pushed the wooden door wide. It squeaked a little on hinges I suspected he left unoiled on purpose.

"If you relaxed a little, you might like it." There was a chilling little laugh. "But tonight, you're going to sit down and have a drink with me."

Oh, Christ. "What are we drinking?"

"Whatever you like. And I am going to have your full attention, Kiss. It's been too long."

Not for me. I stepped into the room, my boots sinking into plush white carpet.

The room was large, and music from below thudded faintly through the floor. At the far end in front of a sheet of tinted bulletproof glass the bed stood—pristine, swathed in white, and loaded with pillows. The wet bar at the other end, to my left, gleamed with chrome and mirrors; artful track lighting showed the Brueghel on the far wall next to the bank of television monitors, some showing interior views of the Monde, others showing satellite feeds of news channels. The walls were painted white. The smell of hellbreed floated thick and curdled on still air.

On the expanse of white carpet, two chairs: recliners in white leather. Which brought up the inevitable choice. Did I sit with my back to the door so I could pretend to watch the television images of death, destruction, and hellbreed dancing, or did I sit with my back to the bulletproof glass and have Perry be the only focus for my eyes?

Choices, choices.

"Sit down, take it off. What do you want to drink?" He moved to the bar, and I swallowed dryly again. He was being far too polite.

Wonder if I should put a new strategy into play? Make him dictate every damn move. It was worth a try. "Where should I sit?"

"Wherever you like, my dear Kiss. Just take that idiot cuff off. I like to hear your pulse."

I reached down, unbuckled the leather, and slowly drew it off. Tucked it in my pocket. Air hit my skin again; the scar tightened deliciously, and I choked back rising panic. What was he going to make me do to him this time? The whip again, or would it be the flechettes?

And would I enjoy it? He *liked* the pain. And sometimes, dear God, I liked making him bleed.

If there was a valley of darkness for hunters, that was it. You can't live with the violence, blood, and screaming for long without getting a taste for vengeance. Every time I made Perry bleed it felt suspiciously close to justice.

It felt good.

"Sit down," he said in my ear, hot too-moist breath brushing heavily and condensing on my skin. I gave a violent start, whirled away, my hand closing around the butt of my right-hand gun. I had to work to make my fingers unloose as Perry cocked his head, the light shining off his blond hair. He held two brandy snifters, an inch of glowing liquid in each. "Oh, come on, Kiss. Tonight's not a night for those games. If you would only relax a little, we could be *such* good friends."

"You are *not* a friend." My hands curled into fists. "You're a hellbreed. Hellspawn. Just one step up from a goddamn *arkeus,* that's all. One more type of vermin."

He shrugged, then held out the glass in his left hand. "And yet you keep coming back."

"I made a bargain. One that allows me to hunt more effectively." My fingers avoided his, I took the glass like it was a snake. The silver ring on my left hand spat a single white spark, reacting to his closeness, the carved ruby at the hollow of my throat gave a single reassuring pulse of clean heat.

The spark didn't seem to upset him, as usual. "Mikhail warned you about me." He pointed at the chairs. "Sit." Incredibly, he chose the seat with its back to the bulletproof glass, settling down and bringing the bowl of the glass to just under his nose. He inhaled, his eyes half-closing.

Almost purring with pleasure, as a matter of fact. He looked tremendously pleased with himself.

Why the fuck is everyone talking about Mikhail now? The ring warmed on my left hand. My chest tightened. "He did."

"What did he say?"

I swallowed memory, set my back teeth against it, and got ready to lie. *He told me you wanted me for reasons of your own, and I'd best remember that. And that a woman always has the edge in this situation. I believed him. I always believed him.* "That nothing you could give me was worth what I'd end up paying for it." I settled gingerly into the other chair. My heart beat thinly. *I still believe him.*

"You didn't listen to him."

"I evaluated the benefits and risk of the bargain." *I'm still alive, aren't I? And still playing patty-cake with you. Still coming out ahead by a slim margin, I'd say.*

Just don't mention how slim.

"Just like a Trader." He looked, of course, amused. And generous, so early in the night's games. He could afford to be.

"I'm not a Trader. I'm a *hunter.* And one day, Pericles—"

"Spare me." His blue eyes turned dark and thoughtful. I began to feel *very* uneasy. This wasn't like the usual visit; he would normally be asking me slip the cuffs on him by now, strapping him into the iron frame. "I find I like you threatening me less and less, Kiss."

"Get used to it." Silver burned against my neck; it was the chain the ruby hung on. And my left ring finger, the burning spreading up my wrist. My earrings were beginning to get warm too, the silver and steel of my jewelry turning against me as I sat in the hellbreed's office with the scar uncovered.

His smile was gone. Instead, he studied me with an interested, somber expression for the first time since our initial meeting. It was a good thing I was already sitting down, my knees were weak.

I was also starting to sweat.

He swirled the liquid in the glass once, precisely, and eyed me. "Oh, I am *used* to it. I console myself with the thought that eventually, you'll beg me. It's only a matter of time."

I decided to go on the offensive. Strobe lights flickered against the huge window behind the bed, red and green drenching the white coverlet. The television monitors buzzed, throwing out blue light. On one, grainy footage of a prison riot played. On another, bombs dropped from a plane's sleek silver belly into a verdant green jungle, giving birth to bursts of liquid orange flame. "What are you, Perry?"

"Just a humble hellspawn. Your most respectful servant, Kiss." He smiled, a thin curve of thinner lips. His tongue flicked once, briefly visible, shocking-wet red. With the cuff off, I could almost see the overlapping scales.

I am beginning to think you aren't so humble. You did, after all, produce hellfire in the blue spectrum. Maybe you're not a hellbreed. Maybe you're a full-fledged talyn instead of an arkeus*? But no. You're physical. You're* real. *I know that.* "I know better. You don't serve, Perry. You like to think you're the one pulling all the strings. Even mine."

"There now." The smile widened. He took a small sip of his brandy, exhaling with a small, satisfied smile. His eyes hooded, glowed bright blue like gas flames. "I told you, you're coming along quite nicely."

All right, you son of a bitch. "I saw Melisande Belisa today." I drew in a deep, smooth breath. "She sends her regards."

That wasn't *quite* true, but if I could distract Perry with the news that the Sorrows were in town I might buy a few minutes without him poking at the inside of my head.

His eyes flickered, but he didn't take the bait. "I find it extremely unlikely that she mentioned me. It was only a matter of time before her path would cross yours again."

My mouth was dry. I badly wanted to bolt the brandy, restrained myself with an effort of will. Sweat slid down the channel of my spine, a cool tickling finger. "You knew she was in town. That's why you were following me. Keeping an eye on your *investment*."

An eloquent shrug, giving me nothing. "You're playing blind."

Aren't I always, when it comes to you. "What do you know about this? Dead teenage hookers and something bullets don't even dent, something hellfire doesn't even touch?" *Though the hellfire may have touched it; I couldn't see. I was hardly a disinterested observer at that point.*

"Tonight is not for business." His tone had cooled. Point one for me.

He knows something. My pulse abruptly slowed. "That's part of the bargain, Perry. Your help on the cases I'm working."

"And your part of the bargain is time spent with me, in the manner I choose. Which you are violating, by the way." The silken reminder closed around my throat.

My temper broke with a brittle snap. "What is it this time, Perry? Am I supposed to whip you until you bleed? Or cut you until you feel like you're real? Or—oh, here's a thought. Maybe I should just beat you up. Give you a black eye and mar that unpretty face of yours. We could probably sell tickets. I'm sure all your fucking hellspawn friends downstairs would love to see you taken down a peg or two again."

He lifted the snifter. "I could simply send a pair of mercenaries to remove your little pussycat from the land of the living. That would, in fact, please me a great deal."

My fingers tightened on the glass. It was suddenly difficult to talk around the lump of dirty ice in my throat. "You leave Saul out of this."

He barely raised an eyebrow. "I allow you your regrettable taste for bestiality. You will do me the honor of living up to your part of our bargain."

You son of a bitch. "Bestiality would be if I was fucking a hellspawn. You're *not human.*"

"Can you call yourself human, after the things you've done? Not to mention the punishment you've meted out to one uncomplaining, passive hellspawn who has done nothing but aid you? Or the countless souls you've sent screaming back to Hell?"

I took refuge in sarcasm. "I do love my work."

"But you don't, Kiss. You don't like causing pain. You don't like it when you have to kill. You don't like it when you have to—"

"I like it just fine," I interrupted. *This is the only part of the goddamn job I hate. This, and looking at dead innocents.*

"They were *all* pregnant, Kismet."

The breath left me in a walloping rush. "What?" I sounded about ten years younger, and breathy as Marilyn Monroe to boot.

He blinked, both blue eyes suddenly much darker than usual. Almost black, indigo spreading and swelling through the whites. And in the back of each was a glim-

mer of light, a pinprick of infinity. "There is much more
to this than you think. And I am warning you, my dearest
little whore of darkness, tread carefully. My protection
may only extend so far in this matter."

Holy fucking shit. I rocked up to my feet, the glass
dropping from my hand and spilling its cargo of liquor
onto the pristine carpet. "Are you telling me what I think
you're telling me?"

"I am telling you it is possible that I can only protect
you *so far.*" He lifted his own glass, carefully. He looked
far more immaculate than usual, his cheekbones seemed
a little higher, his eyes still indigo, swelling through and
staining the whites. Almost . . . well, if he hadn't had
Exorcist eyes, he might have looked almost handsome.
"Though I have made it adequately clear that you are
mine, there are . . . extenuating circumstances."

*Yours? If you think so, you've got another think com-
ing, Pericles.* But there was a more important point to be
addressed. "Extenuating circumstances? Like *what*—like
you know what's going on? Like you're *involved?*" I was
repeating myself. Goddammit. I'd dealt with so many
hellbreed. Why did this one give me so much trouble?

He took another sip, totally unmoved. And yes, friends
and neighbors, he was changing shape right before my
eyes. Still recognizably Perry, but much handsomer,
higher cheekbones and his mouth ripening, his eyebrows
subtly remodeling. Was the blandness a front, or was this
the lie? "You have an hour and forty minutes left to give
me, Kismet. I suggest you rein in your impatience."

An hour and forty minutes. My hand curled around—
not a butt of a gun. No, it was a knife I went for. Was he

trying to make me so angry I attacked him? *I can make him bleed, but I can't make him tell me.*

Not when I'd just gone and given away how interested I was in the whole deal.

The reek of spilled brandy filled the air, fuming. I eased my hand away from the knife, felt the scar on my wrist go hard and hot, infection pressing against the skin, stretching before the bursting of pus. Perry's lips thinned even more, turning up into a facsimile of a smile. His eyes turned depthless, with the sparks of infinite darkness dancing far, far back.

His face finished transforming from bland to sharply handsome, bladed cheekbones and perfect proportions, subtly wrong but still . . . attractive. In a graceful, hell-breed sort of way; the type of beauty that wormed into the apple and ate it from the inside out. Giving a blush of tubercular crimson to the fruit before the blood started to cough up.

I dropped down into the chair and stared at him. *One hour, forty minutes. God help me.* "If you want anything out of me at all, you had better start talking, Pericles." Even as it left my mouth I knew it was the wrong thing to say.

"I could speak to you all night. For example, I could begin to extol the virtues of your mouth and move to your eyes, which are charming in their mismatched splendor. Perhaps I could quote from the Bible. I'm told there is some wonderful poetry in there when one overlooks the rape, pillage, plunder, and murder." The smile touching his lips didn't resemble anything human at all. "Then again, that might appeal to you, *hunter.*"

I crossed my legs and closed my eyes. Deepened my

breathing. He waited, but when I didn't respond I heard cloth shifting, as if he'd moved.

I breathed deeper, deeper. Relaxed, one muscle at a time. One of the wonderful things about being a hunter: you take your sleep where you can get it, and unless you learn to relax in a dangerous situation you don't last long.

Perry didn't see it as a gift, apparently. "You can't escape me that easily. I have your time."

Fine. But it's time I'm going to be spending feigning sleep. I settled myself more comfortably, loosened every muscle. *Saul.* The hickey on my throat burned, a different fire than the scar on my wrist. A cleaner fire.

Not going anywhere, kitten. Saul's voice scratched at the inside of my head, the roughness of his hair under my fingers. Was he right now driving into the barrio, parking my car in some hideous little spot and going into a bar or some little dive to dig for information on the little bit of knotted leather and arrowhead?

I relaxed. Perry wouldn't kill me, and even if I couldn't fall asleep completely I could give a go at faking it. It was a new strategy, I could give it a try.

Then he touched me.

The contact slid against my cheek, warm skin; he traced the arc of my cheekbone. Then his fingertips slid over my lips, trailed against my jaw, and brushed down my throat.

Christ, stop it. Make him stop. Please make him stop. I clamped down on control, heartbeat, respiration, everything. Tension invaded my body. The scar turned liquid, a traitorous outpost on my own flesh.

He'd never done this before.

Another, softer touch brushed my lips. There was no stink of rot, but the breath was too hot and humid to be human, and condensation prickled at the corners of my mouth.

He sipped my breath, and the scar exploded on my wrist, spilling fire through my veins. I heard my own voice, crying out weakly as I spilled off the chair and onto the floor. The riptide of sensation drifted away.

My hips tilted up. My heels dug into the ground, the scar burned again. *No, not again, please not again, please—*

"This does not have to be so difficult," he whispered against my damp cheek. Was he crouching over me? A brushing, feathery sound filled the air.

Tears slid down my face. The scar pulsed. *Oh, Christ. Christ help me. Still a whore. Once damned, always damned.*

The whisper continued, as the scar pounded another hot acid-burning tide of pleasure through my nerves. "All you must do is give in. I can be forgiving. I can wrap you in silk, I can make your life a series of delights, little one. I can be so kind, if you would simply *let* me. If you would only bend just the smallest bit and let me turn you, just a fraction. Just a hairsbreadth. Not so much at all. You are already so very, very close."

I've already turned all I can. I gasped, heard an agonized moan. Like a woman in the throes of love. Or death. *As a new strategy, Perry, this one sucks. I was being fucked better than this when I was fifteen years old.*

The moan sent a hot curdled wave of shame through me. My voice. It was my own voice. I braced myself against the welter of sensation spilling from the scar's puckered little mouth. "Fuck . . . you," I gasped. "*Hate* you." My voice caught, I gasped again.

"Oh, Kiss. My poor, poor Kismet." His breath was against my cheek now, loathsome oily moisture dewing my skin. The scar began to throb harder, the darkness behind my eyelids bursting with fireworks as the ragged leather of my coat rasped against the carpet. "Why do you force me to be so cruel to you?" His hands tensed against the front of my coat. My head fell back, the ruby at my throat hissing a blood-red spark. Perry hissed back in the shapeless grumble of Helletöng. "Shall I show you what you've been missing?"

My hand curled around the knifehilt as he lifted me, the silver ring turning hot against my skin. Hard to think past the spill of desire, the flare of heat as the scar was brushed with a random curl of air, it smashed through me again and my hips tilted, body convulsing with poisoned delight. Fingers clamping down, oiled metal leaving the sheath, I slashed with all the strength I could find and felt flesh part like water.

Fell. My head hit something—a bedpost. He'd *thrown* me, weightlessness and a jarring crash. The impact rang in my head for a moment until I shook it free and hauled myself to my feet. The crotch of my leather pants was warm, too warm, the sodden material of my panties rasped against delicate tissues and I bit back a curse. Turned on just like the whore I was.

No. The whore I *had been*. Now if I fucked someone, I *meant* it. I wasn't a working girl anymore.

Not anymore. Not now.

Not since I'd killed the man who'd turned me out. Not since I'd descended into Hell and been pulled back by the first man to ever rescue me, the man who had knelt in front of my death-altar with his hand knotted around the ruby, our mixed blood dyeing the gem and dragging me back into the light. The first man and only man who had seen not just tits and ass but my anger, my talent, my strength, my reflexes.

My ability to become a hunter.

I gasped, gathering myself. Hoped like hell Mikhail was right and that I had the advantage here.

It sure as shit didn't feel like it.

Perry lifted his bloody fingers to his mouth and delicately licked, his tongue flickering coal-red along thick black fluid. The cut was low on his belly, I'd scored a good hit. "Another sweet nothing, from you."

I lifted the knife. Got my balance back. My head rang. "You do that again, you son of a bitch, and I'll kill you."

"Kill me, and your strength is effectively reduced by a few orders of magnitude." He touched the wound on his stomach again. Thinning black ichor slid down his trouser leg. I'd cut through his suit, ruined another fine shirt. "I'm the devil you know. You should treat me better."

"I don't care if I go back to being a human hunter," I flung at him, getting my balance and my bearings. "You do that to me again, Pericles, and *I will kill you.*"

"I'm only trying to be nice." His smile widened as he licked his fingers clean of blood. "Wouldn't you like me to be nice? I can be very, very *nice* to you."

If you only knew how many times I've heard a man say something similar. "Sit the fuck down." I pointed the knife at the chair. "Now."

He did, very slowly. I decided it was safer if I got away from the bed. My hands shook, but the knife was steady.

Or at least, I hoped it was steady. I took an experimental step. Another. Kept going until I could see his profile, and the glass of brandy spilled on the carpet.

It was time to get back to business. He wouldn't be satisfied with just that exchange, but I might get something out of him nonetheless. "They were all three pregnant? How the fuck do you know?"

He closed both eyes, settled back in the chair. "Ah, now I have your attention. The sum of your regard. The sunshine of your—"

"Stop fucking with me, Perry. What do you know about this?" I licked my lips, wished I hadn't. The scar gave a small twinge, another jolt of pleasure sinking through my bones.

"I know they were all pregnant." He said it like it meant nothing. He did hear all sorts of things, and I would have to check, but it was a damn good clue.

If I could follow it. And if he wasn't lying.

"And?" *How do you know anything about this case at all, Perry? How deep are you in? And what the fuck is that thing that nearly killed me?*

"And nothing more, my dearest whore, unless you pay me."

Oh, God. "In what coin?"

"You know what I want."

Rage rose. The knife *did* shake, perceptibly, as my grip tightened on it. "If you are involved with these murders, Perry, I will—"

"What? Kill me? You've made that threat already. Don't be boring. If I were involved, would I tell you anything? Besides, there are some things even I will not stoop to profit from. But you should beware. My protection, as

I've said, may only extend so far." His voice dropped inti-
mately, like a hand between my legs. "But you could have
all my protection, and so much more besides."

*Some things you won't stoop to profit from? There's a
short list.* I took a deep breath. *Christ, Saul. Come back
soon. Please come back soon.*

"Sit down," Pericles said softly. Almost kindly. "No
more of this, tonight. Though I do love to hear you
whimper."

"Go to hell." It wasn't very creative, but I was kind of
at the end of my leash. This was far worse than any other
encounter I'd had with him. He'd been watching me for
a while, and hellbreed were masters at finding out what
made people tick and taking them apart, piece by piece.

Seducing them.

"Oh, no. I like it here ever so much better. Sit down,
my dear. In a little while I'll fetch another drink."

My breath turned harsh in my throat. But he kept his
eyes closed, the black blood stopped soaking through his
clothes, and the scar didn't erupt on my wrist. He tilted
his head back against the white leather of the recliner.
Resting. As if he was satisfied.

*Christ, Perry. What happened to you? You kept trying
to make me react by making me hurt you, and now you
pull this?* The thought that he might have figured out a
way to make me react the way he wanted was chilling, to
say the least. It meant I would have to find a whole new
way to relate to the bargain I'd made, a whole new way
to deal with him.

Like I don't have enough problems.

Or maybe he was just moving in on me because I was
vulnerable, because this case was bothering me more than

I wanted to admit. I lowered myself down in the chair opposite him, the knife's blade throwing back colored light. Blue from the TV screens, red from the glare in the bulletproof window, gold from the track lighting.

"One day." His voice was very quiet, very soft, and almost human. "One day, Kiss, you will have to face just how much like me you can become before you give in."

"You can't turn me, Pericles." But my throat was dry as sand. I knew better. If he kept getting better at pushing me, things might get sticky.

I'd have to kill him.

"I don't have to. You'll turn yourself, given enough time. Now be quiet. I want to listen to you breathe." All semblance of life left him, draining away until he was only an icon painted on the white leather of the chair, a black-splashed icon with his arm clamped against his side. The silver content in my knife must have hurt like a mad bastard even as it healed.

For the first time we sat there, Perry and I, and he didn't speak. Neither did I. And when the two hours were up I left. I made it to the iron door at the bottom of the stairs, buckling the leather cuff on, before I started to run. I had promised Saul, yes.

But I couldn't stay there a single moment longer.

16

I hit the door still running as the cab pulled away. Tossed my torn and battered coat over the habitual chair at the end of the hall and pounded into the practice space, barely hearing the creaks and echoes as the warehouse registered my presence.

The reinforced heavy bag hung, its scuffed red sides repaired with tape several times. Before I reached it, both my fists were balled up so tight I felt my bones creak.

I began.

Leather and vinyl popped. The charms in my hair jingled. Left hook, uppercut, right hook, combinations Mikhail had taught me, my second-best boots scuffing the mats on the floor, the heavy bag shuddering as sweat began to drip down my spine, my arms, my legs.

My teacher's voice, with its harsh song of gutter Russian under the language we shared. *Use it, use it use it! Zat is best friend right there. Should be able to do this in sleep, milaya, use it! Hurt it! Kill it! Do it!*

How had he seen the potential in me, the scared, skinny, beaten girl in the snow? He'd never told me.

Of course, I'd never asked, too grateful for his care. For the attention he paid me, attention I was starved for. We are supposed to love our teachers, otherwise it's unbearable. You have to trust your teacher with your heart and soul, with the other end of the thin silver-elastic cord that is your only way of escaping Hell once you descend. And Mikhail and I had been lovers, of course—it was inevitable, so much adrenaline and prolonged contact, two people closer than siblings or spouses or even twins.

But we are also supposed to hate our teachers, because they must teach us how to *fight*. A teacher cannot afford to be an apprentice hunter's friend. Soft in the training room means unprepared out in the dark depths of the nightside, and that's something no teacher wants. Losing a fellow hunter is bad.

Losing an apprentice is a thousand times worse.

So to hear Mikhail's ghostly voice was a double-edged comfort. I was making a sound, too. A low, hurt sound, as if I'd been stabbed. The skin on my knuckles broke and bled, leaving wet prints on the thick red vinyl. The blood would grime the ring he'd given me when he accepted me as an apprentice, the ring that was singing a thin distressed tone as my furious pain communicated itself to the metal. The carved ruby spat spark after spark, each a guncrack of frustration.

Sweat fell in my eyes, stinging, and I pounded on the heavy bag. The doorbell rang, but I ignored it. Anyone knocking at my door would either come in and get shot or go away.

Throw elbow, solid, tighten up, hit so zey know zey been

hit! Not like that, want to lose fucking hand? Tighten up! Vurk it, vurk it, vurk it— Mikhail's voice, barking through the painful hole in my memory, the years of training peeling away until I was the girl standing on the streetcorner again, cold wind against the backs of my bare legs as the cars crept by, each with its cargo of hungry-eyed men.

The mousy little brown-eyed, skinny-legged smartass girl. Not *me*. Not Jill Kismet, kickass bitch.

Not me. Not anymore.

The horrible moaning sound stopped. My hands throbbed. Punches slowed, stuttered, I gave one last blow—solid contact, a right cross, the scar on my wrist running with heat—and stood, head down, shuddering, sweat soaking through my clothes as the broken skin on my knuckles melded together, painfully, twitching as it healed.

"God." My voice cracked, fell to the floor. "God. Jesus. God."

I heard a sound. The east door opening; the front door, the only door that gave onto the street, unlocked because I'd been going so fast. Stealthy movement in the hall, probably human.

I whirled, gun coming up, the sound of it clearing the leather holster loud in the deafening cavernous draft of the warehouse. The heavy bag creaked as it swayed.

Standing at the end of the hall, the front door open behind her, was a thin brown-haired girl with a terrific bruise spreading up the side of her face. I had to look under the split lip, the bruise, and the painful, hitching little sounds she made when she breathed before I recognized her.

It was Diamond Ricky's number one girl.

"Jesus fuck," I yelled, my voice slamming through unprotected space, "what are *you* doing here?"

She jumped. She had her hands up, a battered backpack hanging off her thin shoulder. Her legs were bruised and battered too. A short pink skirt and a green sweater with holes in it completed the picture of a woman at the end of her goddamn rope.

And I knew what that felt like, didn't I? I'd once looked like that, standing in the burning snow with my life in flames, a stray cat with no place left to go.

It was official. Perry had gotten to me, and the past was about to swallow me whole. I jerked myself back into the present with an effort that made fresh sweat spring up in the hollows of my armpits and the curve of my lower back.

She would never know how close she came to eating a bullet, this girl.

Holy Christ. Echoes faded, bouncing off walls and ceilings. I took a deep breath. Sweat dripped in my eyes, stinging. "Jesus." I finally managed to get some control of my voice. "What the *fuck* are *you* doing here?"

Her face crumpled a little. Her big brown eyes were the size of dinner plates, and they welled with silent brimming tears.

I put the gun away, sliding it back into the holster with a creak of leather.

"My n-name is C-Cecilia," she whispered. Then she said the magic words. "I . . . uh, I . . . can you h-help m-me?"

I checked her for needle marks, for the nasal deterioration that would mean coke, for the smell of burnt metal that means meth. She looked pretty clean other than the familiar tang of weed and beer. She was also so painfully thin I wasn't surprised as she stuffed herself with leftover penne and steak. "Go easy on that." I poured myself a double jigger of Scotch. *Drinking too goddamn much.* "Don't get all bulimic."

She gave me a pitiful, owlish look, and I immediately felt like the biggest bitch in the universe. I poured her a glass of orange juice, and looked at the clock.

Three-thirty in the morning. How long had she been sitting outside waiting for me? One shoddy human, and I hadn't noticed. Was I slipping? Then again, I was tuned to notice things like *arkeus* and Traders trying to ambush me. Not one skanked-out little girl.

"You're Ricky's number one, aren't you? His head girl?" *The one that keeps all the others in line?*

She nodded, stuffing another mouthful of penne in. I didn't blame her, Saul makes a kickass red sauce. She wiped her mouth with a paper napkin and sniffed loudly. "I . . . I met him when I was in high school. I—"

Jesus. Don't. I shook my head. "Honey, it's all the same story, getting into that life. Don't need to hear it. Now, what's going on?"

She stared down at her plate, seeming to lose her appetite. I tried again, pitching my voice low. It cost me to be gentle.

"Did Ricky bust you up?"

She nodded. Tears welled up, brimmed out of her sad brown eyes. My frustration mounted another notch. It was like pulling teeth. I settled myself down on the stool at the kitchen counter next to her. "Because?"

"I . . . I know some things."

No shit. But what are you doing at my door, woman?
"Like what? What do you know?"

She gulped in air. "I knew Baby Jewel. And Sweet Sylvie. There's . . . you know, an awful lot of the girls have
gone missing lately. It's hard to keep track of people, they
move in and out, some of them go north on the circuit,
some go back east—it's just really hard."

I nodded. Sweat had dried on my forehead, my shirt
stuck to me. I smelled like a hard workout and spilled
brandy.

*And hellbreed. Let's not forget the hellbreed. God-
damn you, Perry.* He had wormed his way into my head
with startling ease, and with a suddenness that left me
breathless. Had he just been waiting for the right moment
and pretending to misunderstand me all along? "I know
what that's like."

She shoveled another spoonful of penne in. Chewed
and gulped it down. "They've been going missing for a
while. There were whispers, before. But it's been really
bad since . . . oh, since spring. When the rain moved in
that one week and we had flash floods."

I remembered, there had been people caught in the
floods. Idiots, mostly, but that rain had made the hunt for
a Trader serial rapist miserable. *You haven't had a week
off since spring,* Saul's voice whispered in my head. He'd
be going back to the Monde to look for me. Dammit.

"How bad?"

"Bad enough that girls are starting to get desperate.
They . . ." She gave me an uncertain look, as if gauging
my comfort level with details about the night trade. It
made me want to laugh. Did she think I was a john or a
nine-to-fiver?

To hell with dead whores, my own voice rose up to haunt me. "It's okay," I said, as gently as I could. "Believe me, kid, nothing you could say could shock me." *I've probably done it all twice if it's human, or killed it at least once if it's nightside.*

She probably didn't believe me, but she continued anyway. "They won't get into cars with a trick they don't know. Everyone's trying to buddy up, to get a good look at the last trick anyone else goes with. But it's hard. And there's been . . . well, Bethie Stride disappeared, and Mercy. And Lucy Long, and Star and Hope and Alexis—and these are all girls who wouldn't leave the city. But the worst is, if a girl gets pregnant she *vanishes.*"

Pregnant. Even with condoms and spermicide it happened. Not a lot of working girls could afford the pill, or could remember to take it every morning. And then there were pimps, and tricks who paid more for skin jobs. An occupational hazard, in the sex trade. "How many pregnant girls are there on the strip now?"

"Not a lot. They all keep disappearing." She tore off a bite of wheat bread; I'd buttered two slices for her.

Pregnant hookers. Pregnant women, with all their organs gone. And their eyes. I frowned at my glass, seeing the amber liquid inside swirl gently as my attention touched it. And those marks, too clean and sharp to be claw-marks. Scalpel cuts.

The scar on my wrist throbbed under the leather cuff. My back ran with gooseflesh.

Profit incentive. "There are some things even I will not stoop to profit from." *What if one of those things is the sale of bodily organs and stem cells?* "Holy fuck," I breathed. "Holy mother of fuck."

"She is attempting an evocation, hunter. She is fuel-ing it with death and acquiring funding from the sale of bodily—"

And I'd fired on Belisa, who may have been trying to mindfuck me with the truth.

Oh yeah. This just keeps getting better.

"Yeah." She pushed her stool back and dug in her backpack as I watched. "Look." And she came up with a thick wad of crumpled, dirty bills. "I've got two grand in cash." She laid it on the counter between us. "Most of it's mine, but five hundred's from Ricky's stash. If I go back he won't just beat me up, he'll mark my face. Maybe kill me. He's done it before." Her eyes met mine. "Can I . . . I mean, they said you could help people. Can you help . . . me?"

Those little words. Those little magic words. *Can you help me? You're my only hope. Help me. Please, for the love of God, help me.* Of all the words a hunter hears, those are the most common. And those were the words that drag us in, again and again.

Well, we sure as hell weren't in it for the money, were we.

"You want out of the life?" I said it as flatly as I could. "You get one fucking chance, doll. *One.* You fuck up with any help I give you and you're on your own. I don't care how you got on the street; if you're determined you'll get the help you need to stay off. But *don't fuck with me.*"

"You think I don't know that?" She yanked her stool back up to the bar and hunched over her plate, beginning to eat again in great starving bites. I saw the deep ugly freshness of the bruise on her face and winced inwardly.

"There's stories about you," she said between mouthfuls. "All sorts of stories. Ricky calls you a witch."

"Not a witch. Exorcist, sorceress, and tainted with hell-breed, but not witch." I didn't have to work for a dry tone. "Don't let that concern you, though. You're better off not knowing." *Believe me, are you better off not knowing.*

She shivered. I didn't try to console her. I was having enough trouble consoling myself.

Fuck Perry. You've got a job that needs doing here, Kismet. You just forget about him for a little while, you're paid up until next month when it comes to His Royal Hell-breedness. One problem at a goddamn time.

I decided. "Okay. I'm going to clean up a little and then we're going to have a nice long chat. Then I'll call a friend of mine who might be able to give you a safe place to stay until this is all over. But I warn you, you'd better not fuck with anyone I call for you. No drugs, no tricks, no nothing. Strictly legit. You got it?"

Her eyes couldn't get any bigger. I squashed the little voice inside my head telling me I was being a bitch for no good reason.

She nodded. "I got it." She sounded about five years old.

"Cecilia. You got a last name?"

She started as if pinched. "Markham."

"Well, Miss Markham, you're officially under my protection as a witness. I'm gonna go get cleaned up. There's more juice in the fridge." I paused, looking down at the grubby pile of bills. "And put that cash away. You'll need it to start a new life."

The way her pinched, bruised, split little face lit up

was enough to make me feel like an even bigger bitch than before.

I am not hellbreed, I told myself as I headed for the bathroom. *I'm a hunter, goddammit. And whoever's harvesting hookers in my city is going to get a little taste of Judgment Day real soon now.*

I couldn't help feeling better.

17

I didn't call Galina; I had already dumped one witness on her. Instead, I called Avery and wished Saul had a cell phone. Then again, if he was down in the barrio, he didn't need any distraction. He'd catch up with me soon enough.

Ave promised to drop by and pick up the girl as soon as he could, which meant three hours since he was on his Sunday overnight shift. One of those hours I spent questioning her. She was bright and relatively observant, and living on the street had fine-tuned her instinct for what was bullshit and what was truth left unsaid.

What Cecilia could tell me was almost as interesting as what she couldn't. The doctor on Quincoa—Kricekwesz—had been taking care of street girls as a profitable side gig for a long time now. Recently, though, whispers had started. The flesh gallery was alive with rumors, because girls that told their running mates or coworkers (if such a word could be used for girls that worked for the same pimp or walked the same bit of street) that they had a little "trouble" started disappearing. And the girls that visited the doctor came back with appointments to see him again—but never got there.

"It's not just girls," Cecilia told me. "Some of the street kids, the young ones, get taken too. And some of the older rummies on the street have started to talk about weird things. Seeing weird things." When pressed, she shook her head. "I dunno. I've heard everything from UFOs to Sasquatch. Real crazy shit."

If other people had seen what Robbie the Juicer had seen, no wonder the street scene was boiling with rumor.

The most interesting piece of news was the pimps all getting together after I'd put the squeeze on Ricky. A meet was something that only happened in dire circumstances, thanks to the egos of the petty thugs involved. There was always fresh meat, but one or two of the flash boys had been grumbling about something cutting into their profit by picking off the girls. Ricky had thrown a fit, but he was small fry even though his girls had some prime real estate.

Another pimp, a heavyset black man with gold-capped front teeth who went by the name of Jonte, had told everyone to shut up, because they would be getting paid plenty. He'd told Ricky in no uncertain terms that the little shit hadn't been let in on the action because he couldn't keep his mouth shut, Ricky had gotten fresh and got bitch-smacked for his pains. Which explained why the smacking had devolved onto Cecilia, incidentally.

And then there was the bombshell. The meeting had also been attended by a representative from the local Mob, Jimmy Rocadero, with two bodyguards. Beyond supporting Jonte's claim that the pimps would be paid plenty for going along with the program, Rocadero hadn't said much, but his mere presence had scared some of the smaller fish in the pond. Every pimp in Santa Luz paid a percentage to the Mob. It was just how business is done.

"Do you know if the strip clubs are having similar turnover?" I asked.

Cecilia, the worst of her scrapes Bactined and a few Band-Aids applied, as well as arnica to take down some of the worst swelling, no longer even looked eighteen. Instead, she looked twelve. A very frightened twelve. She curled up on my couch with a battered teddy bear she'd fished out of her backpack and jumped at the slightest noise. I hoped her ribs weren't busted up; she sounded horrible when she breathed. She had nothing but short skirts and hot pants in her backpack, so I'd rustled up a pair of paint-splattered sweats for her. She shook her head. "I dunno. I never did the strips. By the time I was old enough I was already turned out for Ricky."

I sat on the floor, cross-legged in leather pants and a *Prospero's Housewives* T-shirt, thinking about this. The need for *action* boiled away under my breastbone, but there was nothing I could do right at the moment except get every scrap of information I could from this girl.

I had brought out a package of Oreos, and she was putting them away at a steady rate. *I hope she doesn't make herself sick.* I had a sudden vision of holding her long brown hair back while she retched.

It wasn't pleasant.

I took a closer look at her. She'd been pretty, and bright enough to escape getting hooked on something deadly. I pegged her as smart but terribly needy, probably a cheerleader in high school with a bad home life that she thought running away would save her from.

Like looking into a fucking mirror, eh, Jill?

I pushed that voice away. It was time for the most inconsequential but revealing question.

"So why did you bail out on Ricky?" I tented my fingers and leaned forward, bracing my elbows on the coffee table. Saul's slippers lay neatly underneath, and my knee touched one of them. I found it absurdly comforting.

She actually blushed. Her cheeks turned red, and she looked down at the package of Oreos.

I caught the message. I should have smelled it on her, but under the fume of hellbreed and fury from my own skin and yeast-alcohol beer from hers, it would have been a miracle to catch it.

Christ. "Okay. Please tell me you haven't been out to Quincoa."

"I haven't," she whispered. "But Ricky called the doctor to make the appointment for me. I said I wouldn't go. He . . ."

"That's when he got all nasty on you." I nodded. *Great.* It must have been the last straw.

"I told him I'd go after he hit me. But I . . . there are people who know stuff. I went to this head shop on Salvador Avenue, I told them I was looking for you. That I needed help. The woman there said to come here. I walked the whole way."

And if I'd checked my messages, I'd probably have heard one from Jordan letting me know someone in need was heading my way. Dammit. "All right." I stared at the tabletop, my finger tracing an invisible sign on the wood. "The best thing to do—"

I stopped. Tilted my head a little. *What was that?*

The sound came again. A scrambling, and a stroking of claws on cold concrete. Far away, but growing closer, coming from the east.

Oh shit. The sensation of danger was immediate, palpable, and hair-raising. My head snapped up, my right hand automatically blurred for a gun, and Cecilia gasped.

"Get up," I snapped, leaping to my feet, barking my knee a good one on the coffee table. Wood cracked, but I hardly noticed the brief burst of pain. "Get the fuck up. Come on."

"What's happened? What's going on?" She flinched, her eyes getting even rounder as she saw the gun. I stalked for the recliner by the small table where I did tarot card readings, scooped up my battered leather coat, and shrugged into it, passing the gun from hand to hand.

"Something's coming. I just heard it. It'll trip the first line of defenses and alarms around my house in, oh, ninety seconds." I couldn't restrain a hard, delighted grin. "You don't think I'd sit in here *helpless,* do you? Move, girl. You're going to play mousie and hide in the hole."

It was probably a good thing she was trained to immediate obedience, even if I could have cheerfully ripped Diamond Ricky's nuts off for the beating he'd given an underweight girl. She scrambled up the rickety wooden ladder, her breathing coming short and hard. Her bruised ankles were terribly thin. When she reached the top, her battered face peered down at me.

"Pull this up." I helped her get the ladder up. "Now close that fucking trapdoor and lock it. Stay up there until

I come get you, or until dawn. If it takes me out, go to the precinct house on Alameda and ask for Montaigne. He'll take care of you. I know you don't like cops, but he's all right."

She nodded, biting her lip. Tears rolled down her pale, bruise-mottled cheeks. "Why are you doing this?"

What the fuck do you mean, why am I doing this? I'm a hunter. I protect the innocent. "This is what I do. Now close that door *and lock it, bitch!*"

She scrambled to obey. The heavy lead-sheeted trap-door closed; the little hidey-hole was in the bedroom, where the mixed scent of Were and hellbreed hunter would help mask her fear and human smell.

I'd also wanted the bedroom for the extra ammo stash, and it took a few seconds I didn't have to load up on sil-verjacketed lead, each full magazine slid into the loops sewn in my coat. Better to have the ammo and not need it, especially if what I had in mind didn't work. I wished I could use the bullwhip, but that was for Traders. The little distance a thin bit of leather would give me, critical for facing down a full hellbreed, wasn't going to be any frocking help against something this fast.

So I ran for the practice room, my breath coming hard and harsh in my chest. Skidded against the hardwood and reached it just as the front door shuddered under a mas-sive impact. It had taken the thing two and a half minutes to reach my home; maybe they'd let it out in Percoa Park or down on Lucado somewhere?

I shelved the question as the door shuddered again. *Wonderful. Didn't your mother ever teach you to knock?* I ran along the side of the room, each step seeming to take forever, toward the long shape lying under its fall of amber silk on the far back wall, its shape reflecting in the eight-foot mirrored panels.

The silk slipped in my fingers as it crashed onto the front door for the third time. *I hear you knockin',* a lunatic Little Richard screamed inside my head, *but you cain't come in!*

"Shut up," I gasped to myself, and tore the silk free.

There, humming with malignant force, was the long, fluidly carved iron staff. A slim dragon head snarled at either end. The leather cuff I tore from my right wrist, gasping as air hit suddenly sensitive skin. I felt the humming of etheric force begin to cascade around me as my right hand closed around the staff's slim length.

The iron burned, pain jolting up my arm. "Thou shalt serve me," I whispered. "By the grace of the Destroyer, thou shalt *serve* me!"

The staff subsided as I lifted it down, my knuckles white against its oiled metal gleam. It had tested my will only once, in a massive struggle inside a consecrated circle, the final test before my Hell-descent, before I was a full-fledged hunter in my own right. It rumbled in my hands, restive—too much blood and violence swirling in my aura and way too long since the last time I'd used it, even to drain off its excess charge. I would have to drain it to about half-strength soon, and deal with a couple of days of nosebleeds.

That is, if what I was about to do now didn't drain it, and if I survived.

I really wish I could use the whip. My hands tightened. I whirled, testing the heft, the dragon heads clove the air with a sweet low whistling sound. Then I gathered myself and ran for the front door.

The etheric protections in the walls screamed and tore as the physical structure gave way too. I dug my bootheels in, skidding to a stop in the living room, the staff held slightly tilted in front of me, both hands aching where they gripped its coldness. Then it began to warm, vibrating with eagerness, and the scar on my wrist turned hot and hard again.

"Come to Mama, you hunk of shit," I whispered, and the creature slammed through the crumbling wall. Rebar snapped, chunks of concrete and wooden paneling flying, and the staff jerked up in my hands, coming alive. There was a soft *snick,* deadly curved blades springing from the dragons' mouths. Warm electric light drifted down as the thing came for me, a faint silver glimmer showing at its low unhealthy neck.

As usual when I was holding the staff, things seemed oddly slow. Shift the weight, throwing the hip forward— in both whip and staff work, the hip leads. A sweet low sound as the blades cut the air, the complicated double-eight pattern becoming a blur of motion.

Then, *impact.*

It smashed into me again, the low, fluid somehow-*wrong* shape that my eyes hurt straining to see. The staff jerked in my hands, supple and alive, singing its low tone of bloodlust as it clove both air and preternatural skin. Fur flew, and the gagging stench of it enveloped me, *can't breathe can't fight* but I was going to give it an old college try, something black and foul exploded and the cold smacked through me, a cold like a razor burn with the bile in my throat, good thing I hadn't eaten anything because the Scotch boiled in my stomach looking to escape the hard way.

And as always, when the staff was in my hands and
time blurred around me, the dragons beginning their long
bloodthirsty moaning and the blades slicing the air as I retreated, shuffling, I felt it. The cold clear chill of the world
falling into place, everything stark and simple.

Kill or be killed.

Another gagging, retching breath, pluming in the frozen air as the staff executed a complex maneuver, going
so fast it almost seemed to turn on itself, Mikhail's voice
screaming in my head and the entire world narrowing to
don't get dead move move move, no time for thinking,
only time for pure trained reflex that is nonetheless informed with a great deal of thought. The fastest fucker in
the world can still do something thoughtless and end up
dead. Moving is not enough; one must move *correctly.*

The creature howled and came at me again. It was
vaguely humanoid despite the claws. Which clanged off
one blade—but the staff was working hard, humming to
itself contentedly as if it had finally found something to
wake it up and exercise it a little. My arms ached, especially the scar that was a knot of fire against my wrist,
etheric energy humming through it; but the fierce high
excitement beating behind my breastbone didn't let up,
and I knew who was making that terrible sound under
the snarling and foul nails-on-chalkboard howling of the
creature.

It was a high chilling giggle, clear as crystal and cold
as midnight in a moon-drenched room. It was my own
voice, laughing, crazed with bloodlust. The scar turned
blood-warm, strength like wine flooding my limbs, and
the charms in my hair rattled and struck together with
cracks like lightning.

The creature backed up and snarled. I snarled back, almost twitching in my eagerness to kill, ice painting the air as my breath froze. It was human-shaped, and I was so far gone by then that I peered underneath its scrim of hair and blinding blur. Only for a moment, trying to decipher the silver glimmer at its throat—a chain? A leash? Who knew?

Then it backed up, holding its front left limb up as if I'd wounded it. Black sludge dripped on the floor, smoking in the cold.

I laughed again, that chilling tinkling sound that broke glass and shivered the wooden flooring into splinters. *Kill it. Kill. Kill.*

A crackling bolt of blue hellfire lanced through the shattered air, splashing against the thing's side. It howled again and streaked away, its footfalls heavy and off-kilter now. I heard it drumming the surface of the earth as I whirled on the balls of my feet to meet this new threat.

The scar turned hot and hard. I felt Perry like a storm front moving through, a change of pressure that meant lightning. But that wasn't what made me freeze. Standing amid the shattered wreckage, his eyes dark and infinite, Saul shoved his hands deep in his coat pockets and regarded me. Steam drifted up from his skin. The couch was a shambled mess, the kitchen was torn all to hell, every mirror and window in the place was shattered and crusted with ice.

And still, my hands tightened on the staff. The blades hummed, alert, vibrating with bloodlust. *Kill?* the slim length of iron, old when Atlantis was young, hummed in its subsonic language. *Kill? Kill? Destroy?*

What civilization the staff was an artifact of, I didn't

know. Mikhail hadn't known either. But ever since that
highly advanced people had shaped this length of steel
into a long wand with stylized dragon heads at either
end—and don't ask me how we know they're dragon
heads, we just *do*—it has been used for one thing.

Bloodshed. Destruction. The secret to handling it has
been passed down from hunter to hunter in an unbroken
line since its creation—or so Mikhail told me.

I had no reason to disbelieve him. Once, and only once,
I think I saw what the world had looked like when the
staff was created. The fact that I wasn't howlingly insane
meant I had passed the test and was ready to descend into
Hell—and come *back,* a full hunter.

My muscles spasmed. The terrible battle began, me
trying to wrench my fingers free of the iron, the staff
screaming to be set free, to whistle through the air again,
to cleave flesh and anything harder, anything at all, to
maim and rip and tear. Blood trickled hot down my side,
down my leg, down my arm from my left shoulder, turned
into hamburger by the thing's claws.

But Saul's eyes were dark, and he didn't look away. He
didn't move. The electric current between us—the thing
in him that saw past every wall I've ever built to defend
myself, the thing in me that *recognized* him—went deeper
than all the bloody raw places in my head, deeper than my
breath and bones and blood, and deeper still.

He *knew* me, even now.

It seemed to take forever but was in reality only a few
seconds before I could *make* my fingers unloose. The
staff slid toward the floor, I spun it, turning with a scream
of agonized muscles and a cry that shattered each iota
of broken glass into smaller shards and tore the scrim of

ice into steaming fragments. The staff tore free, taking the skin on my palms with it, and smashed into the wall. Stuck there, sunk six inches into the concrete, quivering.

I let out a low harsh sound. Swayed, the small spattering sound of blood hitting the floor very loud in the stillness. I suddenly became aware that I had been moving in ways a human body hadn't been designed to move, even one with the help of a chunk of meteoric, pre-Atlantean steel and a hellbreed scar on one wrist. Everything *hurt,* a scalding fiery pain.

But my heart still beat, so fast the pounding in my wrists and throat was a hummingbird's wings. I was still taking in great ragged breaths, panting, my ribs flickering as they heaved, fiery oil spreading up my left side. My shoulders felt dipped in molten lead and my legs felt like wet noodles and my *head,* my God, my head felt like it was going to crack down the middle, like some demented dwarf was driving glass pins through my brain.

I swayed again, sour taste of adrenaline in my mouth. Heard someone else moving and knew it wasn't Saul approaching me, *knew* it wasn't him, and moved without thought.

My fingers had turned into claws, and I screamed as my nails tore through Perry's face, the scar on my wrist giving an agonized flare of pleasure. Then Saul had me in his arms, was talking to me as I struggled, he had me caught in a bear hug and took my legs out from under me, we hit the ground among debris and melting ice and I struggled, getting wood dust, glass, plaster, water, all sorts of crap in my hair before Saul snarled at me, burying his face in my throat, and I went utterly still. The sharp edges of his teeth could open my carotid in a moment.

I made a low sobbing noise, gongs clanging inside my head. "Si-si-si-si—"

I was trying to tell him there was a civilian in the house, someone I had been protecting, when I passed out.

18

I woke up with one hell of a hangover.

Using the staff does that. It's not something to be done lightly, as Mikhail had reminded me until he was blue in the face. But really, I was just happy it had *worked*.

I opened my eyes, saw something hazy that qualified (maybe) as light, and let out a low moan. Immediately, someone slid an arm under my head and held the foulest concoction in the whole wide goddamn world to my lips.

The best cure for a bad case of overstrain goes like this: nuke room-temperature Coke until you get the fizzies out, about ten seconds in the microwave on defrost will do it. Then mix it half and half with Gatorade. You dump about a quarter of it and fill up the huge old mug with *very* strong valerian tea. Mikhail always used to spike it with a little vodka, but he was crazy.

It tastes unspeakably foul, especially when your stomach is trying to crawl out through your throat without so much as pausing to say goodbye. But it works. The Gatorade settles your electrolytes; the caffeine and sugar in the Coke bring your blood levels back up and the nixed carbonation settles the stomach, and the valerian if strong enough is almost as good as Valium to calm down a hunter who's just gone through the wringer.

The vodka, of course, was because nothing medicinal could be without a touch of that finest of elixirs. I heard Anja's brews involved imported absinthe, but I've never had the dubious pleasure of having her mix up a concoction. God willing, I never will.

I took down four mugs of it before swearing at Saul and thrashing, trying to get up out of bed. "Calm down," he told me, in a tone that brooked no argument. "Or I'll strap you down, goddammit. You stupid bitch."

"Fuck you," I flung back. My head was splitting. My stomach sloshed. I felt like I'd been put together sideways.

"I told you to fucking stay with Perry."

He was right. And he was furious.

"Si-si-si-*civilian!*" I managed to get the word out.

"She's okay. She's with Avery. Just settle down, Jill. Come on."

I went limp. Lay with my breath whistling in my throat. *Thank you, God. Thank you.*

He stroked my hair back from my damp forehead. "I told you to stay with Perry." But this time, less anger. He sounded worried.

I squeezed my eyes shut. Found I could speak. "I couldn't." My voice cracked.

"Guess not. What'd he do to you?"

How could I answer that? *He suddenly found his way in, Saul. He got to me.* "The usual m-mindfucks." I dragged in a deep breath, let it out. "Saul." It was so hard to *think* through the dragging pain in my head.

"Right here." His fingers threaded through mine. "You want more backlash brew?"

Oh, God, no. "Shit no. What'd you find out?"

"Interesting stuff. Just rest, okay?" His hand was warm, and he leaned in, his lips meeting my cheek. "I'll kick your ass later."

"Promises, p-promises . . ." But I passed out again.

When I surfaced, I felt better, the brew had done its work and my head no longer felt like something monstrous was trying to birth itself from the center of my brain. Late afternoon sunlight fell in through the window; I was in my bed. Plenty of space all around, so nothing could sneak up on me.

Saul was a warm weight on the other side of the bed. His dark head rested on his arm, because as usual he'd thrown off the covers and ditched his pillow. Unlike usual, however, he was clothed, boxers and a T-shirt. He smelled of Were and sweat and musk, and the charms in his red-black hair gleamed under the light.

I sat up slowly. My head felt tender and my body was a little sore, but other than that, I felt surprisingly good. It was the first time I'd used the staff since striking my bargain with Perry, and I didn't feel like I'd been run over by a truck.

I stretched, yawning. *First order of business is to get that goddamn doctor and throttle him until he squeals. And then a quick visit to Jimmy Rocadero, and—*

Saul's hand closed over my wrist. One of his eyes had slid open a bit, and he yawned. "And where do you think you're going?"

"Hey, baby." I didn't have to work to sound relieved to see him. "How are you?"

"Pissed as hell," was his languid reply. "How you feelin', kitten?"

The tension in my chest eased at his calm tone. "Okay. Not going to be running a marathon anytime soon, but I can work. Saul—"

"Goddammit, Kiss. I told you to stay with Perry." He opened his eyes and curled up to a sitting position, shoving blankets aside.

How a man in boxers and a Santa Luz Wheelwrights T-shirt could look so delicious was one of the wonders of the world. I swallowed hard and wrenched my mind away from that. *It's just the survival thing. You know that. Chemical cascades and psychological necessity to prove you're still fucking alive after a dicey situation. No time for that now.* "I couldn't." The words stuck in my throat. *Christ, Saul. I couldn't stay there. Not around that mindfucking bastard.*

"What did he do to you? Huh? *What did he do to you?*" The charms in his hair tinkled, moving against each other; his fingers sank into my arm. I took another deep, lung-stretching breath. A shiver of pleasure went through me. Even though he was holding me hard enough to bruise, I liked it. The thought that he was touching me was enough to make me catch my breath, threatened to make me melt.

What didn't he do? "Nothing. Just . . . *nothing.* Mindfuck. Like usual. There's a reason why I don't want to *stay* there when he's finished with me. Last night it was bad."

"Two nights ago. Perry's been putting the house back

together. Avery has the girl. There are three more bodies. I've got files."

Lovely. Great. Wonderful. I'll read 'em in the car. "I got things to do. We have to get that doctor. And Jimmy Rocadero—"

"Rocadero?" Saul snorted. "He's one of the bodies, kitten. And I want to make it *abundantly* clear to you how fucking unhappy I am with the chain of events that ended up with you, here, facing that thing alone with *no fucking backup*. Very, *very* fucking clear." His eyes glowed with a Were's peculiar lambent orange tint.

"Rocadero's dead?" *Holy shit, that's news.*

"Straight-up dead. But he's still got his internal organs—they're just spread all over his goddamn house. I also found out a few things in the barrio."

I stretched. My entire body ached. *God, I hate using that thing. But I'm alive. Alive. And Cecilia is too.* "What did you find out?"

His fingers flicked, and the length of cluttered leather braid and obsidian arrowhead dangled. A venomous dart of blue light splintered from the arrowhead. "I found out what this is."

"Well?" I stretched, loosely. My skin twitched and rippled with soreness. The headache was returning, circling like a shark, though with less of its former virulence. "You're killing me here, baby."

"Don't fucking say that." His fingers flicked again, the arrowhead vanished. Neatest trick of the week. "Want to wash up, then we'll talk?"

"Okay." But I reached out to grab his arm as he turned away, his skin warm and hard under my fingers, under the T-shirt's sleeve. "Saul?"

"Don't ever do that again." He stared at the window, his profile suddenly clean and classic. His mouth turned down bitterly at the corners. "I dropped by here to pick up fresh clothes and ammo for you so we could track down the leads I found straight from the barrio. Imagine my surprise at finding Perry and that goddamn thing here before me."

"Perry was here?" *What the hell was he doing here so late? Protecting his investment?*

"He'd just arrived, I saw him coming down the street. That thing was tearing up the inside of the house. We came in and saw you beating the shit out of it. You looked . . ."

I winced. With the staff in my hands, I probably looked feral, my hair standing on end as I moved in ways a human body shouldn't. And the laugh, the chilling crystal laugh, bruising the vocal cords as it ripped free. "Horrible," I said flatly.

"Deadly. Beautiful." His eyes dropped. "Jesus Christ, Jillian. You could have died."

I know that. "I had to."

"For one of Diamond Ricky's girls?"

Just a whore, right? Just another teenage hooker on the cold street. I swallowed the words. Saul wasn't like that; I was just . . . edgy. Too willing to think the worst, no matter what anyone said. "A civilian. She asked for my help."

He made a short, vicious growling sound. "And those are the magic words, aren't they? Well, I need your goddamn help too."

Please, baby. Don't do this now. "Saul."

He turned his head, his eyes trapping mine. "You listen

to me. You end up dead and you know what happens to me? *Do you?*"

A Were dies when his mate does, but I'm not Were. I'm human. Fucked-up with hellbreed, but still human. "Saul—"

"I put up with Perry. I put up with you throwing yourself into every goddamn mess in this city. But god-*damm*it, Jillian, I do *not* want to lose you!"

"Saul."

"I want you to meet my people," he said softly. "I want you under the Moon with me."

Holy Christ. My mouth dried up. "That's serious." Then I kicked myself. Couldn't I come up with something less stupid to say?

"Very serious." He removed my fingers from his arm gently. His hand was warm. "As serious as it can get. Need a shower?"

For a moment, I thought the stone in my throat would stop me from speaking. "You offering to seduce me?"

His teeth flashed in a white grin before he levered himself off the bed. "I'd love to, but duty calls. Hurry up."

"Where in the barrio did you go?"

"Couple of places," he said over his shoulder on his way to the closet. "But I found what I needed in a little bar off Santa Croce. A real dive. You'd love it."

I peeled the sheet away. I'd bled on it, nosebleed and from the wounds that were now pink scars, rapidly fading. It had marked me a couple of times. Left side up my ribs, shoulder, leg. I was lucky to be alive. "I suppose it was a smelly place full of nasty characters."

"Just like usual, baby. You've broadened my social horizons, that's for sure." He opened the closet door, and I spent a few moments in artistic appreciation of his boxer-clad ass before hauling myself up out of the bed.

There was work to be done.

I called Hutch from the cordless in the bedroom, but he had still not had any luck digging up whatever *chutsharak* meant. I was beginning to think it was a dead end.

Just like Saint Anthony's spear. Gui and I were going to have a little talk about lying to hunters, just as soon as I had some time.

Hutch did have other news, though. "Hey, it's the end of the Sorrows' three-year cycle this year." His voice whistled slightly with excitement.

"Three-point-seven," I corrected, shoving my feet into my second-best boots. My coat was still torn up, but better than nothing. I wriggled my toes, rocked up to my feet, and accepted a cup of coffee from Saul. It was thick black mud, and I could drink about half a cup before I needed food in me to balance out the caffeine. I nodded my thanks to Saul, bracing the phone against my shoulder. "So they're in the Dark Time now."

"Looks like it. Though if you ask me, those motherfuckers are *always* at thirteen o'clock. So, the Dark Time. Cleansing within Houses, hunting down apostates—and evocations of the Elder Gods."

That rang a teensy bell. "Wait a second. Evocations?"

Saul's eyebrows rose.

"Miguel de Ferrar says it's SOP for a House to evoke their patron Elder at this time. Lots of demonic activity, that sort of thing. It's when they believe the veil between this world and the world of the demons gets real thin, like Samhain for witches."

I leaned back in the chair, taking a sip of coffee. "So. What's necessary for an evocation of this magnitude? Say, if a Sorrow was doing it alone?"

"They *can't* do it alone. That's why houses are collective, it takes a full House to hold a door in the world open for an Elder to reach through even briefly. We're talking granite floors carved with the Nine Seals, perfect-tallow candles, velvet robes, ambergris and amber incense, the whole nine. The *whole* nine, including gold laid in the circle for the Elder, the sacrifice, and the psychic energy needed to rip a hole in the ether." Hutch was sounding more cheerful by the moment. He did indeed love his research.

She is attempting an evocation, hunter. She is fueling it with death and acquiring funding from the sale of bodily—

"So it's a massive financial as well as sorcerous effort," I said slowly. "Hutch, what's the market like in Santa Luz for black-market organs?"

"Organs? What kind of—"

"Human organs. Kidneys, livers, that sort of thing. Stem cells, too."

"Hell, I don't know. But I can find out. Five minutes on the Internet and—"

"Never mind. Listen. Which patron Elder rules the end of this cycle? I know each House has their special dedication, but which one of the Ninety-Nine rules this *particular* cycle in general?"

Saul's eyes met mine. I took a scalding mouthful of coffee.

I heard paper rustling and his breath whistling as he dug around for it. "I just had it, I just had a copy of Luvrienne's *Chaldeans* open . . . ah-ha. Here we are." More paper rustling. "Let's see . . . if we calculate from the Chaldean calendar . . . carry the one . . . leap years . . . the Gregorian . . . okay. This year's winner is . . . oh, *shit*."

"What?" *Hutch, I hate it when you say oh shit.*

"It's the Nameless." His voice dropped to a whisper. "And the cycle ends in four days."

It felt like all the hair on my body was trying to stand straight up. It probably was. The charms tied in my hair tinkled. I set the coffee cup down on the nightstand. "Jesus, Mary, and Joseph," I whispered. "The Nameless?"

"Destroyer of babies. Eater of worlds. He-Who-Rewards—"

"Shut up, Hutch." *I know the titles.* I swallowed dryly. "Listen to me. Leave the bookstore right now. Go over to Galina's. Stay there until I come get you. Take the Luvrienne and de Ferrar with you, I might call there. Okay?"

"Oh, God," he moaned. "What have you gotten me into now?"

"I haven't gotten you into anything, stupid. I just want you safe. Better safe than eviscerated. Get my drift?"

"Oh, shit, Jill. I hate you."

"Galina will be glad to see you."

"You bitch." But I heard more paper rustle, and knew he was getting ready to do as I asked. "Okay. I'm on my way. I'll leave everything locked. If you come in, try not to burn the place down, okay?"

"Hutch!" For once, I sounded scandalized. "I wouldn't ever burn down a *bookstore*. Jeez, what kind of hunter do you think I am?"

"One who's made it her personal mission to get me into trouble. Bye, Jilly."

"Don't call me that." I hung up and stared at my bedroom phone, feeling my forehead pucker. *Holy fuck. The Nameless. Why would a Sorrow break away from her House and do an evocation? It makes no sense.*

Well, there was one person who could explain it. The catch, of course, was if I could trust her explanation.

Saul was silent. He stood by the window, sunlight touching his hair, making the silver sparkle and bringing out the richness of his skin. He had his hands in his jeans pockets, the black *Cazotte Lives* T-shirt strained at his shoulders. The tiny bottle of holy water on its silver chain at his chest glittered, throwing darts of hard light from the glass.

All right, Jill. I looked at the fall of sunlight against his hair. *Think. What pattern do we have here? Having a pattern is the first step.*

If what I was suspecting was really going down, why hadn't there been bodies showing up earlier? Or if there *were* bodies, where were they now?

That isn't a very comfortable line of thought.

I didn't have enough pieces of the puzzle to make a pattern I was happy with logic-wise. Once Saul told me what the arrowhead was, I would have a little more. Hopefully.

And the thing, the clawed and furred thing that I couldn't quite get a mental picture of no matter how hard I concentrated . . . what did that have to do with it? Was it a piece of Chaldean sorcery I hadn't seen before? It wasn't exactly likely, given the study of the Sorrows I'd done. But was the furry thing the *chutsharak?* If it was, and Belisa and the younger Sorrow were fleeing it—

No, that didn't make any sense. Was the furry stinky thing unrelated to the murders? But no, its smell was gagging-strong over the scenes. *That doesn't necessarily mean they're related. Does it?*

I coiled the bullwhip at my side, checked my guns, my knives, and shrugged into my coat. I caught a fading whiff of iron, pre-Atlantean bloodlust, and furry stink on the tattered leather. "Saul?"

"Yeah?" He looked away from the window.

"It's time. You can tell me what that thing is."

"Come on out into the kitchen first."

"Why?"

"You need breakfast, and Perry's here."

Jesus Christ. "*What?* He's still here?"

His dark eyes were fathomless. "Of course he's still here. He's patched up the windows and everything, he thinks he should shadow you until this is over. I happen to agree."

"What?" My jaw threatened to drop completely. The charms tinkled in my hair, and my palms itched with the memory of a slender piece of steel, reverberating with bloodlust. "He left the Monde Nuit and he's in our *kitchen* and you want him to *stay there?*"

He shrugged. "I want him to stick around. You're safer with both of us looking after you."

"Saul—"

He held up the arrowhead. "I found out what this means, kitten. And believe me, you don't want *any* of it."

"Well, spill it."

"Come on into the kitchen and I will. I'll make you breakfast, and we'll strategize." He was utterly serious.

I held up both hands, Mikhail's ring glittering in the thin hard sunlight. "Wait just a goddamn minute. You don't like it when I visit him, whether to track down a hellbreed or pay my dues for the bargain I made. What the hell are you doing playing pattycake with him now?"

"If he's going to help get your stubborn ass through this in one piece I don't care." Saul folded his arms, muscle sliding under the T-shirt's thin cotton. "This is *bad,* Kiss. As bad as you think it is, it's worse."

My heart was doing something strange, pounding so hard I felt faint. I didn't like the thought of Perry in my *house.* The thought of something so bad Saul didn't care if Perry was running around unchaperoned inside the warehouse was even worse. "Why? What *is* that thing?"

"Come out, have some breakfast, and I'll tell you. Then you can decide what you're going to do."

In the end I gave up. Saul had a good reason for anything he asked me to do, and I trusted him. But for Chrissake, something so bad he wanted Perry around as backup. . . .

It was enough to give even a seasoned hunter the willies.

19

Saul set the plate down in front of me. "Eat."

I eyed it. Eggs, pancakes, bacon, more coffee, an English muffin. Another plate of eggs with hollandaise, and a peach, cut up carefully and decoratively. Nothing experimental, and nothing fancy. For Saul, this was the culinary equivalent of a polite non-answer to a question that hadn't even been asked.

Perry hunched on the stool at the end of the kitchen counter, his gray suit sharply and immaculately creased. He seemed not to like the sunlight falling through the windows, and I was secretly glad. For all that, his hair glowed and his eyes burned blue, and the warehouse—while smelling of hellbreed—was neat and repaired, the ice gone, every inch of glass swept up and new panes put in, the wood fused back together, shattered furniture either patched up or replaced. It was a massive expenditure of cash and sorcerous power, and one I wasn't quite sure I liked the thought of incurring.

I finished examining my plate and glanced at Perry,

who snickered into his coffee cup. "Don't worry, Kiss. Saul and I negotiated terms. This doesn't enter into our bargain."

"Is that so." I tried not to look relieved; tried also not to feel a little wriggle of panic that he had guessed what I was thinking. Picked up a piece of bacon, crunched it between my teeth. "Well? Care to clue me in, Saul?"

He leaned against the counter on the other side, and I realized he was keeping Perry in the corner of his eye. "I found out what our hairy little friend is." Saul poured himself a glass of orange juice. "You want the bad news or the bad news first?"

"Just tell me *something*. I'm getting impatient." I tucked in with a will, finding I was indeed hungry and my stomach would, indeed, accept nourishment. Hallelujah.

Perry snickered again.

Saul didn't even glance at him. "It's a wendigo."

I choked on a bite of pancake. "Urf? Mrph murfr *mrph!*"

"They're not myths. I wish to Christ they were." Saul had actually paled. "I had to take the arrowhead to a Moonspeaker in the barrio, an old one. She'd seen a wendigo before and remembered the smell. She said it was a *hund'ai,* part of a fetish meant to control or create a wendigo. The sight of it turned her into a sobbing heap and her mate nearly had my liver and lights for upsetting her. I ended up at a little bar with a werespider; she'd actually hunted a wendigo up Canada way. She started to shake while she talked about it." Saul's tone was dead level. His eyes were as dark and serious as I'd ever seen them.

I glanced at Perry. He stared into the coffee cup, his face arranged in a mask of bland interest. All the same, he looked miserable. My blue eye twinged a little, I could see the edges of his aura fringing a little bit, wearing down.

Maybe our favorite hellbreed didn't like being out during the day. I was suddenly immensely cheered by the thought. Inside his jacket, pants, and open-collared crisp white shirt he looked almost normal, and profoundly uncomfortable.

Don't fall for that, sweetheart. It's just another dirty little façade. If Saul wasn't here we'd see a different Perry indeed.

"Wendigo." I crunched on another bit of bacon. "A flesh-eating spirit, with its lips and nose frozen off. Come on, Saul."

"Jillian, if you don't cut the crap, I'm going to take your breakfast back and drag you into the sparring room. And make you wash the goddamn blood off the goddamn sheets, too. Look at your *coat*. This is no fucking laughing matter." Even, chill, cold. Saul had never spoken to me like this before. "A wendigo is something else. It's a spirit made mad by neglect and violence, a spirit that has done what is *taboo*—tasted human flesh, developed a craving for it."

A craving for human flesh and black-market organs. Why is this fitting together far too neatly for my comfort? And the unearthly, deadly icy chill of the thing rose briefly in memory. I shivered again. "A Were spirit? That thing wasn't a Were. I know Weres."

"It's not Were, it's a *spirit* we know about. Totally different kettle of fish." Saul folded his arms. "Some of the legends say they're maybe Weres dying without burial rites, or a Were who was *taboo* in life. I don't know. The legends are confused. It's not like hunting scurf. Weres *know* scurf. These things . . . humans might get confused about them, but whatever they are, they're not Were."

"Jesus." I was having a little trouble with this. The *last* thing we needed was it getting out that the Were had anything to do with something like this. This thing was as unlike Weres as. . . . My brain failed, trying to come up with the simile. But a non-hunter, even one with some nightside experience, wouldn't understand that. Hell, plenty of nightsiders with grudges against the furkind wouldn't understand it either.

Perry finally weighed in, as if he couldn't help himself. "Really, dear Kiss, you should listen to furball here. He knows more than you think. After all, he didn't go into the barrio to seek facts. He went to confirm."

My fork paused halfway to my mouth, and I looked up at Saul. His mouth had drawn down bitterly, and he pushed his hair back with one hand. But his other hand was on the counter, and his knuckles were white.

What, did Saul think a transparent little ploy like that would work on me? How far inside my head did he think Pericles had wormed his little hellbreed way?

However far Saul thinks he has, he's probably gotten in further. Last night proved that, didn't it? "You suspected it?" I felt like an idiot with my fork in the air, I set it down gently, carefully, on the cobalt-blue counter. "Saul?"

"I didn't know." He picked up his juice again, took a sip, his eyes not leaving mine. But I got the idea that if he could have, he would have darted a venomous look at Perry. "Until I knew for sure, I didn't want to open my mouth and muddy the trail."

I nodded. Looked down at my plate. "Well, that's why

you're my partner." *Nice try, Perry. But no dice.* "So you're absolutely satisfied that this thing is a wendigo?"

He nodded. The silver in his hair tinkled, and his dark eyes lost their hardness and for a moment were lambent orange, a Were's hunting glow. "I'd bet my life on it."

"It's not your life we'll be betting, it's mine." I stared down at my plate, forced my fingers to curl around the fork again. "Whatever it is, I'm taking it down. What kills a wendigo?"

Saul sighed, heavily. "I don't know yet. The legends are . . . confused. The werespider was part of a team that tracked one of those things for fifteen weeks, through a few snowstorms, and finally killed it by driving off the edge of a crevasse and dynamiting a mountainside down on it. The creature and the dynamiting combined to knock out most of her team."

"How many?" Werespiders aren't known for being pack animals; like werecats they tend to be independent, loosely affiliated in tribes rather than in pack-groups. Except werelions, of course. Always excepting werelions. Some bird Weres were highly social, and most of the canine Weres except the occasional albino shaman. Then there were the *khprum* and the scorpiani, who some sources said weren't Weres at all, not to mention the kentauri and the wererats, who are highly social and stratified to a fault. The wererats, incidentally, are the closest in physiology and outlook to humans.

Nobody but me usually sees the humor in that.

"Fourteen in the team. The spider and a wereleopard made it back. The wereleopard died of matesickness two months after; his mate was lost in the dynamiting. If they hadn't been out in the middle of nowhere the casualties might've been higher. Humans and such."

Crap. I mulled this over, tapping my fingertips on the countertop. In an urban setting, this didn't bode well. "An evocation in four days. Bodies being dumped, clean of organs. . . . Saul, where are the autopsy files? I wonder how much other body mass was lost. Muscle, specifically."

"Belly muscle was gone on the ones we saw. Some bites on the thighs and the arms, too." He edged down the counter to a stack of file folders. "But Rocadero wasn't found with his organs gone."

I snorted. "Given his proclivities, I'm not sure his own side didn't murder him." I was chewing on more egg when a terrible idea hit me. "One of the traditional evocations of the Nameless is done with perfect-tallow candles. Victims' omentums would be perfect for that. All you'd need is a place to render it down." My gorge rose; I swallowed it and took a gulp of coffee. "Ugh. This is going to be a messy one. How about Rocadero gets sliced because he's no longer useful?"

"How so?" He slid the folders down to me. Perry had subsided, but I get the feeling he was only biding his time. Some essential quality of scariness had drained away from him in my sunny kitchen, Saul's territory in the middle of my house, and I was grateful for that.

But not grateful enough to relax. Or to think he was finished yet. "Let me pass this theory by you. A Sorrow escapes, she decides for whatever reason that she's feeling a little apocalyptic. She starts laying her plans and moves into Santa Luz, finds a Mob man, and starts supplying him with black-market organs, taking a healthy cut to fund her dreams of world domination. She gets the organs out with the help of a trained doctor—our friend Kricekwesz. Then she throws whatever bits she doesn't need to the wendigo, who sits in the van and snacks until she needs to get rid of an inconvenient hunter." I buttered my English muffin, very pleased with myself. "Only why does she start dumping pregnant hookers?"

"Once-pregnant hookers," Perry corrected, pedantically.

"They were still pregnant when they were killed." I looked at him, hunching on the stool, and had a moment of dangerous pity. He looked miserable.

But even a miserable rattlesnake can kill.

"We don't know that. They were visiting an abortionist." He pronounced the word with no audible weight, just a slight emphasis on the last syllable that made it sound vaguely French.

Where do you come from, Perry? "Thanks for putting my house back together," I said suddenly. "Why did you follow me?"

"The cat wasn't at the Monde to pick you up. I thought you might be in a state to harm yourself."

Well, isn't that decent of you.

Saul pushed the folders closer, hitting my elbow. Subtle of him, but I was glad of it anyway. "Fetal tissue?" he hazarded. "Valuable stuff, to the right buyer."

I swallowed another wave of nausea. *Goddammit.* I needed the nutrition if I was going to stay on my feet and bounce back after using the staff. "Oh, yuck. That's a wonderful thought to have with breakfast." *Not to mention one I've been kicking around for a bit.*

"Troubled by a delicate stomach, my Kismet?" Perry was suddenly all solicitude. The oil in his voice reminded me of the terrible devouring spill of pleasure through my nerves, the mark on my wrist suddenly swollen-hot with his attention.

I closed my eyes, chewing the English muffin. Swallowed. "Our first stop is this Kricekwesz. If he's not in his office I want to tear the goddamn place apart until we find something, anything. I want to get Carp and Rosie to start leaning on the organ trade in town. And I want to find Melisande Belisa. She knows something, and once we get our hands on her I want to make her squeal." My eyes opened, met Perry's. "You ever menaced a Sorrow before?"

Did I imagine it, or did a flicker of a snarl cross his face? "They don't like hellbreed. With good reason." He set his coffee cup on the counter. "If you will agree to stay in my sight until this matter is finished, I will agree to find this Sorrow and make her fit her name."

"I thought your protection only extended so far."

"That was before you were attacked in your own home, Kiss." He slid off the stool, and I tensed. What was it about daylight that made him seem so bloody human? "All bets, as they say, are now off. I want to repair some of the holes in the walls. Call me if anything *interesting* happens."

He glided away, and I sighed. *I don't like this. I don't like this at all.*

Saul muttered something unprintable. I silently agreed. "I don't like this," I said quietly. "So he shows up just in time, both times. I dragged Elizondo in on a slave-ring charge and he was in the Monde after we scorched that hole on North Lucado. And now this organ thing, and a wendigo. Saul, you're *sure*? Absolutely sure?"

"Hundred percent." He hunched his shoulders, his eyes

on me. "The truly bad news is I don't know if we can kill it. It's a *spirit,* kitten. Hunger incarnate, hunger distilled. It's taboo. Not a real physicality at all, now. Just . . . appetite. And ice."

I took a long gulp of coffee that had cooled just enough to be reasonable. "It cut me." The finality in my voice surprised me. "If it can cut, it can *be* cut. There's nothing out there so bad it can't be killed. Except for maybe a god, and we're not facing one of those. Not for four days, at least. What can you tell me about wendigo? How they're created, what can kill 'em, that sort of thing?"

"Not much." Saul straightened, looking relieved. "But I can get in touch with someone who knows more."

"Good." I turned my attention back to my plate. "This is good, Saul. You do a mean pancake."

I didn't look up, but I could feel his smile. "Glad you like it, kitten."

Monty was going batshit.

"What the fuck are you telling me, Jill? Black-fucking-market organs? What the hell?" He stalked through his office as if expecting the perp to be hiding behind a stack of paper. "Why didn't you *tell* me?"

If I'd known, Montaigne, I would have. Don't get pissy. "I had no idea organ heisting was part of it. I was looking for a supernatural explanation. It was the scalpel marks that clued me in."

"Sullivan and the Badger have been tracking a string of black-market organ harvestings that end up leaving the donors dead with a .22 hole in their skull." Monty's tie was loose and his collar crumpled, he was working round the clock. It wasn't good for him.

Then again, police work isn't, strictly speaking, *good* for anyone. Eating your Glock, ulcers, cynicism, depression—the list goes on and on. I took a deep breath. Hunting wasn't good either, but at least a hunter could take the edge off with sex or some hard sparring. "Huh. Maybe they're related?"

Monty's office seemed too small to contain his rage. Not at me, thank God. He stalked behind his desk and dropped into his chair, almost disappearing behind the flood of paper files and assorted other crap. "Go talk to them, look over their files. We'll pick up this doctor, Kricky—"

"Kricekwesz. Polish, I think." *Like it matters.*

Monty rubbed at his eyes. "Whatever the fuck his name is. We'll pick him up. Though if whoever this is decides to take out some more scumbags like Rocadero I might throw a fucking parade."

"For cleaning the streets of pregnant hookers too?" My tone was harder than it needed to be. But goddammit, everyone was forgetting the victims here, the girls that walked the streets, the girls who had been abandoned too many times already.

Don't get up on your high horse, Kismet. You did it too. They're less than human because they're still in the life. On the street. Swallowing God-knows-what and doing what nobody wants to talk about, and turning over a cut of their pay to the professional pimp or the dealer or the man who "loves" them. Christ. Even I look down on them.

And I should know better.

Monty's silence warned me. I dropped my eyes to the tough short russet carpet of his office. Outside the door, Saul waited. Perry was in a limousine circling the block. I was alone in here with Montaigne, who was a good cop—and even more important, a friend. He'd never let me down.

"I'm sorry, Jill," he said finally. "You know it ain't that way."

Carp and Rosie cared about every body they came across; even the pimps and the hookers and the drug lords. There is something so unutterably final about death, some robbing of human dignity from every corpse, even the ones that die naturally. And Montaigne cared too. Even the impossible cases, where the perp was never found, he and his detectives circled like a tongue circles a sore tooth, unable to forget.

"I know it isn't. I'm just fucking frustrated." *This is getting to me far more than it should.* I blew out a long breath between my teeth. "I'm sorry, Monty. Really."

"You're gettin' punchy." *Bitchy* was the word he wanted to use, I guessed, and I was grateful he hadn't. "When this is over, you wanna take some time off? I guess we can keep everything under control for a little while. Mebbe."

Oh, Monty. The fact that he had brushed the night-side once and knew a little bit about it made the offer that much braver. "I'm planning on it." I stretched, my bones still aching and tender from the demands the staff had made on my body, demands engineered to keep me alive. "I'm sorry, Monty. I'm sorry as shit. I should have thought of the organ thing sooner."

He waved one limp, sweating hand. Rubbed at his eyes. "Don't worry about it. Just go out there and stop this shit, will you? I got to go home to Margie one of these days. Okay?"

"Okay." I squared my shoulders. "I'll get this done ASAP, Monty." *Because if I don't and a rogue Sorrow brings the Nameless through with an evocation, all hell's going to break loose. And that's not even half of it.* "Do you want to know any more?"

"Christ, no. What you just told me is going to give me fuckin' nightmares. Get out of my office; get to work. Give Carp and Rosie something new to do, and Sullivan and Badger too. I'll keep the press distracted as long as I can. Just make this shit *stop*."

"Okay, Monty." I paused. "You're good to work for, you know that?"

Another languid wave of the hand. He reached down into a half-open drawer and set a bottle of Jack Daniels and a bottle of Tums on his desk. "Get the fuck out of here, Jill."

"See ya."

I left, closing the door softly. Saul, leaning against a cubicle wall directly across from the door, examined me. I met his dark eyes for a long moment.

"This is getting too big," he finally said, quietly, under the clamor of ringing phones and the shuffling sounds of the homicide division. "We need help. Not just human cops."

What he didn't say, we both thought. *And a hellbreed neither of us trusts.* My tattered coat rustled as I stepped away from Monty's door. "What are we supposed to do? Call in a bunch of Weres to waste themselves on a suicide attack? No. We figure out how to take the wendigo out on our own. There's got to be a way."

"What about this Sorrow?" It was a good question. He fell into step beside me, shortening his stride to mine, and I was so abruptly grateful for his presence that my eyes prickled, both my dumb eye and the smart one.

"If Belisa's telling the truth, she probably knows how to short-circuit whatever evocation this bitch is trying to perform—and if the wendigo's involved. I just have to get a message to her that I'm willing to talk."

"How are you going to do that?"

"Simple. Just drop a word in the right ear, and it'll get to her."

"Which ear?"

"Relax, Saul. It's taken care of, Perry put the word out this morning." I slid my arm through his. "We're going to set Rosie and Carp to digging with the Badger and Sullivan, and then we're going to go have a little chat with this doctor. And after that, we're going to visit Hutch's bookstore and see what we can dig up on wendigos."

The Badger was a short round motherly woman with a streak of white over her left temple, and Sullivan a thin, tall red-haired Irish with a penchant for cowboy hats. They were sometimes called Jack Sprat & Wife by the braver practitioners of cop humor, and put up with it estimably. They had reams of information on the organ trade in Santa Luz, too much for me to absorb. The Badger, bless her forward-thinking little heart, had photocopies of the more interesting cases as well as a few fact sheets.

I read in the car while Saul drove and Perry's limo cut a narrow black swath behind us. I wasn't sure I liked that albatross following us around, especially during the day, but the tightness of Saul's jaw warned me not to say anything about it. I wondered what deal he'd made with Perry. Swallowed the question.

We made it to Quincoa against light traffic, and Saul parked in the same alley as before. Perry's limo, in magnificent defiance of its own incongruity, idled, gleaming and black, across the street. I checked the sky—sunlight, still. He didn't seem as scary in sunlight, but the limo had smoky tinted windows. He made no appearance, and I wondered once again what he was.

Vulnerable to sunlight? Or just not showing himself? Playing a game?

This time we didn't lie in wait and examine the building.

No, this time Saul kicked the hermetically sealed door in on the second try, the deadbolt tearing free of softer metal. I had my gun out, swept the inside of the hall, and recoiled as the stench boiled out.

"Jesus *God!*" The reek drove me back a full three paces, to the edge of the steps. Death, and a loud zoo-like odor. Saul wrinkled his nose, glanced at me. He had drawn his Sig Sauer, he covered the door. I swallowed bile. "What the *fuck?*"

"Stinks. And a sealed door." He didn't sound strained, but I caught the edge of disgust in his voice. "I smell more than one."

"How many?"

"I can't tell."

"The wendigo—"

"I smell it too. But old. It hasn't been here for a day or two."

"Jesus." I coughed, my eyes watering. "All right. Call Montaigne; tell him we've got a scene. I'm going in."

"Jill—"

"Come on, Saul. I'm the hunter. There's a pay phone on the corner. Or there's a cell phone in Perry's limo, if it comes to that. Hurry up so you can come back and cover me." *Though I don't think the thing's here. I don't think anything's left alive in here.*

His jaw set, hard as concrete. Then he was gone, his coat flapping as he took the stairs with a single bound, brushing past me. Silver chimed angrily in his hair. I waited until he was half a block away before I peeled the leather cuff off my right wrist one-handed.

Cool air hitting the scar sent a shiver down my spine. I stuffed the cuff in my pocket and closed my left hand around my secondary gun. Then I stepped forward, into the miasma of death.

Breathe. Dammit, Jill, breathe. The smell will fade.

But I knew it wouldn't. It *wouldn't*. The receptors in my nose might shut off, but the smell would work its way into my skin. And even deeper, into memory. How many bodies?

Let it be only one or two. What do you say, God? Even as I crossed the threshold and stepped into the flickering fluorescent light of a perfectly normal waiting room, I knew it wouldn't be only one or two. No wonder the clinic hadn't been open.

The air was stuffy, dead still. I peered behind the nurse's counter—no, nobody there. A neat stack of files sat next to a keyboard, under a dead dark monitor. I wanted to take a look, but rule one of sweeping a scene is *give assistance to the living.* Of course, I doubted there was anyone in here alive. Not with that smell.

I pushed open the swinging door that should lead to patient rooms and the back hallway, and the odor of death belched out, enfolding me.

I peered into the hall, and my fingers loosened on the gun. "Dear God," I whispered, then wished I hadn't because the smell rushed into my mouth and the vision of . . .

Sweet Jesus, dear God, it burned its way into my skull.

How many of them are there? Arms, legs . . . this is a lair. Or it was. The smell of the creature was fading, but enough remained to make the intaglio of twisted rotting limbs seem to move. Open mouths, eyes torn from skulls, torsos cracked like nuts—

I backed up, the gun bumping against my leg as my grip slipped still more. *Oh, God. God in Heaven.*

The sight scored itself deeper behind my eyes, and the scar on my wrist pulsed, gruesomely warm and wet as if a rough-scaled tongue had licked it. I backed up again, ran into something soft, and leapt, raising the gun.

Perry's fingers locked around my wrist. "Just me, Kiss." His blue eyes glanced past me as the swinging door closed, a soft sheaf of pale hair falling in his face. He looked just the same, and the fringing of his aura had stopped. Of course, there was no sunlight in here. "There is nothing living in this place."

"It's—" Words failed me, and the reek closed thick and cloying. Pressed against my skin like rancid oil. "God—"

"God is not here. Of all people *you* should know that."

His fingers tightened on my wrist, the scar gone hot and swollen. "Catholic, weren't you? A schoolgirl."

I pulled against his grasp. His fingers tightened, but I tore my hand away. My grasp firmed around the butt of the gun.

My shoulder hit his as I pushed past him. He didn't even bother to pretend I could move him, I bounced off and stumbled. I aimed for the door, a rushing sound in my ears and the back of my throat suddenly whipped with hot bile.

"Jillian." Perry's voice echoed with soft chilling glee in the still, muffled air. "You do know that, right? God is a fiction. There is nothing godly about this."

Shut up, Perry.

I made it outside before I threw up. The air was cold and full of knives; I hung over the spindly iron railing and lost everything I'd ever thought of eating.

Perry held my hair back, ignoring the silver charms. His fingers rubbed soothingly between my shoulder-blades until the sirens started in the distance and Saul came back.

Maybe I should have been grateful. But I wasn't.

20

They were stuffed everywhere. Bodies and *bits* of bodies, in varying stages of decomposition; there was not an inch of carpet that wasn't soaked with blood and fouler things. Maggots exploded from torn flesh, noisome liquids ran, and the techs brought the remains out in bags much too small for a human corpse. There was only so much piecing together of individual corpses that could be done at the scene. The rest had to wait for the lab.

The only thing worse than the stench inside was the smell of vomit outside. Even the hardened forensic techs who had seen the worst stumbled out to void their stomachs and staggered back in, grimly determined to do their work. Voices were hushed, even the most cynical and jolly of the homicide deets taking hats off and speaking as if we were in a church.

The whole building was cordoned off, thank God we didn't have to worry about a crowd. This was a quiet part of town. Quincoa was a limbo that only happens in cities—a long seedy street zoned for both industrial and

residential and holding precious little but vacant buildings and the occasional professional office lingering from
better days, when it had been a thriving highway. Perry's
limo sat sleek and black across the street in a parking lot,
not idling but simply . . . sitting. Perry himself stood off
to one side, watching the human hubbub while the sun
went down. Most of the paramedics, cops, and forensic
techs instinctively avoided him, as if he was a cold draft
or a nasty smell. His hair glowed, and his suit was still
immaculate.

The almost-worst had been finding the operating theater, scrubbed and glistening; there was a close narrow
back hall that gave onto a haphazard bay where they had
most likely pulled the van in. A stack of Styrofoam cool-
ers; a supply of dry ice, scalpels and clamps laid out with
gleaming precision. Everything you needed to harvest
organs.

Especially if you weren't too concerned about the own-
ers of those organs surviving the experience.

The medical examiner's office was not going to be
happy with this.

What was even worse than the operating room were
the fading marks of violence, the etheric strings of souls
torn and violated as surely as the bodies had been. My
blue eye could see those marks, where a Sorrows adept
had performed that most foul and tricky of feats: eating a
soul. Taking the psychic energy of death, harvesting it to
fuel something unspeakable.

An evocation of the Nameless, powered by this kind of
terrible agony and brutality, would tear a hole sky-deep in
the fabric of reality. We were looking at a psychic wound
the people of this place would probably never recover

from—and God help us all if the Nameless was set loose. It would mean three and seven-tenths years of indescribable corruption, agony, and degradation, a cancer eating its way into the heart of the world.

Not here, goddammit. Not in my city.

I sat on the curb, my head on my knees. The last failing vestiges of sunlight fell across my shoulders, edging with gold the weeds forcing up through cracked and failing sidewalk. I heard the faint roar of traffic and the mutter of official activity, pencils scribbling and the faint sounds of flashes going off. Footsteps. The dry heaves of someone who had seen all they could take for the moment. The paramedics, talking in hushed tones.

They were treating some of the officers for shock.

I pulled further into myself, forehead pressing into my knees, my arms wrapped tight around my shins.

Since spring. God knows how many there are in there. Right under my nose, a Chaldean whore and a wendigo.

Right under my goddamn nose. Some hunter I am.

Saul sat next to me, close enough I could feel the heat of him. He didn't touch me, though. He knew enough to leave me alone, silently offering his presence while I suffered the worst wound any hunter could ever suffer.

Guilt.

God. Under my very nose. How could I overlook something like this? And the not-so-comfortable thought, *in my city. My city. Why?*

The images were burned into the darkness behind my eyelids. A cavalcade of horrors, Hell reproduced in miniature, and Perry's soft corrupting voice, smooth as velvet and so, so amused.

God is not here. Of all people you *should know that.*

Dark exhaled up from the cold pavement, the sun sliding below the rim of the earth. "How is she?" Rosie's voice, soft and respectful.

"Quiet." Saul's deadpan reply held no trace of levity. "Taking it a little hard."

"I brought some coffee." Wonder of wonders, Rosie sounded shy. "Jill? Want some coffee?"

Get up, Jill. Mikhail's voice, the harshly weighted syllables, as if he was tired and wounded. *Get up, and do your duty. You are hunter. This is what you do.*

I raised my head. Slowly. The sun was on her tired way back down under the rim of the earth, and night was rising.

Rosie's freckles stood out garishly against the paleness of almost-shock. Her hair was pulled sleekly back, but she still looked tired and frazzled. Carp was talking to a forensic tech, leaning against a squad car, a defeated slump to his shoulders. He looked a little green, and his hair stood up as if he'd run his fingers back through it more than once.

"Thanks." The word cracked, my voice as dirty and disused as an empty room. I took the Styrofoam cup of coffee sludge Rosie offered. The laces of her white canvas sneakers were dirty, and that one small detail suddenly filled my eyes with tears. "I'm sorry, Rosie."

"For what?" She shrugged. "Better we find these people now. We have a chance of identifying them. Hopefully, that is." One side of her mouth pulled down. "You look like hell."

Not yet I don't. But soon I probably will. I took a sip of the burned coffee. "Thanks."

"You gonna be okay?"

No. Not even close. No way. "Fine."

Saul leaned over, bumped me with his shoulder. The coffee splashed inside the cup, its surface oils swirling.

"What do you want us to work on, Carp and me? We've been getting up to speed on this organ stuff with Badger and Sullivan."

I returned to myself like a heavy sigh, sinking back down into my body. Leather creaked as I sat up straight, I heard a car door shut quietly. Someone else started to heave. I took another swallow of the liquid masquerading as coffee. "You and Carp can process the scene and keep on the lookout for another one. Other than that, nothing. It's too goddamn dangerous to have you guys poking around, I don't want to lose either of you."

I suppose I should have taken it as a compliment that she didn't argue. "What are you going to do?" She sounded less like a seasoned detective and more like a teenager frightened to death by ghost stories told around a campfire. It just showed how sane she was.

"Find the Sorrows bitch responsible for this," I answered quietly. "Take her out. And her entire happy crew of helpers. Kill them and leave them in stinking gobbets somewhere, and curse their bones so that their souls find no rest in this world or the next. *Nobody* fucks with my city."

A short pregnant pause was broken only by the sound of someone still heaving. Quiet murmurs.

"Well," Rosie said finally. "Nice to know you have a plan. Anything we can do?"

"Keep your heads down." I rocked up to my feet, my knees protesting. I felt bruised and tender all over. "One way or another this is all going to be over soon. Either

I'm going to kill them all. . . ." I glanced at Perry, who had finally moved and came silkily through the organized chaos of processing one of the worst murder scenes in Santa Luz history.

"Or?" Rosie prompted. "Do I really want to know?"

"Or you'll need a new hunter, and quick. Not to mention you'll want to get as far away from this fucking city as possible." I handed the coffee cup back.

"Lovely, Jill. That's really reassuring."

"Not my job to be reassuring. You're a good cop, you know that?"

"Coming from you, that means something." A tired, sour smile lit her face. "I'll go tell Carp the good news. You might want to slide away before he decides to corner you and tell you not to do anything stupid."

"You're not going to tell me that?"

"He thinks you'll listen; I know better. Be careful." She looked up at Saul. "You too, Tonto."

He nodded, silver chiming in his hair. Perry reached us as Rosie stepped away, heading back to Carp.

"Jill—" Saul began, rising like a dark wave.

"Hang on. Perry?"

"Kiss." A tilt to his chin, a raising of one blond eyebrow, and his eyes began to glitter. He looked far more like the hellbreed I was used to seeing inside the walls of the Monde Nuit.

"Find Melisande Belisa. Bring her to me."

He was about to protest, I suppose. At any rate, he opened his mouth as if he was going to say something, then stopped, studying me intently. I was safe enough right now, if the wendigo was going to attack me it would have to find me first. Which wasn't a comforting thought, but we needed someone on our side who knew what this other Sorrows bitch was up to.

And Belisa, damn her eyes, was the only one I could think of. Besides, if she gave me any trouble I'd have Saul and Perry hold her down while I took her spleen out the hard way.

And I would enjoy every goddamn moment of it.

I am not a nice person.

I held Perry's gaze for a long, restless eternity. Then I folded my arms, the ruby at my throat beginning to vibrate. The scar, slumbering since I'd found the bodies, tingled. His aura tightened, the bruised sludge that marked him as hellbreed. Funny, but nothing with an aura like his should be able to produce hellfire in the blue spectrum.

Just what was Perry, anyway?

He dropped his eyes. "Certainly, my dear. Anything for my Kiss. It shouldn't take too long."

"Good." I watched him turn with an oddly uncoordinated grace, and begin walking away. "I want her alive, Perry. But I want her frightened."

He waved one hand above his shoulder, as if I was bothering him with trifles. Saul bumped into me, crowding; I bumped back. The taste of ashes, burned coffee, and sourness still hung in my mouth. The scar on my wrist pulsed, but quietly, a soft mouthing caress, scales rasping seamed and puckered skin.

"Saul." My voice sounded strange, as if I was several miles away and hearing myself talk. Pushing everything else away, boiling everything down to the simplest possible essence.

Distilling it.

"Right here." And he was. I could feel his attention like sunshine on my face—but from far away.

From very far away. I focused on the gleaming paint of Perry's limo as dusk spread over the sky, turning the blue to purple and tinting the clouds with pink in one last gasp of brightness. "I need you to go down into the barrio and find out what kills a wendigo. Keep digging until you find something, then come back to me. Take the car, I won't need it."

"Jill—"

"No. I need you to do this for me."

"What are you going to do?"

"Some things." *Things I don't want you to see me do, Saul. I love you.*

"What kind of things?"

Bloody, screaming things. I watched as the headlights turned on and Perry's limo smoothly banked out of the parking lot, heading north on Quincoa. "Please, Saul." *Don't make me say any more.*

"Try not to get into trouble," he said, heavily. "Give me your keys."

I dug in a pocket and handed them over, still staring at the spot where Perry's limo had sat. My eyes blurred, and I felt the final *click* that meant I was lifting off, sliding away from the earth, into the space where there was no room for what I was feeling. The space that would hold me until it was safe to feel something again.

I have had enough. My city. They are trying to do this to my city.

"Jill?" Saul bumped into me again. Just like a Were, crowding me so I knew he cared. "I'll come find you as soon as I know how to kill it. I promise."

That made me smile, a gentle abstracted smile I could feel against the foreign material of my face. I turned my head and looked up at him. "You don't need to promise."

"I like to. So you know I'm serious." His dark eyes scorched mine for a moment, and feeling threatened to come back. I shoved it away. "Jill?"

"Go. Find out what kills the thing." I pushed him, gently. "Then come get me. Okay?"

"Okay." A short nod, his hair falling forward over his shoulders. Silver glittered, and his high cheekbones caught the last of the dusky light. He always looked good in dimness, and even better in strong light. "You got it." He turned and headed for the Impala. I don't know if he looked back, because I took the opportunity to fade into a pool of shadow between the unnecessary SWAT van and an ambulance, then ran soft and light for the alley that cut between an old abandoned grocery store and a newer but equally abandoned building that had been an auto parts supply store. I could cut over to 142nd and get a cab there. I had enough cash for anywhere I would need to go tonight.

I did not look back. I kept going.

21

The flesh gallery was just starting to pulse with nightlife. Long legs in ragged fishnets under short skirts, the motion of hips back and forth, the glitter of eyes under mascara and thick eyeliner, cheap jewelry and the ubiquitous jackets now that the wind had risen. Coming down off the mountains, the winter wind was cold, full of the smell of sage and stone. It whistled in the canyons between skyscrapers, and here on Lucado it filled the night with knives.

The girls were nervous, and I didn't blame them. I examined the street from a good vantage point on the roof of a tenement, pulling my tattered coat around me. I waited, taking deep lungfuls of the cold wind.

The street danced; they were like shoals of fish glittering and turning in sync. Clicking of platform heels against concrete, the sound of car wheels, catcalls as the girls stamped their feet and tried to keep warm. Cars pulling in, cars pulling out, doors slamming, windows creaking as they slid down.

I had stripped the cuff from my wrist, and the scar

burned under the cold kiss of wind. The night came alive, colors and sounds curdling under the lash of preternatural attention, my mind open, still, receptive.

I saw it. The Cadillac.

It slid like a stiletto through the shoals of tired girls, and some of them cast frightened glances at it afterward. I *moved,* brief wind in my ears as the world turned over and gravity caught me, plummeting, hitting the ground and rolling to bleed momentum. Cold concrete, pebbles digging into my back, then I was sliding through the shadows, just a flicker of motion in the darkness.

The scar, the scar, I'm moving like a hellbreed. Like a Trader. A five-story drop off a roof and here I was, running.

By the time I reached the quiet little brownstone he was already inside, and one of his muscle troop was on the front steps. The muscle, thick and heavy in a long coat with a bulge under his left arm where the gun was, never even saw me. I simply came straight out of the shadows and hit him, the crack of bone breaking in his face a sharp sweet sound.

Then I was inside, and the other thug was at the end of the hall. I took him too, a short tubby man powerfully built for all his lard, smelling of *frijoles* and grease; with the heatless scent of a killer on him too. *Well, Ricky certainly doesn't skimp on the help, does he?*

The short one went down easily and quietly, I pulled the strike at the last moment so as not to break his neck.

I slid up the stairs on cat-soft, cat-quick feet, and burst into the bedroom.

Diamond Ricky had a girl in there with him, a half-naked child with high brown breasts who was rolling the top of a stocking down her thigh. I saw her from very far away and spared her less than half a thought. There was a low table with a mirrored tile fouled with cocaine holding down a fan of twenties, a white leather couch; the ceiling held mirrors too as well as the closet on the far wall. Electric light was soft and dim from three green and blue lava lamps on a glass shelf; the nightstand held a paper bag (full of something illegal, judging by the smell) and a 9 mm that would do him no good.

The thick musky-green smell of pot filled the room, both old and new; Ricky had just lit a joint and was reclining on the bed, his hand inside the open fly of his trousers. He saw me and his mouth fell open, the joint falling from his fingers over the side of the bed. I was on the bed in one leap, my left-hand fingers sinking into his throat and the gun in my right hand rising up to lock onto the girl, who hitched in breath to scream. Her face hadn't lost its baby-fat yet, she was barely old enough to be walking to school by herself, let alone be in a room with a pimp.

"Shut up," I snarled, cutting through her gasping inhale. "Shut the *fuck* up."

She did, clutching an incongruous bit of feathers to her chest. Some kind of lingerie, probably Ricky's contribution to the fun and games. Her long dark hair quivered, and the lipstick smeared on her lips made her mouth into a wet dark hole.

"Pick up the money." I pointed the gun toward the table, she edged over and looked at Ricky, then jerked the money out from under the tile. The cocaine scattered on the tabletop. Snow on glass plains.

I made a tiny motion with the gun toward the door. "Go out the back door, or you'll be shot." The softness in my voice made it a promise. "Go home, if you have a home.

If you don't, check into a hotel. But if I see you on the street tonight, or if you tell *anyone,* I will find you."

It was an empty threat. I wouldn't have cared. But she believed it, and her eyes darted toward Ricky. I tightened my fingers in the pimp's throat, and he moaned, a shapeless sound of terror.

She scrambled for the door, and I heard her bumbling along as she tried to get dressed on the stairs while running. I listened—yes, she went out the back door.

Good girl. I turned my attention to Ricky, who was choking as my fingers tensed. "Ricky." I sounded meditative. The gun swung around, settled against his forehead. "Now you and I are going to have a little chat, *cabrón.* A very cozy little talk. You're going to tell me about your playmates, and we are going to have a lovely special moment right here on your bed. Bet you like that, don't you?"

Ricky was wet with sweat; it rolled in great beads from his brown skin. He had a hard-on, and he smelled of oil and smoke, as well as fried cheese. A thin curl of smoke lifted from the joint on the floor.

The smile pulled my lips back into a snarl of effort as the scar on my wrist pulsed, every fiber of my body straining to pull the trigger. But instead, I loosened up a little on his throat.

"Now," I whispered. "Your meeting. With Jonte and the boys. Who else was there, and what was said? Take it from the top."

He did.

Pimps are predictable creatures. They have their routines and their habits, and the fact that most of them are into petty drug dealing doesn't change that. If a pimp gets picked up, his girls bail him out, usually with the help of his lieutenant.

But if a pimp ends up dead, with his second and his muscle crippled, the girls freefall for a while. The drugs come from other dealers, some of whom are weak and move into the power vacuum to become pimps. Or they come from new pimps that rise like maggots from a corpse to take the place of the old one.

I wish it was harder for them. God, do I wish it was harder.

Wish in one hand, Kismet. Spit in the other. See which fills up first.

I followed the chain up, each pimp telling me a little more, and saved Jonte for last. He was a big, broad, soft-in-the-middle black man with a wide genial smile and two front teeth cased in gold that rang sweetly against the floor the second time I backhanded him. Eleven pimps, each of whom had been at the meeting with Rocadero, who was dead probably because the redheaded Sorrow didn't need him any more. The pimps being alive either meant that they weren't important or that she still needed them to supply something, whether it be flesh or cash.

It was from Jonte that I got the most important piece of news.

It would take a stronger man than a pimp not to give up everything he knows when a hellbreed-strong fist flexes and a testicle pops like a grape. At heart, the men who make their living like that are cowards. It's why they engage in the mindfucks instead of getting real jobs. What they don't realize is that the mindfucks eat them alive too.

Now's not a time for philosophy, I told myself as the

boneless body of the big man slumped to the tiled floor.
Jonte had a nice place, for all that I'd busted up a good
deal of it. He'd also had some half-decent help. I was
bleeding down one side of my face, and there was a fresh
bloody hole in the left thigh of my pants, closing rapidly.

*Now is the time for showing these fucks what happens
when you mess with* my *city. Had enough, I have* so *had
enough of this. The* scar on my wrist pricked wetly, a thick
welter of heat spilling up my arm. Fresh cold wind poured
in through the busted French door, glass broken in sharp
slivers in the tide of sticky blood that washed across the
tiles.

I let out a long soft breath as Jonte gurgled his last,
pieces falling into place. Taken separately, the pimps
hadn't known much. But putting all the pieces together
gave me a picture. Just like a jigsaw, even if you don't
have all the pieces you can make a guess if you have
enough of them.

And now I knew, too, where the redheaded Sorrow had
her little bolthole. It was a stroke of genius, one I admired
coldly while I considered how to break in and kill her.

The pseudo-adobe house groaned under the lash of
wind. I'd taken four men with assault rifles, three with
handguns, and another two that apparently had little use
other than as hangers-on. They were only human, all
of them, and I'd found Jonte gibbering with fear in his
kitchen, crouched under the counter and trying to load a
.38 revolver—whether for himself or me I wouldn't want
to guess. And now that the shooting and moaning was
over I heard something else.

I tilted my head. Scratching sounds.

Mice in the walls, Kiss? The voice, strangely enough,

was Perry's; his jolly happy tone when he'd just discovered something to make me flinch. *Little mice fingers scratching at the plaster. Mmmh.*

Glass crunched under my feet. The sound was coming from downstairs, in the basement. Jonte was quite a successful pimp, probably because of his connection to a few of the larger drug dealers in town. He actually had a suburban house, in depressed real estate less than five minutes on the old highway from the strip downtown where his girls paraded. All the comforts of home but close enough to keep a tight leash on his moneymakers. Yes, ol' Jonte was quite the operator.

"Was" is the operative word. Now he's pimping in Hell. The thought brought another one of those frozen smiles to the surface of my face.

The house was utterly silent except for the scratching and the faint whimpers. If I'd been wearing my cuff, I probably wouldn't have heard it.

I had both guns out. Jonte's taste in furnishings was Mission-style, with a few tribal touches; it was nice for a fatass pimp, I supposed. The kitchen gave onto the living room, I stepped past the body of one of Jonte's thugs, the one dressed all in night camo. *Where do they find these people? Then again, reputable mercs don't like to work for pimps; they prefer a little higher on the food chain where the money's better.*

I turned into the entry hall, lifting both guns. There was a door at the end, probably going down to the basement and locked with a shiny brand-new padlock. Behind it was whatever was making those stealthy sounds.

Hamelin Town's in Brunswick, by famous Hanover

City; the poem rang inside my head with dark glee. *Vermin, 'twas a pity.*

The hammers on both guns clicked back. *Focus, Jill. What the fuck is that?*

I caught a muffled sob, and the sound of movement again. More than one.

What lovely little surprise do we have waiting for Kismet in here?

I approached the door, cautiously, quietly. More muffled sobs. *What the fuck?*

I holstered my right-hand gun, closed my fingers around the padlock. Drew on the scar for a quick hard yank, and metal squealed, snapping. I twisted, tossed the padlock, and drew my gun again.

It pays to be careful.

I backed up. "Come out," I called, ready for submachine gun fire, zombies, scurf, or anything else that might pop out to surprise a hunter who had just had a very bad day.

Anything except what confronted me. More sobs from behind the door, which was thick heavy old wood. Women's sobs. But I kept the guns level. There was simply no telling, and I was here without backup. *I hope Saul's having some luck in the barrio.*

The door creaked. They were fiddling with it from the inside.

"Goddammit!" I yelled. *"Come out right fucking now or I will come in there shooting!"*

More soft sounds of distress, and the heavy iron doorknob twisted violently. A slice of darkness widened as the door slid open, and my fingers tightened on the triggers.

A naked human woman emerged, blinking. She carried

a long splinter of wood that looked utterly useless as a weapon, and for one of the longest and most exotic moments of my life (and that's saying something) we faced each other over the expanse of tiled floor, under the gently tinkling chandelier Jonte must have paid a fortune for.

She had wide dark eyes and close-cropped dark hair, and she couldn't have been more than eighteen. She also recovered first, as another girl—this one just as naked, and quite obviously just as young or younger—stepped blinking out into the light.

"Are you one of them?" the first one demanded. "If you are, goddammit, I'll kill you."

Brave of her, considering how I must have looked. And considering that I was armed, I was smoking with violence, I was spattered with blood, and I was ready to kill whoever I had to.

What the fuck is this? I stared. "What the fuck?" I couldn't come up with anything better. Then I recovered, slightly. "I just killed Jonte. What the hell were you doing in the basement?"

Her shoulders went back and her chin lifted a little. I heard more soft sounds behind her. More women? Naked women? "What, you think we *wanted* to be locked up down there in the dark?" She lifted the splinter of wood, and I remembered I was holding both guns on her.

I lowered them, slowly. A horrible idea began forming under the surface of my conscious mind. "Are any of you pregnant?"

"What?" She stared at me. It was another exotic moment. "Are you fucking *high?* We've been down there for *weeks!*"

I decided this would be a good time to holster my guns,

did so. "I just killed the pimp who owns this house," I said. "Let's call 911 and find you ladies some clothes."

The suspicion she eyed me with would have been insulting if I hadn't suspected that I'd stumbled across the reason why Jonte had been left alive by the redheaded Sorrow. Three days to the invocation of the Nameless, and a clutch of young girls held here in a pimp's house, fed and trammeled like prized rabbits.

Oh, God. And what she said next convinced me I was maybe right. She stared at me like I was her own personal nightmare.

"You're *her,*" she whispered. "You're the one who bought us."

"I don't buy people. Nor do I sell them." My voice was a little sharper than usual, and the chandelier overhead tinkled restlessly. I must have been wearing my mad face, because the girl gasped and dropped the splinter; it clattered on the tiled floor.

It was a good thing I had the cuff off, because otherwise I might not have heard it. But I had been functioning with preternatural senses most of the night. Sensitivity is a wonderful thing, once you get used to it.

Clawed feet brushing the earth like fingers on a drumhead, incredibly fast. Far away, but getting closer.

Much closer. Someone was coming to dinner. The hair on the back of my neck stood straight up, and the charms in my hair tinkled together sweetly. The sound was suddenly loud in my hellbreed-sensitive ears, moving to the forefront. Impossible to ignore.

I whirled, the tattered edges of my coat flaring out. Stared at the half-open front door, the one I'd busted through. "Holy fuck," I whispered, forgetting the naked women for a moment. I heard individual heartbeats; there had to be a good twenty of them in there. Defenseless, and from the smell, sanitation hadn't been as good as one could wish. But they were in good health, so they had probably been fed.

Just the thing to fuel your evocation of a hungry Elder God with.

Shit. Goddammit. I turned back to the women. The girl behind the leader had folded her arms over her bare breasts defensively. I saw more spilling out, none of them a day over twenty if I guessed correctly. They clustered behind the dark-haired girl, who was obviously the leader, and I saw a glint in her eyes I recognized from a lifetime ago and miles away.

She wasn't ready to die yet, and she was one tough cookie.

What am I going to do here? "Listen to me. Jonte's got cars, the keys are hanging in the kitchen. Be careful, there's broken glass. Get the fuck out of here, all hell's going to break loose."

She took it better than I thought she would. "Where should we go? Shut *up!*" She yelled the last, over her shoulder, and I heard the sniffles and soft moans behind her quiet down. Wide wet eyes were wiped, the girls holding on to each other, more pushing up from what looked like dark stairs. "Goddammit, I'm going to get us out of this, but you have got to stop *whining!*"

I like this girl, I decided. "Get downtown. I think he's got a fucking Humvee in there, get downtown and get to a police station. Tell them Kismet sent you. Got it? K-I-S-M-E-T. Kismet."

"Kismet. Okay. Show me the car, I've got my learner's

permit." Yes, she was definitely the leader. "Amy, Conchita, you two get the girls organized. Let's go. Come on. Quit crying, Vicky; hold her up." She sounded like a battlefield general, but I heard the quick thunder of her pulse. She was scared half to death. And so young.

Holy fucking shit. I can't just leave them here. "Come on." The chandelier overhead tinkled again as I spoke. I sounded two short steps away from murder. The scar abruptly cooled on my wrist, turning chill as an ice cube pressed into the flesh. "What's your name?"

"Hope," she replied, moving forward, seemingly utterly unselfconscious of the fact that she was completely unclothed. But I saw the bruises on her thighs and the way she held herself, as if she couldn't stand to even have the air touch her. "Hope Melendez." Goosebumps rose on her skin, and I heard the footsteps in the distance stutter, pause . . . and redouble their effort.

Shit. Fucking shit.

"*Move* it!" I yelled, and several of the girls flinched. "This fucking way, and hurry up. Hurry *up!*" I had a good guess where the garage was, and Jonte was known for his car collection.

I've got to get them to a car or two. Christ, I hope more of them know how to drive.

Then I've got to hold the wendigo until they can get away.

22

Two of the longest minutes of my life later, we were in the garage with the huge door creaking open. "They kept us down there in chickenwire cages. I've been working on tearing a hole through the wire in one." Hope held up her left hand; her fingertips were mashed and bleeding. "We heard the gunshots, figured either we were next or we were going to be left down there in the dark. So I broke open my cage. They told us we'd been bought by a woman, and that she was coming to take us away." She shivered. *"Jesus."*

Closer. It was getting closer. I didn't have time to offer any comfort. They were barefoot and naked, and miserable. But I got them all loaded into two cars—a black Humvee and a silver Escalade; Jonte had certainly liked pimp rides. Finding the keys was no problem, there was a neat pegboard with all the keys we could ever want. Seatbelts *were* a problem, but if it was a choice between seatbelts and getting them out of here I'd pick getting them *out.* They were packed like sardines, some of them openly sobbing now.

Hope clambered into the driver's seat in the Humvee. Her second-in-command, a plump blonde girl with wide blue eyes and bruised, blood-crusted thighs, was already strapped into the driver's seat of the Escalade.

"Jesus, this is big." Hope's breathing was short and rapid, and I thought some of the girls were going into shock.

"Go easy on the brake. If you get pulled over, it's okay. Tell them my name and they'll take care of you." The garage door finished opening, I flinched as the sound of the creature's footsteps—distinct from a thousand other sounds—pounded my ears, communicating itself up through my bootsoles. *I'm sensitive to it now. Of course I am, it almost fucking killed me.* "And for God's sake be careful. It might help if everyone in there prays. Turn the heater up as soon as you can, you don't want anyone going into shock. Okay?"

"Who the fuck are you?" Her eyes were wide and haunted. "Jesus."

"Kismet," I repeated. "Tell the cops I sent you." I spelled it out for her again. "Now go. For fuck's sake, go. *There is no time.*"

The footsteps were very close now, drumming against the earth. The cars roused themselves, and the Humvee pulled out, slowly. The Escalade followed, torturously slow, and slid down the circular driveway. *Oh, please, oh please . . .*

I saw them make the turn out onto the street, so god-damn slowly, the footsteps almost on top of us by now and coming from the north. Which made not much sense, if she was hiding out where I thought she was, where Jonte had told me he had "taken a few bitches."

It didn't matter. I wondered if it had slipped its leash and come hunting or if the redheaded Sorrow had let it loose in another part of town.

Then it howled, a long chilling spun-glass growl of bloodthirsty hunger rising from the north. My skin crawled like it wanted to run away from both me and the creature; I turned around, hitting the button to close the garage door. *Fucking Christ. I could have been out of here already.*

I wanted to examine where they'd held the women, but it was enough to know that they were supposed to be kept alive and relatively unharmed except for rape. Opening up a door in the ether and bringing a Chaldean demon through requires a massive effort, and that effort could be fueled by harvested death. But something simpler was fresh death, done ritualistically; Traders sacrificed snakes, rabbits, dogs, horses, goats—anything they could catch and get rid of the husk afterward. But to bring through the Nameless, not even the death harvested from organ theft would do.

And to bring him through and bribe him into doing something nice for a renegade Sorrow would take even more. It made sense. Appalling, wasteful, *mad* sense, but still, it was a pattern. It was a workable theory.

Now I just had to stay alive long enough to figure out the rest of it and *stop* it. Brooding wouldn't help—and the slight nasty thought that the renegade Sorrow might have killed Jonte herself for allowing his boys to play with her sacrifices was amusing and gratifying, but wouldn't help me now.

I ducked under the garage door and set off across the driveway, my legs aching with the need to run. *Decide which way to go, Kiss. Move with a plan, for Christ's sake don't do anything stupid, taking off like a rabbit. This thing is fast, it's deadly, and you've got the scar, your whip, your guns, your knives—all of which are fucking useless if it gets too close—and you've got your teeny little noggin. Which has to save you now.*

This was a bad part of town to be trapped in. But if I cut across the old highway and ran for a bit, I would be at the edge of the barrio's dark, night-pulsing adobe warren. I knew that warren, knew some good hiding spots and shortcuts.

Going into the barrio was a good way to end up dead. But still, given the choice between killing me and killing what was chasing me, I was comfortably sure self-interest might strike the deciding blow in my favor.

It was getting close. Very close. Night wind brought the first threads of its scent, a noxious stink that raised the hairs on the back of my neck. Gooseflesh prickled up under my skin.

That thing almost fucking killed you. You have no staff now, goddammit, and it's fast. It's too goddamn fast. Oh, God. Oh, God.

I told the rabbit-panicking part of myself to shut up, reached the street, and picked up the pace, my coat flapping and the sour taste of fear on my tongue.

23

I don't mind being shot at. I don't *like* it, mind you, and I don't seek out flying lead. But I don't mind it. I don't mind knives, I don't mind a bit of fisticuffs. I don't even mind it when someone springs a trap on me and does their best to kill me.

I am a hunter; it comes with the job.

But Lord God on high, I hate to be *chased*. I hate to run with no other thought but the rabbit's thought of finding a way to escape certain death.

It was too fast. I paced myself, and drew on the cold, pulsing scar on my wrist as hard as I could. But even though I had the benefit of hellbreed-bargained strength, I was seriously flagging by the time I reached Merced Street and the Plaza Centro.

The PC isn't really a plaza. It's a gutted five-story building full of tiny shops, botanicas, and bodegas, with a vast central well thronged with people at any time of the day or night. It takes up a whole city block and was once a train station before the barrio reached in from the slum edge of town and took it captive.

It also has the biggest concentration of Weres in the city. Something that smelled this bad and was obviously intent on mayhem was likely to attract some notice. And while I didn't like the thought of luring the wendigo right through a heavily populated area and risking some casualties, I also didn't like the thought of meeting my death on a lonely street where there was no bloody *cover.* Weres mean smell, and smell was likely how this thing was tracking me. If I could confuse it, maybe I could escape.

These considerations flashed through my mind as I turned down Merced and saw the lights of the Plaza Centro in the distance, glimmering like fool's gold. My boots pounded the pavement, the scar no longer cold on my wrist but *hot,* so hot I expected it to steam in the chill night air. It poured pure etheric force into me, and I spent it recklessly—speed was imperative, since I could *hear* the thing behind me, and whenever the wind shifted I could smell it too. How it was tracking me through windshift I didn't want to know.

I didn't even want to guess.

At this point, I would settle for just keeping my miserable life. My breath rattled in my chest, my ribs heaving, it had almost caught me once on the top of a tenement on Colvert and Tenth. I knew my city, knew every dip in the streets, knew every shortcut and back alley, and it was only knowledge that kept me one scant sliver ahead of it, this thing—wendigo, whatever it was—that roared its glassine screech behind me doing its own personal imitation of a Wild Hunt.

Christ I'm glad it's not smart, if it was smart I couldn't have fooled it and it would have me by now. I pounded up the slight slope, flagging badly now, headlights blurring past. If the normal humans sensed me at all it was only as a cold draft, a flash out of the corner of the eye, something not-quite-right but gone before they could take a second look.

A ghost.

Grant me strength in battle, honor in living, and a quick clean death when my time comes—The prayer trembled just at the edge of my exhausted mind. *But don't let it come yet. Please, God. I have served well; help me out a little here. God? Anyone?*

Then, the impossible, the smell of the thing gaggingly close, I had slowed too much, no alley in sight, no way to jag left or right, I was running for the PC and maybe an escape in the tunnels underneath but oh *God,* I was tired. So tired. And I was hit from behind, a massive impact that smashed *through* me as the thing collided with its prey and sent me flying.

I heard the scrabble of claws and the screams as I flew, trying vainly to twist in midair, get my feet under me, something, anything, and heard the snarling crash into a wall behind me.

Hit. Hard. Snapping and shattering glass, I'd gone through a window and fetched up against shelving that fell over, bottles breaking, glass whickering through the air and the sudden smell of smashed vegetables all around me.

Lay for a moment, lungs burning and heaving, legs and arms too drained to move, scar a burning cicatrice on my wrist. *Oh God oh God, let it be quick, if it has to take me let it be quick, Saul, oh God Saul. Saul*—

Then, as if a gift from heaven, something familiar. "Get up. Jesus Christ, Jill, *get up!*"

A familiar voice, a prayer answered. I levered myself up just at the thing smashed through the glass searching for me, a massive ball of hunger and gagging stench suddenly freezing the air. It moved too *fast* and I was tired, so tired, arms and legs weighted with lead.

Crash. He hit the thing from the side, screaming his warcry, a roar halfway between man and cougar. Flame suddenly belched out, garish in the darkness and the fluorescent light of the grocery store, I heard screams and popping sounds as the fire, bright crimson-orange, speared through the night. More vital, more impossibly real than regular fire or hellfire, heat scorched the air so badly it stripped the hair back from my face, a holocaust of flame.

More screaming, and the barking, coughing growl of more Weres. I heard chanting—a shaman's voice lifted in the high keening screech of Were magicks, those bloody, animalistic, and strangely pure works of sorcery that are their peculiar heritage.

Saul yelled his warcry again, moving with fluid grace as the shining thing he held glittered with heat. More glass smashed, the smell of mashed vegetables and fruit suddenly turning caramel-brown shot through with the disgusting stink of the cancerous thing that screeched and tried to bat Saul away.

Seeing a Were fight in midform, dancing between human and animal, is . . . We never really think of how they shift to animal forms, forms that are precise and graceful. In most cases, far more graceful than human beings ever manage to be. And in their human forms they're graceful too, blessed with quick reflexes, regular features, an uncanny ability to move economically and efficiently through space.

Midform, they have the best of both worlds, a beauty that is so weird and alien it catches at the throat and dries the mouth. The movies don't do them justice at all. And midform is not somewhere they linger, unless they are rogue—or unless there is no other way to fight.

Saul was somehow not there as the creature swiped with its bloody claws, and seeing its speed and power up close I slumped to my knees, jaw hanging open in wonder and my breath rasping in my throat. It wasn't fair, it just wasn't *fair,* that I had to bargain with a hellbreed to get even a fraction of his grace and *still* I was so much less.

So acutely aware of being so much less.

Steam billowed. The thing Saul held, its flame liquid and hissing, broke the soul-devouring cold of the creature. Another scream from the shaman, and a massed snarling tide of power rode through the air. Were magic, tasting of nights out under open skies, black air against the back of the throat like champagne, hard crusted snow under feet no longer human, and the joy of *running* on four legs, the air alive with scent and the hard cold points of the stars overhead singing their ancient songs of lust and slow fire to those of us on the ground who had ears to hear.

The glowing thing, a long slim wand, struck. Saul yelled, ducking aside as the wendigo clawed for him, slowed by the weight of furred heavy power smashing through the interior of the store. More glass shattered, cardboard exploded, and the smell of cooking food shaded through goodness and into burning.

Saul *kicked,* a perfectly placed *savate* blow, then somehow twisted, using the kick to propel his body back and up, uncoiling to avoid the creature's claws as it fumbled for him again. The slim shape, burning white-hot, scored through my eyes, I flung up a hand to shield them and heard a death-scream unlike any other. Clapped my hands to my ears and screamed as well, a little sound lost inside the massive wrecked howl like frozen mountains colliding.

If glaciers feel pain when they rub against each other and split off whole mountainsides, they would scream like that. It . . . no, there is no way to describe the enormity of that cry. It broke whatever had not broken and flung me back; I hit the wall with my boots dangling six feet off the floor and slid down, landing in a medley of shattered glass and exploded packets of meat sizzling in the heat. Smelled my own hair burning as the silver charms heated up.

The scream stopped just before my eardrums burst. I rolled free of the bubbling, steaming mess, gained my knees again, had to try twice before I could make it up to my feet. The air abruptly chilled, became the normal cold of a Santa Luz winter night.

Steam and vapor drifted in the air. There was murmuring, the ancient words Weres mutter when they come across death from bad luck or humanity. A forgiving of the spirit, in the midst of clear red rage. They have never had to translate that prayer.

You don't need to, if you've ever heard it. No translation is necessary.

My breath sounded harsh in the sudden silence. I was suddenly aware of my legs, strained and unhappy, making their displeasure known. My ribs, heaving, almost pulled loose by the demands placed on them. The scar, pulsing obscenely against the inside of my wrist, as if Perry was kissing my arm again and again. Pressing his hellbreed lips to human flesh, his scaled tongue flickering and his hot humid breath condensing on cooler human skin.

Veils of mist in the air parted. Saul stood over the shattered body of the wendigo; he tossed the arrowhead with its cargo of leather, feather, and hair onto the mess. Now that it was dead, it was a twisted humanoid figure running wetly with icy gray fur and long bits of different colors where its victims' scalps had been plastered to its mottled hide. Its face was tipped up, the eyes collapsing into runnels of foulness, its lipless mouth open in a silent blasphemous scream. And its claws, obsidian-tipped and deadly, lay twitching against the prosaic bubbling linoleum of a devastated grocery store.

It looked strangely small now, its face like a wizened ugly child's despite its frozen, rotted nose and nonexistent lips. Its genitals were pendulous, and black with frostbite.

And around its neck was a thin silver chain, winking in the light, squirming with unhealthy black Chaldean sorcery. The chain was broken about a foot below its jaw. Had it escaped and come looking for me?

Shoved through its heart was a spike of glossy black obsidian-like material, popping and zinging as it shrank. It had been white-hot just moments before. The steam whooshed away, evaporating into the night.

I sounded like I was dying of pneumonia, my breathing was so hard and labored. I half-choked at the titanic stink in the air. Bile caught in my throat.

Oh please don't let me throw up again. Oh please.

The hair of cougarform had melted from Saul; he stood straight and in profile, staring down at the defeated creature, his lips moving with the prayer of the massed Weres, their eyes bright and their mouths cherry-beautiful, crowded in through the window. I saw several different types: a kentauri tossing his long silvery mane, a werespider whose face was gray and haunted under her mop of silken hair, another werecat who folded her hands and had closed her eyes, mouthing the ancient sounds. There were others, but I was too tired to see them. And then, in the back of the crowd, I saw a pair of familiar blue eyes, a sheen of pale hair. Perry. Had he found Belisa?

At the moment I didn't care. I closed my eyes. The breath that knifed into my lungs was not less sweet because of the stench it carried. No, it was *air,* and I was still alive to breathe it, no matter how foul it smelled. *Oh, Saul. Saul. Thank God for you. Thank God.*

Then I stumbled away, looking for a place to throw up. There was nothing left in my stomach, but I felt the need to purge anyway.

24

I had never been so glad to see my own four walls again. The warehouse clicked and rang as I collapsed on the couch, keeping a wary eye on Belisa as she moved to perch on a chair opposite, glaring at me through her good eye while she clasped the pack of ice to the other side of her face. When she wasn't avidly peering at the interior and the furnishings, that was.

Storing up little bits of deduction to mindfuck me with later, no doubt.

Perry stood slightly behind her. He was immaculate, gray suit, the first two buttons of his crisp white dress shirt undone, his shoes shined to perfection. He looked very satisfied with himself, in his bland blond sort of way.

Belisa was moving gingerly, and her blue silk shirt was crumpled, her slippers were battered. It had probably been a hell of a fight, but for tangling with Perry she was strangely unharmed. I wondered if it was because I'd threatened him.

Not likely.

Saul went straight for the kitchen. I heard the cupboard opening, glass clinking. "Anyone who wants whiskey better speak up now," he said, calmly enough.

"God, yes." *Oh, Saul. Thank God for you.* I rested my head against the couch's back, almost beginning to feel like I could breathe again. Leather creaked, I hadn't bothered taking my coat off.

"If you have anything decent, I'll take it." Perry's eyes rested on me. Under the leather cuff, the scar ran with rancid flame, trailers of heat sliding up my arm. Smoky desire, sliding through the map of my veins as if he was touching me, running his fingers up the inside of my elbow.

I didn't look away, but I did clamp down on my self-control. I was vulnerable now, exhausted after expending so much power. And any time human animals get close to death, sex is the easiest thing to tempt them with afterward. "Belisa?" I kept my tone neutral.

She almost flinched, recovered. "That would be nice."

Perry leaned on the back of the chair. "What?" It was a soft inquiry, and I saw the blood drain from her face.

She looked terrified, and I couldn't blame her.

"That would be nice, mistress." All the color had leached out of her tone too. She shivered, hunching her shoulders.

Mistress. The term for a bitch-queen, a Sorrow higher in status than herself. What had Perry done to her? Abruptly, I felt sick all the way down into my stomach. He'd found her and brought her, and from the looks of it she'd resisted; and now he was rubbing it in. For her benefit, and also for mine; just to drive home that I owed him for bringing her in.

Christ. Well, you knew what he was when you struck the bargain, Jill. Don't pretend otherwise. "Drinks all round, then." I sank into the couch.

The two cars full of naked women had made it to the police station; Montaigne had left a message on my answering machine, alternately swearing at me and thanking me, then swearing at me again. I'd sort it out later.

Right now I had other things to worry about. A few clipped sentences in the Impala, with Perry's limo right behind, had laid out the chain of events for me: Saul had gone into the barrio and poked around, not finding much of anything until Perry showed up with Melisande Belisa in tow and a long thin iron-bound case—the firestrike spear Father Guillermo knew was hidden under the altar in the seminary's main chapel, a secret kept by Sacred Grace since its inception. Perry swore whatever was inside should kill the wendigo.

The catch? He hadn't actually opened the case yet. Both of them felt my wild plunge into the barrio, Saul had left Perry to corral the bruised and beaten Sorrow and set off as fast as he could to find me and either kill the thing chasing me or buy me enough time to escape.

He didn't want to talk about killing it, and he didn't want to talk about how the spear had burned his palms. *It doesn't matter,* was all he would say. *It's fine.*

Saul brought the bottle and four glasses. He poured, slamming the bottle down when he was done, and left two glasses on the table. He handed me a glass half-full of amber liquid. He took his own and settled on the couch, and I wished I could cuddle up next to him, feel his heat.

But he was still angry, the musky fume of fury hanging on him. He was wound tighter than a clockspring, I knew enough to leave him to himself right now. Were-cats are dangerous and unpredictable; if he snapped now I would have to calm him down the old-fashioned way. The thought sent a spike of heat through me, cleaner heat than the spoiled spillage of the scar, and I tossed down half my drink in one motion. I didn't think Perry and Belisa were to be trusted poking around the warehouse while Saul and I attended to some demons of our own.

Besides, there was this redhead bitch of a Sorrow to catch.

But first things first. "So Rourke lied. It wasn't Saint Anthony's spear. I *knew* there wasn't such an artifact."

Saul shrugged. Belisa leaned forward, took a glass, and handed it up to Perry, flinching. Then she took the last one for herself.

I don't think I like the looks of that. I eyed her over the rim of my own glass. Whiskey exploded in my stomach, another clean brief heat as my metabolism burned through it. *I'm alive. Alive. Thank you, God. I'm alive.*

Saul's tone was carefully neutral. "Gui didn't want to lie to you, but he'd taken an oath to keep the secret. I wonder what else they're hiding in there."

I don't care right now. Sort it out later, too. I shivered. The thing had glowed, white-hot, and part of the smell of burning had been Saul's hands charred down to the bone. "How are your fingers?"

He wriggled them, almost fully healed. I caught a flash of pink scarring rapidly shrinking. "Hurts a little. But fine." He spared me a tight smile, the corners of his mouth and eyes crinkling. Even though smoky musk rage pounded in the air around him, he still wanted to put me at ease.

I love you. The words choked me for a moment. I looked back into my glass. Another piece of the puzzle fell into place. "So *you* were looking for the spear, too. And your brother."

Belisa hunched her shoulders, staring into her glass. The warehouse creaked and muttered around us. The ice crackled against her face; her other eye, black from lid to lid, seemed oddly unfocused. "The plan was simple. We were to find the spear, kill the creature, and bring back Inez Germaine. Use her to buy our way back into the good graces of our House. It was my inattention that allowed my brother to escape, and we were both due for punishment and liquidation once we were returned unless we achieved something . . . extraordinary, something that could be legitimately seen as needing an escape as part of the plan. I visited him, explained the plan; he was to bring me the firestrike once he found where it was hidden. The New Blasphemy priests hid it well, and we were running out of time. When I visited him he had *still* not located the spear. And our House sent the Chaser for my brother, and—"

"And I got involved. So you decided a little mindfucking was in order?" I couldn't help it. *I should kill her right now. Goddammit, she killed Mikhail and she's sitting on my goddamn couch. In his house, the house he gave to me. Goddammit.*

"I know you have reason to hate me," she said evenly. "You've killed my brother. Tit for tat, we're even. Are you happy? We have less than a day before the evocation of the Nameless will alter the balance of power in every Sorrows House in the *world*. Inez isn't just playing in your little city, hunter. She will be a new Queen Mother above even the Grand Mothers, and we will—"

I choked on my whiskey, my protest that he had cracked his own poison tooth with no help from me dying in my throat. "Wait just one goddamn second. Less than a day? But the end of the cycle isn't until—"

"It's tomorrow. Your calculations are off. They usually are, when you add the Gregorian calendar to the mix." Belisa's shoulders hunched even further. "We are doomed. All of us, doomed."

Oh, for Christ's sake. "I'm not going to give up yet. When *exactly* does the cycle end? Tomorrow, *when?*"

"At 1:15 P.M. And thirteen seconds." She eased the ice away from her face and took a gulp of the whiskey. She looked as dejected as it was possible for a Sorrow to look, but her black eyes were oddly empty. As if they were painted on.

Perry took a small mannerly sip, raised his eyebrows, and took another. But he was crackling with awareness; he looked ready to leap on Belisa if she so much as twitched. I found that comforting—but still, seeing her flinch away from him rubbed me the wrong way.

Hard.

I finished mine and reached for the bottle. The bottle neck chattered against the mouth of my glass. I poured myself a tall one.

"Jill?" Saul. Carefully, quietly, his *you want me to kill someone or what?* tone.

"One in the afternoon." I settled back on the couch, leather creaking. The charms in my hair chimed, shifting, the scar on my wrist pulsed as Perry's eyes rose to meet mine. Why was I looking at him? Because he was right in front of me, and I didn't want to look at Belisa. "Will freeing the human sacrifices help stop it?"

Belisa shrugged. "For an evocation of this nature, she would keep them close at hand. The ones you freed were probably decoys, or only to reward her human tools. You said they had been used?"

Used. What a pretty little euphemism. "They were raped." My voice was flat, and loaded with terrible anger. "Probably repeatedly." *They're probably going to need therapy for the rest of their lives.*

Belisa nodded. "And several of the victims were pregnant?"

I nodded. The ruby nestled in the hollow of my throat was comfortingly warm.

"Then it's simple." She took another gulp of whiskey. "The harvested fetal tissue is probably to provide a base matrix for the Unnamed's entrance and physicality. She's going to create a *Vatcharak*—an Avatar." Admiration, probably unconscious, shaded her voice. "The other organs went for cash to build her new House, and still others went to feed the creature. Which was insurance, I would guess. The chain around its neck carried a powerful control spell. I wonder if she created it herself?"

I don't know and I don't care. "Why dump the bodies?" Of all questions, that was probably the most useless, but the one I most wanted to have answered.

"Probably because she had run out of places to hide them. And also, every place where a victim of this evocation lay slain would become a node-point when she succeeds in bringing the Unnamed through."

"A node-point." *I sound shocked.* "Of course. So the Avatar could have ready-made taplines into the ambi-

ent energy of the city, draining it like an orange. Which
would widen the psychic scar in the ether and give it a *hell*
of a lot of power."

She nodded, like a teacher pleased with a good student.
"Very good. I begin to see why your file is red-flagged."

"Red-flagged? Forget it, I don't want to know. Why
did this bitch pick my city, huh?"

"You allow no House here. No House, no scrutiny by
other Sorrows who might discover her plans."

What, so it's my fault? I swallowed the flare of temper and closed my eyes, tilted my head back against the
couch, and swore inwardly. Blew out between pursed lips,
not quite a whistle. "Jesus *fucking* Christ."

"I can get almost every Were in this city ready in a few
hours," Saul said tentatively.

"And there are hellbreed who can be coerced—" Perry
began, his voice a dark thread, for once not supercilious.

Well, would you look at that. Even Perry's scared.
"Not enough time. And once this is dealt with, there'd be
a free-for-all I'd have to sort out." I sagged into the couch.
*Tired. So fucking tired. I need a vacation. God. How many
other graves are there out there, do you think? And other
bodies. God. Dear God.* "Why a wendigo?"

"I suspect she came across it in her travels and thought
it could be useful. She was in the Alps, and there have
been . . . stories." Belisa shuddered. *"Chutsharak."*

Curse my curiosity, I had to know. "What is a *chutsharak,* anyway?"

"It's House slang, not the ceremonial shorthand-
garbage you know. It means—well, the best translation
is, *oh fuck.*" Belisa managed to sound amused. "Or something of that nature. It depends on inflection."

Well, one mystery solved. For a moment I was tempted to just curl up on the couch and go to sleep. Just let whatever was going to happen, happen. The animal inside me just wanted to bury itself in a hole and sleep off the shakes and unsteadiness that came from almost-dying.

Silence crackled, tense and deadly. Unbidden, padding soft and clean into my head, came the sound of Mikhail's voice. Not singing the prayer in Russian, but growling it out in his accented English, every word a slap against the gray cotton of shock and apathy threatening to close over me. My own voice following along, uncertain and tired, but strong enough.

Cover me with Thy shield, and with my sword may Thy righteousness be brought to earth, to keep Thy children safe. Let me be the defense of the weak and the protector of the innocent, the righter of wrongs and the giver of charity. In Thy name and with Thy blessing, I go forth to cleanse the night.

That is what you swore, Mikhail's voice continued. *That is what you prayed. And that is what you will do, milaya.*

I gathered myself. When I opened my eyes I found Perry and Belisa staring at me. Black eyes and blue, waiting avidly. For what? It was in Perry's interest to keep me alive—at least, until he got tired of my resistance. And Belisa? If she could get me to distract this Inez bitch for long enough, she might have a shot at stepping into her shoes.

I rolled my head along the back of the couch, looked at Saul. He was staring into his glass, the musky smell of anger draining away. *Look at me, Saul. Please. Let me know what you're thinking.*

He might even have heard the thought, because he glanced at me, his mouth pulled tight in resignation. No, he wasn't happy at all. But he said nothing, merely giving the slight headshake that meant he would wait until we were alone.

Uh-oh. I made up my mind. "All right. Perry, you can take the Sorrow back to the Monde and wait for me. If all hell breaks lo—"

"No." Perry leaned against the back of the chair. Belisa cringed away from him, and bile rose in my throat. *Stop it. Don't feel sorry for her. That's like feeling sorry for the rattlesnake a bobcat's playing with.*

But still, she cringed just like a hooker waiting for a pimp's slap. And I knew what that felt like, didn't I.

Every blessed thing about this case seemed engineered to remind me what that fucking felt like.

"Excuse me?" The temperature might have dropped a few degrees, or it might have been my tone. "Last time I looked, Perry, you weren't the one in charge here."

"I brought you the Sorrow. You promised to stay in my sight for the duration." The scar on my arm prickled wetly, as if he had just licked it, and I steeled myself.

"I didn't—" I began.

Perry gestured languidly with the glass, his tone laden with flat finality. "The creature's dead. Very well, very good. But you are my investment, dear Kiss, and I am not about to let another little viper such as this one interfere with my very *interesting* plans for your education. That wouldn't be very wise of me, would it."

"You're not known for wisdom, Perry. A certain type of cunning, maybe, but not wisdom." It was out before I could stop myself. "Cut the crap. You want to go along?

Why should I let *you* wander into a fire zone where I'll have to split my focus between worrying about what's in front of me *and* worry about you slipping a knife into my back?"

Even I couldn't quite believe I'd said it. Saul didn't move, but I felt his attention sharpen, and reminded myself that he was Were. If Perry moved on me, Saul might try to stop him, and however fast and dangerous a Were was, a hellbreed who could produce flame in the blue spectrum was not my idea of a good time.

And I needed Saul alive.

Amazingly, Perry laughed. But Belisa was suddenly examining me, her mouth slightly open, as if a new thought had occurred to her.

"There are more enjoyable things to do than slip a knife between your ribs, my dear Kiss." He saluted me with his glass, then downed the rest of the whiskey, rolling it around in his mouth and swallowing. "Now, just tell us where the icky little Sorrows hidey-hole is, and we'll finish this matter and turn our attention to other things." He reached down and gently, delicately smoothed Melisande Belisa's sleek dark hair. "Like what I should do to teach this viper some manners. We have a room at the Monde specifically reserved for—"

White-hot rage boiled up. I snapped.

I had the gun out, barely aware of drawing it. I was on my feet, my shins hitting the coffee table with a short sharp sound. Then I'd leapt on the coffee table, still forward, and ended up with my feet between Belisa's, the gun pressed to Perry's forehead.

Oh, Jesus Christ, Jill, you stupid little prat.

I didn't look down. "Your services are no longer neces-

sary, Pericles," I informed him. Even, level, and with my
unprotected belly less than three feet away from a Sorrow
who probably wouldn't cry too much in her coffee if I
ended up with a serious case of dead.

*But she needs someone to take on Inez for her. That's
why she bothered meeting me at the hospital, that's why
she let Perry catch her, that's why she's still sitting here
instead of trying to escape. Isn't it?*

His eyes were so deeply, infinitely blue, indigo cloud-
ing the whites along traceries just like veins. His pale fingers tensed on the glass. "Put the gun down, Kismet."

*You will not take a woman into that room at the Monde
Nuit if I can prevent it. I have had enough of seeing women
raped tonight.*

That room at the Monde . . . I knew what it was used
for.

I'd seen it used. I'd seen what happened afterward.

My thumb reached up, pulled the hammer back. The
sound of the 9 mm cocking was very loud in the sudden
hush that seemed to have descended on the warehouse.
"Get. Out." I had to work to get the words out through the
obstruction in my throat. "Of my house. Get. *Out.*"

"I am losing patience with you, Jillian. Or should I call
you Judith? Didn't you prefer tha—"

Shock slammed through me. How did he know that?
How *could* he know that?

I *squeezed.*

Saul yelled, a short sharp cat-coughing bark of surprise. Perry fell, dropped like a stone. Blood gouted, so
much thick black blood, shooting a hellbreed in the head
is messy.

No more. My hands shook and my breath came hard and harsh. *No more.*

No more of it. No more women raped, no more mind-fucking, no more of it, *no goddamn more.* I could take no fucking more. And if it took killing Perry and slaughtering a houseful of Sorrows and an Elder God too, I would do it.

It was that motherfucking simple.

My hand dropped. The scar on my wrist began to burn, tearing in through my skin toward my bones. I looked down at Belisa, whose head was bowed. Her shoulders were shaking under the blue silk.

Don't worry, I wanted to say. *I fixed it. I stopped him. He won't hurt you now.*

The faint voice of rationality piped up. This was a *Sorrow,* the one who had killed my teacher. What the hell was I doing protecting her?

She's still a woman. And no woman deserves Perry, dammit. Or gang-rape by hellbreed. "Saul." My voice cracked, my throat denying itself a killing scream. "Go get the car warmed up."

"Jill—"

Goddammit, Saul, I'm not safe right now. I think I just did something stupid. "Do it."

He got up, I heard the couch squeak. Then he was gone. I heard the front door slam as I stepped back from the Sorrow who hunched in the chair, her hair falling forward over her face. The smell of rotting blood cooking in a gun barrel painted the air. My hands were shaking. *Point blank, you shot him point blank, hope that's enough. Pray that's enough.*

And under that, the other thought, repeating like a

bad record. *No more. Not to another woman. No fucking
more.*

"Belisa?" *I still sound like a stranger. What have I
done?* "Melisande?"

Her shoulders were still shaking. And God help me,
but my fingers tightened on the gun again, and it was all I
could do not to shoot her too.

"Goddammit, get up. Let's go. We've got a world to
save, you Chaldean bitch."

Then her face tipped up, her black eyes meeting
mine, and I saw she was laughing. Tears rolled down her
cheeks, and she smiled, a death's-head grin that told me
she was having a hell of a good time. Her hand stabbed
forward, the broken glass ampoule spewing something
that smelled oddly sweet; my body sagged, not hitting the
floor because of her slim iron arms around my waist. Her
fingers were at my throat, I heard a snap as she tore the
ruby away and tossed it, its sweet chime as it hit the floor.
I choked on the poison and heard her laughter ring in the
rafters. She laughed as if she had just heard the world's
funniest joke.

Laughed, in fact, fit to die.

Blackness. I floated.

*I'm dead. Any minute now I'll see Hell again. I'll sink
into it, and they'll start on me, every hellbreed I've killed,
everyone I've laid to rest. I'll start screaming, and it will
never end, and I'll be back on the streetcorner with the
wind on the back of my legs and that car coming toward
me. I will. In a moment. When I finish being dead.*

Something hard against my back. Cold hardness seeping into my skin. My nerves were on fire with pain, creeping up my arms and legs. Any minute now I would wake up to find myself in Hell. There was no reason to fight it. I was dead.

Dead. Floating in a blackness that started to sting in all my fingers and toes, as if I was wrestling with a jellyfish.

Belisa. The traitorous bitch.

Did she kill me? Why? She wanted me for a diversion so she could take out this Inez bitch.

Didn't she?

A nagging little idea began growing in the back of my mind. I tried to push it away, to concentrate on being dead, but it wouldn't go away.

The file on you is red-flagged for a reason. She had given a picture-perfect imitation of being scared to death of Perry, and she probably had been. One false move, one note out of tune, and he might have killed her before he could bring her to me. I certainly wouldn't put it past him. But she'd had an ampoule of something. Poison, the Sorrows trademark. Poison in word, deed, and fact.

Belisa knew too much. This was, again, Mikhail's voice. *Far too much. How she know what the redhead bitch is planning? And here is thought, milaya, is there reason why you haven't seen zis redhead Sorrow yet? There's such a thing as wigs.*

But that made no sense, did it? Nothing about this made much sense.

Wake up, kitten. The tone of my conscience changed, mutated into a voice I knew as well as my own, deep and soft. Saul's voice, whispered in my ear. At least he'd been outside when Belisa made her move. *Time to wake up. Come on.*

But I was dead, and I was so *tired*. So goddamn tired of it all. Being a hunter is just one disgusting fight after another, and there were endlessly inventive ways people could be shot, stabbed, tortured, burned, hurt. Every hunter got tired of seeing it, even if we were luckier than the cops who only dealt with humans. A hunter had to remind himself—or herself—about *why* we did this. Why we put ourselves through this.

Well, why, cream puff? This time the voice wasn't Saul's or Mikhail's. It was another voice, one I knew very well, the voice of a man who had picked up a lonely shivering girl and made her feel worthwhile, made her feel *loved,* before he'd turned her out on the street and set her to earning her keep. *Why d'ya do it at all, then?*

I didn't want to hear Val; I'd *killed* him. I pushed that voice away with an effort so hard it felt physical, heard a shapeless sound. It sounded like someone was moaning, coming to, swimming up out of dark water. Metal clashed, and the fierce cold against my back and my heels ratcheted up another notch. It burned across my buttocks, my shoulders, digging into the back of my head and my neck. And the inside of my right wrist hurt, a sharp stabbing pain.

Oh, *shit*. Maybe I wasn't dead.

Val's voice wouldn't go away. *Why d'ya do it, baby-doll? Huh? You don't do it to save the world or any fucking shit like that. You want to know why you put yourself through this?*

I pushed that voice away again. I knew why I did it. I didn't need to be reminded.

Why are you a hunter, kitten? Saul's voice, on the edge of breaking. We did fight, sometimes volcanically, and he had asked me once or twice *why* I seemed so determined to fling myself into the worst trouble I could find. There's no retirement plan for hunters—none of us live that long. There's also no Higher Authority, even though the Church trains a lot of us. If a hunter wants to quit he just *quits,* just disappears. You aren't a hunter because you're forced into it, or because you fill out an application and have to find a replacement.

No, a hunter *chooses* to put his body on the line. And each hunt is another conscious choice. Nobody would blame you if you stopped, backed out, laid down the sword, and walked away. As a matter of fact, that was the sanest option—part of finding an apprentice is doing everything possible to dissuade the candidate from even thinking about taking the training.

We all do zis for one reason, milaya. It is for to quiet ze screaming in our dreams. It is for to kill our own demons. And they call us heroes. Idiots. Mikhail, again. Why was I hearing voices? I could even smell him. Vodka metabolizing out through the skin, the smell of someone raised in a different climate, foreign darkness and the smell of his hair as he leaned over me to correct my form, the copper charms tied in his hair tinkling sweetly.

His voice dropped to a whisper in the very center of my head. *Now is time for ze waking up, milaya. Wake up.*

I didn't want to. I wanted only to drift. But the stinging in my fingers and toes sharpened, as if they were coming back to life.

As if I was coming back to life.

If you do not wake up, milaya, I will hit you.

I lunged into consciousness, fully aware and awake, because when Mikhail said that he never lied. Metal clashed as I tried to leap to my feet, springing up—and was grabbed mercilessly at wrists and ankles, my head hitting cold stone as I was yanked back. Stars slammed through my head, actual bright points of light.

Shit. Oh shit.

I was on my back on cold, hard stone that felt glassy, like obsidian. And I was chained, the cold cuffs closed around ankles and wrists. Stretched out like a virgin sacrifice.

Well, if that's what they wanted they certainly have the wrong girl. My forlorn little laugh half-choked its way out of my throat, I blinked, breathed in a long lungful of air so cold it burned, and looked around.

I pulled against the chains first. No give, and they were orichalc-tainted titanium, just the thing to hold down a hellbreed-strong hunter. Stronger than they had any right to be, and probably with staples driven deep into the granite of the floor and concrete underneath. I pulled all four chains until I was sure I couldn't just wriggle out. It wasn't likely, but sometimes even Sorrows made mistakes.

Not this Sorrow. A respectable foe, smart, accurate, canny, and unwilling to take chances. Just my luck. The chains were too tight for me to pop a shoulder out of its socket and wriggle around, too.

Dammit.

Vaulted ceiling, made of poured concrete, ribbed and beautiful, in perfect proportion. Hammered into the concrete were the Forms, the squiggles and sharp curves carved and filled with thick gold wire, glinting as they channeled etheric force. The place was humming, alive with sorcerous power.

By craning my head I could see the floor was granite

blocks fitted precisely together, and was also full of wrist-thick gold lines twisting; the altar was inside a square, set inside a pentacle, set inside a triple circle that held the Nine Seals, each in its prescribed place. Between the pentacle's outer orbit and the beginning of the triple circle was another smaller altar, this one curved like a dolphin's back without the fin. Channels were carved into this concrete curve, deep fresh channels that were already dark and crusted.

The first sacrifices had already been performed.

Candles burned, their flames hissing in the dimness. Candles that smelled sickish-sweet. In the trade they are called perfect-tallow.

The layman would call them, with respectable horror, *made of human fat*.

"Christ," I whispered, and the sound bounced off the high vaulted roof. There were braziers, and heat simmered up from each of them. This little hole hadn't come cheap, especially with all the gold. She must have funneled an amazing amount of cash into it.

Perhaps the final indignity was that I was naked except for the leather cuff buckled securely over the scar—*under* the chain-cuff. My ruby was gone, and I could tell the silver ring Mikhail had given me was gone too. The silver charms in my hair, each one painstakingly braided in with red thread, were gone as well. There was no comforting weight of silver in my ears either.

Which made me feel even more naked.

Crap. Well, I'm still alive, aren't I? That's one. But the sinking sensation under my breastbone just wouldn't go away. Because if Belisa had drugged me, stripped me of my jewelry, and dragged me here, there was only one reason why.

The deep sharp blood-channels cut into the smooth glassy surface of the altar underneath me told me just what they had planned for me.

Saul. Did she hurt Saul? How did she get me here? I shut my eyes. *Don't panic, Jill. Don't you fucking dare panic.*

How could I not panic? Had she hurt Saul? *Had* she? Or had she just dragged me out of there, content to elude him?

The prayer rose under the surface of my mind. *Thou Who hast given me strength to fight evil, protect me. Keep me from harm. Grant me strength in battle, honor in living, and a quick clean death when my time comes—*

"Fuck that," I whispered. I didn't want to die at all.

There had to be something I could do. Even if the preliminary sacrifices had already been performed, I still had at least an hour. Or at least, I hoped I did.

Time to think fast.

25

The stone was cold and my head hurt. I kept my eyes closed and my breathing steady, and the scar had turned hot. *Very* hot. As if a blowtorch was held against it, the skin crisping and turning black, burning down to bone but never quite getting there, *burning.*

Was Perry dead? Probably. I'd shot him in the head with silver-coated ammo. If he wasn't dead he was very unhappy—and unlikely to forgive me. He would probably peel the scar off me himself, and overload my nervous system with sick wriggling pleasure while he did it.

If he does that, Jillian, you'll be alive to feel it. Which will mean you'll have escaped this. So don't worry about it right now.

The scar was *hot.* And when the first acrid scent of burning found its way to my nostrils I was elated—but not so happy my concentration slipped.

Fire, from a hellbreed mark. Part of the bargain, even if Perry was mad at me.

He shouldn't have called me that. Shouldn't have

threatened to have a woman raped, even if it was a Sorrow.

The thought disturbed my concentration, but the heat didn't slip. I heard a rustling, and swallowed hard, opening my eyes just as the last shred of the tough battered leather charred. I couldn't see it under the metal cuff that held my arm stretched at an awkward angle, just in the precise place that robbed me of any leverage. It was the same with my legs.

The Sorrows are good at trussing people up.

The soft sounds were velvet capes, brushing the floor. I heard another soft, chilling sound.

A long drugged moan, impossible to tell if the voice was male or female. The cold air brushed my skin, and I shivered.

The sudden wash of sensation from the scar was enough to make gooseflesh rise all over my body. I could, if I wanted to, look down and see if my nipples were hard.

A fine time to be naked and chained to an altar, Jill. With you the fun times never end. I drew in a long soft breath, watching as they came in two by two.

Two. Four. Six. Eight.

I was beginning to get a very bad feeling about this. I had assumed that Inez was a rogue Sorrow, but that was because Belisa had told me so. For there to be more than one Sorrow here was bad, bad news. Which one of the robed bitches was the one who had killed my teacher and maneuvered me so neatly?

Ten. Twelve; these two carrying between them a long pale shape that was a woman's body. The shapeless moan came again, it was from *her*. Drugged.

Oh, thank God, she won't feel a thing if I can't save her in time. Christ, how am I going to get out of this?

They were hooded and draped in black-blue velvet, but the thirteenth entered with her hood thrown back. A sleek shock of darkish hair glowed with bloody highlights in the candlelight, and she walked to one of the brass braziers—the one nearest the curved sacrificial altar—and tossed something in. Sizzling filled the air for a moment, then sweet smoke billowed out.

Ambergris. Amber. And clove.

The incense of evocation. My skin chilled again. I was going to go into shock.

Stop it, Jillian. Listen. Look. Plan.

What plan? I was trussed up tighter than a Christmas turkey. But the stink of charred leather told me I wasn't completely helpless.

Think, Jill. And open your goddamn eyes.

"It won't help, you know." Her voice was soft, accented with fluid French and wrapping its velvety ends around me; digging in, squeezing, looking for a way inside. She glided up to the altar on cat-soft feet, this blood-haired Sorrow.

I found myself looking at a strong-jawed, not unpleasant face; her eyes were black from lid to lid and the bruising of her aura was deep and severe. I caught a whiff of something else, too, a fume that shimmered out from her robe in waves of olfactory scarlet and gold.

She was far more than a Sorrows adept. That fume could only mean one thing.

I was looking at a Grand Mother of a House of Sorrows, one of the most efficient praying mantises the world has ever seen. Just one step below a Queen Mother, a brooding termite capable of hiving off Houses and *calling* potential suicides to her as Sorrows Neophyms.

In other words, I was in deep fucking shit.

My brain jittered like a rabbit; I inhaled sharply, and she smiled. Set just under her hairline, above and between her eyes, was her mark: the three circles, the black flame, and a colorless glitter that was the seal of a Grand Mother.

I cleared my throat. "Inez Germaine, I presume." My voice was harsh, cracked, and only human after the softness of hers. Like the cawing of a raven after a dulcet song.

Quit it, Jill. She's a fucking Sorrows mantis, she'll chew you up if you're not careful. I gave her my most winning smile. She was going to have to work harder than that to squeeze her way in through my mental defenses. I was toughened by so many exorcisms that I wasn't even sure I could let something in if I wanted to.

I didn't want to test that theory, though. Not at all.

She put one hand down, and a velvet sleeve brushed my belly as her fingers closed around my left breast. I made my face a mask, but she smiled, a very gentle smile that sat incongruously on her strong face. Her thumb moved a little. "Inez Germaine Ayasha, if you wish to be specific." She paused, examining me thoroughly; scalp to toenails. If I'd been embarrassed by nakedness, now would have been the time to show it. But dating a Were will give you a whole new definition of naked, and having a hellbreed kiss on your wrist will too.

But her hand let go of my breast, trailed down my ribs. I sucked in a shallow breath. *No.*

Her fingertips brushed my belly, passing over old

ridged scars and the furrows of abdominal muscle from hard training. I was too stringy, really, not much room for big curves when you're fighting like hell all the time and having a hard time taking in enough protein to fuel that sort of muscle burn.

Sometimes I wondered if Saul would have liked me a little softer. A little more feminine.

The touch lightened as she brushed my pubic hair. *"Tranquille, enfante,"* she murmured. Calmly, lovingly. "I would not crack so fine a vessel."

Her fingers dipped, and my entire body closed. My eyes rolled up into my head, and I curled up into the quiet space inside my own head. That space was small, and dark, and smelled like a kid's closet stuffed with shoes and plush animals. Bad things could batter at the door, men could howl outside, but inside I was safe.

It was the space that I used to go to whenever Saul touched me. With Mikhail it had been heat and combat, but with Saul . . . it had been gentleness.

He had coaxed me out with infinite patience, one night at a time, holding me when I sobbed. Stroking my hair, reassuring me, easing me along. Until I could have my body belong to me again, and like anything that belonged to me it could be shared.

But not now. Now I didn't want to share. I went rigid, sweating, my jaw so tight my teeth ground and sang a thin song of agony, red and black explosions playing out behind my eyelids as she probed with first one finger, then another.

I made a low harsh sound. Metal clashed as I struggled, hit my head against the stone altar, and suddenly knew that if she kept going I would beat my skull against the stone until one of us broke.

And I didn't think it would be the altar.

She finally returned her black eyes to my face, sliding her fingers free and stroking my belly again with the flat of her palm. "You should have been born into a House, *cherie*." Her tone was gentle, kind. "We would have known how to bring out the best in such a . . . delicate temperament as yours, without causing such regrettable side effects."

High praise, from a Sorrow. "Horseshit." *If you think I'm going to beg, bitch, think again.* "Nice trick, sending Belisa to play the Sorrow in distress. That brother bit almost got me."

"Melisande's brother was genuine. I picked both of them, *ma cherie*." The smile widened. "So brave." Her fingers stroked, came back up to cup my breast, and I could feel that my nipple was indeed hard. Hard as a chunk of rock.

Goddammit. But six years of Perry's scar burning on my wrist and his fiddling with my internal thermostat was now paying off in prime. My heartrate stayed the same, though my breathing was a little harsher than I liked. I felt soul-bruised, savagely stretched, and just one thin hair away from raped.

If I belong to me, then I can share or not share, and I don't want to share with you, you bitch.

Besides, if she wanted to mindfuck me with just a paper file to work from, she was going to have to work for it. Perry was harder to deal with.

No he isn't, goddammit. Perry's interested in seeing you remain breathing so he can break you. This bitch is

*going to kill you anyway; she's calling you "dear" as if
you're her Neophym. You're dead. Get something for your
pains, Jill.*

"The bodies were to draw me out and create taplines."
I sounded steady. Steady enough for being chained naked
to a rock. "Belisa was just to spice the mix, draw me in,
keep me around. But why the wendigo?"

She laughed, a marvelously soft sound. I sucked in a
deadly breath as her warm fingers continued to stroke my
breast. "You think I'm going to make the mistake car-
toon villains make and tell you my plans while you work
on burning away that ridiculous leather bracelet?" She
tweaked my nipple with her fingertips, I kept a straight
face. Heard more soft moans.

Oh, God. They're starting the second sequence.

"I see the lamb's voice disturbs you more than mine
does, hunter. The wendigo was a useful tool, and its habits kept you looking in the wrong place. But your first
encounter with it was carefully scripted."

"You were on the roof with a bow." I sounded bored.
But I wanted to look past her to the curving altar. Con-
trolled myself. "Killing your own employees."

"They were men, my darling. Useful, expendable, but
overwhelmingly useless—"

"I'm female, and just as expendable." Interrupting a
Grand Mother is a good way to piss her off; they were
the rulers of their Houses. Big egos and big brains, not to
mention enough sorcerous ability to power a blimp. Her
eyes were so *black,* from lid to lid, infinite holes in her
pleasant face. Deep. So deep.

The scar on my arm was growing hotter by the moment, as if Perry had breathed on it, turning it to lava. I

could almost feel acidic saliva trickling down my wrist, too. The pain scored up my arm, jolted me out of the sticky web of her eyes.

"You, *ma belle,* are not expendable. You are my greatest achievement. The pregnant victims were selected for fetal tissue, yes, but that tissue has already been harvested and sold to the highest bidder. They paid for the vault over your head."

Well, that's a fucking relief. Thanks for giving me that wonderful piece of news. I was beginning to get a very bad feeling about this. "You're doing an evocation," I said flatly. "And you want me to be the host for your psychotic little fucknut of a—"

The blow came out of nowhere, smashing across my cheek, my head rang and I saw stars again. Then her fingers were back on my breast, caressing, kneading my flesh. I felt a warm trickle of blood trace down my chin and rolled my head back to look at her. "Damaging the merchandise, bitch." My voice was husky.

"You are merely required to be whole, not undamaged. Think of it. One of the Old Ones, the *summa* of negation, inside a body—a female body, a body capable of creation and destruction, a body strengthened with a hellbreed mark and possessing a soul gifted with murder and mayhem in the finest degree? You are a fit vessel, and once you are filled there will be enough blood, enough *destruction,* to remake this world as it once was. The Elder Gods will live through you, hunter." Her smile was calm, beautiful, and so sane it was crazed, and I began to *really* get a bad feeling about this.

I heard the last breathless sigh of the drugged woman near the door. *Oh, God. Please, God. No.* Then a terribly final *cessation,* the act of slitting the throat down to the vertebrae. And the gurgle of life and blood leaving the body.

The golden marks on the ceiling writhed, a fresh humming charge flooding them. "Try again, you bitch," I whispered. "I'm a hunter. Your Chaldean filth won't stick to me."

"A hunter who has just killed a dozen men." Inez Germaine's smile broadened. She stroked my breast once more, lovingly, and I jagged in a sharp breath. The gentle touch reminded me of Saul, something I couldn't afford. "You slaughtered them like pigs, *bebe.* You heard the screams for mercy and you disregarded them. You were judge, jury, and executioner, you took your God's place."

It wasn't like that. "I did not."

"You killed them, didn't you?"

"They were your accessories. Willing, in Jonte's case. Unwitting in others. But they were—"

"We're all aware of your feelings about pimps, Judith."

That *name* again, the name of a dead girl. The air left me as if I'd been punched. Oh, Belisa had gotten her money's worth when she'd rifled Mikhail's private papers.

Stop it, the voice of reason said, desperately. *Stop it. Of course she's dug that up. You aren't her anymore. That girl died and you came back from Hell. That's not you.*

But my voice was ragged. "Cogs in a wheel, bitch. One steps out, the next steps in. Try another sticky-finger attempt to get inside my head. You've failed."

"Pas necessaire." The smile that broke over her face now was a marvel of sincere serenity. I heard more vel-

vet shushing and another slow, disoriented moan. Another victim. The second sequence.

The touch on my breast gentled. "The ritual will proceed, *cherie belle*. And when you look in the face of the Old One who will inhabit you, we will see how much your protests avail you." A final gentle tweaking of my nipple and she was gone, shushing back in her long velvet robe. The sound of the candles hissed, and there was another soft gurgle as blood spilled, steaming, into the air. The copper reek thickened.

I looked up at the ceiling. Golden marks revolved in their stately dance, thick gold wire scoring new channels through the concrete, twisting and healing their former runnels without a sigh. And as soon as Inez Germaine cleared the square around the altar, the golden border of the square flushed with etheric force and began to move too.

By the end of the second sequence of sacrifices the pentacle would be revolving as well. Then the third sequence, but that one would be the harvested death Inez was carrying behind her black eyes, ready to release with a Word. A Word in Chaldean, which would charge the Nine Seals and the triple circle, containing the psychic force and enforcing the collective will of the Sorrows hive on the space inside.

After that, the final sequence, which would rip open a hole in the fabric of reality. And I was right at ground zero. A tasty little snack.

Her voice was soft and utterly merciless, dropping into my head like a bean into a furrow. Ready to germinate, the seed of doubt. *You slaughtered them like pigs, bebe. You heard screams for mercy and you disregarded them. You were judge, jury, and executioner, you took your God's place.*

And what had I told Saul? Told him to go to the barrio, because I didn't want him to see what I was capable of. What I could do, once I decided it was *necessary.*

My breath hissed in my throat. Hopeless. It was fucking hopeless. Nothing left to do but pray.

Cover me with Thy shield, and with my sword may Thy righteousness be brought to earth, to keep Thy children safe. Let me be the defense of the weak and the protector of the innocent—

I balked, sheer stubbornness rising up under the words, shunting the prayer aside. It would work when I was gearing up to face Perry, but not now. Not now. Oh God, not now, I didn't want to die like this, stretched out like bad fantasy-novel art on a moldy old twenty-five-cent paperback.

I was going to die.

Fury rose in me. *Shit on that, Jillian Kismet. Shit all over that. You're a hunter, there's work to do and your city to save. Think up a way to get out of this one, you stupid whore. You didn't even tell Saul where her little bolthole is. How could you be so stupid? Assuming, of course, that Belisa left Saul alive.*

Another breath, this one deeper and smoother.

You're chained naked to an altar and they're killing people over there, and there's a Sorrows Grand Mother who is crazy as a bedbug with a thumb in your door. And all hell's about to break loose.

It wasn't working. Panic set in. I thrashed, once, twice, the chains jangled.

I heard it again, the gurgle of another life wasted.

Women, probably, the reserve Inez had kept here in this place, a Sorrows House hidden so wonderfully well in my own city. Hidden so well I hadn't had a clue—but I'd been busy since spring, hadn't I? Dreadfully busy. A spike in violence and crime that was a clear sign of Sorrows moving in, with twenty-twenty hindsight I could solve *every* fucking problem, couldn't I?

They were killing people. People from my city. *My* people.

But why should you care? You killed eleven of them last night. Not twelve, like that bitch said—unless you count Perry and he's not a pimp, he's a hellbreed. Just one step up from a pimp in my personal pantheon of evil, but still.

The voice was soft, seductive, stroking me. *Why should you care, Jill? Why should you care how many they kill?*

"Mine," I whispered, and closed out the sound of the candles burning and the sudden hiss as someone threw a gout of incense into another brazier. "My city. *My* city."

Santa Luz was *my* city; and whoever was in it—especially anyone a Sorrow would want to sacrifice—was under my protection. *I* kept the law in my city, goddammit, and if this jumped-up praying mantis thought she was going to kill pregnant hookers and Mob bosses in my town and without my say-so, she had another think coming.

But doesn't that make you just like them, Jill? Doesn't it? You decide who lives, who dies? Judge, jury, executioner?

The scar on my wrist turned excruciatingly hot. Pain rolled up my arm, a great golden glassy spike of pain. The scream burst from me, raw, wrecked, and agonized, like the dying scream of the wendigo. I'd killed it too, hadn't

I? No matter that Saul had held the spear, I had caused its death.

Who was I to decide that?

I am the law, goddammit! I protect them, the innocents. I am the sword of righteousness.

But I'd murdered, hadn't I? Eleven pimps. Eleven *men*, never mind that they'd given me the information I needed. Never mind that the world was probably better off without them.

Cogs in a wheel, bitch. The world is not better off without them. More will rise to take their place.

And with every pimp I killed I bought some hooker on a corner a little breathing room. Not much, not ever enough—but some.

It was worth it.

I sagged against the altar's cold unforgiving glass at my back. The chains clashed. The golden marks on the ceiling were twisting madly now, running with the black crackling lightning of Chaldean sorcery.

Another gurgle. Guilt slammed through me, a hot steamy nauseous guilt. I had fallen right into the trap, and people were dying for it. Innocent people.

I tilted my head over, tucking my chin, and *looked*.

Black lightning ate the body whole once the blood had been spilled. Where there had been a pale human form, veined in black fire, now there was nothing; the etheric discharge of death, visible through my blue eye, was trapped and funneled, the soul tearing itself free and disappearing, the etheric strings holding it to the body snapped. Cleanly severed. The wendigo's violence and reek had covered up the signs of theft on the other bodies. How many of them? How much death was the blood-haired bitch carrying?

No wonder she's fucking mad, I thought, and it was like a slap of freezing water.

They dragged another drugged naked form in, and ice slammed through me. Pure, clean, marvelous ice, the little *click* as I disconnected again, taking off, rising. Becoming that other person, the Jill Kismet who could go from house to house like the Angel of Death, sparing and striking according to her will.

The girl had long sandy hair, and was drugged out of her mind. She didn't struggle, but suddenly it wasn't her I was seeing. It was another girl, with long brown hair and a severely bruised face, whose ankles were thin and bruised too, who flinched when I yelled.

Oh, dear God. I knew it wasn't Cecilia; she was with Avery. Or at least, so I hoped.

But goddammit, the light wasn't good, and when I looked at the pale body they bent back over the curved altar all I could see was Cecilia's face. The face of a tired young hooker who had once been a bright needy little girl, who had escaped from Hell between four walls of a home and found a different hell out in the cold world, in backseats and hotel rooms and up against walls and wherever a dark corner could be found and sometimes, not even then.

And under Cecilia's face, I saw another face. A face of a girl with dark hair and brown eyes, a very intelligent but terribly crippled child who had grown up too fast.

She's dead, Jill. The only one left alive is you. She went into Hell and you came back.

I struggled, but silently. Pulled. *Pulled.*

I pulled against the chains, my breath coming out in a long *huuuuuungh!* of effort, veins popping out and muscles protesting. The scar turned white-hot, agony bolting up my arm, and I heard a slight groan of overstressed metal.

I was still looking when they tipped her head back, the vulnerable curve of her throat glaring-white in the smoky dimness. More incense had been thrown on the braziers. The air crackled with humming etheric force, the thick golden wires whispering now as they remade themselves, livid lurid golden fire writhing and undulating through granite floor and concrete vault.

They use curved knives, the Sorrows. Curved black obsidian blades, with hammered gold in the blood groove.

I screamed as the knife descended, my cry taking on physical shape and smashing through the incense smoke, my back arching as if in the throes of orgasm. I convulsed with every iota of strength, mental, physical, *everything,* straining, tearing at the prison of metal around my wrists. My left shoulder popped, tendons savagely stretched, almost dislocating itself, and I heard a scream of metal stretching and stone bubbling hot. Heat blasted up, reflecting from the altar's surface and careering across the cold vault in a gunpowder flash.

Inez Germaine Ayasha laughed, and she pronounced the Word in Chaldean that set loose the third sequence and tore the three circles into screaming life.

Then everything broke loose.

I think I passed out. At least momentarily. But that moment contained a lifetime.

Darkness enfolded me, smothered me, pressed down deep upon me. A bulging pressed obscenely against the fabric of the physical world. Spacetime curving, the black curved mirror *slanting,* a pregnant hollow of cancerous pus as something, sensing its time was near, strained to be let out. Strained to rip through etheric and physical reality, strained to unzip the barrier of the world and step through. There had been much work to prepare for this, much toil and suffering, and there was a body ripe for the taking. A matrix of probabilities meshed, caught, turned . . . and *tipped.*

It dropped like a baby's head into the waiting hollow of the pelvis, descending preparatory to labor. The mother draws a deep breath, relieved for the moment, unconscious that around the corner lies the straining of birth.

And then, it *pushed.*

Screaming, torn past rationality, an animal shriek as if my guts were ripping out on glassy sharp claws. Screaming as if the veil had been torn away and I'd seen the naked face of existence leering down at me.

Maybe I had.

The howl was an animal's, yet it shaped *words,* a language that had not been spoken since the War between the Chaldean gods and the Imdárak, the Lords of the Trees. The Imdárak were gone, their victory in banishing the Chaldeans from this plane Pyrrhic in the extreme, something only whispered faintly of between hunters, passed down in the dead of night as part of a hunter's inheritance. Yet I screamed aloud in that language, tearing my vocal cords until the screaming trailed off in a long rasping gurgle as if my throat was cut.

It bore down on me. An immense weight, seeking to get *in,* to crush me and fill me, boiling wine trying to shatter the cup it was poured into. Or lava, forcing its way through a brittle stony crust. Forcing its way into me, to possess me.

Something in me resisted. A hard piece of tinfoil between the teeth, a small germ of irritation, a pinprick to a creature this mighty. Every exorcism I'd ever done—had it felt like this to the victims? Locks smashed, drawers pulled out, mental furniture reduced to matchsticks, personality shredded, *breaking,* the essence that was me stretching in a thin film over something too horrible to be described, like the shape of a monster under a blanket that is so instantly *wrong* you know it cannot be human.

Is nothing even close to human.

Then, pain. Fresh pain, a slice straight through the middle of me. A fist curled in my hair and *yanked,* metal snapping at my wrists and ankles, and I spilled off the altar in a boneless heap, my head hitting granite with skullcracking force. The gurgle died in my throat, giving way to a whimper.

Like a beaten dog, whining in the back of its throat.

"No," Perry's almost-familiar voice said, and the scar on my wrist suddenly turned blowtorch-hot again under the metal of the broken cuffs. And every pain in the world was suddenly a thin imitation of this agony, excruciating because it was physical and yet a relief because it wasn't the soul-destroying violation of my innermost self.

"She is *mine,*" the voice continued, calmly but with a terrible weight of anger. "Signed, sealed, and witnessed, Elder. She is not for you."

The world stopped on its axis, though I could now hear other sounds. Crimson sparks danced behind my eyes, and I heard clashing, screams, and the coughing roar of a Were in battle-fury. *Saul?* My dazed brain staggered.

The *thing* spoke again, a long string of those horrible, horrible alien sounds. I cowered, chains clashing as I clapped my numb hands over my bleeding ears and huddled against something solid. Something absurdly comforting, twin hardnesses poking into my ribs, as if I was at the foot of a statue. I choked on blood and bile, drew in a shuddering breath, and the scar turned to liquid on my arm. Pleasant oiled honey, sliding under my skin. Soothing.

OhGodplease let it be over, please let it be over. I sobbed without restraint, huddling down and making myself as small as I could.

"Let's ask her, shall we?" Perry's voice turned cheerful, razor-edged with sheer goodwill, and I flinched. I knew that tone. I knew that voice, though I had never heard it unveiled in its full aching power before. "I think she likes me better. But then, I'm handsomer."

More screams, more sounds of bloodshed, the steady roar of an enraged Were doubling, trebling. How many were there? *Saul? Is that you? Oh, God. God help me.*

It was my first coherent thought, and I welcomed it, even as I clung to someone's feet. My eyes cleared, bit by bit. The air was full of ambergris, clove, copal, and a horrid, foul, rotting stench; a smell so alien the brain shuddered each time it drifted across the nasal receptors. *Oh, God. God, thank you. Thank you.*

It spoke again, that sound tearing at the world. With it, quiet seemed to envelop us, the choking quiet of a nuclear winter.

A laugh like a flaming steel sword to the heart. "How very crass, Elder. Wherever you have been, you have not learned manners. No wonder they banished you. Did you not hear me the first time? I said *no*. This one is *mine*. See?"

The scar bloomed hotly again, and I moaned against his feet. Spilled over onto my back, my body not obeying me but I had to look, had to see. He was hellbreed, and he was *dangerous,* but he was better than that . . . that *thing*.

Perry stood, his hands in his gray trouser pockets, immaculate as always. There was an angry red healing mark on his forehead, perfectly placed, and his blue eyes blazed with holocaust flame over the indigo spreading through the whites like a cobra's hood. I was looking from beneath, from the floor, so he seemed taller than he should have, and thinner, and his face was full of a wasted light like the dying of the sun on a knife-cold winter day. His pale hair had become a halo, and a breeze touched my face, choking with the smell of dusty feathers and spoiled, rotten honey. I heard buzzing—wasps? angry hornets? flies?—and couldn't tell where it came from. He stood straight and slim as a sword, and his face was no longer bland but terribly, sharply beautiful.

Beautiful in the same way a mushroom cloud or the sterile white light of reaction is beautiful. A devouring beauty.

Above the altar, darkness pulsed. Only it wasn't darkness. It was like the wendigo, shapes running like ink on wet paper. Shapes that were so completely divorced from the geometry of our normal space that I tried to throw up again, seeing them twist and try to leap free.

If that carnivorous thing broke through . . .

It spoke very softly, the words still dimpling and scoring the fabric of reality. But it was fading, drawing away like the cry of a distant train. It was no less menacing and alien.

Perry shrugged. It was a marvel of Gallic fluidity, that shrug, expressing resignation and uncaring disinterest. "Perhaps. But you are *there,* and I am *here,* and I own *this.*" His foot moved slightly, nudging my hip now since I had turned onto my back. The scar boiled with spiked honey, pleasure creeping up my arm and spilling down my chest. Soothing, calming. I heard my own shapeless, helpless moan again.

Just like one of the drugged victims they had slit open.

Oh, God. God help me.

The thing replied with a thick burping chuckle, like poisonous mud boiling. I twitched against the sound, the raw places inside my head stinging under another salted lash.

"Empty threats bore me, Elder. Go contemplate cold eternity elsewhere. It is *our* time now."

Reality closed together like a camera lens shutter, and I convulsed as it tried to drag me, but Perry's foot came down on the skein of my hair, nailing me in place with a jolt. A soon as the telescoping hole closed I shuddered again, strength spilling back into my bones.

But not enough. Nowhere near enough.

Perry glanced over his shoulder, gauging the situation. Then he squatted, his left hand dangling, his right reaching down to thread through my hair. There was no silver for him to avoid. He made a fist, pulling my head up. My throat curved helpless, and the cold floor scorched my hip, my back, my buttocks, my heels. "Look at this," he said softly. "My poor darling."

His blue eyes burned into my brain, even as the scar writhed with curdled pleasure. "Here." A jolt smashed through me, as if I was in cardiac arrest and had defib applied. I cried out, weakly, the cuffs on my ankles and wrists chiming and clattering against the floor.

Just like a newborn screaming.

"My poor, poor Kiss," he whispered. "Look at this mess."

I was getting very tired of him saying that. I couldn't help myself. "Saul," I whispered in reply.

Perry's face didn't change, but I flinched nonetheless. "Oh, stop it." He sounded annoyed. "You'll tire of him soon enough. Can you stand?"

I'll sure as hell give it a try. "No . . . dancing," I managed, in a thick choked voice sounding not at all like myself. "For a . . . while."

He actually laughed, a chilling, happy little chuckle. "Brave to the last. Stand, I'll help."

The growling of Weres had subsided. Now I heard only moans and the soft low thunder of still-angry shapeshifters; the battle was evidently won. He slid his arm behind my shoulders and picked me up as if I weighed less than nothing. I'm tall for a girl, and muscular, but he handled me as if I was made of straw.

Or spun glass.

"One moment." His fingers curled around the metal of the cuff over my right wrist, sank in and twisted. He tore the metal as if it was cardboard, freeing my hand. Then he closed his warm fingers over my wrist, the scar pulsing in his palm. My head lolled, resting against his shoulder. "There. Isn't that better?" The fabric of his suit was expensive, rich, soothing against my cheek, and I felt muscle flicker underneath as he stroked my hair. Warmth spilled through me, strength like wine flooding through my abused flesh. Unhealthy strength, like the jitter of a drug smashing through my system—but I'd take it.

Perry sighed. "Just relax."

Delicious, wonderful safety spilled down my skin. "Saul," I whispered against Perry's suit.

"The cat is in fine form, little one. No worries. We have averted a little unpleasantness. I think we shall renegotiate your visits to me, no? Come. Walk. You can walk."

"Ch-chains—" I was trying to tell him to take the other cuffs off.

"Let them be a reminder," he replied, inexorably. "You should have listened to me, Kiss. You've racked up a heavy debt."

"Fucking . . . romantic." Humor would help, I decided. My brain shivered, jagging between the unreality of the Chaldean obscenity straining to break through into our world and the sanity of a normal day.

Normal for a hunter, maybe.

"I've never been accused of romanticism before." Perry's fingers dug into my upper arm as he steadied me. Just short of bruising.

Broken bleeding husks in velvet robes lay scattered, the fluid golden wires of the Nine Seals and the three circles pale and still, useless. There was a blackened path—Perry's passage through the circles and the pentagram, breaking into the center, slashing through the careful work Inez had done.

All that work, all that life, wasted. I slumped against Perry, metal anklets clinking and the broken bits of chain chiming sweetly against the floor.

There were Weres in the shadows, a whole contingent of them. Among them I saw four lionesses from the Norte Luz pride, and two 'pards, both shamans, from the Anferi confederation, and then there was Saul and two more werecougars—and, oddly enough, Theron from Micky's, his dark eyes luminous orange in the candlelit dimness. Some of the candles had been knocked over, and someone was snuffing the braziers. Of course, the smell would make the Weres nervous. I also saw a werefalcon, his feathery hair ruffling as he checked the borders of the room, passing his hands over the walls, checking for hidden doors.

Where did they come from? I didn't want them in on this, Sorrows are dangerous for Weres.

Saul approached, rage crackling in the air around him. He didn't pause, shucking his hiplength leather coat as he walked. He had recently *shifted,* I could see the glow swirling through his aura. The deepest thrumming snarl was coming from him. Muscle slid under his T-shirt; he was armed to the teeth and had a dark streak of warpaint on each high, beautiful cheekbone.

He took me from Perry with a single scowl, his lip lifting. But he didn't fully bare his teeth, Perry didn't protest, and in short order Saul had the metal cuff off my left wrist and the coat closed around me. The clean musky smell of him rose, and warmth flooded me. I felt like I could stand up, but I leaned into him. The coat swallowed me whole, sleeves hanging far below my fingertips and the hem coming down to my knees. "Christ," he whispered into my hair. Then he swore, vilely, in deep guttural 'cougar. "Are you all right? *Are* you?"

No, Saul. I'm very far from all right. But there was work to be done. "How many bodies? Theron? How many?"

"Ten dead, hunter." Theron sounded grim. "The other two are unhappy, about to be worse."

"Show. *Show* me." I coughed, rackingly, my throat afire. I wanted to sink into Saul's arms, shut my eyes, and scream. I wanted to black out, flinched away from the screaming well of darkness threatening to swallow me whole. "There's another one. *Find* her. There are probably prisoners, too. Search this hole, but for God's sake don't do it alone. Go in pairs. How many do we have on our side?"

"Twenty or thirty, Boss. There's already a group scouring for survivors. Let us work." Theron waved one long-clawed hand in an elegant brushoff.

Saul lifted a silver hipflask to my lips. Brandy burned my throat and exploded in my empty stomach, I retched, managed to swipe at my lips with the back of one hand while he picked me up and hugged me with ribcracking force. "Jillian," he whispered into my hair, his breath a warm spot against my skull. The butt of a gun poked into my ribs, a blessed sensation. I felt a little better now.

A little. Not much. The scream boiled under my skin, I pushed it down. Trembling weakness settled into my bones. *Alive. I'm alive.* "Show me." *I have to see. I have to.*

Perry laughed again, a bitter little sound. "Have no fear, little one. These vipers are most dangerous in darkness. *Fiat lux,* and they are vulnerable as maggots." He stood a little distance away, his hands back in his pockets and his shoulders slumped. "Belisa is not here. But the head viper is."

Saul half-carried me to the crumpled bodies; two of the Weres were methodically checking them. Wet crunches came as the necks were snapped, Weres believe in being thorough. They were searching for marks once the necks were snapped; all of them were Sorrows, probably Adepts.

Dear God. It had been close. Very close.

I could have died. Or worse, definitely worse. That was definitely worse.

"Casualties?" My voice was husky, a ruin, I'd broken it screaming on the altar. The inside of my head echoed with the filthy squealing of Chaldean; I pushed it away with an effort that left me shaking again. *Please God, be kind. Tell me nobody died rescuing my stupid ass from this.*

One of the 'pard shamans looked over her shoulder. "Not on our side. They were all looking the other way, didn't even have a guard." She was a lean, rangy female, gold earplugs dangling as her head moved; her sleek short spotted hair was chopped and feathery. Like most Were shamans, she kept her arms bare, cuffs closed around her smoothly muscled biceps. The tattoo on her left shoulder slid under the skin, its inked lines running almost like the gold wire had in the ceiling and floor.

Nausea rose sour under my breastbone. I wasn't sure I was still alive, after all. Saul was warm and solid and real, but everything else wavered, dreamlike. The world was retreating into the fuzziness of shock, dangerous if I passed out now. Holding on to consciousness with teeth and toenails; I had to make *sure.*

Two Sorrows left alive. One of them was Inez Germaine, her red-dark mane draggled and slicked with blood, chewing at the leather gag as Theron finished tying her legs together. He snarled at her, lifting his lip, and I saw the other 'pard shaman—this one a male, his spotted hair pulled back in two high crests—reach down to cup the other Sorrow's face in his hands, tenderly.

"Go in peace," he said, huskily, and made a sharp movement. The crack echoed through the room.

My gorge rose hotly again. More killing. Christ.

Theron reached for Inez's head.

"Stop." This was from Perry. "Give her a gun, Saul."

"You're out of your fucking—"

"He's not talking about Inez." The weary huskiness in my voice cut through Saul's automatic protest. My head lolled, I gathered my shattered strength. Heard movement, stealthy cat feet padding; they were searching this place, however big it was. *Be careful. There could be little traps set in here, it is a Sorrows House. Right under the Santa Luz garbage dump. Perfect, absolutely perfect. No wonder everything reeked so bad. How did they find me?* "He means give *me* a gun, and I agree." I stopped to cough, a deep racking sound I wasn't sure I liked.

I am really going to feel this in a little while. But for right now, I was in shock, standing just outside myself, watching as a hollow-cheeked, almost-naked woman with bruised wrists and long tangled dark hair missing its usual silver stood next to Saul, swaying. He steadied me before reaching down and unholstering a Sig Sauer.

"This do okay?" he asked, and tears rose in my throat.

I denied them. *Oh, Saul. Thank God for you.* If I started to cry I was going to laugh, and if I started to laugh I was going to scream, and if I started screaming now I wouldn't stop until I passed out or battered myself senseless. I nodded, reached up with my right hand. Closed my fingers around the heavy gun.

The scar throbbed, and cold air kissed my exposed skin. My legs shook, Perry's borrowed strength not covering up the deep well of exhaustion underneath. With the gun weighing down my hand, I eased Saul's arm aside and made my way, unsteady as a newborn colt, to the spill of black velvet and draggled slicked-maroon hair.

Her black eyes stared up into mine. Her wrists were working against each other, trying to loosen the Were-tied bonds. Good fucking luck—when a Were tied something up it *stayed* tied.

At least, most of the time.

I shook. Tremors spilled through me, each wave followed by another feverish-warm tide of false strength from the puckered, prickling mark on my wrist. I looked down at her, the broken bits of chain from the anklets making sweet low sounds against the floor.

Lifted the gun. Sighted. Right between those fucking black eyes, just below where the colorless gem glittered at her hairline.

You slaughtered them like pigs, bebe. You heard the screams for mercy and you disregarded them. You were judge, jury, and executioner, you took your God's place.

Her soft, merciless voice chattered inside my head. So close to being outplayed. I wondered who had tracked me here, Saul or Perry, and I wondered just how deep into debt with Perry I'd gotten.

The thought of paying off that debt made me shiver.

Maybe she mistook it for weakness, or indecision. Her eyes lit up, sparks dancing in their infinite black depths, and her mouth curved up despite the distortion of the cruel gag. The Weres learned a long time ago not to take chances with a Sorrow.

So did I. I should have killed Belisa on sight. But I hadn't.

"Judge, jury, executioner," I said, harshly. The rest of the world fell away, leaving us enclosed in a bubble of silence. "Just like you, you fucking Sorrows bitch."

Her eyes widened.

"There's just one difference, Inez." My mouth was dry, I wanted another swallow of that brandy. I wanted to start screaming.

Most of all, though, I wanted to stay in that clear cold place where nothing mattered but the job at hand, the killing that had to be done. Everything there was so fucking simple. It was mercy that fucked things up; it was kindness and compassion that tangled everything together.

The smile spread razor-cold over my face, and watched as her struggles to free her hands intensified. She began to move on the floor, velvet whispering and a thin choked sound bubbling up from behind the gag.

I took a deep breath, air so cold it burned going down. "I'm a hunter. I *am* the fucking law in this town, bitch. Sentence pronounced."

I squeezed.

The muzzle flashed and her body jerked. Her head exploded—Saul had loaded with the hollowpoints, and as tough as Sorrows become, they are still human at the bottom. Not like Perry.

Did that make them bigger monsters, or smaller?

I lowered the gun slightly. Squeezed the trigger again. Again.

He must have had a full clip. I kept squeezing, firing

into her body again and again and again as it twisted and jerked. Then there were only dry clicks, two, three, four, five of them before Saul twisted the gun out of my weakening hand, took me in his arms, and dragged me out of there. I wanted to stay, to find Melisande and kill her with my bare hands, I raged in my cracked and unlovely voice that I was going to do just that. I did, until the shakes got so bad my teeth chattered and cut the words into bits.

Then I screamed, again and again, in Saul's arms until he carried me outside, where the reek of the garbage piled around was overwhelming but at least there was sunlight, thin and sad through high clouds. But it was Perry who clapped a hand over my mouth, finally, and hissed a word in my ear. It was Helletöng, a long sliding subvocal whisper, and it sent me into a sleep that was, again, like death.

And I went gratefully.

26

I'd been wrong. It had been Perry who had tracked me, through the scar, disregarding the wound in his head. It had been Perry who suggested spreading the word among the Weres about the trouble I was in. They had stopped by Micky's and made Theron their first contact.

The Weres had come because I was a hunter, and because I was Saul's lover—but, more important, because they respected me. It was nice, I supposed, to know I was regarded so highly among them. They're notoriously hard to impress.

I spent the first two days in a deathly daze, dealing with one thing after another in between passing out and having Saul threaten to tie me down in bed if I didn't stop and take some time to heal. Belisa had escaped, her trail led out of the House underground in the very heart of the Santa Luz garbage dump and then . . . vanished.

There were no surviving sacrificial victims. They recovered eight bodies, Belisa had stopped long enough on her way out to slit a few throats herself. They were all vanished prostitutes, not a one over twenty, and they were folded into the murder statistics for the year. Five of them had family, but I wasn't able to attend any of the funerals. I wanted to, but I just . . . I had my hands full with other fallout.

Demolition boys from the Santa Luz bomb squad brought out some type of explosive, wired the underground complex while the Weres guarded them, and blew it. There was a rumbling sound, a crater, and the slight depression in the ground was buried under tons of refuse.

Montaigne finished another economy-sized tub of Tums. Juan Rujillo filled in the requisite forms to report a Major Paranormal Incident as well as requisition hazard pay for me from the FBI's backstairs funding since the mercenaries had come from out of state, sent it off in its courier pouch, and told me to get some fucking rest. Montaigne seconded that emotion, and thanked me with profanity-laced gruffness for sending him two carloads of naked sobbing women who understood very well they were not supposed to talk to the press about their ordeal. The women had been turned over to counselors and social services; in a few years they might be okay. Maybe.

Two of them had already committed suicide. But not Hope; I asked specifically after her. "Tough cookie," Montaigne had sighed. "Keeps asking difficult questions about you."

"She'll get over it," I said, rubbing the new leather cuff Saul had made to go over the scar.

Montaigne paused, leaning back in his chair. Saul was just outside the door, and the sound of phones ringing and people moving was so comforting I almost closed my eyes right there. Swayed on my feet.

Monty cleared his throat. "About those pimps."

I braced myself. *I won't apologize, Monty. What are you going to do? Fire me? Bring me up on murder charges?*

His mouth twisted up on one side. It was a facsimile of a smile, more like a grimace of pain. "Turf wars. Wish they'd kill each other more often." Monty dropped his eyes to his paper-strewn desk.

Bile rose in my throat. *Judge, jury, executioner. You took God's place.*

It was true. But like most truths, it had an edge that would cut—and an edge that didn't cut me. I found out, with relief, which one was pointed at me. "Monty—"

"Shut the fuck up, Jill."

"I was only going to say thank you."

Mónty told me to get the hell out of his office, and I complied meekly.

I missed Carp and Rosie's visit, being sound asleep for once. They came, Rosie left a bouquet of flowers, Carp left a bottle of Jack Daniels. Nice of them.

Father Gui called, offered to come by and pray with me. Saul told him in no uncertain terms where to stick it and hung up. I guess he was still upset. At least it saved me the trouble of hanging up on the priest. I wasn't ready to forgive him yet.

And I was still weighing whether or not it would be worth it to go down and tear apart that fucking church to find what else he had hidden from me.

The Weres, of course, said nothing. Except Theron, who came by the warehouse and squatted down by the couch, which was the only place I could stand to sleep. I kept staring at the chair Belisa had sat in. My eyes would close as I heard Saul moving around the warehouse,

cleaning up, cooking exquisite little meals I tried to force
myself to eat.

I usually woke up screaming. Nightmares are usual
after something like this; better a nightmare than waking up to the real fucking thing. You go long enough with
post-traumatic stress from nightside fun and games and
you learn that very quickly.

Theron examined me for a long time, his dark eyes
moving over my face. He was here on business, not so-
cially, so he didn't try any of his usual little games with
Saul. Instead, he simply *looked* at me. Saul had tucked
a wool blanket around me, pulled it up to my chin, and
spent some time braiding more charms into my hair. My
throat felt naked without the ruby, and Mikhail's ring was
probably gone.

The Sorrows don't like holy objects. Anything consecrated with love is anathema to them. The ruby, a soul-
link between me and my teacher, would be doubly so.

"You weren't planning on calling in Were backup,"
Theron finally said, his hands dangling loosely as he
crouched with peculiar ease. "Right?"

I blinked. Shrugged under the blanket. "Sorrows." My
voice was husky. "Dangerous."

He waved that away with one sharp, economical movement. "You need to take some time off and clear your
fucking head out. That was a stupid fucking decision,
hunter. We're allied with your kind for a *reason*."

"I didn't know what it was." I sounded exhausted even
to myself. And pained.

"When Saul came 'round asking questions about wendigo, that was the time we started taking notice. We could
have trapped it more effectively if you'd coordinated with

us." He sighed. Eyed me speculatively before getting to the point. "Mikhail would have kicked your ass for this Lone Ranger shit."

Mikhail. I'd failed him; his killer had outplayed me and gotten away. Again.

Theron shifted a little, as if preparing to stand upright. "We put the word on the wind, Jill. Wherever that bitch goes, sooner or later she's going to run across a Were. She's under the Hunt."

"But—" I started to protest. Sorrows were *dangerous,* and Weres coming across them often died.

"But fucking nothing. We'll deliver her head one of these days, or she'll come back to fuck with you again and we'll joint her like a pig. Quit the Lone Ranger shit, Jill. It's detrimental to the safety of the citizens of Santa Luz." His smile broadened. "Besides, your ass is a lot cuter than Mikhail's. I'd hate to have to chat up a whole new hunter."

"I heard that," came Saul's voice from the kitchen. "Get out of here, Theron. Go chase some chickens."

"You're a fine one to talk, Dustcircle. I'm going." Theron rose to his feet with the fluid grace of a Were. He leaned down and touched my forehead, smoothing my hair back. His voice dropped. "Peace in your dreaming, hunter. We'll bring you a head one of these days."

Then he was gone, and I shut my eyes, curling into the couch, and cried. Saul left the kitchen and half picked me up, held me, we ended up on the floor under the blanket while I sobbed and he murmured soothing nonsense in my ear, until I fell asleep again and woke up in my own bed with him beside me, trying to calm me down as I screamed from the dream of being chained to the cold glassy stone and feeling the thing from *outside* try to force its way into me.

But Saul was there. And his warmth was enough to keep that thing at bay.

I shrugged into my new leather trenchcoat, my fingers running over the handle of the new bullwhip. Replacing gear gets expensive, but the FBI's hazard pay was a nice chunk.

"You sure you want to do this?" Saul's mouth pulled down bitterly. Afternoon sun slanted through the windows, bars of thick gold. Spring was right around the corner, or at least I hoped so.

I held up a hand, watched it shake just a little. Concentrated, and it kept steady, my fingers easing. The scar was warm under the new leather cuff. "I've got to tell him I'm going on vacation. Five minutes."

"You shot him in the *head*." Saul folded his arms. His dark eyes rested on me, then slid down to the floor. "He wasn't happy, kitten. He said some pretty nasty things."

"He broke through a Sorrows circle and faced down a Chaldean god to—"

"Because he thinks he owns you, kitten. Because he's hellbreed. He'd rather kill you himself than have another demon touch you. Why don't we just go?" He'd already loaded the suitcases in the Impala, and I wasn't due to get a new pager for another three weeks.

Because I have to finish this. I checked the action of each gun before I holstered it; the knives were new too. "I wish we could have found my gear," I muttered. "Goddammit."

Then another fit of trembling hit, and Saul was suddenly there, his arms around me. He hunched down a little so I could bury my face in the hollow of his throat and breathe him in, deep. All the way down to the bottom of my lungs.

But still, I smelled ambergris. And a breath of foul reek that seemed to stay on my skin no matter how raw I scrubbed myself.

Andy's apprentice was staying up above Micky's, in the apartment kept for visiting hunters. Anja's apprentice, nearly a hunter himself, was due in on the evening train; Galina would meet him and get him settled. The Weres would come out of the barrio and run regular patrols. But it had been quiet since the demolition of the Sorrows House.

Thank God.

Saul stroked my back, slid his hands under the coat, and pulled my T-shirt up. His palms met my skin, he flattened his hands and pulled me closer, closer. I could barely breathe, but that's the way I wanted it.

The waves of trembling went down, silver charms shifting and chiming against each other in my hair. Each wave was a little less intense than the last. He murmured soothingly, little nonsense-words, purring in 'cougar until they stopped. Even then he held me.

I swallowed the lump in my throat. Breathed him in. Musk, male, leather, the best smell in the world. Safe. I whispered his name, over and over again.

The fit passed. He rubbed his chin against the top of my head, his heartbeat thundering against mine. "Sorry," I finally mumbled into his chest. "Sorry, Christ I'm sorry—"

"Mmmh. What the hell for?" He kissed my hair. "I like holding you."

My eyes were squeezed shut, dampness slicking my cheeks. "Saul?"

"Jill."

"I did something wrong. I . . . I'm not a nice person." That wasn't what I wanted to say.

I didn't want you to see what I was capable of. I didn't want you to know. What am I going to do? I can't stand to lose you. Oh, God, I can't stand to lose you.

I wanted to tell him. I wanted to tell him about the little click inside my head, how I could move outside myself and calmly, coldly, commit murder. How I had slaughtered eleven men who hadn't had a chance, because they were human and I'm a hunter. And not only that, I'd ruthlessly used the advantage of my bargain with Perry not only to get information but also to . . . to what? I could have gotten the information and left them alive. Crippled, maybe, but alive.

I could have. But I didn't. I evened the score, *my* score. I played God.

"No," he agreed. "You're not."

Silence. His hands tightened, pulling me even closer.

"But." He nuzzled my hair. "You're a *good* person, Jillian. Not nice, but good."

"I killed them." The words were dust in my mouth.

"Yeah." Neutral agreement.

"I killed them because of someone else, what someone else did to me." Another shudder slammed through my abused body. He steadied me. "Don't leave me," I whispered, so softly I wasn't sure he could hear, even with a Were's acuity.

He sighed, a heavy movement that pushed against my own ribs. "Not going anywhere, kitten. Count on it."

Relief smashed into my heart, a pain so sharp and sudden I might have been having a cardiac arrest. "Saul—"

"I want you to meet my people," he said, slowly and clearly, as if talking to an idiot. "The sooner we get this over with, the sooner we can go and get formal. Hitched. Under the Moon. Full ceremony, with a feast afterward. You thinking of backing out?"

"No. *No.*" I shook my head, rubbing my chin against his shirt. "Good God, no. I just . . . I'm not a nice person, Saul. I'm *not.*"

"Hell, kitten, I knew that when I met you. It's part of your charm. You're a *hunter.* Being nice would be a weakness. Right?"

He sounded so sure.

Is mercy a weakness, Saul? Doesn't killing like that make me worse than what I hunt?

"Right?" he prodded, moving slightly to bump my hips with his.

I wish I was as sure as you sound, catkin. I swallowed the stone in my throat. "Right. You bet."

"So let's get this visit to that goddamn hole out of the way so we can get out of town. Okay?"

I firmed my jaw, set my shoulders, and gently slid away from him. He let me. I touched the handle of the bullwhip. "Okay."

But I sounded more like a scared teenager than a hunter. He didn't mention it, just picked up the duffel with spare weapons and ammo in it and motioned me toward the door. "Let's go, then."

Oh, Saul. Thank God for you.

27

The Monde was just getting ready for the night. Outside, winter sunlight was slanting thinly toward the end of the day, cold breath of wind coming not from the mountains but off the river, filled with a chemical tang.

There was a new bouncer at the door, daytime muscle, but he just nodded and let me by. Food for thought—or maybe, even as drawn and haggard as I was, I looked like nobody to mess with.

Riverson, his gray-filmed eyes widening, was at the bar. The charms in my hair shifted and rang as he reached behind him for the vodka bottle. The air turned hot and tense, the few hellbreed having crawled out of their holes before dusk suddenly stilling, several Traders clustered around a table near the dance floor looking up, disturbed by this new feral current.

I passed the bar for once and headed for the back, for the iron door behind its purple cord. I heard Riverson call my name.

"Kismet! *Kismet!*"

Sounded like he was trying to warn me. Nice of him, really, considering we hated each other.

I stepped behind the purple velvet and reached for the doorknob. It was unlocked, as usual. I twisted it, pushed it open, and went up the stairs, stopping halfway to lean against the banister and try to calm my racing heart.

What are you doing, Jill?

Only what I have to, I replied. *Only what I must.*

And Mikhail's voice, barely a whisper. *Head high, guns out, milaya. Meet what chases you.*

I pushed the creaking wooden door at the top open and the room hove into sight: white carpet, pristine, no sign of spilled brandy or blood. The glimmer of glass and chrome that was the bar. The other two doors, neither of which I ever wanted to see what lay behind. The bed, perfectly made, as always.

The two chairs, facing each other.

Perry stood straight and slim in front of the bank of television monitors, his hands clasped loosely in front of him. His back was to me, and I could see he'd gotten a haircut. A nice, short, textured cut, the latest thing for boys this season. Nothing but the best.

He wore, for once, jeans and a pale ash-gray sweater instead of a suit. A pair of dark leather engineer boots. Blue light from the monitors touched his hair, picked out paler highlights in the blond.

I closed the door behind me. Waited.

"It is not safe for you to be here," he said finally, very softly. Static blurred across the monitors, they cleared up. On one satellite feed, Court TV was just getting underway with a serial killer's trial. On another, explosions ripped through a Jerusalem restaurant in slow motion. There were more explosions on the third, some Eastern European country purging again, riots in the streets.

I took a deep breath. "Three things."

He waited. The trembling started, I leaned against the door. *Stop it, Jill. Just stop it. You planned what you were going to say. Do it quick.* The scar pulsed under the new cuff, sweating.

Push him off balance, Jill. "First of all, thank you. For saving my life."

He didn't move. His shoulders were absolutely straight. More static fuzzed across the monitors, moving in an oddly coherent pattern; a cold breeze touched my cheek. Spoiled honey and dusty feathers. The air behind him shimmered like pavement on a hot day; the shimmer swept back and forth, combing the air.

Double or nothing, Jill. Do a mindfuck of your own. Make your teachers proud. "Second of all . . . I owe you an apology, Pericles. I should have listened to you about Belisa. I should have let you kill her. It . . . what I did to you wasn't right. I'm sorry. For shooting you in the head and for not listening to you. You didn't deserve that."

The static drained away. The silence in the room was now shocked, as if I had walked into a high-class party and started yelling obscenities. A murmur slid through the air, circling; the shimmer behind him died down.

His shoulders were still straight, but some essential quality of murderous rigidity had drained away. I waited.

"Surprising." His tone was flat. "But not entirely unexpected."

Holy fucking shit. It worked. I peeled myself away from the door, cautioning myself not to get too cocky.

Next came the trick of the week, if I was good enough to perform it. "What do I owe you?"

His laugh made the glasses rattle uneasily at the bar, the hanging material over the bed billowed as if caught in a breeze. Glass bottles of liquor groaned, chattering against their shelves. "More than you can comfortably repay, Kiss. More than you can *ever* repay. I have angered an Elder for your sake, though I was well within my rights. You are *mine*."

I don't think so, Perry. "The deal was that you would help me in my cases in return for a slice of my time. That hasn't changed."

Another fluid, almost Gallic shrug. "If it pleases you to think so, by all means, continue."

Now for the sting. I braced myself and tossed my dice. "There's just one thing." My right hand rested on the butt of a gun, a new Glock 9 mm. I wouldn't need to draw it. At least, I hoped not. I was in no condition to deal with him if he got nasty.

But I'd certainly give it a go if this went south.

"What?" This was a snarl, more glass rattling. The windows looking down over the empty dance floor flexed in their frames.

"How much did she take *you* for? Belisa, I mean. How deep in their venture did you have your tentacles?"

Silence.

A warm bath of satisfaction started at my toes and worked its way up. *I guessed right. You fucking hellbreed bastard. God damn you.*

It had become clear to me in a blinding flash while I stood shaking in the shower trying to scrub the smell of the Nameless off my skin yet again. Just before I'd shot him in the head, Perry had spoken that name, the name of my dead self. A name he could have had no fucking way of knowing unless he'd chatted cozily with someone who had taken a peek at Mikhail's private papers.

Someone like Melisande Belisa, who had put the information in the Sorrows file for Inez to read too and taunt me with.

I'd suspected, of course. A Trader known for slaving showing up in the Monde when I'd blown all his other boltholes, Perry trailing me before he should have known I was in serious danger, his warning that his protection might only extend so far—which by itself would have meant nothing, since he liked to pretend he knew everything going on in the city. But with everything else, it added up to a pretty picture.

A *damning* picture. Not to mention him finding her with a minimum of fuss, and her only showing up with a black eye and tender ribs.

Just to make it look good.

I continued, surer of myself now. My arms and legs stopped shaking. "She crossed you, didn't she. They moved into town and I was kept busy chasing my tail on other cases, but you didn't know Inez's big plan was to have *me* in the starring role when her lord and master came calling. That's also why you intervened when it came to Elizondo, he was a bit player but you couldn't have him talking to me." I swallowed dryly. "How much, Perry? How much did you lose on the deal?"

Another shrug. "Money. Only money." His tone told me he was lying. He'd lost something else too.

And I had a pretty good idea of what that *something*

else was. "Belisa played me like a fiddle. And she played you, too."

"The cat was supposed to be with you," he informed me, flatly. "When the wendigo was allowed out. You were not the beast's target."

That's why they were in a holding pattern. Only I sent Saul away; they couldn't have known I would do that. My skin went cold, flushed hot. "But nobody expected us to be searching for a witness down on Broadway." We were supposed to be out there canvassing the street scene for clues about missing hookers, not meeting with a witness.

Oh, Christ. And once Saul was gone, was I supposed to turn to Perry for solace? Fat fucking chance.

Belisa had probably told him to wait, to bide his time and she'd take care of Saul. She had maybe even set the wendigo free the second and third time—not guessing that the creature, balked and hurt when it came for Saul the first time and Cecilia the second, would fixate on me. Hard to get much coherence out of a thing built only for appetite and destruction.

Though the silver chain around its neck had been broken. Maybe the wendigo had broken free on its own. I didn't know. I would probably *never* know.

So Perry had been waiting, not just watching over me but waiting for the assassination of my lover to step in and take his cut of the whole rotten deal. And once I had bloodied my hands cleaning up the expendable bits of their operation, Belisa had to have guessed I wouldn't take kindly to Perry moving on me. That I would, to some extent, *identify* Perry with the men I'd just killed.

And with the man I'd killed before I ever became a hunter.

She had only to wait until the ticking bomb inside my head went off. Belisa had applied the pressure neatly, and if Perry hadn't been so all-fired eager to use his newfound psychological leverage on me himself I might have been a little less likely to shoot him in the head.

It was so neat, so perfect, that I began to laugh. I leaned against the door to his little chamber of horrors and chuckled. I damn near *guffawed*.

No hellbreed likes to be laughed at. But Perry suffered it, static crawling over the TV screens, while I fought for breath, tears running down my cheeks.

"You poor bastard," I finally wheezed, hanging onto the door, wiping at my cheeks with the back of my left hand. "You poor silly bastard."

He twitched, and I jerked the gun up out of the holster. His hand clapped around mine, shoving it back in; he leaned into me. The door creaked, Perry pressed his body against mine, and I could feel he was shaking.

And he had a hard-on. A quite respectable one, as such things went. Shoved right up against me.

Well, at least now we know he's generally built like a human. Hellbreed usually are, but reserve judgment, Jill, he could have something else in there entirely. Like his tongue.

The scar went white-hot. Desire spilled hot through me, my legs turning weak; his breath was hot on my lips. It smelled of dry hot desert winds and spoiled boiling honey. At least it wasn't the clotted reek of the Nameless.

The devil I know, at least. Be careful, Jill. Oh, God, be careful—Saul's right outside.

"Do not," he breathed against my skin, "make the mistake of thinking you can treat me like I'm *human*. You made a bargain with me."

He was strong, wiry-strong. I went limp, not even trying to fight, staring unblinking into his blue eyes. They were human, maybe a little *too* human, except for the hellbreed sheen to them and the spreading indigo stain. And the far points of distant light in the very center of his pupils. A remote, shimmering spark, of no color I could have identified.

The static twisting behind him came up to twin high points, combing the air.

My throat wouldn't let me speak, so I whispered. "You broke the bargain when you sold me out."

"Then I will make you a new one. I will leave the cat alive, and you may play with him all you wish. But you will give me your time as always, Kiss."

The pinpricks in his pupils revolved, swelled. I stared through them, the scar thundering on my wrist, pulsing in time to my heartbeat. Heat curled through me, down low.

Whore, I heard in the furthest-back reaches of my memory, from the dead time before I'd been a hunter. *You whore. Spread your legs for anyone, won't you.*

Not anymore, the hunter's voice of steel replied. I found my physical voice, a raw, cranky whisper. "No deal, Perry."

Then I brought my knee up, swift and sharp. He avoided the blow, but I shoved him while he shifted his weight and he let himself be toppled over. He sprawled on the plush carpet, and the gun left the holster in one smooth oiled movement. Slender, silver-coated bullets, and his head would explode just like Inez's. And I wouldn't just count on one shot to do it, either. Not now. I would fill him full

of silverjacket lead and when he was down I'd hack off
his head with one of the knives I carried. Then, just to be
sure, I'd smash a few bottles of liquor and set his carcass
ablaze; and with enough etheric force spilling through the
scar I could burn this whole place down.

That is, if the scar was still a conduit for a hellbreed's
power after he was dead.

He leaned back against the carpet on his elbows, looking up at me, one eyebrow slightly raised. "Fun and
games, Kiss? Go ahead. Pull the trigger. Show me how
far you've come."

The gun trembled. *Judge, jury, executioner. Playing
God.*

Downstairs there was a clatter, and a loud swearing.
Riverson. The sound brushed my ears, not as acute as they
would be if I'd stripped the cuff off. Still, I heard it, and
the red haze over my vision cleared. My heart pounded
in my ears.

I reached over with my left hand, unsnapped the cuff.
Slid it off, and fresh strength flowed through my veins.
My skin turned exquisitely sensitive, brushed with the
chill air and my clothes, hot and confining. The leather
crumpled in my hot sweating palm, creaking slightly.

Perry took in a small avid sip of air, tensing.

My right hand tightened. The hammer rose, clicked
into the up position. I stared into those blue, scorching,
mad, inhuman hellbreed eyes and temptation dried my
mouth, made my hand shake. My pulse roared in my ears.
The low grumbling sound of Helletöng rattled through the
building, the hellbreed on the first floor conversing.

Mikhail's voice rose again in my memory, swirling and
trembling. It was a good memory, of his gruff voice in

English and my own lighter tone repeating each line of
the prayer.

*Cover me with Thy shield, and with my sword may Thy
righteousness be brought to earth, to keep Thy children
safe. Let me be the defense of the weak and the protector
of the innocent, the righter of wrongs and the giver of
charity. In Thy name and with Thy blessing, I go forth to
cleanse the night.*

I stuffed the scrap of leather in my pocket. "I'm going
on vacation, Perry. When I come back, I'm not visiting.
When I need you, I'll call. And if you 'arrange' for anything to happen to Saul, I'll put a bullet through my own
fucking head and spoil all your pretty plans for me. So
you'd better take *real* good care where you drop your
quiet words."

His face froze. I could almost feel the air pressure shift.
"Sooner or later you will come to me." He said it quietly,
as I groped behind me for the doorknob with my sweating, suddenly clumsy left hand.

I felt the smile sink into my face, my lips pulling back
from my teeth. "Hold your breath until I call, hellbreed."
My fingers closed around its slick roundness. My right
hand quivered, but I managed to ease the hammer down
with my thumb. The big muscles on the front of my thighs
were shaking too.

"You can't escape it." His voice rose as I backed out,
my foot seeking behind me for the first step, finding it.
Lowering me down. I backed up another two steps, swung
the door closed. "Come back and kill me or walk away
now, it's all the same." His shout rattled the door as I
pushed it closed. The click of the latch catching seemed
very loud. "*I will have you, hunter! I will have you!*"

"Not today," I muttered, and made it down the stairs without having to stop. It helped to be going down.

I pushed the iron door open, stepped out. Slammed it behind me. Leaned against it for a moment, studying the room.

Riverson stared at me. The hellbreed, all frozen, stared at me. One of the night bouncers, leaning against the bar for a quick drink before going on duty, stared at me.

All eyes on you, Jilly.

I walked across the Monde Nuit with my head high, the heels of my third-best steel-toed boots clicking against the floor. The boots would need hard use before they were as soft and comfy as my favorite pair. I was going to have to figure out a better way to get blood out of boot leather.

"Kiss. *Kismet.*" It was Riverson, out from behind the bar. Nobody made a move to help him as he stumbled for me, his hands out. As if he was truly blind, and not more capable of finding his way around—at least in here—than anyone else.

I didn't stop, didn't slow down. But he reached me anyway, and grabbed my coat sleeve. "Kismet."

"Fuck off." I didn't have breath or energy to waste on him. I had to get out of here.

He grabbed my hand, shoved something into it. A box, a small cardboard box like they have for jewelry. "God-damn you." His fingers bit into my sleeve. "Take it and go, you fucking bitch. Take it and go if you know what's good for you. Don't ever fucking come back here."

Oh, God, I can kill you now if you push me. Don't push me. "Fuck *off*, Riverson."

"These are yours," he insisted. "Fucking take them, or

he'll destroy them. And for the love of God, *don't come back.*"

He let go of my sleeve, and I made myself keep walking. My fingers crumpled the edges of the box, I felt the harshness of some kind of ribbon. What kind of present would Riverson give *me*?

These are yours. Take them or he'll destroy them.

That was a laugh. How much more could Perry take or destroy?

Nothing but what you let him, Jill. It's that goddamn simple.

I was past the bar and four steps away from the door when I heard shattering glass and a screech of inhuman rage from above. The air turned hot and tight, but I didn't pause, and nobody moved on me.

Outside, I stepped past the day bouncer. The parking lot was filling up, and the sun was sinking. The sky was fantastic, crimson and gold, indigo moving in from the east. Night's dawning, ready to spread over the vault of heaven.

I stopped, looked down at the box. It was wrapped with a piece of silvery ribbon that slid off because I had crushed it. But I felt a familiar tingle in my fingers, and tore the top of the box off.

There, sitting on a cushion of white padding, was a silver glimmer. Mikhail's ring. And tangled around it, the supple silver necklace and the chunk of carved ruby, glowing and pulsing with its own inner light.

The gem that Mikhail had held as he pulled me out of Hell, and the ring he had given me when he accepted me as an apprentice. Both shining with their own inner light here, at the edge of the brackish pond of hellbreed energy.

My eyes filled with tears. I fitted the ring on my left third finger, clutched the necklace, and dropped the box. Looked up.

My orange Impala was parked in the fire lane, like the good girl she was. The engine was running, and Saul had lit a Charvil. I made it to the passenger's side on unsteady legs and dropped into my seat with a sigh. Slammed the door. Locked it.

Saul said nothing.

I rubbed at the top of my right wrist. There was a paler patch of flesh where the cuff had protected and softened the skin, a bracelet of weakness. The marks from the Sorrows' chains had healed over.

The ruby glowed up at me. My fingers fumbled with the clasp of the necklace, the ruby settled right in the hollow of my throat. Home again, home again, Jill Kismet.

Pulled out of Hell.

Who was holding the line this time?

Jesus. Jesus Christ.

If Perry had planned to give them to me, why did Riverson have them? Had he filched them from his master? I always stopped at the bar first; did Perry think it would soften my mood to have the blind man present me with my own jewelry?

Take them or he'll destroy them.

Saul's profile was even, serene. He watched the door of the Monde, the Charvil dangling from his left-hand fingers, his other hand on the wheel.

I found my voice. The ruby warmed against my skin,

settling into its familiar tingling readiness. "Ready to go, baby?"

He tossed the cigarette, touched the wheel with both hands, his fingertips gentle as if he was stroking my back. "Born ready, kitten. You?"

"Get us the fuck out of town, catkin." I swallowed roughly, closed my eyes. Felt Saul shift into first. "Let's not stop for a few hundred miles."

"You got it." The Impala slid forward, he cut the wheel, and as we pulled out of the Monde's wide broad lot, he slammed on the gas and left a respectable streak of smoking rubber. I slumped in the passenger seat, and didn't open my eyes until we hit the freeway.

Glossary

Arkeus: A roaming corruptor escaped from Hell.

Banefire: A cleansing sorcerous flame.

Black Mist: A roaming psychic contagion; a symbiotic parasite inhabiting the host's nervous system and bloodstream.

Chutsharak: Chaldean obscenity, loosely translated as "oh, *fuck*."

Demon: Term loosely used to designate any nonhuman predator with sorcerous ability or a connection to Hell.

Exorcism: Tearing loose a psychic parasite from its host.

Hellbreed: Blanket term for a wide array of demons, half-demons, or other species escaped or sent from Hell.

Hellfire: The spectrum of sorcerous flame employed by hellbreed for a variety of uses.

Hunter: A trained human who keeps the balance between the nightside and regular humans; extrahuman law enforcement.

Imdarák: Shadowy former race who drove the Elder

Gods from the physical plane, also called the Lords of the Trees.

Martindale Squad: The FBI division responsible for tracking nightside crime across state lines and at the federal level, mostly staffed with hunters and Weres.

Middle Way: Worshippers of Chaos, Middle Way adepts are usually sociopathic and sorcerous loners. Occasionally covens of Middle Way adepts will come together to control a territory or for a specific purpose.

Neophym: A Sorrow between an Acolyte and a Terephym/Mother in rank. Females go on from Neophym to become Mothers and Grand Mothers; males never reach higher than Terephym (soldier-drone) rank.

OtherSight/Sight: Second sight, the ability to see sorcerous energy. Can also mean precognition.

Possessor: An insubstantial, low-class demon specializing in occupying and controlling humans; the prime reason for exorcists.

Scurf: Also called *nosferatim,* a semi-psychic viral infection responsible for legends of blood-hungry corpses, vampires, or nosferatu. Also, someone infected by the scurf virus.

Sorrow: A worshipper of the Chaldean Elder Gods.

Sorrows House: A House inhabited by Sorrows, with a vault for invocation or evocation of Elder Gods.

Sorrows Mother: A high-ranking female of a Sorrows House.

Talyn: A hellbreed, higher in rank than an *arkeus* or Possessor, usually insubstantial due to the nature of the physical world.

Trader: A human who makes a "deal" with a hellbreed, usually for worldly gain or power.

Utt'huruk: A bird-headed demon.

Were: Blanket term for several species who shapeshift into animal (for example, cougar, wolf, or spider) or half-animal (wererat or *khentauri*) form.

extras

www.orbitbooks.net

extras

about the author

Lilith Saintcrow was born in New Mexico, bounced around the world as an Air Force brat, and fell in love with writing when she was ten years old. She currently lives in Vancouver, Washington with three children and a houseful of cats. Find her on the internet at: www.lilithsaintcrow.com

You can also find out more about Lilith, and other Orbit authors, by registering for the free monthly newsletter at www.orbitbooks.net

if you enjoyed

HUNTER'S PRAYER,
look out for

REDEMPTION ALLEY

Book 3 of the Jill Kismet series
by Lilith Saintcrow

*R*ight before dawn a hush falls over Santa Luz. The things that live and prey in the dark are either searching for a burrow to spend the day in, or for one last little snack. *The closer to dawn, the harder the fight, hunters say*. Predators get desperate as the sun, that great enemy of all darkness, walks closer to the rim of dawn.

Which explains why I was flat on my back, again, with hellbreed-strong fingers cutting off my air and my head ringing like someone had set off dynamite inside it. Sparks spat from silver charms tied in my hair, blessed moon's metal reacting to something inimical. The Trader hissed as he squeezed, fingers sinking into my throat and the flat shine of the dusted lying over his eyes as they narrowed, forked tongue flickering past the broken yellowed stubs of his teeth.

Apparently dental work wasn't part of the contract he'd made with whatever hellbreed had given him supernatural strength and the ability to set shit on fire at a thousand paces.

I brought my knee up, hard.

The hellbreed this particular Trader had bargained with hadn't given him an athletic cup, either. The bony part of my knee sank into his crotch, meeting precious little resistance, so hard something popped.

It didn't sound like much fun.

The Trader's eyes rolled up and he immediately let go of my trachea. I promptly added injury to insult by clocking him on the side of the head with a knifehilt. I didn't slip the knife between his ribs because I wanted to bring him in alive.

What can I say? Maybe I was in a good mood.

Besides, I had other worries. For one, the burning warehouse.

Smoke roiled thick in the choking air, and the rushing crackle of flames almost drowned out the screams coming from the girl handcuffed to a support pole. She was wasting both good energy and usable air by screaming, almost out of her mind with fear. Bits of burning building plummeted to the concrete floor. I gained my feet with a convulsive lurch, eyes streaming, and clapped the silver-plated cuffs on the Trader's skinny wrists. He was on the scrawny end of junkie-thin, moaning and writhing as I wrenched his hands away from his genitals and behind his back.

I would have told him he was under arrest, but I didn't

have the breath. I scooped up the handle of the bull-whip and vaulted a stack of wooden boxes, their sides beginning to steam and smoke with the heat. My steel-reinforced bootheels clattered and I skidded to a stop, giving her a once-over while my fingers stowed the whip.

Mousy brown hair, check. Big blue eyes, check. Mole high up on her right cheek, check.

"Regan Smith." I coughed, getting a good lungful of smoke. My back burned with pain and something flaming hit the floor less than a yard away. "Your mom sent me to find you."

She didn't hear me. She was too busy screaming.

I grabbed at the handcuffs as she tried to scramble away, fetching up hard against the support pole. She even tried to kick me. *Good girl. Bet you gave that asshole a run for his money.* I curled my fingers around the cuffs on either side and gave a quick short yank.

The scar on my right wrist ran with prickling heat, pumping strength into my fingers. The cuffs burst, and the girl immediately tried to bolt. She was hysterical with fear and wiry-strong, choking, screaming whenever she could get enough air. The roar of the fire drowned out any reassurance I might have given her, and my long leather trenchcoat was beginning to smoke. I was carrying enough ammo to make things interesting in here if it got hot enough.

Not to mention the fact that the girl was only human. She would roast alive before I got *really* uncomfortable. I'd promised her mother I'd bring her back, if it was at all possible.

Promises like that are hell on hunters.

I snapped a quick glance over my shoulder at the Trader

lying cuffed on the floor. He appeared to be passed out, but they're tricky fuckers. You don't negotiate a successful bargain with a hellbreed without being slippery.

The roof was falling in. More burning crap fell down, splashing on the concrete and scattering. A lick of flame ran along a runnel in the floor, and the girl made things interesting by almost twisting free.

Dammit. I'm trying to help you! But she was almost insane with fear.

It probably messes your world up when you see a short woman in a long black leather coat beat the shit out of a Trader with a bullwhip, three clips of ammo, and the inhuman speed of the damned. The silver charms tied in my long dark hair spat and crackled with blue sparks, and I'm sure I was wearing my mad face.

I hefted the girl over my shoulder like a sack of potatoes and spent a few precious seconds glancing again at the motionless Trader. Burning bits of wood landed on him, his clothes smoking, but I thought I saw a glimmer of eyes.

She beat at my back with her fists, but I hefted her and sprinted down the long central aisle of the warehouse, lit with garish flame. Fire twisted and roared, stealing air and replacing it with toxic smoke. Something exploded, a wall of hot air mouthing my back as I got a good head of speed going, aiming for a gap in the burning wall.

This might get a little tricky.

Rush of flame, a crackling liquid sound, covering up her breathless barking—she had nothing left in her to scream with, poor girl—and my own rising cry, a sound of female effort that flattened the streaming flames away. The scar ran with sick wet delight as I pulled force through it, my aura flaming into the visible, a star of spiky plasma light.

Feet slapping the floor, back burning, I'd wrenched something when I'd brought my knee up. *Probably feel better than he does. Hurry up, she can't take much more of—*

I hit the hole in the wall going almost-full speed, my cry ratcheting up into a breathless squeal because I'd run out of air too, darkness flowering over my vision and starved muscles crying out for oxygen. Smoke billowed and I hoped I'd applied enough kinetic energy to throw us both clear of the fire.

Physics is a bitch.

The application of force made the landing much harder. I don't wear leather pants because they make my ass look cute. It's because when I land hard, something snapping in my left leg and the rest of my left side taking the brunt of the blow, trying to shield the girl from impact, most of my skin would get erased if I wasn't wearing dead animal.

As it was, I only broke a few bones.

Concrete. Cold. The hissing, roaring of the fire as it devoured all the oxygen it could reach. The girl was still feebly trying to struggle free.

It was a clear, cold night, the kind you only get out in the desert. The stars would be huge bonfires of brilliant ice if not for the glare of Santa Luz's streetlamps and the other, lesser light of the burning warehouse. I lay for a few moments, coughing, eyes streaming, while my leg crunched with pain and the scar hummed with sick de-light, a chill touching my spine as the bone set itself with swift jerks. My eyes rolled up in my head and I dimly heard the girl sobbing as she stopped trying to get *away*.

She'd be lucky to get out of this needing a few years of therapy and some smoke-inhalation treatment.

Sirens pierced the night, far away but drawing closer. *Here comes the cavalry. Thank God.*

Unfortunately, thanking God wouldn't do much good. I was the responsible one here. If that Trader was still alive and the scene started swarming with vulnerable, only-human emergency personnel . . .

Get up, Jill. Get up now.

My weary body obeyed. I made it to my feet, wincing as my left tibia and my humerus both crackled, the bone swiftly restructuring itself and all the pain of healing compressed into a few seconds rather than weeks. My hand flicked, the bullwhip coiling itself neatly and stowed at my hip, and I had both guns unholstered and ready before the warehouse belched a torrent of red-hot air and the Trader barreled through the hole in the wall, flesh cracking-black and his eyes shining flatly, the sick-sweet smell of seared human pork adding to the perfume of hellbreed contamination.

Traders are scary-quick. I tracked him, bullets spattering the sidewalk as my right arm jolted under the strain of recoil going all the way up to my shoulders, broken bone pulling my aim off.

Mikhail insisted on me being able to shoot left-handed, too. I caught the Trader with four rounds in the chest and dropped the guns as he reached the top arc of his leap, his scream fueled with the rage of the damned.

I'm sure the fact that half his meat was cooked didn't help.

My hands closed around knifehilts. Knife-fighting is my forte, it's close and dirty, which isn't fun when it comes to hellbreed or Traders. You don't want to get too close. But I've always had an edge in pure speed, being female and little.

The scar helps too. The hard knot of corruption on the soft inside of my wrist ran with heavy prickling iron as I moved faster than a human being had any right to, meeting the Trader with a bone-snapping crunch.

The idiot wasn't thinking. If he had been, he might have done something other than a stupid kamikaze stunt, throwing himself at a hunter who was armed and ready. As smart and slippery as Traders are, they never think they're going to be held to account.

The knife went in with little resistance, silver laid along the flat part of the blade hissing as it parted flesh tainted by a hellbreed's touch.

The Trader screamed, a high gurgling note of panic. My wrist turned, twisting the knifeblade as we landed, right leg threatening to buckle as momentum drove me back. I stamped my left heel, the transfer of force striking sparks between metal-reinforced bootheel and concrete.

My other hand came up full of knife, blurred forward like a striking snake as the blade buried itself in his chest, and I pushed him *down*, pinning him as the shine flared in his eyes and roasted stink-sweet filled my mouth and nose.

Hunting is a messy business.

A SORCERER'S TREASON

Sarah Zettel was born in California in 1966. Since then, she's lived in ten cities, four states and two countries. She has written four science fiction novels and many short stories in the sf, fantasy and horror genres. Her debut full-length work, *Reclamation*, won the Locus Award for Best First Novel. Sarah now lives in Michigan with her husband and their son.

BY SARAH ZETTEL

A Sorcerer's Treason
The Usurper's Crown